AT THE MERCY OF NATURE

"Ben?" Natalie yelled, but the wind tossed her voice aside. "Ben, where are you?"

There was only the sound of the wind. Then she saw him. He was up in the tree's lower branches, one foot balanced on the plane's mangled nose.

"Can you get in that way?" She climbed up toward him, scrambling over half-buried pieces of metal. "Last night, it was filled in with snow."

He didn't answer, so she hooked an arm over a limb and pulled herself forward.

"Didn't you hear me yelling at you?" she asked.

Still no reply. She climbed up next to him and braced herself against the trunk. "Hey, dammit, I'm talking to you. What's . . ."

Her voice faded out all by itself. The snow, which the night before had clogged the Lear's windshield, was mostly gone now. Dug out of the way. Inside the cockpit, a mountain lion was crouched beside Landry's body.

Its normally white chin was stained a darker, deeper color.

Natalie froze in place. The big cat's eyes were a golden-amber color. There was very little snow on its long tan and brown body. It had probably been inside the cockpit awhile, judging by what was left of Landry. The cougar, so thin that Natalie could see its exposed ribs, looked from one of them to the other, its small ears flattened against its head.

Then it opened its mouth and showed them a double row of blood-pinkened teeth.

"RELENTLESS is a damn good novel. Franklin can write suspense."

Stephen Coonts

RELENTLESS

Kris Franklin

ZEBRA BOOKS
KENSINGTON PUBLISHING CORP.

ZEBRA BOOKS are published by

Kensington Publishing Corp.
475 Park Avenue South
New York, NY 10016

Zebra and the Z logo are trademarks of Kensington Publishing Corp.

First Printing: November, 1993

Printed in the United States of America

Thank you, Marcia

Prologue

"I'm telling you I don't know where he is."

Eugene Cleese poured Diet Coke into a glass full of ice. He ran a latex-gloved finger across his forehead; then he flicked a fat bead of perspiration toward the fireplace.

"I promise . . ."

The room was large and rectangular and luxuriously furnished, and its showcases were the huge stone fireplace and a west-facing glass wall that overlooked the ocean. It was a gloomy early morning out there, even for February. Muted, panchromatic shades of white and gray like an old movie.

Or a recurring dream.

"That rain," remarked Cleese, and wiped a droplet of Coke off his iron gray mustache. "Just keeps on keeping on."

"Gene, listen to me . . ."

Shelly's voice broke a little just then, took on the edge of a whimper. Cleese couldn't blame her.

"Why would I lie? I know you, Gene. Dammit, I know you!"

Not as well as you thought, Shelley-girl.

Cleese could feel where sweat had puddled the armpits of his gold V-necked sweater. It was an uncomfortable, *used* kind of feeling he didn't much care for. He stood up and pulled the V-neck over his head, glancing by habit at his reflection in the glass wall. Not too bad for sixty-one

7

years old, sixty-two come April. He wiped his trim torso dry with the sweater.

"Gene, please . . ."

Ben's clothes were still hanging in the bedroom closet, and the size was near enough. Cleese leaned down and pushed the Stop button, then walked along a thickly carpeted hallway. The bedroom was the way they'd left it—pillows on the floor, tangled sheets, half-open drawers. Cleese had a wide selection to choose from. He loved bright colors. Warm colors.

He returned to the living room, smoothing down a lemon yellow pullover of some sweat suit type material. A poly-cotton mix with a velour texture. He sat on the wide leather couch and took another sip of Diet Coke. Hit the Play button.

"Dammit, Gene! Don't! Gene . . ."

It got a bit repetitious at that point, Shelley being tougher than expected, so he pushed Fast Forward. Found a better spot.

". . . sometime tonight. That private airstrip over by Brawley." Shelley's voice had gotten hoarse, probably from all the screaming, which was hard on the throat.

"Where are they taking him from there, Shelley?" Cleese had never cared much for his voice on tape, but everyone promised it sounded just like him.

"Flushing, I guess. Or maybe into Teterboro first, if they can fly at all tonight with this storm . . ."

Cleese pushed the Stop button again. He took his time finishing the Coke while he considered his commitments. Prioritized them. The mall would take a while; everything had to be just right. Then out to Kaydra's. . . .

The telephone rang.

The phone had an answering machine, and Cleese considered letting it play out. He walked over and picked up the receiver instead.

There was silence on the line. Silence at his end, silence at the other end. He stood very still for about thirty seconds and listened for any background sounds. There were none.

8

"She's not here, Ben," he said, after a while. "Metaphysically speaking."

There was something, maybe like a faint sigh. An expulsion of air. Then a soft click, and the dial tone.

"Goodbye, Ben," said Cleese, and hung up the phone.

He took his glass into the long, narrow kitchen—all California pseudo-Mexican tile and chrome—and dumped the ice. Then he washed his glass and replaced it behind some others in the cabinet. He went back into the living room and put on his hooded rain slicker. He looked around the room, then gathered up his gold V-neck and the Coke can and the cassette recorder.

"You got me all sweaty, Shelley," he said, and stepped over her on his way out the back door.

Life and death, they're meaningless, boy. That's what his father had told him. And—with one exception—he'd seen nothing since to change his mind.

The nearest house was nearly one hundred yards away, south along the beach. The kind of privacy Malibu money could buy. From Shelley's back deck Cleese saw someone over there, moving around near a retaining wall, little more than a shadowy silhouette through the hard rain that slanted in off the ocean.

That house had been deserted when Cleese first arrived just past midnight. He'd checked to be sure, on the chance things with Shelley might get loud before they were done.

Cleese stepped back into an alcove created by the glass door, and watched the figure. Moving casually, apparently making sure the storm-swollen tide was no threat, the man had probably driven out early this morning. Probably heard the weather report, and come out to see if there was any need to sandbag around his property. Probably arrived well after the noise died down over here.

And there was the covering sound of the rain, anyway, as well as that heavy surf booming up on the beach. Which was partly the reason Cleese had picked this particular night.

This shouldn't be a problem. He really preferred not to go next door if it could be avoided.

He watched until the figure disappeared around the far side of the house; then he put up the hood on his slicker and crossed Shelley's rain-soaked deck, his characteristically erect posture unaffected by the storm blowing across him. At the edge, where an advancing high tide was already licking at the bottom stairs, he removed his shoes and socks and rolled his pant legs up over muscular calves. Then he stepped down into the cold water.

Cleese disliked cold, gray things like this incoming tide, but sometimes there was no choice.

He waded north along the beach. The wind and rain tore at his slicker, and the tide obliterated each footstep as quickly as he made it. He wasn't surprised to be completely alone, considering the weather. That was part of the plan, too.

Half a mile north he came to a public section of beach where there was a parking lot back in the low dunes. The lot was deserted except for a fire engine red Jeep Cherokee, a single spot of warm color in this gray morning. Cleese raised the back hatch to stow the things he'd carried from Shelley's house, then climbed into the driver's seat and turned on the engine and the heater.

An AM station was airing a weather bulletin. Continued rain along the coast, changing over to snow in the Sierra Nevada and the Great Basin farther east. A Winter Storm Warning was being declared for the Colorado Rockies.

Not the best flying weather, decided Cleese. Especially for someone like Ben McKee, who was afraid of airplanes to begin with.

He switched over to an FM station that was playing Jimmy Buffett. A bouncy song, fresh with the images of sunshine and blue skies and warm sand. Cleese sang along while he drove out of the lot. Headed north back into town.

After the mall, it took him forty-five minutes to drive to Del Mar, time enough—with some occasional fast forwarding—to listen to the entire Shelley cassette again. Traffic was slow, barely moving. Southern Californians were congenitally terrified of rain.

He cut his car engine half a block away so that he could glide silently up to the house. He was chuckling to himself by the time he got everything on the porch and rang the bell.

Kaydra opened the door with her usual flat smile. The one that never quite reached her eyes. She stretched up to kiss his cheek.

"That's all fine and good." Cleese kissed her back, somewhere in the vicinity of her left eyebrow. "But where's my *real* darling?"

"Gramp?" The blond-haired little girl was tearing down the stairs just inside, green eyes alight with excitement.

"Genie!" said Kaydra. "You be care—"

But the child had already hit the entry running. "Gramp!" she squealed, and leaped into Cleese's outstretched arms.

"Oh, my God." Kaydra was looking at the packages all over the porch. "Dad, you promised me . . ."

"Birthdays are once a year, Kaydra." Cleese spun Genie around so she could see, too. "And granddaughters are once in a lifetime. Help me get this stuff inside before it gets any wetter."

It took Genie less than ten minutes to tear the brightly colored wrapping paper off her birthday presents, but some of them—like the hand-carved antique dollhouse with its perfectly scaled furniture—took a while to set up. Cleese and his granddaughter spent several hours in her room, creating fantasy scenarios for the inhabitants of the dollhouse, who Genie decided were a rock star—or maybe MacGyver—and his fashion model wife. Finally, Cleese looked at his watch and climbed regretfully to his feet.

"You let her watch too much TV," he said to Kaydra at the door. "MacGyver, my foot. You should get her

11

reading more. *Black Beauty, The Wind in the Willows. The classics, Kaydra.*"

It was still raining when he got back in his car and headed for Brawley. He had a couple of stops to make along the way.

Tuesday night—
Wednesday morning

SHELTER

I am not bound to honor any master;
where the storm drives me,
there I turn for shelter.
—Horace, *Epistles, Book I*

Chapter One

When she walked out of her cabin, the storm engulfed her. Swallowed her whole. The night was a shifting, blinding twilight of black and white and gray against the background scream of the wind. And the wind had Rick's voice.

Nattie my love. . .

Natalie Kemper battled her way through it. She wanted to look back, to make certain the small cabin was still there, but she didn't. Instead she gritted her teeth and swore under her breath, and tried to shut out the sound of his voice . . .

Nattie . . .

. . . riding the wind. She held one arm across her face to shield her eyes from the hard pellets of wind-driven snow and followed the cone of her flashlight, struggling toward the edge of the small clearing and the square outline of a glass-fronted wooden cabinet that seemed a mile away.

Or maybe ten feet. When wading in waist-deep snow, right into the teeth of a Rocky Mountain blizzard, distance could be somewhat relative.

Forever, Nattie . . .

She broke through into the natural well around the cabinet and grabbed its edge with a gloved hand to pull herself forward. Behind their glass protection, all the instruments in the weather array were going crazy, of course. Temperature, twelve degrees and falling, which

15

combined with the anemometer's wind-speed readings of forty miles an hour out of the northwest to create a windchill factor of maybe thirty-five below zero. Humidity, only in the seventies so far, since this was dry, powdery snow. But the key number behind the glass was on the barometer. Twenty-nine point forty-one inches of mercury, and dropping like a rock.

"Good God," murmured Nattie, and the wind carried her voice away so quickly she never heard the sound.

There's something about nature out of control, she thought. *We* like to believe we're the ones in charge . . .

And this was just the advance guard for the main storm, still gathering itself out in the Great Basin. Like Starvin' Marvin Stone had commented on the headset earlier that evening, this one was going to be nuts-deep on a tall moose.

The FCC could yank him for language like that, but Starvin' Marvin knew they wouldn't. He was the single link to the winter people high up in these mountains surrounding Walker Lake, and that left him pretty much bulletproof.

Nattie unhooked the safety chains on the cabinet's metal doors, then pushed them closed and latched them. The next set of readings would wait for morning. She had her mind fixed on a hot bath, a *very* hot bath, and then some sleep. Those new barometric numbers would have to go in first thing tomorrow.

The latch on one of the doors was working its way loose again, she noticed. She made a mental note to bring a Phillips screwdriver with her the next time out.

Nattie found returning toward the cabin much easier than coming out to the weather array had been, since she was now headed downwind and also following her own trail. The storm shoved her along ahead of it, a giant and not-so-gentle hand in her back. All around her, the huge Engelmann spruce trees were bending before the power of the wind. If one of them snapped . . .

But they wouldn't, of course. Bend but don't break, Nattie. A lesson for us all.

She passed the big BLM dumpster, at the moment little more than a rounded hump in the snow, and noticed that the ravens were gone. A significant fact. When that bunch of raucous freeloaders—everpresent around the dumpster at all hours and in all weather conditions hoping to scavenge the plastic trashbags Nattie stored there—went looking for shelter from a storm, you knew it was going to be a biggie.

Another lesson for us all. Time to make like the animals, Nattie. Get in out of the storm.

She homed in on the sliver of pale yellow lamplight through her cabin's shuttered west window, closer than it appeared, and finally found a corner mostly out of the wind. She stomped loose snow off her Sorels and whacked her gloved hands together. She was already feeling that hot bath water. . . .

Something coming from her left. Moving fast.

"God . . ." She spun away, but too slowly. The hurtling shape hit her chest-high, knocked her flashlight flying, and her feet slid out from under her. She landed on her back in the snow, the thing on top of her. Licking her in the face.

"Dammit, Jack!" She grabbed the dog's floppy ears, just as his tongue slurped her in one eye. "You . . . idiot! You scared the hell out of me, did you know that?"

Jack the Wonder Spaniel apparently didn't care. His spotted brown body was coated solid white, and there was a clump of powdery snow stuck to his nose.

"Damn dog." Nattie clambered to her knees. "I should have left your furry butt on death row."

Jack had long since forgotten he was a refugee from the dog pound, and was unimpressed by empty threats. He leaped away from her, then down in front with his hindquarters in the air. His standard let's-nail-Nattie attack mode.

"Where have you been, anyway?" She found her light and headed toward the cabin's east side, with Jack bounding around behind her like a moderately backward child. "You *do* remember your woodland pals, Leo and

Laura? Who keep wanting to know if you can come out and play? If they eat you, I'm getting a goldfish next time."

She lifted one of his paws, webbed between the toes and completely impacted with frozen snow.

"You're not tracking that stuff into my house, bud," she muttered. "And don't give me that poor Jackie look, either. You need to remember who's the human and who's the dog around here."

With very little cooperation from Jack, Nattie managed to get most of the snow from between his toes; then she stepped up onto the raised platform of two-by-fours that served as the cabin's front porch. She opened the heavy door carefully, so the wind wouldn't yank it loose from her, and followed the dog inside.

The Bureau of Land Management cabin, leased for weather research by the non-profit foundation that employed Natalie Kemper, had a simple floor plan. A single room, rectangular in shape, it had space for a bed on one wall, directly opposite a small alcove that served as a pantry. With Marvin Stone's help, Nattie had hauled in some personal items, like an old Bristol rocking chair and a small oval mirror that hung on a side wall above an antique washbasin. The bed, the table and its four chairs, and the generator-powered shortwave radio were provided by the foundation, as was the large black Fisher woodstove with cooking plates on its top.

There were few personal items in the cabin, other than the rocker and the mirror—and a single framed photograph sitting next to the washbasin. A picture of a small, slender man holding up a trophy-size cutthroat trout and smiling at the camera.

The shortwave, over beneath an unshuttered side window, was cranking out static when Nattie came in the door, but she headed first for the warmth of the woodstove.

"First things first" being axiomatic because it was the truth, she decided.

She backed up to the stove and groaned with pleasure

18

as its heat penetrated first her icy clothing and then the bone deep chill beneath the garments. Jack, afflicted as usual with the odor of WCS—Wet Canine Syndrome—squeezed in next to her.

"You smell a lot like a dog," she informed him. "And I should probably tell you that your eye-boogers are back, too. And don't even think about shaking off next to me. Go over there in the corner while I find a towel . . ."

Jack gave her the doggie equivalent of a grin, then shook himself vigorously, spraying water and snow and ice all over Nattie and the woodstove. The hot metal sides of the stove hissed where the drops hit it.

"Oh, thanks loads." Nattie peeled off her gloves and cap. "Looks like I'm the one who needs the towel, huh?"

The Wonder Spaniel left her to drip, and ambled over to his water bowl, which he proceeded to empty. His tank was probably low, Nattie decided, from the continuous process of hiking his leg on every bush and tree around the clearing.

"All that territory marking's thirsty work, isn't it, bud?" she asked, and was about to expound on the thought when her shortwave started up again. More static, and maybe the trace of a voice in there somewhere. She went over to the set and was reaching for her hand-held microphone when the noise stopped.

Just as well. It was probably Marv down at Walker Lake. When she'd talked to him that afternoon, about the time the blizzard was beginning to really make itself felt, he'd tried to convince her to snowmobile on down to the comm center. Ride out the storm down there, just in case.

Fat chance, she'd thought to herself, but she'd thanked him anyway. Marv was a nice old guy, though he could talk you into a coma once he got started.

Which had nothing to do with Nattie's reasons for preferring to stay up here, alone in her cabin. She could take care of herself, and her ongoing solitude was something she'd purposely sought out in taking this job, for reasons Marv knew nothing about.

When she'd interviewed with the foundation nearly a year ago, the solitary nature of the work was the first thing the personnel man mentioned. Stan Bishop had obvious concerns about the concept of a woman alone in the mountains, but being politically correct—there were few places on the planet more PC than Boulder, Colorado—he wasn't about to confess that he'd had a man in mind for the job.

"There's nobody up there, Natalie," he'd told her, looking properly earnest and concerned. "Just that little cabin, eleven thousand feet above sea level and nearly ten miles from the communication center down at Walker Lake. You'll be all alone . . ."

When a certain nationally syndicated cartoonist—one whose political views were somewhere to the right of *Reader's Digest*—caricatured liberals, he always drew them to look like Stan Bishop: thin and balding, with a scraggly beard and granny glasses. The stereotype old hippie.

Or maybe Peter and Paul, singing on either side of Mary. That folkie group had been a favorite of Nattie's father, though she could never remember which guy was which.

"You'll be all alone up there, Natalie." Bishop's vast expanse of forehead had knitted in a frown. "Especially in the winter . . ."

Since he knew nothing of her history, other than the fact she was a college-educated, divorced woman in her late twenties—which was to say he didn't *really* know anything about her at all—he'd naturally assumed she'd consider the continuous solitude to be a drawback.

But she'd gotten the job anyway, to her mother's undisguised dismay, and here she was. And she wasn't giving away her privacy now, just because of a winter storm. In this country you were never far from the edge—the weather was only one of the many hazards ready to rise

20

up and bite you—so you just went on with whatever it was you had to do. Speaking of which . . .

Nattie took out her notebook of foundation data sheets and made all the weather entries before she forgot them. She dated the page February nineteen, along with the time—almost exactly eleven P.M. on her trusty Timex—and then stood up to close the window shutter . . .

When she saw something moving out there in that gray-white, swirling darkness. Not snow, and not tree limbs blowing in the wind. Something out at the weather array.

Maybe one of the dumpster ravens, out of its shelter and disoriented by the storm. Or maybe . . .

Maybe it was Leo or Laura. Or both of them. Nattie glanced first at Jack, who was entertaining himself by batting around a rag-filled cloth ball next to the stove, then at her old four-ten shotgun leaning in the pantry alcove. She hated guns, but Marv had talked her into bringing this one.

"Just fire a little birdshot over their heads," he'd suggested. "They'll take off like a pair of scalded cats . . ."

Really big scalded cats

". . . and that'll be the last time they bother you."

Nattie took a closer look out the window and decided the movement she saw out there wasn't anything alive. Too regular, flapping in the wind like . . .

Like that metal door to the weather array. The one with the loose latch.

"Well, hell," she muttered, and started looking for her flashlight and her Phillips screwdriver.

It had to be fixed. Either fixed or chained back open again, which wasn't a good idea in this storm. The weather array was expensive, and Nattie's job revolved around those instruments.

She sighed, and pulled back on her cap and gloves. That hot bath would have to wait a bit longer.

"No way." She gave Jack a severe look when he jumped to his feet and hurried over to the door, his

21

stumpy tail wagging. "That ship's done sailed, bud. You had to drink all that water; you can hold it for a while."

She waded back out into the storm, which seemed to have intensified just in the time she was inside. Following her own tracks out to the array, where one of the doors was flapping back and forth, made it a little easier than the first time.

Luckily, the screws were still halfway in the latch, and it took only a couple of minutes to tighten them. This time, everything shut securely.

Should've done this when you first noticed it the other day, Nattie my love. Rick's voice in her head took on that pleased, I-told-you-so tone. *Could've saved yourself a trip . . .*

She was turning back toward the cabin when she heard something that shut Rick's voice off in mid-gloat. A sound *different* from the howl of the wind.

"What the hell . . ."

Above her. A kind of *WHOOSH*.

Nattie spun around and looked up just in time to see a faint row of lights passing overhead. Dropping down into the storm.

"Oh, sweet Jesus," she whispered.

Chapter Two

Take your time, Nattie. That was always the trouble with you, you know? Always running off half-cocked, taking in strays, like that stupid mutt. There's nobody out there, anyway. Nobody alive . . .

Nattie felt her old Polaris Indy snowmobile bottom out. Probably a buried creekbed. The vehicle's rear end slewed sideways and dropped down, and the engine died.

See what I mean? Running off half-cocked . . .

"Dammit," she snapped, and snow blew through her wool face mask and into her mouth. When in a blizzard, Nattie, one should always curse downwind.

She slid off the narrow vinyl seat into a waist-deep drift and pulled up on the snowmobile's lateral rear shaft. She could feel herself sinking as she did it, but the thing finally popped free. She climbed back on and yanked the starter cord, lurched up and out of the buried creekbed, then angled between a pair of huge Engelmanns, each nearly a hundred feet tall.

Nattie was operating on dead reckoning at this point. The plane had gone over her cabin roughly west-north-west, in other words directly into the wind. If the pilot was attempting to belly-in with no power, that was the direction he'd take. Anything else, this storm would swat him down like a deerfly.

The snowmobile's single headlight found the best route through a screen of bare-limbed oakbrush. Nattie drove into an opening, ducked beneath some wildly swinging branches, and found herself in the clear. The wind slammed her head-on, so hard it seemed the old Polaris would rear up like a horse in a western movie. Snow was sweeping laterally toward her in small, hard pellets that stung even through all the layers of her clothing.

The open area ahead had to be Cat Meadow, named for the pair of mountain lions she'd christened Leo and Laura, who hung around, as close to settled in as those nomadic creatures ever got, whittling down a deer herd that foraged there—with Jack the Wonder Spaniel as the designated hors d'oeuvre, if they could ever catch him.

Nattie pointed the front skis of her snowmobile upwind and followed the single cone of her headlight. If this was Cat Meadow, there was a serious drop-off over there past its far side. Probably fifteen hundred feet, more or less straight down, into the frozen canyon of Walker Creek. If the plane had cleared those last trees up ahead and then failed to climb . . .

Shades of Patsy Cline.

But that wasn't what had happened. About halfway across the huge oval meadow, Nattie saw the first gouge torn out of the snow. An irregular shape, probably twenty feet by thirty or forty, and all the way down to the meadow grass and underbrush. Even the snow falling at the rate of two inches an hour had put no more than a shallow covering into the bottom of the hole. Nattie's headlight picked up a scurrying pika that probably figured it wouldn't see daylight until May.

The plane had hit and bounced, she decided, and made a detour around the crater. She tried to hurry, because whoever had brought the plane in was very good. The low trajectory could mean survivors up ahead, with a little luck.

Farther on she came to a second imprint, longer and more shallow. Then a third after that, this one continuing in a straight skid—right into that towering wall of spruce and Douglas fir that formed the western edge of Cat Meadow.

24

It wasn't the pilot's fault. He'd simply run out of room.

Even following the skid, it wasn't easy to locate the plane itself. Nattie's headlight showed shadowy mounds all beneath the trees. Some were probably just snow, bulldozed into piles by the impact. Then she spotted a straight line, not that common in the natural world, and realized it was a wingtip.

"Jesus H. Cryminy . . ." she murmured, and pulled her snowmobile in closer.

The plane was a small jet, maybe one of those executive Lears. It was white, which didn't help much, and it had dark trim. Black or navy blue, it was impossible to tell in this limited light. The plane was tilted slightly toward its left side—that was its right wing she'd seen first—and it was nearly buried under the snow. She saw the wingtip, a twisted piece of what could be its tail, and a longer hump that was probably the main fuselage. The whole thing was covering over fast. In a few hours, there'd be nothing but a smooth layer of whiteness under the trees.

Nattie drove the Polaris in as close as she could, until its tread began to slip in the torn snow. Like most snowmobiles, it had no reverse gear. She got off, left the engine running and the headlight aimed toward what should be the left side of the plane. She dug a large Coleman flash from beneath her ice-climbing equipment in the storage slot, and started wading her way forward.

Or swimming. In snow this deep and soft, you had to stroke your way through. Create some firm underfooting in each spot before moving on.

She was wearing a blue one-piece snowsuit, with her Sorel boot tops tucked inside, but she could feel a few small trickles of cold and wet already. By the time she reached the side of the plane, she was damp all over. Partly exertion and sweat, even in the freezing grip of the storm.

"Hey!" She banged on the fuselage with the butt of the flash. "Hey, can you hear me in there?"

There was no sound except the wind.

She saw a long, horizontal rip in the metal above her head. She pushed handfuls of snow down around her feet and stomped it firm. Made herself an escalating platform.

When she got a little more height, she was able to see the nose of the airplane. What was left of it, at any rate. It had smashed straight into the side of a big, double-trunk Douglas fir, and the lower limbs of the tree had nailed the cockpit area like it was a cork dartboard.

Forget what she'd thought earlier. It was going to take a *lot* of luck.

Nattie lay forward against the curve of the fuselage and pushed the Coleman's nose into the crack.

"Hey!" She tried again, but up this near the top, the wind blew her shout right back down her throat.

It was like trying to peek into an abandoned cellar, she thought. The light showed a facing wall, with what looked like storage compartments. Some of them were standing open. A row of seats, lower down, was shrouded and lumpy. Jeez, the whole cabin was full of snow. If there were bodies under there. . . .

"Nobody home," she said. Maybe they were flying empty of passengers on this trip. Doing a turnaround, was that what they called it?

She leaned a little left and played the light beam farther to her right. Back toward the rear of the cabin, something was humped up in the farthest seat. Dark colors beneath the white, and her light reflected on . . .

A tiny face staring back at her. With . . . an eye patch?

It was a dark-colored jacket of some kind, with the lighter shaded logo of . . . the Los Angeles Raiders. It was that eye-patch pirate's head, with the football helmet and the crossed cutlasses. The Raiders logo on a black jacket.

"Hey!" Nattie got her mouth nearer the jagged rip and cupped one hand beside it. "Hey, you! In the plane . . ."

One passenger, not moving.

She started digging for the door. It should be on this

side; they usually were. And a little below the horizontal rip she finally found it. Buried deep.

Natalie Kemper weighed about one hundred and five pounds after a big meal—if she could ever overcome the sound of Rick's voice inside her head long enough to eat one—but she was wiry and strong. Even so, it took a while to dig out the door. When she was done, she was standing in a half tunnel, the sides higher than her head.

She used her pocket knife to force the impacted snow and ice from the door's seams, and from around its recessed handle. Then she gave it a try.

It didn't move.

What if. . . . She didn't know much about these little private jets, but what if the door had to be released from inside? Some kind of safety feature. . . .

Nattie dug her feet down into the snow and got some leverage against the fuselage, then tried again. Maybe if she could push *in* on it first, then turn.

There's nobody alive in there anyway, Nattie . . .

"Shut up, damn you." She pushed harder, in a burst of reflexive anger at that much-too-familiar voice in her mind, and the handle released. So suddenly she had to duck backward to dodge the door—which opened down rather than to the side—as it hit the end of its safety catches.

An odor came out of the cabin into the fresh, icy air, and Nattie wrinkled her nose beneath the face mask. A smell of wood and evergreen needles and . . . something a little like old copper pipe.

The door had steps built into it, and she led with the Coleman flash. Oddly, when she climbed through the opening, it felt colder inside than out.

The cabin lay under a crystalline layer of blowing snow. The seats and the walls and the aisle seemed to shift and contract in the tunnel of her light.

Like being down a mine shaft, she thought, and fought back a familiar surge of claustrophobia . . .

The blackness . . .

That, or inside the belly of some animal, huge and ancient and frozen dead.

To her left was an open hatchway to the cockpit. Her light picked up glistening tree sap beginning to freeze on gashed limbs that were sticking out of a wall of snow at the front.

There were two men sitting in the cockpit, both dead, their bodies impaled by the thick branches. One was in his fifties or sixties, it looked like, with a slightly overfed face and a wide, fleshy mouth set in a grin. The other was somewhat younger and very large, with a bodybuilder-type torso that reminded her of Rick. Even with his eyes closed, he looked startled. Like something had sneaked up on him when he least expected it. The coppery smell had come from the blood all around both of them, freezing into a blackening paste in the tunnel of her light.

No surprises here. The outside of the plane had pretty much told the story. Nattie backed out of the hatchway and went to the rear of the cabin, back to where the figure in the Raiders jacket was rapidly disappearing under a thickening layer of snow . . .

The figure moved.

"Jee-*zus!*" Nattie reflexively lunged away and tripped, and found herself sitting in the narrow aisle, looking at the snow-shrouded body above her, distorted into scarecrow lines by the angled light of her flash.

It moved again, just a twitch, but a tiny avalanche of powdery snow slid down across the jacket's logo. Nattie climbed to her feet and began brushing the snow away.

It was a man, wrapped in blankets and pillows, except where the blanket had slipped in front. He was sitting yoga-fashion, his legs crossed, and his head was slumped forward on his chest. Nattie raised his chin and saw his eyes were closed.

She removed her fleece-lined Hotfingers mittens and touched her hands to his face. He felt like frozen marble, but just then his eyes opened. In the light of the Coleman flash, they were a startling pale blue.

28

"Cleese," the man said, with perfect clarity. "You murdering sonofabitch."

Then his eyes closed again.

Nattie stood there and stared at him. The wind howled past her, and a fresh spray of snow blew into the metal tomb and lashed her back. And the man didn't make another sound.

The man was fairly tall, or at least he looked that way a while later, all stretched out on the wooden floor of the BLM cabin. Of course, when you were five feet three, as Nattie was, a lot of people looked tall.

He was probably in his mid to late thirties, she decided. Forty at the most, based on her observation that he didn't have any gray pubic hair.

"It'll be ready in a minute," she said, seeing his eyes were opening more often now. She stuck a finger into the water half filling the old metal bathtub she'd dragged into the center of the room. Nearly hot enough.

"Maybe one more bucket." She nodded to Jack, who'd given up growling at the naked man and had adjourned to lie in the relative coolness on the other side of the tub. Nattie went over to her woodstove, which she'd stoked so high its iron sides were turning a dull cherry red. She wiped a trickle of perspiration from her cheek, then used oven mitts to carry the bucket to the tub. When she poured it in, it hissed on the metal sides, and a thin vapor-fog billowed up around her.

"Okay, bud. Bath time." She knelt behind the man's head to grab him under his arms. His eyes opened again as she rolled him forward, and he looked around without much apparent comprehension, until he glanced down and saw he was naked.

"Hey, don't worry about it, bud," said Nattie, and hoisted him into a seated position. "I've seen one of those before."

The man tried to put his hands over his crotch.

"No, honest, I *like* guys with tiny little peckers." Nattie pulled him to his knees. "Usually they have a nice personality and are good dancers."

He said something about that, but she couldn't tell what it was. Because he was tall, she had to fold him over the side of the tub. He went in with a splash that doused Nattie's flannel shirt and scattered Jack from the other side.

"Don't drown me now." She propped his head on a towel she'd draped over the back, and watched the water level stabilize just below his shoulders.

"God, that's good," he mumbled; then his eyes closed again.

Acute hypothermia. Nattie didn't have a thermometer—at least not one she could detach and use on a human—in the midst of all her meteorological equipment, but she was pretty sure from personal experience this guy was running mid to high eighties by the time she got him to her cabin. A close call.

Frostbite was always a possibility, too, though his fingers and toes looked okay. One of the Denver hospitals—a facility Nattie was a little *too* familiar with, for an entirely different reason—had a hyperbaric chamber, resembling a miniature submarine, where pure oxygen and elevated atmospheric pressure were used to treat frostbitten tissue by boosting the metabolism of the affected cells and oxygenating the blood that fed them.

But this cabin was a long way from Denver.

She pumped another bucket of water from her aluminum snow melter on the back wall and carried it over to the stove to heat up. Then she sat in her old Bristol rocker and let her head relax against the scarred oakwood frame. Jack, who hated and feared men, especially large ones, settled next to her uneasily, watching the tub and whining softly while one of her hands rubbed his floppy ears. Outside, the blizzard was escalating just like she'd forecast, pounding and screaming at the cabin walls.

She hadn't realized how tired she was, probably because she'd been so kited on adrenaline the whole time.

The process of rescue—dragging this guy out of the plane and up the hand-dug trench to the snowmobile, attaching him to her, literally, and to the machine with hook-end bungee cords, and finally that nightmarish ride sinking and floundering overweight through the storm—had all seemed surreal in time. But it was a little past three A.M. now, and she'd seen the plane go over around eleven.

The man mumbled something else, which started Jack growling again, but it wasn't clear. The only lucid comment he'd made the whole time was his reference to Whatzizname the murdering sonofabitch . . .

"Not that easy," said the man, and Nattie sat forward with a start. He was lying in the tub with his head still propped on the towel at one end, but his eyes had opened, unfocused in the lantern light. "Not like Shelley, you god . . ."

He faded out halfway through the expletive, just as the water on the stove came to a boil.

Nattie went over and set it aside to cool a little before she added it to the tub. The man continued to mumble, and she thought she heard that name—Cleats?—again; but his eyes remained closed.

Classic hypothermia. In and out, and the mind rambling off . . .

Not that easy . . . you murdering sonofabitch . . .

. . . along its own agendas. Once, during a hazardous early autumn climb of El Diente Peak, over in the San Miguel Range near Telluride, she and Rick had gotten caught halfway along the difficult Mt. Wilson traverse by that season's last surge of the summer monsoon. They'd been poorly prepared for weather like that, and had been soaked to the skin, but of course Rick wanted to summit. To bag another Fourteener. On the way down she'd begun to shiver uncontrollably, and only her fear of her husband's wrath had carried her—stumbling and incoherent with hypothermia—back to their base camp in Navajo Basin, where it was George Van Zandt who got her out of her wet clothes and into an insulated sleeping bag.

It had been the end of some things, the beginning of others.

Nattie carried the bucket of hot water over to the tub and poured it in, careful not to splash. The man's eyes didn't open, but she saw a faint smile.

A nice smile. The man wasn't handsome in the brooding TV soap-star way Rick was. Few men were. But this one had a nice smile and a square-jawed, pleasant face and dark hair. And, judging from what she'd already seen, he looked to be in pretty good shape. . . .

Oh, cut the crap, Nattie. If there's one thing you don't need in your life right now . . .

But she wondered who Shelley was, anyway.

She went over to her old shortwave and tried to raise Starvin' Marvin down at Walker Lake. There were newer, more high-tech comm sets available, but she'd never found one more dependable. Maybe she had an aversion, she considered, not for the first time, to the new flashy stuff with all its bells and whistles. . . .

You'd look sharper, Nattie my love, with a shoulder-length cut and a perm. More nineties, you know? That hippie-girl stuff went out of date with your mother.

Handsome Rick—dressed in his eye-catching black, of course. Sharp enough and nineties enough for both of them, and still kicking around up there somewhere in her frontal lobe. . . .

Maybe that was why she liked her old, scarred Bristol rocker and her old, dented Polaris snowmobile. And this shortwave.

She couldn't raise Starvin' Marvin, or anyone else along the dial, but that wasn't the equipment's fault. In a storm of this magnitude, nobody could get through. Those two men out there, dead and freezing solid in the buried plane, had to be reported. But it would have to wait.

One of the few positives about hypothermia was how quickly the victim recovered, provided he received proper care. By tomorrow this guy would be able to fill her in on all the pertinent information. Maybe by then she'd get a window in the storm—which wasn't uncommon in these big three- or four-day blizzards—and she'd be able to at least let people know what had happened. Evacuating him, probably by helicopter, that might be another story.

We may be stuck with each other for a while, stranger.

She went over to the tub and touched the man's forehead. He was sweating lightly, which was good. It meant his own metabolism had started to kick in.

"Okay, bud. Let's get you under the covers." She leaned down next to him, and her braid fell across his face for a moment. "You suppose you could help me a little? Maybe we can avoid flooding the place this time."

He opened his eyes and looked up at her. "Name's not bud," he mumbled. "Name's Ben."

"Hey, you say potato and I say potahto." For a moment the man's gaze had been very clear and penetrating, and Nattie quickly looked away. Down into the tub, which was even worse. "So come on, Ben-bud." She tried to cover a surge of embarrassment. "Lean on me, as the old song goes, when you're not strong . . ."

Which he wasn't. She got a lot wetter helping him out of the tub and toweling him dry, something else she hadn't thought about in advance. Since his clothes, including his underwear, were still damp, she put him into bed naked.

"I have some Jockies For Her you might fancy," she said, pulling the blanket up around his neck. "Assorted colors, in fact."

But he was already asleep.

Way to go, Nattie. Something gets a little too close to the bone, and you don't know how to handle it, so you crack wise like always. Only this one's not even staying awake for the punchlines.

"Gotta get some new material," she decided, and dug out dry towels to mop the floor around the tub. She put one hand into the bathwater, which had finally cooled enough for normal human tolerance . . .

And found herself, almost without thought, unbuttoning her shirt.

After she'd undressed, she stood by the tub for a minute or so, watching the man. The lamplight flickered across his face, but he didn't open his eyes.

"Not only is my stand-up routine a wash," she muttered. "Now they're even sleeping through the stripper."

She unbraided her long hair and climbed into the tub, then slowly sat down in the hot water. Frowned at an imaginary fold of flesh across her flat belly . . .

Did you weigh this morning, Nattie?

. . . and leaned gratefully against the metal back. Jack padded over next to her and lay his furry chin on the tub's edge, a whine down deep in his throat.

"I guess we've got a man in the house, Jackie," she whispered, and rubbed his ears some more. "And I know you don't like it, but don't go ballistic on me, okay? It's only temporary."

Jack appeared unconvinced.

She lay back and looked at the beamed ceiling above her head, which was probably safer than watching ol' Ben-bud. After a while, her eyes closed.

Outside, the storm continued to batter the small cabin, howling past the shuttered windows in a fury of denied access while snow fell and deepened into drifts against the weather array. Natalie Kemper lay in a tub of cooling water, shadowed by lamplight and the glow from the woodstove, and petted her dog. And made it a point to think of other things besides the man sleeping in her bed.

Less than a mile from the cabin, snow blew across Cat Meadow and the torn carcass of the Lear jet. Shapes that had been sharp and straight became rounded and indistinct, and merged into each other. The wind found all the inequities and smoothed them. The snow found all the openings and filled them. The gouge marks torn in the meadow floor began to level out. In a high-mountain blizzard, the snow was always the ultimate undertaker. Burial was its business.

And inside the plane, the battery-powered Emergency Locator Transmittor pulsed steady and true.

Chapter Three

Under a brilliant sun, Eugene Cleese and his granddaughter are at the beach. It's one of those rare, smog-free southern California days, all blue sky and blue-green water and powdered-sugar sand, and Genie's shoulders are a golden tan above her red swimsuit.

A day of bright colors. Warm colors.

"Swim out with me, Gramp." Genie's smiling down at him, and slipping her small hand into his. Trying to tug him to his feet. "Swim out to the sandbar with me, okay?"

"In a little while, darling," he answers. "Right now the tide's going out, and it's too . . ."

That's when he sees something. Something that doesn't belong.

"Carter?" says Cleese, and stands up, realizing immediately this is a dream. "What are you doing here, Carter?"

Will Carter is hurrying along the sunlit beach toward them, that familiar waterbird-looking-for-lunch walk, all skinny legs and long arms and half-bald, bobbing head. He's wearing a swimsuit, too, since this is a dream, but his skin isn't golden tan. More of a gray-white, which is to be expected.

"Carter, you get the . . ."

(But Cleese never swears, not even in a dream)

"You get out of here, Carter. You're going to scare . . ."

Then Cleese sees Carter isn't alone on the beach. He has Shelley Gallatin with him, and Shelley's also wearing a

36

swimsuit. One of those new one-piece tank suits, cut high on each hip and showing a lot of gray-white flesh.

There are others there, too.

This is not a new dream. It's everchanging, which makes it unpredictable, but it's not new. And, as always, Cleese sees the bright colors around him disappear and shift, like a dark cloud crossing the sun, into shades of gray and white.

"Go away," says Cleese. "All of you go away before Genie sees you. She doesn't know . . ."

Which is when they each raise an arm, arced outward and oddly double-jointed at the elbow. The index finger of each hand is extended, the other fingers hanging below like pale gray lace, and the finger points. Not toward Cleese. Toward the ocean. And Cleese turns in that direction, already knowing he'll see . . .

Genie. In the water. No longer blue-green, the water is a boiling gray-white now. And so cold . . .

And pulling her out. Pulling her, caught in the rip of the outgoing tide.

"Gramp!" she screams. "Help me!"

And Cleese is running. Running through gray-white sand that freezes his feet, running past the gray-white figures on the beach who are pointing out at the child. The child who's disappearing beneath the water.

"Genie!" yells Cleese, and he's running with his terror riding so high into his throat he can't breathe. And the figures on the beach open their mouths

And the sound they make . . .

"Wha . . ." Cleese sat up in bed. Next to him, on his end table, the telephone was ringing. He grabbed for it with a hand gone clumsy and trembling, and knocked it onto the floor.

"Gene?" The voice was faint until he brought the receiver to his ear. "Gene, are you there?"

It was Des Pruitt.

"What time . . ." Cleese looked at the illuminated face

of his bedside clock. A digital read-out, flipping over onto 2:46. Outside his second-floor window, the rain was still beating down.

"I'm afraid we've got a problem, Gene," said Pruitt. His voice, as always, was matter-of-fact. Looks like rain. The Lakers aren't the same without Magic. Your grand-daughter has drowned again tonight. Matter-of-fact.

The dream was still there, stark and everchanging and always the same.

Genie . . .

"Call me back, Des," said Cleese. "Fifteen minutes."

"This is important, Gene."

"Fifteen minutes," said Cleese, and pushed the disconnect. When he got a dial tone, he punched in a set of numbers. Listened to one ring, then another.

"Come on," whispered Cleese.

Kaydra answered on the fourth ring.

"Kaydra, is Genie all right?"

"Dad? What time . . ."

"Genie. Is she all right, Kaydra?"

"She's asleep." Cleese could hear that familiar edge of irritation in his daughter's voice. "It's nearly . . . my God. It's nearly three o'clock."

"Are you sure, Kaydra? Go and check for me, okay?"

"Dad . . ."

"Check for me, Kaydra."

There was some grumbling on the other end of the line, then silence. Cleese sat in the dark on the side of his bed, holding the phone receiver tight against his ear and listening to the rain. Gusts of wind were sweeping it against the windows, a cold . . .

gray-white

. . . kind of sound. He shivered and watched the faint ambient light outline a silver-framed photograph on his end table next to the phone. A picture he didn't need any light to see. Taken last summer at the beach by an amiable passerby, it was one of the few times since his PRU days in Vietnam that Cleese—always careful—had allowed himself to be photographed. It showed Genie in her red swimsuit, sitting astraddle Cleese's broad shoulders. Both of them smiled squinty-eyed grins, hers made more interesting by the absence of two baby teeth she'd pulled herself the week before.

She'd already become well aware of the Tooth Fairy's financial possibilities.

"Dad?" Kaydra was back. "Are you still . . ."

"Is she all right?"

"She's fine. She'd kicked off her cover, and she was a little goose-bumpy, but that's all. What on earth possessed you to call at this hour of the night?"

A dream, Kaydra. A dream is what possessed me . . .

"Just a feeling," he answered aloud. "Grandfatherly intuition, maybe."

"Yeah, well, your intuition blew it this time, Gramp. You know, she tried to take that dollhouse to bed with her. You spoil her without mercy."

Cleese heard the bitter edge in that last statement.

"That's my job description, Kaydra." He felt his pulse slowly returning to normal. "Listen, I'm sorry to wake you. Go back to sleep, okay?"

"Already gone." Kaydra's voice softened slightly. "This is a recording, in fact."

"Good night, Kaydra." Cleese hung up the phone. His digital clock read 2:58, so he got up and went into his bathroom. After he urinated, he went over to the lavatory and turned on the light.

A Cleese-in-disarray looked back at him from the mirror. From habit, he took a brush and smoothed his headful of thick gray hair into place, fixed the collar of his silk burgundy pajama shirt, then ran an index finger across his mustache.

Better. A business acquaintance had once remarked to Cleese that if he had a mustache he'd look a bit like that character actor Richard Farnsworth. A little taller, a little younger, but that same rugged outdoor look.

Cleese had shrugged it off at the time, and changed the subject, and later grown a mustache. He couldn't remember the business acquaintance's name, but he remembered what happened to him. Bad things, as was sometimes the case.

The telephone rang. Cleese switched off his bathroom light and walked back to his bed. He lifted the phone on its third ring, just as his clock clicked onto 3:04.

"You're late, Des," he said. "By three minutes."

"I'm afraid we've got a problem, Gene," Pruitt said again—as though the first conversation never occurred. He was an essentially humorless man, motivated solely by self-interest, and that made him predictable. A comforting quality.

"What problem is that, Des?" asked Cleese, as he lay down on the bed.

"There was an accident. An airplane accident." Predictably, Pruitt would now shift into double speak. To Pruitt, there was no such thing as a secure phone line.

"And?" Cleese felt like he was in a scene from *The Godfather*. WASP-Mafia doublespeak at three in the morning.

"And . . . there was an unexpected result."

"Such as?" Cleese shifted the phone to his other hand. "Speak English, Des. This line gets swept twice a week, and I'm sure yours does, too. Tell me what you're talking about."

There was a silence for maybe fifteen seconds. Des Pruitt deciding whether to take the plunge. If he did, then it *was* important.

"Okay." A deep send-me-to-San Quentin sigh on the other end. "The plane. The Lear. It went down in the Rockies."

"Somewhere between the Four Corners and Colorado Springs, I'd venture. Give or take a hundred miles," answered Cleese. "Rugged country, especially during the winter."

"What did you use?"

"Something new," said Cleese. "Why?"

"Not a . . . uh, device?"

"You mean a bomb."

He could almost hear Pruitt wince. The line was silent.

I didn't know what he was talking about, Your Honor.

"No, Des," said Cleese, after a few more seconds. "Not a . . . uh, device. I used a liquid polymer. Would you like for me to explain how it works?"

"It didn't. Work, I mean."

"What?" Cleese sat up straight in bed. "You said the plane went down."

"So it did. And the reason we know that is because, at about eleven P.M. Mountain Standard Time, ten o'clock here, it began transmitting on its ELT."

Cleese didn't say anything about that for a minute.

"Since we knew the approximate geography involved, we took the trouble to monitor the nearest search-and-rescue agencies. They're uncertain what to do about it at the moment, since the signal is evidently quite faint, probably because of the mountainous terrain and the weather. They're also preoccupied by the early stages of a storm system that reaches all the way from the rain we're getting here to blizzard proportions in the Colorado mountains, and . . . Gene, are you still there?"

"I'm here," said Cleese. His mind was already moving ahead with this thing, balancing scenarios and outcomes, but it was politic to allow Des Pruitt his lecture.

"Anyway, as near as we can pinpoint, we're talking about somewhere on a line east of Telluride and north of Durango in southwestern Colorado. That's the San Juan Mountains, the largest and most remote chain of the Rockies."

Given that location, it had to be the Lear, all right. Cleese didn't believe in coincidence. Karma, either.

"What's the nearest airport?" he asked.

"There's the one at Telluride and the one southeast of there at Durango. They're both closed down right now by the weather, and probably will be for the next couple of days, which is quite fortunate for our—"

"A crash beacon doesn't necessarily mean survivors, Des," murmured Cleese, just to see what Pruitt would say. "That plane's probably augered into the side of a mountain with three *very* quiet passengers on board."

41

"But it does mean the plane wasn't totally destroyed, Gene," replied Pruitt. "Why didn't you . . . uh, take the more usual approach? Then we wouldn't be having this conversation."

"Technology marches on, Des," said Cleese, who had no intention of telling Pruitt his real reason. "Given the right scenario, the polymer's virtually undetectable by an Air Safety Board investigation, in case the plane turns up. And this plane *will* turn up, considering who's looking for it. You know that."

"But in the meantime we can't take the chance, Gene. That they're not all . . ." Pruitt's voice faded out.

"Quiet? I agree with you completely."

"Some people are concerned, Gene. This is . . . not satisfactory, I'm afraid."

"For me, either," said Cleese. "But it sounds as if I have a little time to make it right. In a storm the size of this one, nobody will be getting to the crash site for a while. A day or two, at least. I'm going to need some things, Des. A private plane to get me as near as the weather will allow, then access from there. Snowmobiles, or maybe a helicopter in case there's a break in the storm at any point. Also, check for me on some Data Sheet or C-4, whichever would work better in those conditions. And I'll be needing funds for my own subcontracting, of course."

"I don't need to stress, Gene, how important this is."

No, you don't, Des. You certainly don't. More important to me than to you, Des.

"I'll meet you at . . ." Cleese glanced at his clock. "At five-thirty. Is that enough time for what you need to do?"

"It will have to be," said Pruitt, and hung up.

Not too happy, thought Cleese, and went back into his oak-paneled bathroom. Middle management was like that, caught it coming and going. If Eugene Cleese messed up, it could very easily reflect back onto Des Pruitt, and Pruitt . . .

"Pruitt knew-it," said Cleese, and stared into his own

pleasant grandfather brown eyes in the mirror. "Pruitt knew-it, and he thinks old Gene blew-it."

The polymer was a space-age synthetic, a form of liquid plastic in a way, that adhered to the kerosene monomers which were the primary component of jet fuel. Over a measurable time span, the hybrid monomers enlarged into molecules . . .

Why didn't you . . . uh, take the more usual approach?

. . . that would eventually clog the injector next to the turbojet's combustion chamber where the fuel mixed with air. The result would be the same as trying to fly on empty tanks. Except in this case, with the added bonus of a fuel-laden plane on impact, the resulting explosion and fire would reliquify the polymer and then burn it off with the kerosene. If you didn't know what you were looking for, good luck with the investigation.

Which, of course, had very little to do with the *real* reason Cleese used the polymer instead of a bomb this time.

For some people, bombs were much too quick.

But something had obviously gone wrong. Cleese had realized, with this particular scenario, there'd be a radioed distress call from the Lear when the engines quit. That was the inevitable trade-off for the long, screaming ride down, and not a problem really, since it would serve as a form of confirmation. But an emergency locator transmitter meant the plane was at least partially intact . . .

What was that pilot's name? Bill Taliferro? Was he that good?

Or maybe just lucky. Either way, Pruitt was right. They couldn't take the chance. Not with Ben McKee.

What would be a real kick in the pants would be if McKee wasn't on the plane at all. If Shelley had lied . . .

"Trying to read Shelley Gallatin," Will Carter once said, "is like playing Liar's Poker with God."

. . . but Cleese was certain she hadn't. Shelley was as

tough as nails, but he'd seen the realization finally come into her eyes. There at the end.

Life and death, they're meaningless, boy.

Cleese glanced over at a small oak bookcase, there on the far wall beneath the framed battalion insignia and the fire team photos. At the tattered old Bible he was always about to throw out, but never did, for reasons that had nothing to do with Christianity. EUGENE CLEESE, SR. was lettered in gold on the cover.

Cleese felt a bitter taste well up in his mouth. It tasted like lye soap.

He had a quick shower, then went downstairs to the exercise room which comprised the back section of his multilevel stone and redwood house. The chromed Universal machine and the Stairmaster gleamed under dim track lighting, and a pair of fixed climbing ropes hung near the two-story-high rear wall. He dressed in layers, folding a Day-Glo orange polyurethane snowsuit—not much for camouflage, but he liked its warm, bright colors—into a large duffel next to his worn old Sorels. He packed in a fifty-meter length of multicolored Edelweiss eleven-millimeter rope, and put a pair of jumars and his ice ax on top, next to his cloth-wrapped crampons and some extra carabiners. Closed the duffel's top.

Then he opened a walk-in closet and took out four weapons. One was an Austrian-made Glock Seventeen, a nine-millimeter automatic pistol with a seventeen-shot clip. One was an Ithaca Magnum-10 over and under shotgun, gas operated, semiautomatic, its full-choke barrel sawed off to ten inches. One was a Mauser thirty-caliber rifle with a Weaver 3-9X scope. One was a Henley Buckmaster knife with a narrow, serrated eight-inch blade.

Also a powder blue Du Pont Kevlar vest with Velcro side straps. Pruitt wasn't the only one who was careful.

Cleese went into the other side of his closet and took down a pair of new Tubbs Katahdin aluminum snowshoes, lighter and shorter in the tails than the older models. He loaded the snowshoes and all the guns except the Glock Seventeen into a long canvas bag. Then he put on a leather fatigue jacket and found pockets for the Glock and the sheathed Buckmaster.

It was fifteen minutes past four on Cleese's wrist watch when he carried his bags through his warm, brightly lit house and into the terrazzo-tiled entry area next to his garage door. He went over to a wall phone and began making calls.

Calls to Liam Riley, Milton Wallace, and Arturo Garza. Wallace, an airplane mechanic turned gentleman grape farmer with the profits from his previous work for Cleese, was already awake at his Gold Hill vineyards up near Vacaville. Likewise Riley, who was luckily still at his hotel suite in Century City. After a couple of tries, Cleese reached Garza, the youngest of the group and a one-time East L.A. gangbanger, just arriving home from a Rave in a Pasadena warehouse. With each of them he talked circumstances; then he talked terms. Garza was ready—he was born ready, he said—and Wallace asked only about the possibility of a bonus. Riley, packing for his trip home to Massachusetts after some recent free-lance work, wasn't really interested, but that was no surprise. He was never really interested until he got there; then he was the best of the three—a man who'd courted death from Saigon to Belfast to Boston, pursued it like a star-struck lover.

Cleese made arrangements with them; then he closed up his house and set his security alarm system. As always under circumstances like these, the last thing he did before leaving the house was to remove his Academy ring. He left it on the entry table by the phone, in plain sight, sitting on a sheet of paper with the word "GENIE" printed in all capital letters.

The rain was increasing again by the time he backed out of his garage and down his shrub-lined driveway. Rain here, snow where he was going.

Blowing snow, driven by a blizzard wind. The colors

45

there would be muted. They would be charcoal shades of gray and white, like a Gustave Dore illustration of hell.

Like his recurring dream of Genie and the beach. Gray-white and cold, the ocean and the sand . . .

And dead flesh.

The poets and the painters were wrong about the color black. Gray and white were the colors of death.

Cleese backed his bright red Jeep Cherokee into the street, then headed south toward the freeway. It was five minutes past five.

Chapter Four

At five A.M., Mountain Standard Time, a general Weather Emergency was declared for the southwestern mountains of Colorado. The National Weather Service, in cooperation with the Colorado Highway Department, announced the immediate closure of the seven highway passes through the San Juans. All forms of travel were officially discouraged due to blowing snow and near-zero visibility. Emergency situations—those which could be dealt with at all—would be handled on a priority-first basis.

Though couched in the language of public relationese, the message was clear enough: Stay out of the high country, unless you were already there.

And if you were already there . . .

(A figurative shrug at this point)

. . . then you were on your own.

Ben McKee awoke from a dream of falling.

His eyes opened to a kind of flickering dusk all around him. Near blackness, with lighter shadows above his head . . .

And the memory of that dream. Something to do with high walls of stone and ice, and a swirling, blinding emptiness below that he knew went on and on . . .

Forever. As far as he could fall and scream. Which was also forever. At least in the dream.

When he opened his eyes again, he realized he was looking up at a ceiling. There were wooden beams up there, cross-patterned below a sloping roof, and those shadows flickering . . .

Were from the light below it. From an oil lantern, sitting on a table next to the bed.

He was lying on his back in a large bed, covered by heavy quilts and a wool blanket, listening to a soft, droning kind of sound that was nearly drowned out by a stronger, deeper noise. The noise of the wind outside.

He was inside a darkened room. He saw a square corner of walls over there, then another. There was a faint glow from what appeared to be a stove, combining with the oil lantern to cast a flickering, rust-reddish twilight that turned everything to elongated shadows. A table and chair, a low, bulky shape . . .

One of those old metal bathtubs. Ben wasn't certain how he knew that, but it triggered a memory somewhere. A memory of someone's face, and a momentary sense of warmth. And something else . . .

Someone else. Bare skin, bathed in firelight.

He shivered, which stirred a different sort of memory. God, he'd been so cold. So cold. . . .

His eyes opened wider, and he felt his heart lurch hard in his chest. Because, in that moment, he'd remembered the airplane.

Hearing the engines quit, even above the roar of the storm outside the compartment window. First one engine, then the other a minute or so later.

Hearing Taliferro swearing up there in the cockpit. Hearing Landry screaming. Feeling the Lear nose forward. . . .

Why was he in that goddamn plane? Ben McKee, who *hated* airplanes, had hated them ever since he was ten years old and his dad's friend Tom Something-Or-Other took him up in an open cockpit puddle jumper. And tilted so far to one side on his turns that Ben felt himself—he truly believed it—sliding out of his seat belt. Then out of the seat and down the wing . . .

48

Falling.

. . . toward the multicolored earth hundreds of feet below.

He wasn't sure that had been the beginning of his paralyzing fear of heights, but it seemed logical.

So why was he in the Lear, flying through a storm in the middle of the night? Leaving Brawley in the rain, then heading east through that fifty-thousand-foot-high monster blizzard. . . . ?

Because he had to. Stupid question. If he was going to stay alive, he had to.

You'll be fine, Benjamin. Trust me.

Trust you? Shelley, if you're lying . . .

But I never lie, Benjamin. At least not to those I don't love.

The Lear's engines quitting, one at a time. Then the realization that they were dropping out of the sky. In absolute silence, except for the sounds of Taliferro on the radio, trying to raise somebody . . .

Broadcasting in the blind, they called it.

. . . and Landry praying. Dropping out of the sky, and then Taliferro saying something about a clearing below.

"Could be a meadow, boys. Course it could be a boulder field, too. We're gonna need some luck . . ."

Bracing for impact, his face in the pillow, and his breath smelling like the roast beef and mustard sandwich he'd eaten at the safe house.

I'm alive, he'd thought at that moment. I'm still alive, and I can *feel* myself alive . . .

And then hitting the ground.

And later . . . much later, that smell coming back from the cockpit. Like tarnished pennies.

And the cold. Leave everything, they'd told him at the beach house. *Everything.* So all he had on was his blue crewneck sweater and his faded cords and his scuffed old Rockports. And the satin Raiders windbreaker he'd bought mostly to irritate Shelley, who was big on the Redskins, quite naturally.

Shelley . . .

She's not here, Ben. Metaphysically speaking.

The last thing he remembered was the cold. Or . . . maybe not the last. He remembered movement, and the wind all around him. He remembered a voice, saying something that embarrassed him at the time, but he couldn't recall what it was. He remembered the sudden warmth of that bathtub . . .

And something else. Someone else, bathed in firelight.

The droning noise he'd heard earlier got a little louder, more audible now above the muffled scream of the wind—coming from somewhere to Ben's left, it sounded like, though his head felt so thick and fuzzy he wasn't certain of anything. Maybe this was only a continuation of the dream. He struggled up onto one elbow, surprised at both his lack of strength and the renewed wave of shivering that broke over him . . .

He was naked, apparently.

. . . and tried to locate the source of the sound. In the shadows next to the bed, a pair of eyes returned his gaze.

Ben thought he jumped, and maybe cried out, too. But probably not. He was too dizzy, too disoriented to do more than stare at the small dog that was glaring right back at him. And showing some teeth in the process.

The dog's soft growl—the droning sound he'd heard—seemed to intensify a little.

Ben managed to move farther from the edge, and then he heard something else. The faint sound . . .

Of someone breathing.

He turned to his right, toward the oil lantern, and that was when he first realized he wasn't alone in the bed. A bundled shape over there, hugging the far edge. The faint outline of a head, partly covered by the wool blanket.

He heard the same noise again. Like the sound of congested breathing. A quick indrawn gasp, followed by a slower, trembling exhalation. That, or maybe. . . .

Then he saw the shadowy silhouette of the body twitch convulsively, and he realized this other person was asleep. Asleep, and crying very softly.

Someone else with bad dreams.

Ben felt his dizziness returning, and he laid his head back on a mashed old feather pillow that carried the faintest edge of a scent, not unpleasant, like the smell of clean hair . . ,

Another trace of memory.

. . . before he felt his senses starting to fade again. Also not unpleasant. All things considered, a little oblivion at this point wasn't necessarily a bad thing.

His last thoughts, before he spiraled down into the windblown darkness where he continued to fall and fall forever, were of Shelley and Cleese.

And the disk, of course.

After a while, when the man's breathing became slow and regular again, Jack rose from where he crouched on the floor and walked to the edge of the bed. The smell from there, the man-smell, raised his hackles along the curly brown and white fur of his spine, and he began to growl softly again.

The smell was in his nose and, therefore, in his mind. It stirred a mix of memories, uneasy images. Of loud noises and pain, and of fear. For himself, but mostly for the woman.

He sniffed the edge of the blanket, and his lips curled back over his teeth. He was angry and frightened all at the same time, though he didn't remember exactly why.

When he finally decided the man wasn't going to move again, Jack padded around to the other side of the bed. The woman was there, like always. Lying at the very edge of the bed, like always. And making those soft, disturbing sounds as she breathed. Like always.

Somehow, the sounds she made merged with the man-smell in Jack's consciousness, and attempted to trigger a connection of some sort he wasn't capable of making, but one that brought back the images of noise and pain and fear. He sat next to the bed and tried to push his head beneath the woman's hand which was lying half-curled and twitching beside him. For a moment, her fingers moved in a familiar caress along his floppy ears, and everything—whatever it was that was making him angry and frightened—went away, and he whined softly down in his throat. He loved the woman in the way that occurs when love has only one singular focus for its existence.

After a few more moments, the woman's fingers were gone, and she turned away on the bed, still making the soft sounds in her sleep. Jack continued to sit beside her for a while, his head resting in the warm spot where she'd been; then he went back to the other side. He lay down, but he didn't sleep. He watched the man through the night.

Natalie Kemper awakened a little before seven o'clock and reached over to turn up the burnt yellow flame on the oil lantern by her bed that she never allowed to go out completely at night. Early rising was an ingrained habit, because the information from the array had to be compiled, then transmitted down to Walker Lake if possible. She would have awakened even without the noise of the storm roaring outside her cabin.

And even without the stranger in bed with her, who was propped up on one elbow about six inches away—it seemed—and studying her intently.

"Where'd you get that scar?" he asked. His eyes were still very blue.

"Good morning to you, too." Nattie automatically pulled the patterned Pendleton blanket higher, caught in that peculiar mix of anger and panic she experienced when any man came this close. "And how would you feel about getting the hell out of my face?"

His reference to the scar only made it worse. An intersection of memory.

"Sorry." He smiled—still a nice smile—proving the night hadn't been a dream after all. He pushed himself up toward the log wall that served as a headboard, which caused the blanket to slide down around his waist.

52

"I thought I had some clothes," he said. "Last I remembered."

"They're . . ." Nattie almost pointed toward them, draped across some chairs near the woodstove, but she had a sudden, irrational flash of this man leaping out of bed, giving her a deep bow from the waist, and then tap dancing over to the stove.

"Don't move," she said, and climbed out onto the cold wooden floor. "I'll get them for you."

"Thanks." He leaned back against the wall. "What do you . . . uh, call those?"

Nattie glanced down at her navy blue Damart Thinsulates, and felt a faint blush burn her cheeks. But she made herself give him a cool stare.

"Usually I call them insulated underwear," she replied. "That, or maybe just Bob when there's nobody around. What about them?"

"Nothing." He smiled again. "Except I don't believe I've slept three in a bed since I was a little kid. You and me and Bob."

"Two of us were probably less impressed than you were." Nattie gathered up the dry clothes. "You appear to have recovered quite a bit since last night."

"Thanks to you." The man's smile faded, and he seemed to be listening to the storm for a moment. "Christ," he murmured, and shuddered slightly. "Things are still a little hazy, but I remember enough to know I owe you my life. I'd like to thank you."

This change of pace caught Nattie off guard. She quickly looked away from him, especially those eyes, and made a pretense of folding the clothes.

"My name's Ben McKee, by the way," he said. "Little c, capital K. And you are . . . ?"

I are in love. That old joke popped into Nattie's head, obviously out of context, and her blush deepened. "Natalie Kemper," she said aloud, and covered the awkwardness of the moment by tossing his clothes onto the bed.

"I'm glad to meet you." Ben McKee nodded toward

53

Jack, who sat near the foot of the bed staring at him. "Is he as unfriendly as he looks?"

"You've got his place, speaking of three in a bed." Nattie grabbed her jeans and a tan sweater, and purposely turned her back. "The last guy who tried that's over in Salt Lake now. The Mormon Tabernacle Choir hired him to sing all their high notes."

"Ouch," the man muttered. "That does remind me of one thing I remember from last night, though. Some remark about the . . . uh, size of my anatomy?"

Oh, dammit, thought Nattie, and stumbled into her jeans while standing—no mean feat. My big mouth . . .

"Probably you dreamed it," she replied, still facing the window, and pulled the thick sweater over her head. "Or maybe it was your subconscious talking to you."

"Probably." It sounded like he was standing up now. "Is it safe for me to move, or does he do vertical vasectomies as well?"

"He doesn't much like men." Nattie went to the heavily reinforced wooden door and pushed it open a crack. "C'mere, Jack." Even here, on the east side of the cabin, the wind was blowing so hard it nearly yanked the knob out of her hand.

"Pottie break, bud," she said, and held the door open just enough for the dog to squeeze through. He went reluctantly, glancing back behind her.

"I'll be fine, Jackie." She patted his head. "You just keep an eye out for Leo and Laura."

"Your neighbors?" Ben was there beside her, helping pull the door shut.

"In a manner of speaking." Nattie instinctively stepped away from the man and turned for her first real look at him in an upright position. He was around six feet tall, give or take an inch, roughly the same as Rick, though probably at least forty pounds lighter. "Leo and Laura are a couple of mountain lions from over near where your plane nosed in. They've been trying to invite Jack for dinner."

"Mountain lions? Good God." Ben looked around him. "Where the hell am I?"

"Well, let's see." Nattie went to the old rectangular table and pulled over one of the high-backed chairs she'd used to drape the man's clothes. "You're approximately eleven thousand feet above sea level in a cabin that's six miles from the Walker Lake communication center, which is east of Telluride, Colorado. North of Silverton and Durango. Smack in the middle of the San Juan Mountains." She sat in the chair and looked up at him. "Oh, and you're also surrounded by the early stages of what may turn out to be the biggest winter storm around here in a decade. That's where the hell you are."

Which was maybe laying it on a bit strong, but she hadn't liked his tone.

"Okay." He took a deep breath. "Then, I guess my next question is, where's your bathroom? Or do I just follow Jack's trail?"

"Only as far as the first corner." Nattie kept a straight face. "Then you hook a left—"

"No way." He stared at her. "Hey, I was only kidding. No way you're going to tell me you've got a—"

"If the blizzard's left it standing." She gave up on the straight face. "But, listen, I just redecorated yesterday. Stapled down a brand-new piece of two-inch-thick blue Styrofoam. No splinters, that's a guarantee of the house."

After Ben McKee struggled his way out the door—giving a wide berth to Jack, who came back in coated with a solid layer of snow and a serious wet-dog odor—Nattie tried her shortwave again. Still just static coming over the headset. No response from Starvin' Marvin at Walker Lake, or anyone else along the entire range of the band. Then she went over to the alcove in the corner, next to her walk-in pantry, where she'd hung her small oval mirror. Its glossy wood frame had made the long mule trip unscathed, but she kept a square of thick carpet directly underneath it, just to be safe.

"What does she need with that thing?" her mother had asked.

"She's not a little girl anymore," had been Warren Kemper's reply. *Then he'd turned to where she stood watching them, fourteen years old, her eyes wide with surprise and delight.*

"Every young woman should have a mirror of her own," he had said.

And then he'd smiled at her . . .

"Morning, Daddy," she whispered to the single photograph sitting on the washbasin.

Nattie was always surprised for a moment when she saw herself without makeup. Rick had been insistent upon her use of eyeliner and mascara at all times, though other people told her that her thick-lashed green eyes didn't really need the help. This morning, those eyes were slightly dark-circled anyway from lack of sleep. Nature's own eye makeup.

Her long, dark blond hair—finally losing its summertime streaks of lighter color—was in tangles halfway down her back. She reached for her brush and went to work on it. Parting it in the center . . .

That hippie-girl stuff went out of date with your mother . . .

. . . she brushed it over one shoulder before she tied it back out of her way with a red ribbon. She looked for a moment at the diagonal scar just beneath her lower lip.

"Where'd you get that scar?" Ben McKee had asked.

There are visible scars, she thought, and touched it with a fingertip, *and there are invisible ones. All things considered, she'd been pretty lucky that night—speaking strictly in terms of visible scars.* . . .

Nattie pushed that set of images onto a back burner of her consciousness, as she always did. Or tried to do. This morning it was a bit tougher than usual.

She dipped her toothbrush in a glass of water, and then

layered on a blue curl of Crest gel. If she were the proper hostess . . .

The hostess with the most-est, her mother—who still believed Rick was perfect except for his little temper problem—used to say.

. . . then she'd have a spare toothbrush for Ben McKee. But he was no doubt happy enough just to discover she'd been joking about the toilet facilities. He'd probably gone out into that blizzard expecting an old two-holer with a quarter moon carved in the door, sitting half-buried in the snow. What he'd found was primitive enough —this wasn't the Little Nell in Aspen—but at least it was attached to the cabin wall.

He might be less amused when he realized that the latched back compartment opened directly into the cabin's storeroom at the rear of the pantry, but the fresh air trekking all the way around the outside would be good for him.

"Y'know, you're a prickly one at times, girl." That was what Starvin' Marvin had said to her. "Never know what's gonna set you off. Remind me not to get cross-ways with you, okay?"

Damn straight.

"You wouldn't think you could hear something like that." Ben McKee sat watching Nattie mix powdered milk with hot water. "With the storm so loud, I mean. But I heard it, all right. The engine on the left quit first, and the plane kind of tilted that way."

Nattie glanced back from where she was standing next to the woodstove, but she avoided looking directly at him. Ever since he'd come walking in through the store-room, never mentioning how she'd sent him the long way around through that raging storm, she'd been feeling a little ashamed of herself. In her usual Defiant-Nattie sort of way, of course. No point in getting carried away about it.

"It must have been terrifying," she murmured, and poured Quaker Instant Oatmeal into the pan.

"The other engine quit right after that." Ben was studying the wall above the stove, it looked like. His eyes were vacant and vaguely glassy, as they had been ever since he started this narrative. A one hundred and eighty degree mood swing. "I guess I realized what kind of trouble we were in when I heard Taliferro start cursing."

"Taliferro?"

"Bill Taliferro. The pilot. He was from Texas, had one of those thick Bubba accents, you know? I hear him mumble, 'Well, shee-it.' Then he was on the radio, calling out numbers."

"Was he the older guy?" Nattie divided hot oatmeal into three plastic bowls. "The one sitting on the left?"

"That was him."

"He was smiling." Something about that memory from last night had stayed with Nattie. "When I looked in there. His eyes were closed, but he was smiling."

"I . . ." Ben took the bowl Nattie gave him, and she saw his hand was trembling. "I closed his eyes. His, and Landry's, too."

"So you were in the cockpit." Nattie put the third bowl on the floor for Jack, then sat across from Ben. She placed a sugar container and a small tub of margarine between them. "After the crash, I mean. It's safe to use that margarine, by the way. I keep it in a cold-box out in the storeroom."

Ben started to reached for the sugar, then pulled back. His fingers were still unsteady.

"Let me do that." Nattie took his spoon. "I like mine pretty sweet, 'cause there was a time I couldn't . . . didn't use any sugar at all. So you'd better say when."

"Landry was really scared, and he was showing it." Ben didn't give any indication he'd heard her. "He started screaming bloody murder when Taliferro turned the plane into the wind . . ."

He looked up at her.

"I'm sorry," he said. "I know you don't need to

hear this. It's just that all of it keeps coming back to me . . ."

"Hey, no problem, bud." Flipness was something she could always manage. "But eat some of your breakfast before it gets cold. I slaved, in case you didn't notice."

He mustered a faint smile and took a spoonful, but his hand stopped halfway to his mouth.

"Taliferro flew gliders, did I tell you that?" Ben said. "On his days off. Out over the ocean toward Catalina when the wind was right. And he brought that little jet down, into the wind. Like it was a glider."

He remembered the spoon, and took a bite.

"Still hot." He nodded. "And it's very good. But I'm not really hungry." He put the spoon down beside his bowl and went back to staring at the wall. "I was sitting there in the back, and I was thinking how that damned little plane was just like a flying coffin. Teakwood and brass on the inside, all it needed was a satin pillow and some handles. God, I hate airplanes. And it was . . . so quiet in there. Like being in the middle of a ball of cotton. I knew we were falling out of the sky, and that I was going to die in a few minutes, but it . . . didn't feel like anything at all. Just being in the middle of a ball of cotton."

Nattie kept quiet. She'd long since realized Ben McKee needed to tell this, to get it out. She could relate to that, having a demon or two of her own . . .

Nattie my love . . .

She poured him some coffee.

"Then I heard Taliferro say something about seeing an opening down below, and for me to put my face into the pillows on my lap. He said the ELT would engage automatically on impact, then he said good luck, and he closed the cockpit door."

"You came down in Cat Meadow," said Nattie. "It's the only open area that size anywhere around here. Speaking of luck."

"Yeah." He looked at her. "For me. But not for Taliferro and Landry."

"It wasn't the pilot's fault. Those trees . . ."

"We bounced a couple of times, and I got whip-sawed side to side pretty good. Then we stopped. When I got out of my seat-belt, I could see snow pouring in through a rip above the door. Except for my back aching, I wasn't hurt at all. So I got up into the cockpit . . ."

"I know," said Nattie.

"Landry was still alive, even with those . . . those tree limbs." Ben swallowed some coffee. It was scalding hot, but he didn't appear to notice. "He kept saying how we'd made it, by God. How lucky we were, and how we were going to be okay. Just babbling on. He sounded like some damn football coach in a locker room. Then I saw Taliferro was smiling, over there in his seat, and I thought to myself, why not? He brought us down, didn't he?"

"He did." Nattie nodded.

"Down out of the storm, flying blind past the mountain peaks, and finally into that meadow without any engines. Turning a Lear jet into a glider. I remember thinking that he deserved to be proud. I reached over to close his eyes, and when I turned around I saw Landry had died. I closed his eyes, too."

Ben looked at the bowl of oatmeal, then at Jack. "You mind?" he asked.

"No. But he probably won't take it from you."

Ben set his bowl on the floor next to the empty one. Jack backed away from it.

"I couldn't get out of the plane." Ben's fingers fidgeted the coffee cup. "I released the door's safety bar . . ."

"It's a good thing you did," said Nattie.

". . . but it wouldn't open. The compartment was filling with snow from that tear in the fuselage, and it just kept getting colder. So I took all the pillows and blankets I could find, and I put on my jacket, and I just wrapped up in one of the seats."

"Your L.A. Raiders jacket." Nattie nodded. "You do know this is Denver Broncos country, I guess. If a real hard-core Raider-hater Broncomaniac had found you, he might've just left you there."

"Or fed me to Leo and Laura." Ben smiled, and, as before, it transformed his face. A dynamite smile, no question about it. "Anyway, that's all I remember until this morning, except for little snatches of things . . ."

He looked at her intently for a moment, then away. "I remember being dragged somewhere, several times," he continued, "and riding on something that was bumpy as hell. I remember the hot water 'in the tub. God, do I remember that."

He looked over at her. "And I remember your face."

Nattie pretended to concentrate on her food.

"Oh, and one other thing, or maybe I dreamed it. Did you . . . take a bath last night? After you put me to bed?"

So much for sleeping through the stripper.

"Hypothermia'll give you some weird dreams, all right." She stirred her oatmeal fiercely. "Hallucinations, in fact."

"That's for sure. I don't suppose you have a small birthmark, or maybe a bruise, down low on your left hip . . . ?"

"Right next to my Born To Raise Hell tattoo, you mean." Nattie tried for just the right expression. Faintly amused, that was the plan. "You certainly have a vivid dream-life, Mr. McKee. Now, let me ask you something for a change. What do you think caused your plane to go down?"

He'd been smiling at her, feeling good enough about having talked out the demons of that terrifying fall from the sky to tease a little. But now the smile faded.

"The engines quit," he said, and took a drink of his coffee. "How would I know why? I know computers, not jet airplanes. Some kind of accident . . ." His voice trailed off.

Some kind of accident? *Not that easy. You murdering sonofabitch.* That's what he'd said, rambling in and out of consciousness. Nattie had only asked the question in order to change the subject from her late night bath, but now she sensed deception. And her radar was still razor-sharp in that area.

"Who's Cleats?" she asked.

Ben McKee's face had been slowly regaining its color. Now it went pale again. Pale as last night in the frozen plane. The color of old bones.

"Who?" he asked.

"A name you mentioned." Nattie studied him. "Sounded like Cleats, or maybe Cleese. Also someone named Shelley."

He tried to smile. Failed utterly.

"Hypothermia," he replied, after a moment. "Like you said, it'll give you some weird dreams." He swallowed convulsively.

"Uh-huh," said Nattie, and decided to take a different tack. "Where were you headed? In the Lear, I mean."

"New York." He still wasn't looking at her. "Business."

"From California, I guess." She glanced at the Raiders jacket. Some people apparently dressed informally for business. "Must've been pretty important, just one passenger on that plane."

"Computer business," he shrugged.

"Do you know if the pilot's distress call got through?" His head snapped up, and he stared at her.

"I don't think so," he answered after a moment, then frowned. "At least I didn't hear any response if it did. He was fighting the headwind, and he had Landry calling off the altitude readings to him. Said something about the high peaks, and how we were going to need some luck . . . After that I don't think he radioed anymore. He didn't have the time, and Landry didn't know how."

"I thought Landry was Taliferro's co-pilot."

Ben glanced away again. "More like a friend, I guess. I do remember he said that part about the ELT."

"Then it's probably still operational." Nattie rose from her chair. "When I was outside before breakfast, I checked my weather gauges. Blizzards this size nearly always have what they call dry pockets, small windows in

62

the storm like the eye of a hurricane. It looks like we may hit one sometime this morning, and maybe I can finally get through to Walker Lake."

She went over to her shortwave and unshuttered the window above it. The storm was still roaring out there, blinding snow driven laterally by that hundred decibal wind, but it wasn't quite as bad as when she'd fought her way out to the sealed-up array an hour or so earlier. The barometer was the most telling indicator, and it had stabilized somewhat overnight. Just temporarily, probably, as the worst of the blizzard was yet to arrive, but it could be the first of the dry pockets coming through.

Nattie suddenly found herself wanting to hear Starvin' Marvin's voice very badly. She'd been uncomfortable with this McKee from the time she awoke to find him lying next to her. Watching her. Granted, there had been moments when that discomfort had taken some unexpected directions, even stirring some feelings she thought had died forever in the glaring white lights of a Denver hospital's emergency room. That smile, and those eyes . . .

But then he'd lied to her. To his credit, he lied poorly, as if it wasn't a habit, but . . .

Still, he'd lied. Nattie had known too many liars.

She checked the charge meter on the small generator beneath the table, then glanced at her watch. It was a few minutes past nine. "Marvin'll get the word out if I can reach him," she said to Ben, remembering his reaction to the idea of the radio and the crash beacon. "I guess someone will be looking for you by now."

Ben McKee had walked over to the window, and was staring out. She saw his jaw tighten in the pale gray-white light from outside.

"Someone," he said.

Chapter Five

There was static on the shortwave, but it had been like that all morning. Marvin Stone turned back to his piano, and the second verse of "Camptown Races."

Doo-da, doo-da . . .

The right-hand fingering was a bit more intricate through here, but Stone wasn't worried about screwing it up. That was hard to do on a player piano. Just follow the dancing keys.

G'wine to run all night, g'wine to run all day . . .

Stone was getting into it now, and the elderly piano bench creaked beneath his weight. He was a large man, a little over six feet tall and extremely fat, weighing two hundred and seventy pounds. He had curly hair that was an equal mix of red and gray, and an even curlier red beard with a fringe of gray at the chin. Little china blue eyes stared out from behind a pair of glasses with gold circular rims.

The player piano, like the large mirror mounted above it, had originally belonged to Stone's ex-wife, Etta, who had no more musical talent than he did. He'd learned the trick of pretending to play it from her. Quick fingers, and you could fool a lot of people. She'd certainly fooled him . . .

In several ways.

The static scratched again, and Stone turned away from the keyboard to glance at the shortwave over by his front window. The piano didn't mind. It went right on without him.

Bet my money on the bobtail nag . . .

Better check it out, he decided, even though he was fairly certain he wouldn't get a coherent signal in this weather. It could be any of the half-dozen winter people scattered around the Walker Lake communication center in a rough twelve-mile arc. He hoped it was Nattie Kemper, up above Empinado Canyon. She was his favorite, in spite of being so close-mouthed about her past, and he always looked forward to her calls.

Stone stood up from the piano bench, which caused the top button of his size forty-four Levis to pop loose, as always. He left it like that, since it was more comfortable anyway, and he wasn't expecting company in this weather unless a Sasquatch decided to drop by. He poured a cup of coffee from the hot plate atop his file cabinet, then ambled across the comm center's large front room to the window. Behind him, the player piano began the last verse.

When he'd come in from delivering up the canyon that day and found Etta gone—no note, not even a screw-you-and-the-horse-you-rode-in-on Dear John letter—he'd also discovered she'd taken with her most everything that wasn't tied down, including his collection of autographed baseballs from his boyhood in the Bronx. Hank Bauer, Whitey Ford, Tony Kubek, The Mick, and Yogi, which was the toughest one to lose—thirty years and a hundred pounds ago, Stone had been a pretty fair minor league catcher for a couple of seasons in Class C ball at Roswell, New Mexico. But even someone as determined as Etta couldn't haul that four-hundred-pound piano out of here. One might say he had it to remember her by.

Which was why he fetched it an occasional kick in passing, depending on his mood. Fortunately for the state of musical culture in the Walker Lake area, Stone's moods were usually as jovial as his appearance. Actually he didn't miss Etta—who had a mouth like barbed wire—any more than a person misses an abscessed tooth once it's removed. He would've liked to have those baseballs back, though. Especially the one signed by Yogi.

Outside, the storm continued to slacken. Just temporary relief, according to Nattie Kemper, who certainly had enough weather-related equipment at her cabin to know, but it was nice to have some visibility for a change. Still gray-white and gloomy out there, but the wind had dropped down. Stone could see across the frozen expanse of the lake and about halfway down toward the dam and its locked-up pump station. On the far side, steep, wooded slopes disappeared into low-hanging clouds.

If the lull continued a bit longer, he might be hearing from the coyotes over on that slope, especially if they heard the piano. They'd be holed-up right now—having better sense than humans—but they'd be out once the snow stopped.

They seemed to like the piano, occasionally chiming in with some two-part harmony. Some people didn't care much for their howling, said it was a desolate, lonely sound, but Stone didn't agree. It reminded him of crisp summer nights, with so many stars visible in the high altitude sky that the flatlanders all went home with cricks in their necks.

Marvin Stone was ready for summer, and baseball season. Eight more weeks 'til opening day. That guy from Ouray claimed the satellite dish he'd be installing—once they dug out a spot for it up behind the snowmobile shed—would get both the Yankees and the Mets games, though Stone could take or leave the Mets.

He adjusted the shortwave's frequency to slightly above three thousand megahertz, which, though near the low end of the SHF band, usually worked best with the convoluted interference patterns in these mountains. The set scratched out some more noise.

"Come on back." Stone depressed the transmit button at the base of his microphone. "That you, Nattie?"

Just static.

"Wait one," he said, and adjusted his needle on the band. "Try it now."

More static.

What if it was Nattie, and she was in some trouble up there? Stone sipped his coffee while he considered. Not likely—she was little, but she was tough—but possible. In weather like this, anything was possible.

It was six miles to her cabin, if you happened to be a crow. Or the Human Fly, and were therefore able to scale the frozen, vertical wall of aptly named Empinado Canyon, up past the deserted summer cabins at the headwater of Walker Creek. Just thinking about that sheer, ice-coated granite face made Stone a bit queasy, though he knew Nattie was all over it with her climbing gear in the summertime. But, in the middle of February, it was nearly ten miles by snowmobile to Nattie's place, using the mule trail that was currently underneath at least five feet of snow.

The shortwave squawked again, just as the piano's music roll played out, and in the silence Stone heard the suggestion of a voice, still drowned by static.

"Come back." He released the mike button, and listened for a few seconds. "Whoever you are, if you can hear me, keep trying. The storm's letting up some, and . . ."

Marvin Stone's mouth fell open, and he forgot what he was about to say. Because, out in front of the snow-buried comm center, something was descending. Angling down into his view from out of the low, leaden clouds.

It was a helicopter.

"Jesus Lord!" said Stone, and wasn't aware he'd dropped the mike. "Oh, you crazy bastard . . ."

The copter was a Bell LongRanger with a single horizontal rotor, similar to the type the TV stations in Denver used for traffic reports. It was white with red and blue trim, and it had bulky lake pontoons covering its skids.

Stone hadn't seen a helicopter at Walker Lake since that idiot tourist—from Texas or Oklahoma or someplace equally flat—decided to sit on her raincoat and slide down a snowfield near the old mine up in Empinado Canyon. When she reached terminal velocity shortly thereafter and went airborne for fifty feet into the boulders below, seriously wrecking a number of bones and various other innards, the Flight For Life helicopter had hauled her off to Denver and a future filled with physical therapy.

But that was back in July, sunny and warm. And the helicopter that day was a big, twin-rotor army Chinook, better suited for adverse conditions than one of these LongRangers. Who in hell would fly such a small chopper in this weather? Even now, with the wind dropping and the snow reduced to flurries, who would take such a chance?

Somebody crazy. Or desperate.

The helicopter bounced and bucked in the wind currents, continued dropping toward the long slope between the comm center and the lake. When it entered ground effect, its blades kicked up a secondary blizzard around it, snow devils spinning away downwind, and Stone could make out only a silhouette.

"Goddamn fool." He shook his massive head in disbelief and hurried to the coat rack to grab his parka. "That snow's five feet deep out there."

The pontoons would spread the weight, of course. With a good enough pilot, it might work.

When Stone stepped out onto his covered front porch, the wind struck him like a blunt instrument. This might be a lull in the blizzard, but it wasn't much of one. He saw the copter was resting lightly on its pontoons, still using its whirling blades to keep part of its weight suspended.

The portside bubble-door opened, and a figure in a Day-Glo orange snowsuit climbed down onto a pontoon. The figure was wearing snowshoes, and stepped quickly off into the deep powder. Two more figures, dressed in white, followed behind.

"Hey, you people are absolutely nuts!" Stone yelled at them. "You know that?"

The wind whipped his words away.

The figure in the lead raised an arm in a wave. All three were making good progress, using that distinctive snowshoe shuffle and hardly sinking at all. Those guys are in shape, thought Stone. Maybe a search-and-rescue outfit, though he couldn't see the Mountain Rescue logo—a blue circle with a mountain peak in the center and a white cross on the peak—anywhere on the chopper. He stepped back to give them room on the porch.

"I wasn't sure we could find you." The leader bent down to unfasten the bindings of his snowshoes. "Looks like our coordinates were on the money, though."

"You people are nuts, flying a chopper in a blizzard." Stone motioned them toward the door. "And then trying to land in this kind of snow."

"Milt's very good." The man nodded toward a figure barely visible inside the helicopter, where the rotor wash continued to throw up a blinding spray. "He's flown in worse than this."

"Hey, *vato gordo,*" said one of the other men. "You got some coffee, bro?"

"Yeah. Yeah, sure. Come on in."

The two others came out of their snowshoes—new Tubbs Katahdins with the abbreviated aluminum tails—and filed into the comm center behind Stone.

"Let me at that fire," said one of them, pulling off goggles and a snow-covered cap as he hurried toward the woodstove on a side wall. "I still can't believe I let you talk me into this."

He was an extremely tall man, three or four inches taller than Stone, but probably a hundred pounds lighter. He had dark, curly hair, cut short, and a thin face bracketed with smile lines.

"It'll grow on you, I imagine," replied the man in orange. "It usually does."

The tall man flashed a wolfish smile, and continued to brush snow off his shoulders. He reminded Stone of that movie villain, the one who was the hired gun in *Shane*.

"Coffee?" said the other man in white.

"Over there." Stone nodded toward the hot plate on the filing cabinet. "Cups are clean."

"You're Mr. Stone, I guess." The man in orange had removed his cap and goggles, and Stone saw he was somewhat older than the other two. Very fit-looking, though, about six feet tall with gray hair and mustache, and friendly brown eyes. An erect, square-shouldered bearing like a military officer.

"Yeah, Marvin Stone." Stone offered his hand. "Folks around here call me Starvin' Marvin."

"Starvin' Marvin?" The coffee drinker was a short, burly Hispanic—the youngest of the three—with long black hair pulled back into a ponytail and a closely trimmed beard. He looked over at the man by the wood-stove.

"Era panzon tenia una panza," he said, and inclined his head in Stone's direction. *"Yo no miente."*

The tall man laughed, and Stone felt a sudden twinge of uneasiness. He did his best to like everyone—except Etta, maybe—but he wasn't sure he liked these two.

"Mr. Stone, I'm glad we found you." The gray-haired man's gloved hand was large, and his grip was powerful. "I'm hoping you may be able to help us."

This guy was a little more like it. "You're search-and-rescue, I guess," replied Stone. "You'd have to be, riding that damn chopper in this weather."

"It's brutal out there, isn't it?" The man nodded. "We're looking for a plane that went down somewhere around here late last night. A small private jet."

"Last night?" Stone watched the tall man walk over to the piano and sit on the bench. "I didn't hear a thing, or see anything either. Course, with that storm, the damn thing could've landed right out there where your chopper's sitting and I probably wouldn't have heard it. Be careful of that piano, okay?" he said to the tall man. "It's kind of an antique."

The man looked back at him with that odd, sunless smile, then turned to brush long fingers across the keys.

"The plane has an ELT," continued the gray-haired man, "which activated about eleven o'clock . . ."

"Well, that's a low frequency signal, you see," replied Stone, one eye still on the tall man. "Maybe thirty, forty kilohertz. I'm not rigged to pick it up."

He grinned, and shrugged. Saw the Hispanic guy watching him over the rim of his coffee cup.

The gray-haired man nodded. "That's what I thought," he said. "But we figured, since you're the only comm center in the area, we'd give you a try."

The tall man had switched off the music roll and was playing the piano, softly and expertly. That old Irish song, what was it . . . ?

"You gotta realize," said Stone, looking back and forth between the two, "that around here communication center's a relative term. If the weather lets up some more, maybe one of my—"

". . . back, Marv." The shortwave crackled.

"Hey, all right!" Stone hurried over to the set. For some reason he couldn't quite define, he was very glad to hear someone else's voice. The old guy was nice enough, but those other two . . .

Watching him like a pair of green-eyed cats studying a crippled sparrow.

"Starvin' Marvin here." He depressed the mike button. "That you, Nattie? Come back."

". . . Marv." Her voice was breaking up with static. ". . . tried to reach you . . . morning. Come back."

"It's this damn blizzard." Stone picked up his coffee cup and leaned closer to the set. "You're breaking up pretty bad. Are you okay? Come back."

"I'm . . . guy up here . . . crash last . . ."

Stone was aware the gray-haired man had moved over beside him, and that the piano had stopped. "Nattie," he

71

said. "Is that a plane crash? A private jet? Come back."

"Yeah. Two dead . . . survivor. How'd you know? Come back."

Stone grinned at the man. "'Cause I've got search-and-rescue right here, that's how. They're out in a chopper, looking for the plane. Where'd it go down? Come back."

". . . Meadow . . . survivor named Ben Mc . . . my cabin . . ."

The gray-haired man smiled at Stone, a warm, paternal kind of smile. Patted him on the shoulder. "This is first-rate, Mr. Stone," he said. "Please tell her we'll be up there as soon as possible. You can give us directions, can't you?"

"Oh, sure." Stone nodded toward a large topographical map that covered most of the wall near the woodstove. "Natalie Kemper. I've got everybody around here marked on that map, even the summer people. Nattie?" He depressed the mike button again. "Can you still hear me? Come back."

". . . you fine. Why can't you . . . ?"

"Probably because that set of yours is about ten minutes older than dirt, that's why." Stone felt the man's hand, still on his shoulder. "Listen, these guys're coming up there if the weather holds. Maybe you better ride back down with them, just 'til the storm plays out. Come back."

". . . for them, Marv. Out."

"I knew what she'd think of that suggestion," laughed Stone, and half-turned toward the gray-haired man. "She's a warrior, that Nattie. You couldn't budge her—"

It happened so quickly that Marvin Stone thought he'd dreamed it. Sudden pressure at the base of his skull, then a blurring of his vision, fading to a pinpoint of light. The piano began, "I'll Take You Home Again, Kathleen," he realized, and the pinpoint of light was gone. Only the music, so soft and lovely and dark . . .

Then it was gone, too.

* * *

72

"When snow piles up like this," Nattie was saying to Ben McKee, who she could tell wasn't really listening, "its ice crystals are changed by water vapor, which leaches toward the surface. That creates a prime requisite for avalanches, something called depth hoar . . ."

"Say what?" He stopped pacing for a moment, and looked over at her.

"That's spelled h-o-a-r, so you don't get it confused with any of your friends back in L.A." She felt a surge of irritation at his obvious lack of interest. Okay, it was pretty dry stuff, but *he* was the one who'd asked about her work.

"My grandma used to pronounce it 'hoor.' " Ben managed a distracted smile. "An all-purpose term for any female who smoked or drank or wore eye makeup."

"I don't smoke and I don't chew," quoted Nattie. "And I don't go with the girls that do."

"Something like that." He walked past Jack to look out the window, where snow was blowing past in light flurries. Jack showed his teeth briefly.

"That dog's slow to get acquainted," said Ben.

"He's always been an excellent judge of character." Nattie felt the same tiny kernel of irritation trying to take seed, and she wasn't sure exactly why. "And he doesn't like men. I told you that. But don't worry. You two won't have each other to snarl at much longer. Search-and-rescue'll have you back to the big city before prime time. Probably all you missed was an *Oprah* rerun."

"Oprah's not so bad," he said. "And neither are cities, for that matter. Lots of things to do in a place like New York or L.A. . . ."

"Besides duck and reload, you mean?"

"Beats ending up as lunch for a mountain lion." Ben nodded at Jack. "Are you two going to ride back with us, like that Marvin guy suggested?"

She looked at him for a moment, then away.

"Get real," she said.

The problem was, she *was* exactly sure why she was getting irritated. That was the problem.

73

Look at him, pacing up and down, about as relaxed as guitar strings, ever since Marv's message about the helicopter. He can't wait to get out of here.

And she couldn't wait to have him gone, she decided in that moment. If he was already tired of her . . . well, she was twice as tired of him.

Get her life back on schedule, that was the plan. Everything . . .

Safe again. All alone, with just Jack and the cabin and the mountains, and her work. There were worse things than being alone; she could definitely testify to that. A lot worse. . . .

Admit it, Nattie, the guy scares you . . .

Nobody scares me. Not anymore.

. . . even with those blue eyes and that smile . . .

And that lying mouth.

I hate liars, she thought, and watched him pace back and forth and look out the window. I don't know what this one's real story is, all that stuff he was mumbling last night, and I'll make a guess I'm better off not to know. But I do know one thing. He's been lying to me this morning.

I don't need another liar in my life.

I won't hurt you, Nattie. I promise. Let me in, okay? I just want to talk.

"So . . ." Ben McKee looked at her. "You study snow. That's what you're saying."

You don't care, she thought. You don't give a large rat's rump, in fact. You're just killing time 'til the helicopter gets here to whisk you back to La-La land. And you purposely grabbed on to this subject, right from the moment I got off the shortwave, so I won't ask you any more questions.

Well, don't worry about that, bud.

"I do climate research," she answered aloud, figuring why not? "The snowpack here in the Rockies is one of the planet's key indicators for global warming. And the molecular makeup of this snow, its carbon dioxide and sulfate content, for instance, also gives scientists a broader spectrum for the computerized simulations they're doing on acid rain. You said your field is computers, didn't you? So you're probably familiar—"

"Scientists, you said. You're not a scientist, then?"

Slippery to the bitter end, wasn't he?

"No, I'm not," she replied. "My degree's in English."

"Yeah? If you're not a scientist, what are you doing holed up in this cabin in the middle of nowhere?"

What are *you* doing mumbling about murder, and then lying about it? she thought. I do believe what we have here is a standoff.

She looked at him. Jack looked at him, and growled down in his throat.

He looked at both of them. "Hey," he said. "Forget I asked . . ."

Jack jumped to his feet, a second before Nattie heard the helicopter.

"Saved by the bell." She went over to the window and looked out. "I believe your train's just pulling in, dear. Do you have the right tokens . . . ?"

She'd turned back toward him, and her voice faded when she saw his face.

He's scared, she realized in that moment. I'll be damned . . .

"Helicopters aren't so bad," she said, and inwardly cursed herself some more for this sudden rush of concern over a man who'd done nothing but lie to her. "I've ridden in one or two myself."

She couldn't help it, apparently. "They'll have you out of here before you know it," she went on. "You'll be fine. There's still a little time before the next part of the storm hits."

He tried to smile. Didn't have much luck. The sound of the rotor blades overhead was louder.

What if . . . The thought blew into her head so quickly she didn't know where it originated. What if . . . it's not the helicopter he's afraid of?

That was stupid.

"They'll have to land over past the trees." She continued to watch him while that same stupid thought danced around in her head. "There's no room close by. So it'll be a few minutes yet."

"Listen." He seemed to relax some. "Before they get here...I don't feel like I've really told you how grateful—"

"Hey, no sweat, bud." She turned away from him. "I didn't have my merit badge in airplane rescue, anyway. Thanks to you, I'll be the first on my block."

From its sound, the helicopter was moving off to the east. Which was where they'd set down, in a small clearing just past the shallow ravine over there.

"Nattie." She felt his hand on her arm, and when she turned, the expression was set on her face. Friendly, in an impersonal sort of way, that was the plan.

"You're not going to let me thank you, are you?" he asked. His hand was still on her arm, which had Jack growling again.

"You already have." She moved before he could feel her beginning to tremble, then grabbed her old green cap with the earflaps and her heavy blue parka as she headed toward the door. "Better see if I can spot those guys."

The need at that moment to put space between herself and Ben McKee was nearly overwhelming.

"C'mon, Jackie," she said, and opened the heavy door slowly, so the wind couldn't yank it away from her. The dog bounded past her out into the snow.

The storm was still in a lull, which didn't mean it had stopped. Snow blew over her and past her, peppered her unprotected head with hard pellets while she pulled on her wool cap.

She glanced back and saw Ben McKee standing at the front window, watching her. His mouth was tight, etched with tension. His face looked nearly as pale as the night before, when she'd seen him for the first time.

The color of old bones.

Come on Nattie, she thought, looking away from him. If you'd been the only survivor of a plane crash, you might not be so eager to jump into a helicopter either, especially in this weather. Don't make something out of nothing.

In a little while it'll all be beside the point anyway. He'll be gone, and everything will be . . .

Back to normal.

She saw figures moving between the trees fifty yards away. Four of them, one in Day-Glo orange and the other three in white. She raised an arm to wave.

The lead figure waved back at her. Yelled something, but his voice was swept away by the wind.

Nattie turned back toward her cabin. Ben was still at the window, so she pointed at the approaching figures.

He nodded, and a few seconds later he opened the door. He was wearing his Raiders jacket and a red wool toboggan cap she'd lent him, but he'd never get far in those street shoes.

I guess he doesn't have to, she thought, and decided not to analyze it any further than that.

"They're here," said Nattie, and stopped about ten feet away. He was staring over her shoulder.

This next part was going to be awkward for someone who'd grown so accustomed to solitude. She'd have to bring the four men inside—a tight fit—then give them coffee and her version of the previous night's events. Search-and-rescue was notorious for being hung up on detailed reports.

She just wanted them to go away and take Ben McKee with them. Leave her alone.

He's so damn hot to get out of here, take him.

She glanced up, as part of that thought, at Ben, who was still in the doorway. His eyes were wide.

Glassy and wide with shock. Or something. . . .

She spun back and looked at the men, who had fanned out in a semicircle around the clearing. The snow blew across them, made them blurry and ghostlike in their stillness.

The one in orange was smiling, and Nattie saw twinkling brown eyes behind his goggles.

"Hello, Ben," he called, and brushed snow off his gray mustache with a gloved index finger. "How was your flight?"

Chapter Six

What happened next happened very fast.

Nattie heard Ben McKee's voice . . .

"Nattie, get back!"

. . . at the same moment she saw the guns come up. Some type of automatic pistols in web-sling harnesses . . .

"Get back!"

. . . and glimpsed a blur of movement from her right.

"¡Chingale!" yelled one of the men, and spun that way. Just as Jack hit him chest-high.

"Jack!" screamed Nattie, and started forward before a strong arm grabbed her from behind.

"Get inside!" shouted Ben McKee, and she felt herself being lifted into the air . . .

"Jack!"

. . . while the sound of gunfire surrounded her, deafened her. Whizzing sounds past her head, breaking glass . . .

A single, high-pitched yelp of pain.

. . . and she was inside the cabin. Ben was dropping the wooden brace across the door.

"The windows!" he yelled, as one of them exploded and showered her with a razor storm of flying glass. "Get the shutters closed!"

Nattie stumbled to a window, and swung the heavy wooden shutter inward. A surge of heat rushed next to her head, an instant before she heard a zinging sound go past her ear . . .

Oh, Jesus. Oh, Jesus Christ.

. . . and she latched the shutter. Across the room Ben had done the same. The little cabin went twilight dark, lit only by the illumination from the woodstove.

"Who are these people?" she yelled at Ben. "What the hell are they doing here?"

"Cleese." Ben had crouched beneath the front window. "You hear me, Cleese?" he called out.

"What the hell is going on?" Nattie demanded.

"I hear you, Ben." The voice was from outside. Windblown. The gunshots had stopped.

"This is kind of messy for you, isn't it, Cleese?"

"Kind of. That dog was unexpected." The voice was faint. "Why don't you come on outside?"

"Maybe you should just come in." Ben's face was a pale blur in the twilight. "We're unarmed in here. Helpless as babies."

"Dammit, McKee!" hissed Nattie, but he made a shushing gesture with his finger on his lips.

"Is that the truth, Ben?" The voice had moved farther to one side. Or maybe it was just the wind increasing again. "Should I believe you?"

"Why not? What do you have to lose? Send in one of your goons first if you're scared."

No reply.

Nattie crawled over to where Ben was crouched. "He's moved," she whispered.

Ben nodded. "Keeping us busy. Do you have any weapons in this place? A gun?"

"I have an old four-ten." Nattie pointed at her shotgun, propped in the alcove by the pantry. "But all it shoots is birdshot."

"Better than nothing," he replied. "Get it, but stay low. Knives?"

"Kitchen knives. A pocket—" She stopped. "You hear that? One of them's on the roof."

Ben looked over at the woodstove, then up at the ceiling, where one of the beams creaked again.

"That's not the wind?" he asked.

She shook her head.

"Christ," he muttered. "Get the shotgun. Do it quick."

Nattie crawled away from him, one small part of her mind registering the sudden change in the man.

He's okay now, she thought. Maybe it was the uncertainty, the waiting, before. Whatever, he's okay now.

Thank God.

Who were those people outside? One of them, the old one, he was Cleese . . .

Cleese, you murdering sonofabitch

. . . and the rest sure as hell weren't search-and-rescue. Marv had made a mistake.

Marv . . .

Nattie looked over at the shortwave, but there was no time. Not with those four men out there, shooting . . .

Jack. Oh, God, Jackie, I'm so sorry.

He'd saved her, at least for now, sweet little floppy-eared mutt. The split seconds he'd gained for her were the reason she and Ben McKee were still alive.

It was the second time he'd saved her life, this time at the cost of his own.

She felt her throat closing up, and a rush of tears blurred her vision.

Not now, dammit. She wiped away the tears with the back of her hand. There was no time for that either.

Outside, the wind was increasing again, wailing past the corners of the cabin. And, up on the roof, she heard the scrabbling of steps along the slick propanel.

"Ben?" The voice had moved, close against the wall this time. "Ben, you don't want to get that young woman involved any further, do you? This doesn't concern her."

"I guess I could send her out." Ben shifted quickly to the other side of the window. "You'd probably just let her leave, wouldn't you, Cleese?"

"This has nothing to do with her, Ben."

"Just like you did Shelley."

"Shelley was a player, Ben. Ms. Kemper?" The voice was louder. "Can you hear me, Ms. Kemper?"

Nattie had reached the four-ten. She looked back at Ben. Saw him shake his head.

"Ms. Kemper, I'd like to keep you out of this business if there's any way I can. All I need for you to do is leave. Just walk away right now. We'll all be gone from here long before you could create any problems for us."

Nattie looked at Ben. Saw the truth in his eyes.

"This has nothing to do with you, Ms. Kemper. I have a daughter about your age . . ."

Nattie broke open the four-ten's bore, and saw the shell. The problem was, it was a single shot, and a weak one at that. She'd brought it only to zing a little birdshot toward Leo and Laura, try to scare them away if they came too close . . .

Hunting for Jack. She began to tear up again. Bastards. Those sorry bastards out there. . . .

She wiped her eyes brusquely and popped down the four-ten. Who were they? She didn't know. Why did they want Ben McKee? She didn't know. And, for that matter, who the bloody hell *was* Ben McKee? She didn't know that either.

What she did know was they'd killed her dog. And they'd probably kill her, too, if they got the chance.

"Ms. Kemper . . . ?"

"Asshole," she muttered, and cocked back the four-ten's pin action hammer . . .

Just as smoke started wisping from the woodstove.

"Ben!" she said, and pointed, sliding back over to where he was.

"They plugged the chimney." He looked up at the ceiling. "I was afraid of that. They're going to smoke us out."

"Not with a woodstove they won't. It's self-contained, not like a fireplace."

"That smoke has to go somewhere."

81

"It'll just put out the fire," replied Nattie. "From a lack of oxygen. Unless . . ."

"What?"

"Unless it catches the creosote buildup in the stovepipe on fire first. If that happens . . ."

She looked at the stovepipe, rising vertically to the ceiling. Its entire length was beginning to glow a dull cherry red.

"It could explode," she said, and felt her stomach clench involuntarily. "It's only made of tin. I've heard of it happening."

"Then what?"

"First it'll blast hunks of hot metal all over this room. Then the whole cabin'll probably go up like a dead tree in a forest fire. Everything in here's made of wood."

"Ms. Kemper, can you hear me?" The voice outside had moved again. Away from the cabin, it sounded like.

"We've got to get out of here." Nattie nodded toward the storeroom. "Thank God for semi-indoor plumbing."

Smoke was slowly leaching from the seams of the stovepipe now. It rose to hang near the ceiling, drifting gray and hazy among the beams. Nattie heard the red-hot metal begin to ping, like the sound of an overheated car engine.

"Come on," she said.

They moved in a crouch across the floor, past the table and then the shortwave.

"I'm going to call Marv," said Nattie. "It'll only take a second, and he can send for—"

"Nattie." Ben took her arm and pulled her past the set. "Cleese was there with Marv. There's nobody left for you to call."

His words hit her hard, so hard she pulled free of him.

"Listen to me, Nattie." He held her with his gaze. "I know Cleese. There's nobody there for you to call."

"You sonofabitch." She stared at him. "What have you people done to us? What have you done to our lives?"

She pushed past him, more angry than afraid in that

moment, and cut through the small storeroom with its laden shelves. Opened the narrow connecting door . . .

Right into the path of the huge man who was crouched directly behind it.

The man straightened up, smiling at her, and at her little four-ten shotgun.

"Hello," he said.

And she pulled the trigger, pure reflex, just at the moment the stovepipe blew. And all hell broke loose.

The explosion of the pent-up gases hit the confined interior of the cabin point-blank. Everything went a brilliant orange, then flame red, as chunks of heated tin sprayed the room with shrapnel. Dishes and cups sailed across open space to smash against the far wall, and a piece from Nattie's old Bristol rocker flew up toward the ceiling beams, where a chunk of the roof was simply no longer there.

The entire cabin shifted minutely; then it began to burn.

Nattie heard a scream of pain. "Ben?" she yelled, then realized it was the big man screaming . . .

The man she'd shot.

. . . and scrambling backward, through the open door of the outhouse.

"Go!" Nattie felt Ben McKee pushing her from behind. "Go, dammit!"

She crawled through. Saw open sky, all gray-white and snow-filled. Felt the ice of the wind that was soothing compared to the heat building behind her.

Saw the half-buried outline of her old Polaris snowmobile, parked out there where she'd left it the night before, behind the rounded hump of the BLM dumpster.

"Goddamn sonofabitch . . ."

Cleese heard Liam Riley's voice, somewhere to his left, off in the trees. That nasal Boston twang.

". . . shit, shit, shit!"

Riley had been on the roof when the cabin blew. Normally a man of few words, he was obviously more angry than injured.

"Gene?" Arturo Garza crawled up next to Cleese. Garza looked okay, too, except for a little blood on the wrist of his snowsuit where the dog had bitten him.

"What happened to that cabin, bro?" asked Garza.

"I'm afraid someone had an accident, Artie." Cleese had to smile, the way things sometimes worked out. Apparently, he wouldn't be needing the C-4 after all. He stood up from where he'd leaped behind a big evergreen when the explosion occurred. Brushed snow off his face and shoulders.

"My guess would be whoever lived in there had an accident with their stove," he added. "People should be more careful."

He watched the cabin burn. It was becoming an inferno, and he retreated a few more steps away from its heat. Smoke billowed up into the falling snow.

Garza looked at the fire, then back at Cleese. "*¿El mundo es muy peligroso, verdad?*" he said. "*Llena de cenizas, esqueletos y secretos, me siento decirlo.*"

"Ashes, skeletons, and secrets." Cleese, who could manage in three languages and fake it in a couple of others, nodded. "That about sums it up, doesn't it?"

He shivered, in spite of the heat radiating out from the blazing cabin. Once they'd removed the traces of their presence, he wanted to be away from this place. This place of cold gray-whiteness . . .

The color of bad dreams.

"Oh, man, Milt," said Garza. "What happened to you, *hermano?*"

"Little bitch shot me." Wallace came stumbling out of some oakbrush, holding a bloody handkerchief to his forehead. "God, if I hadn't ducked . . ."

"It's just birdshot." Cleese moved the handkerchief for a closer look. "A little lower, though, and it could've been tough on your eyes."

"Hey, you an' Ray Charles, man," said Garza. "You got the right one, ba-bey . . ."

84

"Suck it, Artie." Wallace's big fingers were probing the bloody lumps near his already receding hairline where pieces of birdshot were imbedded beneath the skin.

"Pelame la verga, pendejo," replied Garza in kind. He and Wallace were always at each other. It was nothing new.

"She shot you, you said." Cleese watched Riley walking toward them across the clearing. "You got inside?"

"Not quite." Wallace continued to probe his scalp. "I found another door in the back, led to an outdoor crapper built onto the wall of the cabin. I'd just opened it when she opened an inside door. Face-to-face, man."

"Fast on the draw, huh?" said Garza.

"Annie goddamn Oakley. Lucky for me it was just a four-ten."

"Then what?" asked Cleese.

"Then the cabin blew." Wallace shrugged. "Blew me, too, like a bloody nose. Straight backward."

"What about the woman?" Riley, who was limping slightly but appeared otherwise okay, had caught the last of the conversation. "You think she got out?"

"I doubt it, man," said Wallace. "She was still halfway in the cabin."

"We'd better look, anyway." Cleese glanced up at the huge trees around them, bending before the wind. "I think the storm's picking up again . . ."

He heard the sound of an engine.

"What the hell . . . ?" said Wallace.

"Snowmobile, bro." Garza reached for his Ruger Mini-14, hanging in its web harness. "That, or the world's biggest chainsaw . . ."

"Over there!" Riley pointed toward some trees beyond the cabin, and Cleese spun that way just in time for a glimpse of movement. Something dark, moving fast, and then gone into the gray-white of the falling snow.

"Two of them," said Riley, whose eyes were the sharpest of the group. "The woman's driving."

So much for tidy scenarios, thought Cleese. He felt the

taste of an oath, right there on his tongue, but he never swore.

"Let's get to the copter," he said instead. "Milt, can you see to fly the thing?"

"Shit." Wallace pocketed the bloody handkerchief. "You're kidding, right?"

The four men managed a running shuffle through the deep powder, their snowshoes a hindrance as well as an aid. In moments they were gone.

In the deserted clearing, Natalie Kemper's little cabin continued to burn. Heat from its fire had already melted the snow around it down to muddy earth. Some of the nearer trees downwind were singed and smoking, but the steadily increasing snowfall prevented them taking flame.

After a while, the walls of the cabin collapsed inward, and the fire began dying from hunger. By afternoon, there would be only a smoldering ruin in the clearing. That, and Nattie's glass-fronted weather array standing next to the body of a little brown and white dog.

Before the snow finally covered it all.

The old Polaris could carry two, if it was babied along at low speeds. Nattie gunned the three hundred c.c. engine full bore, and thought about that.

It was going to overheat if she kept up this pace. And soon.

She throttled down slightly and cut through a narrow gulley. Overhead, the trees were groaning before the power of the wind, and the snow blowing past her was getting thicker.

The dry pocket was nearly gone.

Nattie felt Ben McKee's arms around her waist, and his body squeezed against her back by the snowmobile's small one-up seat. Even through her padding of a parka and sweater and long-handle top, she could feel him shivering.

Because he wasn't padded at all. That thin wind-breaker over a cotton shirt and crew-neck sweater. Corduroy pants and street shoes, no gloves. Not the best rehab program for someone less than twelve hours past hypothermia.

Plus, since he was a lot bigger than she was, riding behind her wasn't giving him any real protection from the wind.

No help for that right now, she thought, and steered toward the edge of Cat Meadow. Besides, in this case, being cold beat the hell out of the alternative.

Speaking of which . . .

She slowed, and cruised laterally to the open area on her right, where she hugged the edge of the trees, spooking a half-dozen snow-laden elk into lumbering flight down a ravine, their pumpkin-colored haunches disappearing into the storm. She listened for any sound that might be the helicopter.

Do we cross the meadow, or not?

Starvin' Marvin's mule trail, buried under probably five feet of snow, crossed Cat Meadow, then turned south before the ridge of Empinado Canyon on the far side. From there, it was a continuous series of switch-backs down toward Walker Lake and the comm center, which lay two thousand feet below the elevation of Nattie's cabin. A long, slow descent totaling nearly ten miles.

Which, once again, beat the hell out of the alternative. Namely, go all the way to the other side of the meadow, climb up through a thin stand of evergreens on the ridge top, then peek over the edge if you have the stomach for it.

Into the depths of Empinado Canyon, looking down toward the ruin of the Ojo del Plata mine near the headwater of Walker Creek. Fifteen hundred of that total two-thousand-foot descent, right there in one giant step . . .

Nattie, take one giant step.

May I?

Make that, must I?

Not likely. Her ice-climbing gear was in the storage compartment of the Polaris, as usual, but that was for places like the frozen waterfall over on Pascoe's Bluff. Nobody messed with Empinado Canyon in the wintertime.

"Why are we going so slow?" Ben McKee leaned forward.

"The trail down to the comm center," she answered, and got a faceful of blowing snow when she turned to look back at him. "It's across this meadow."

"And?"

"And it's a big meadow. Wide open. If that copter's still able to fly in this weather . . ."

"Can't you work your way around its edge? Stay in the trees?"

She shook her head. "The oakbrush gets too thick on that south side over there. I don't think I have enough gas for all the backtracking we'd have to do, and this snowmobile's too old to go bushwhacking through heavy brush."

"So," he said, and shifted his weight closer to her.

She nodded. "So, what are we waiting for, right? Until your pals showed up, I didn't realize you were such a man of action."

He shrugged. "Banzai," he said.

"Right." She revved the throttle. "Hang on, Rambo."

The Polaris shot forward, and Nattie made a long, sweeping turn to her right. Out of the partial protection of the trees, and out into the storm. Straight across Cat Meadow.

She bent forward and watched the red line of her tachometer. Hold together, babe, she thought. Hold on.

The blizzard was increasing in what seemed to be geometric progression. Worse than last night, when she'd crossed here alone, looking for a downed airplane.

Hold on, babe. We're halfway across. We have to be. Start looking for the trees on the other. . . .

Above the sound of the wind, there was another noise behind them. The helicopter.

"Oh, Christ," she heard Ben say.

Don't look back. Don't hesitate. Drive for the trees; they're somewhere ahead. Redline it . . .

Another noise. A whizzing sound.

"They're shooting!" Ben wrapped his arms up over her shoulders. "Step on it, dammit!"

"What the hell do you think I'm doing?" she snarled, in the split instant before she realized he was shielding her with his own body.

But there was no time to think of that right now. More whizzing sounds came, a chorus of them, and a plume of snow exploded upward just to her left.

She began to zigzag, felt Ben lurch side to side behind her. Another gout of snow blew out, on her right this time.

Can't let them get me bracketed.

She smelled the struggling little engine of the snowmobile overheating. She heard the steady *thwack-thwack* of the copter's rotors, above and behind her. Then off to one side . . .

And she saw the faint edge of something dark up ahead, swimming into her vision through the blowing snow.

Trees.

Another zip of sound, so close she *felt* its heat . . .

As it smashed into the snowmobile next to her left knee. The Polaris jagged hard right on her, and she fought for control. Pulled it back straight.

"Hey, I think . . . they're going down!" yelled Ben. "Hot damn, they're going down!"

Nattie didn't look. She concentrated on the trees ahead. But she could no longer hear the noise of the helicopter rotors above her. Just the howling of the wind . . .

And the ratchet, metal-on-metal sounds coming from the snowmobile's engine.

God, no. "Come on, babe," she whispered.

She throttled down to half speed, but the grinding noises only got louder.

"We're leaking oil." Ben leaned forward to speak into her ear. "Lots of it."

"Dammit," mumbled Nattie. "One of the bullets hit us."

"How much farther can this thing go?"

"The trees are up ahead. Maybe . . ."

The engine noise was increasing. A wisp of greasy-smelling smoke curled up from beneath the cowling and blew back into her face, and the Polaris began to buck and jolt.

It was going to be a near thing.

"Did they crash?" Nattie kept her eyes on the trees ahead. Her mouth was sour with the taste of spent adrenaline.

"The copter? I don't think so. The wind's gotten so much worse, I think they went down so they wouldn't crash."

"They'll be coming, then." Nattie's vision was obscured now by the smoke as much as the blowing snow. "And they have snowshoes. If we have to cross this meadow on foot, we'll sink waist-deep. And with those guns of theirs . . ."

"Where's the plane from here?"

Nattie looked up from trying to hold the Polaris in a straight line. "Over that way, I think." She pointed a little to her right. "Northwest edge of the meadow. Why?"

"Can we get there?"

"Maybe. Why?"

"Those two men, Taliferro and Landry. They had guns."

"What?" Nattie twisted to look back at him. "Why in hell would two pilots . . . ?"

Then she thought, in that moment, of the four men

90

chasing them. Of Ben McKee's incoherent mumbling in the night, and his evasions the next morning.

Of lies, and liars.

"Never mind," she said, and guided the shambling, dying machine toward the distant trees.

Chapter Seven

"Everybody okay?" Cleese had to do a modified sit-up to reach forward and unfasten his safety harness. He felt a moment of pride that he did it so easily.

"This is getting old." Riley pulled up next to Cleese, one long arm reaching for the door. "Blown off a roof and crash-landed, all in the same day."

"You love it, Liam," said Cleese. "Fess up."

Riley smiled.

"Hey, pretty nice flying, *parejo.*" Garza clapped Wallace on a huge shoulder. " 'Specially for a blind dude."

Wallace, his forehead crusted with drying blood, just grunted a reply. He looked over at Cleese, who was next to him in the front area of the cockpit.

"We're on the ground, Gene," he said. "Probably to stay, if you get my drift . . ."

"Drift," snorted Garza, and looked out the window at the snow piled up around the helicopter.

". . . 'cause this bird's probably turned penguin for the duration. What now?"

"Better load up," said Cleese. "Full gear . . ."

"Lock and load." Riley smiled at Cleese.

". . . and snowshoes. The longer we sit here, the farther ahead they get."

The four men loaded their packs, then crawled out Cleese's door, the only one clear of the drifts. When they stepped off the pontoon, the weight of their gear took them deep, even wearing snowshoes. Especially Milton

Wallace, who already carried two hundred and forty pounds on his massive six-four frame.

"I had them due west," yelled Cleese, over the scream of the wind. "Let's fan out, try to pick up that snowmobile track."

It was about fifteen minutes later when one of them found it. Riley, of course.

And it was ten minutes after that when they came to the first of the oil, slick-black and still visible beneath a deepening layer of snow.

The Polaris made it to the trees. Barely. With its oil completely gone, the engine went metal on metal. After a few more grinding lurches forward, it died.

"I don't see the plane." Ben McKee climbed off the snowmobile. By the time he'd slogged a few feet away, Nattie could barely find him through the blowing snow.

"It's here," she yelled, over the strengthening roar of the wind. "I remember that big double-trunked fir."

"If you say so." Ben headed off in that direction, wading forward. Under the huge evergreens, the snow was less deep, but his progress was still slow.

Nattie went a different way, angling to her right. Her tracks from last night were long gone, of course, even the half tunnel she'd dug, but she was pretty sure. . . .

She put a gloved hand next to her face to shield it. God, what she'd give for her snow goggles.

Forget that. Those goggles were melted lumps by now, along with her Bristol rocker and her little oval mirror and her father's picture. And everything else in that old government building she'd come to think of as her home. Her cabin. Either melted, or burned down to ashes.

Like my life, she thought. You fall down, pick yourself up, Nattie. You get knocked down . . .

So hard all you can see are lights. Emergency room lights.

. . . you pick yourself up again. Start over. Make it rhyme.

You get burned down . . .

She wasn't sure how many more comebacks she had left in her.

To hell with that. Nattie shook her head angrily, and a layer of snow sprayed off her green wool toboggan hat. There'd been no time for this crap, this galloping self-pity, in the cabin, and there was no time for it now.

She was stronger than that. She'd proven it before, and she'd keep right on proving it . . .

To Ben McKee?

. . . to *anyone* who doubted. Herself, included.

Nattie worked her way toward a long, narrow hump maybe ten yards away. Its general shape was right, but she couldn't see it clearly since she was moving almost directly upwind. Snow blew into her face. Tried to blind her.

She didn't know where Ben McKee had gone. Off to her left somewhere, underneath the big fir's branches, toward what should be the nose of the plane.

Then her hip struck something hard. She stumbled, and nearly went face-forward.

She crouched, which brought the deep powder shoulder-high, and felt around in front of her. Could be it was only a tree stump . . .

Or not. Her hand closed over something so cold it hurt her fingers, even through her insulated glove. Something long and smooth and flat.

Nattie dug snow out of her way, down to where she could see part of the Lear's tail assembly.

Which meant the fuselage, and the door she'd left open the night before, were right over . . . there, somewhere. She rose to her feet and waded forward.

The plane was tilted toward its left side, she remembered. And considerably more snow had fallen since last night—maybe as much as another two feet. By the time she reached the little jet's mid-body, she was floundering chest-deep.

The rip in the fuselage was no longer visible. Gone beneath a rounded, shifting blanket of white. Nattie

94

knew she'd completely disappear, too, like a swimmer wading off into deep water, before she could reach the door.

She was going to need some help.

She pushed her way toward the fir tree and the front of the plane. She passed beneath low branches whipping fiercely in the wind and shaking a thick curtain of snow down over her.

The night before, she'd seen the Lear's front only by flashlight. Now, in this twilight gray landscape, she saw the full damage. The nose of the airplane was jammed backward, crushed into a concave shape by the tree trunk. Huge branches, the thickness of a man's leg, had shattered the cockpit glass.

Nattie remembered that part well enough. From the inside looking out.

"Ben?" she yelled, but the wind tossed her voice aside. "Ben, where are you?"

There was only the sound of the wind.

She'd seen him go in this direction. There were his tracks, in fact, in a long furrow . . .

Then she saw him. He was up in the tree's lower branches, one foot balanced on the plane's mangled nose.

"Can you get in that way?" She climbed up toward him, scrambling over half-buried pieces of metal. "Last night, it was filled in with snow."

He didn't answer, so she hooked an arm over a limb and pulled herself forward.

"Didn't you hear me yelling at you?" she asked.

Still no reply.

She climbed up next to him and braced herself against the trunk.

"Hey, dammit, I'm talking to you. What's . . ."

Her voice faded out all by itself.

The snow, which the night before had clogged the Lear's windshield, was mostly gone now. Dug out of the way. Inside the cockpit, a mountain lion was crouched beside Landry's body.

Nattie froze in place.

The big cat's eyes were a golden-amber color. There was very little snow on its long tan and brown body. It had probably been inside the cockpit awhile, judging by what was left of Landry.

Its normally white chin was stained a darker, deeper color.

The cougar, so thin Nattie could see its exposed ribs, looked from one of them to the other, its small ears flattened against its head. It opened its mouth . . .

"Oh, Christ," whispered Ben.

. . . and showed them a double row of blood-pinkened teeth.

"Don't move," murmured Nattie.

"No shit," replied Ben.

The mountain lion watched them, and Nattie saw its long, black-tipped tail moving in agitated twitches.

"It's wagging its tail," muttered Ben.

"This is not Lassie, McKee. Haven't you ever seen a pissed-off house cat?"

"Oh, Christ . . ."

"Be still, dammit. It's scared and hungry, and it's trying to decide how badly it wants the food."

"*It's* scared?"

In spite of their predicament, Nattie couldn't help the grin she felt nudging the corners of her mouth.

"Pretend you're back in the city," she whispered. "Watching TV. Pretend it's 'Wild Kingdom.'"

"Then, where the hell is Marlin?"

The lion was getting more nervous, its eyes shifting from one of them to the other; but it was slowly starving in this abnormally severe winter, and it wouldn't easily give up the food. It was trapped in the airplane, and knew it, and Nattie hoped it wouldn't retreat into the passenger section. If it did, only an absolute lunatic or someone with a death wish would crawl through that windshield.

Meanwhile, they were at a stalemate. With Cleese and his men still out there somewhere. . . .

Then the wind gusted, harder than before, and ripped

loose a tree branch. The limb slammed down onto the plane's roof.

The big cat leaped forward.

"Holy shit!" yelled Ben, and dove sideways from the plane's nose. Nattie flinched back against the tree trunk.

The cougar was graceful and quick. It cleared the windshield in one fluid movement, pivoted off a branch not three feet from Nattie's face, and landed in the deep snow. She saw it for an instant, tawny gold against the gray-white of the storm; then it was gone, bounding away through the trees.

Nattie slowly let out her breath. She hadn't realized she'd been holding it.

Ben McKee came climbing back up toward her. He was totally covered with snow.

"Is it gone?" he asked.

"Long gone," she managed to get out.

"Hey, that's okay." He regained his spot on the nose of the plane. "You can laugh if you want . . ."

"Thanks loads."

"I don't care. I'm a city boy. See how you'd do up against a tenement rat."

"How long had you two been like that? Staring at each other, eyeball to eyeball."

"About six years, it felt like." He shook his head. "Leo the lion."

"That wasn't Leo. That was Laura."

"You can tell them apart?"

"Sure." Nattie nodded. "It's easy. Leo's big."

"Leo's big? Jesus Christ, Leo's *big?*"

He saw her laughing, and stopped in mid-rant. He grinned at her, a little sheepishly.

"Let's get those guns," he said.

Cleese crouched in deep snow one hundred yards from the trees. The blizzard pounded down over him, slamming him with the full force of its wind, covering him in a thickening white layer that didn't move because he didn't move.

He crouched and watched the trees, visible to him only as a faint, dark silhouette through the blowing snow. Waited for the others.

Most of his assignments had moments like this, vastly different but basically the same. Periods of waiting. He got through this one the same as always.

One part of his mind was alert, concentration honed in for any movement on any side. Someone stalking him, even from behind in this senses-numbing environment of cold and endless noise, would have received a very nasty surprise.

But another part of his mind had gone away. To a golden beach, all warm sun and bright colors, and to Genie.

I love you, Gramp. You're the very best gramp in the whole wide world . . .

Someone watching him carefully at that moment might have seen his lips move beneath his ice-braided mustache.

I love you, Genie . . .

Except, it was difficult to keep her in focus here. Here, in this cold, ice-cold, dead-cold world of swirling gray and white. The color of dead flesh.

And bad dreams.

Des Pruitt had said one time—in a rare display of pique—that Cleese's job description was pathology, not treatment. And Cleese would do that job well again today. He always did, though people like Pruitt would never know the *real* reason. They only sent Cleese when the situation was bad. Worse than bad. When the walls of the fortress were in danger of crumbling.

Because if those walls crumbled, the world would see what was inside. Every dark thing that was in there, including Eugene Cleese. The world would see everything.

And so, eventually, would Genie.

You're the very best gramp . . .

Cleese wouldn't, *couldn't*, let that happen. He had few good memories of his former wife Ruth, who'd died of lymphatic cancer a few years after they divorced, and her icy hatred had clearly begat this stiff, uneasy politeness between him and Kaydra—who was also divorced, and bitter about it—that he'd long since realized was never going to change. But Genie . . .

Right from the first, it had been special for them. Right from the moment he'd taken her, crying fitfully, from Kaydra's arms, and watched a wide-eyed little smile form on her tiny face. She knew it, from the very beginning, and he knew it, too, and they both accepted it. Relished in it, and in each other.

Genie was Cleese's granddaughter and his namesake, a surprising gesture on Kaydra's part—or maybe not, all things considered—but she was much more than that. Genie was the one soft refuge in Cleese's soul, and he would gladly die, or kill anything in his path, to keep her from ever seeing into that fortress.

That dark place where her grandfather lived.

Sometimes Pruitt and the others got a little uneasy. "You're the best I've ever seen, Gene, but you take these things too personally. They're just assignments, not enemies."

But it *was* personal. Always. It was much more than life and death, which were trivial by comparison. It was a matter of sheer emotional survival.

And this time, he'd allowed his personal rage toward one such enemy, Ben McKee, to cause a mistake. Because he knew about McKee's fear of heights, of airplanes . . .

And, for this particular enemy, this one especially, a bomb was much too quick.

But it was a mistake he'd fix. That was what he did, wasn't it? Fix things that weren't right? And then he'd be away from this cold, gray-white world of dead flesh and bad dreams. Back on a warm, sunny beach with Genie.

And she'd be safe again.

"Gene." Liam Riley came out of the storm from off to the left. Cleese had been aware of him for a while.

"See anything?" he asked.

"Saw a cougar." Riley dropped to one knee next to Cleese. Snow blew over his head, tried to cling to the white polyurethane of his snowsuit. "Big sonofabitch, running down through the trees over that way." He pointed in the direction of his own tracks. "There's a ridge back there, maybe a hundred feet wide, and a canyon behind it. Straight down and solid ice."

Cleese nodded. "They can go to the left or right, sounds like. But they can't go forward or back."

"I left Artie over there to seal off that side," said Riley. "He wanted to charge the trees, of course. He wanted to shoot that mountain lion, too."

"I'm afraid Artie's first impulse toward his fellow creatures is not a kind one." Cleese wiped a gloved finger across his goggles to clear them. "He has a straight-ahead attitude, which is a valuable trait at times. Can you see Milt?"

Riley stood up for a moment, then back down. "Nope," he replied. "And he's hard to miss."

"Problem is, we don't know how they're armed. That little shotgun was a surprise, remember."

"Milt remembers." Riley smiled.

"Why don't we try this?" Cleese rarely gave his people direct orders—a necessary part of command, but he'd never cared for it. He preferred to give them suggestions instead, which they always followed anyway. "How about if you work your way over to the right? Cut that direction off."

"Sounds good," said Riley.

"Maybe you'll run into Milt. Meanwhile, I'll move forward from here. I think we can do this gradually, just squeeze in from three sides."

"No rush." Riley rose to his feet again. "They've painted themselves into a corner."

"That's how it seems to me, too." Cleese nodded.

100

* * *

Each of the dead men was wearing a shoulder rig beneath his jacket. The pistol each carried was a Smith and Wesson thirty-eight-caliber Airweight.

"Cop gun, isn't it?" asked Nattie, and glanced over at Ben McKee. He was digging a heavy brown leather bomber jacket out of a storage locker behind Taliferro's seat.

"I don't know much about guns," he replied.

"Uh-huh." She studied him. "You'd better get those gloves, too, while you're at it. And his boots, if they'll fit you."

According to Nattie's watch, they'd been inside the Lear's cockpit for nearly ten minutes. A steady stream of snow was blowing through the shattered windshield, but it still should have been warmer in the plane, out of the blizzard's direct impact. Instead, like the night before, she felt an icy coldness that seeped inside of her.

"I want to get out of here," she said, and shifted a step farther away from Landry's mangled remains, still mostly odorless, thank God, because of the intense cold.

But not to Laura the Lion, obviously.

Ben had on the jacket, its fur collar turned up around his face and neck, and was shoving his feet into a pair of tan, high-topped western boots that looked a bit small for him.

"And go where?" he asked, picking up the gloves. "Your snowmobile's finished, Nattie. Anyway, what's out there, besides the blizzard and more of these damned mountains? Unless we hike over to the nearest grizzly bear den and book a room for the night. Give bed and breakfast a whole new meaning."

He saw her glance at the bodies on either side of them. "At least in here we're out of the wind," he added. "We can crawl back there, into the passenger section . . ."

"Where I found you last night, frozen half solid. Remember?"

101

"I was alone then." A faint edge of a smile touched his mouth. "I didn't have another warm body on board."

"Good idea," she replied. "And maybe you could also leave a message outside. Here we are, guys. Feel free to drop in, weapons optional."

He frowned.

"You said their helicopter went down," she continued. "But it didn't crash. You also said you know that Cleese guy. Is he the type to hole up inside it and wait for the weather to change? When they have snowshoes and winter survival gear?"

Ben returned her gaze for a few moments, and his blue eyes were bleak. "No," he finally answered. "He won't quit. Not ever. He's relentless."

"He wants you pretty badly, doesn't he?"

He nodded.

"I guess you know you owe me one hell of an explanation," said Nattie. "For all this. But I don't think we have time at the moment. Right now, we have one chance, and that's to get down to Walker Lake. To the comm center."

"Nattie, I told you, Marvin's—"

"Maybe so." She cut him off before he could say it. "Maybe so, but there's nowhere else to run. All the winter people are strung out around Walker Lake. The comm center's as close as any of them, and Marv has that high-powered radio set."

Ben glanced out the front of the plane, where snow was blowing past the fir tree. "Can we make it there on foot?"

"I don't know. It's close to ten miles . . ."

"Ten miles? In this storm?"

"What's our option?" she replied. "We can't stay here. We're sitting ducks in this plane. And my cabin . . ." She felt a sudden burning behind her eyes. "It's gone, isn't it?"

She blinked her eyes to clear them. "Most of that trail down to the lake's through the trees," she continued. "The snow won't be as deep in there. We really don't have a choice, Ben. We've already stayed here too long."

He looked at her for a moment. Then he nodded. "Let's go," he said.

They were on the ridge, just starting south from the plane, when Nattie saw the first man.

"Get down!" she hissed, and yanked Ben's coat sleeve. Both of them ducked behind a tree.

"What?" he muttered, his mouth next to her ear.

She pointed.

The man was crouched next to another tree, no more than twenty or thirty yards away. He had one hand cupped over the top of his goggles, and the other holding his automatic weapon.

Nattie realized the snow had the man blinded. Looking in their direction was looking nearly straight upwind.

A lucky break, at least for the moment.

"Can we get around him?" whispered Ben, still against her ear.

She shook her head. The man had chosen his spot well. The ridge was narrow at this point, open meadow on the east and the canyon on the west.

"What, then?" asked Ben. "Shoot him?"

The thought made Nattie's midsection go hollow. She'd fired her four-ten at one of them, but that had been mostly a terrorized reflex action. Could she take cold aim at a human being . . . ?

"Could we even hit him from here?" she whispered.

Ben appeared to be measuring the distance. "I know I couldn't," he answered. "I think you have to be a lot closer with one of these snub-noses. And with that gun he has . . ."

He pointed toward the plane. "Maybe we can swing wide of him in the meadow."

He took a step in that direction, then quickly pushed her down again. "There's another one," he said.

Nattie looked through an opening between frozen branches. She saw a second man, much larger than the first, moving slowly past the trees on the other side of the buried Lear. The man appeared to be looking out into the meadow.

Probably for reinforcements, she thought.

"We're cut off," whispered Ben. "Both ways . . ."

"They don't see us." She put a gloved hand over his mouth. "And they're not moving. We're not cut off yet."

What she was thinking at that moment froze her blood. Colder than the screaming wind around them . . .

But what was their choice?

"I'm going to try crawling up on that first guy." Ben slipped the thirty-eight out of his pocket. "When you hear the shots, I want you to run like—"

"No." Nattie held him in place. "That's a bad idea. I have a better one. I want you to start working your way down that far side of the ridge."

"Over there? I thought you said—"

"I know what I said. Just do it. And don't shoot anybody 'til I get back."

On the far side of the ridge, the ground fell away rapidly, and Ben McKee stumbled across rocks buried under the snow. The wind was worse there in the open, howling across him in downdrafts toward a vast, yawning emptiness just at the edge of his vision. Finally he found partial shelter by crawling next to a shattered boulder. He crouched down, his face pressed against the rough stone.

He didn't know where Nattie Kemper had gone, or if she'd be back. Maybe she'd had some second thoughts.

His gloved hand curled around the textured grip of the thirty-eight Airweight, and he tried to flex some feeling back into his numbed fingers. If it came down to it, the first sonofabitch around the corner of this rock was going to be very sorry. He hoped it would be Eugene Cleese . . .

Let it be Cleese.

. . . even as poor as that would make his chances.

104

Shelley Gallatin was dead, like Will Carter before her, because Cleese was very good at his work.

But your work isn't finished yet, is it, old man? Somehow or other, the legendary Eugene Cleese screwed up with me. I'll bet the big boys at Machtel didn't like that. A few Maalox moments at the latest board meeting.

So here we both are, out here in this god-awful storm in these godforsaken mountains, winding up our unfinished business. Maybe that's the way it should be.

Except we've made an innocent bystander a part of our business. And changed her whole life, just like that. I'll bet she wishes she'd stayed indoors last night.

What have you people done to us? What have you done to our lives?

You're heading on down that trail toward the lake right now, Nattie, if you're smart. And not looking back. You can get away from these goons by yourself.

I wouldn't blame you at all.

He granted himself a few moments for the luxury of thinking about her. Her face, with the small scar below her mouth. The first thing he remembered, after that slow slide down into darkness inside the frozen plane. Then again, when he woke up next to her in the night and heard her crying on the other side of the bed.

And this morning, watching her open her eyes. . . .

If he'd met her a few years ago, before all this started. Six months, even. . . .

If. Forget ifs. These high mountains were no if, and neither was this storm. And neither were those four men.

Ben McKee squeezed his body in closer behind the rock. He listened to the roar of the wind blowing past him, and he listened to the steady thump of his own heartbeat inside him. After the plane crash, after the cabin explosion, after the barrage of gunfire from the helicopter, he was still alive. He wasn't done yet.

I'm a survivor, Shelley. He remembered saying that.

That remains to be seen, Benjamin. Her voice was in his head for a moment. Half-mocking and amused, as always.

He sat very still, no longer even shivering. Motionless, except for the slow turning of his head, side to side. His eyes were slitted against the flying snow, and he held the gun poised at chest level as he watched for movement at either corner of the boulder.

I hope it's Nattie, he thought. Even though that would be a mistake on her part. If it's not . . .

Let it be Cleese.

Nattie slid out from behind the last of the trees and into the full force of the wind. She kept the shape of the buried airplane in the corner of her vision and crawled toward a smaller lump, rapidly covering over, at the meadow's edge.

You don't really want to do this, Nattie. Let's think about this for a minute. How none of this has anything to do with you. Cleese said so.

Shut up, Rick. There's no time.

When she reached the Polaris, she used it for cover. Then she raised up slowly to look out into the blowing, shifting whiteness of the meadow . . .

And saw something out there, at the very edge of her vision. A faint speck of . . .

Orange.

Your cabin is gone, thanks to this McKee. Your cabin is burned, your dog is dead, and you have four stone killers on your tail. And why is that, Nattie my love?

With one hand she unsnapped the compartment behind her seat, reached inside and pushed past the Coleman flash. Felt her fingers curl around the rope.

It's because you're the same ol' Nattie, aren't you? Still taking in strays.

The rope slid out, fifty meters of blue and red Maxim kernmantle, already yoked. Then the razor-toothed Footfang crampons and her bag of ice screws and a figure-eight descender, fastened to its rappel harness and some carabiners with a short length of bungee. Finally her white plastic Petz climbing helmet, with its hand-

106

lettered decal on the front, and her pair of Charlet Moser sixty-centimeter ice axes.

You have gear for one, Nattie. Not two. What are you going to do about that?

She saw the speck of orange move, out there in the blowing whiteness of the meadow. Getting closer. . . .

It's him they want, Nattie. Not you. I suggest you make a little detour right now, while you can. Find another spot to descend. If they have him, do you really think they'll follow you down a cliff in this blizzard?

Nattie thought about the men and their guns, and how easy it would be to elude them in this storm. If she were alone.

I wouldn't want anything to happen to you, Nattie . . .

And she thought about Ben McKee, who'd come uninvited, out of nowhere, to tell her lies and wreck her new life.

And who'd shielded her with his own body.

Nattie looked at the decal on her helmet and remembered the day she put it there. The day her new life began.

ALL EMPTY ROADS REQUIRE FAITH TO TRAVEL was what it said.

Back past the trees again, Nattie found Ben McKee. He'd taken cover where the ground began to fall away below the ridge top, next to a huge splintered boulder. He swung the thirty-eight in her direction, then lowered it.

"You were gone awhile," he said. "I was beginning to think you'd decided you'd have a better chance without—"

He saw the climbing gear.

"Bull*shit*," he said. "No way, Nattie. No way in hell."

She began to rope up. "There's no choice," she replied, feeding the rope through the figure eight. "I saw them when I was coming by the plane. They're squeezing in on it, Ben. From every direction except this one. Another ten minutes, and they'll be inside. Ten minutes after that, they'll be on us. We're leaving a trail they won't miss, and they can travel twice as fast in those snowshoes. We've got to be gone by then. Someplace they can't follow."

Ben leaned out for a moment, then quickly back. "I don't much like heights," he said. "Airplanes, tall buildings, bottomless pits. Probably I should have mentioned that before now."

"Probably." Nattie pushed her boot into the toe bail of a crampon. Set the heel clamp and snapped the buckle of the ankle strap.

"In fact, I'll probably get nosebleeds just wearing these cowboy boots."

Nattie looked over the edge. This upper section of cliff was so sheer it seemed to curve back in. To overhang. She knew that only because she'd been here before, during the summer. At the moment, she could see no more than fifty or sixty feet below her. The rest disappeared into the storm. Into emptiness. A churning, blowing emptiness that made the inside of her mouth suddenly taste like old coins.

You're making a mistake here, Nattie.

She looked at Ben. "There's no way around it," she said. "It's pretty much climb or die."

"What makes you think the two are mutually exclusive?" he answered, but he got to his feet anyway. He was looking at her, not the edge. "You've climbed here before, right?"

"Right." She nodded, and saw no point in mentioning that was in the summer, on a dry, sunny day.

"I had a dream about this." Ben McKee's voice was faint. "During the night, before I knew where I was."

"What . . . ?"

"This." He looked down for the first time, over the edge of the cliff, and she saw him shudder. "I thought it was about something else, but I was wrong. It was about this."

"Ben, we have to go."

"Okay." He took a faltering step toward the rim, then another, and his eyes were once again locked on hers. Out of the shelter of the boulder, the full force of the blizzard blew across them. Roared past them in spiking downdrafts of blinding snow, over the edge into the invisible depths of Empinado Canyon.

"Okay," he said again, and took a deep breath. "Tell me what to do."

Wednesday—Wednesday Night

EMPTY ROADS

All empty roads require faith to travel
—proverb

Chapter Eight

When he pushed his way through the front door of the Walker Lake communication center, the first thing Rick Macon saw was the woodstove. Or maybe the second. What he actually noticed first was himself. There was a large mirror mounted on the far wall, above an old piano, and it reflected back a wide-angle view of the room. And of Macon standing just inside the front door, rivulets of snow sliding down the slick surface of his black REI parka.

Mirrors drew Rick Macon, the way a woodstove drew a frostbite victim.

Which he very nearly was, he decided. He gave himself a quick once-over in the mirror, then went to the stove. And found the damn thing a lot less rewarding than he'd expected.

"What the hell . . . ?" He removed a heavy snowmobile glove and carefully placed his hand against the black metal. It was warm to the touch, no more.

"Anybody home?" Macon looked around the deserted room, then saw a partially open door on the rear wall near the piano. "Hey! There in the back . . ."

No response. The place was silent, except for the howl of the wind. Outside glazed windows, the storm continued to pound the building, roaring past in near-lateral sheets of blinding whiteness. Macon's rented snowmobile, a Yamaha Venture 485, was out there, parked in the lee of a storage shed behind the main building, but it might as well still be back in Ouray—twenty miles north-west of here—as far as seeing it was concerned.

Goddamn blizzard. And it was getting worse again, which didn't seem possible.

"Hey!" He tried again, but all he got was the same silence, deepened by its contrast with the storm roaring outside.

"Hell with this," muttered Macon, and cranked the woodstove's twin handles inward and then down to open its square, wrought-iron filigreed door.

The firewood inside was down to gray ash, except for a couple of lumps of scrub oak, harder and therefore slower to burn than aspen. Now that he'd been inside a few minutes, Macon could feel the chill in the room.

That numbnuts—Stone, they'd said his name was—had let his fire go down.

Rick Macon slipped out of his heavy snowmobile parka and dropped it on the floor, where it immediately began to puddle the worn, brown indoor-outdoor carpet. No great loss, since there were dried stains everywhere, including a small, fresh-looking one over by the short-wave radio. He grabbed two handsful of split aspen kindling from a cardboard box by the wall and fed the wood into the stove, cross-patterning it around the lumps of oak. As he'd expected, there was enough fire smoldering in the ashes to ignite the dry kindling without having to use wadded-up paper.

He partially closed the woodstove's door, leaving about an inch for draft, and checked the damper on the back. When the insides heated up, he'd add a few pieces of oak.

There was a right way and a wrong way to do things. Rick Macon did things the right way.

Or if he didn't, he damn well *made* them right, sooner or later. Natalie Kemper Macon, or whatever she was calling herself these days, being a case in point.

He'd come a long way to make that one right.

"Did your job for you, Stone," he announced to the room in general. "Wherever the hell you are."

Macon went over to the door on the back wall. It was ajar by about a foot. He tapped on it with his knuckles. With the edge of his large college ring.

"Stone?" he said. "You in there?"

A big fat guy, that was how the snowmobile people in Ouray had described Marvin Stone. A lardass like that, in this weather, maybe he'd keeled over from a heart attack . . .

Which would be no more than he deserves, Macon decided. A person with any self-respect, any sense of pride, takes care of his body. Nothing is more important than your body. It's what tells the world who you are.

Macon pushed the door the rest of the way open, half expecting to find a purple-faced corpse on the floor. What he found instead was an empty bedroom.

It was colder back there, away from the gradually strengthening heat of the woodstove. And the sound of the wind was louder. . . .

Another noise, sudden and sharp, and Macon jumped involuntarily. He spun in that direction, big fists clenched . . .

And then recognized the sound. Over there in one corner of the dimly lit room, a refrigerator motor had kicked on.

"Shit," he said, and slowly raised up out of his crouch.

Getting jumpy, and for no good reason. Except maybe the silence of this place. The sense . . . of *something* having happened here, like when you come upon the scene of an accident . . .

After the casualties have been removed.

"Rick, my man," said Macon. "Your imagination's getting the better of you."

He did a quick tour of the room: A saggy-looking bed that curled his lip with disgust, especially where the mattress bowed out on one side. A spindly thrift store dresser with no mirror, next to a large, double-wide refrigerator—humming quietly now—and a stove that smelled like burned grease, near an outside door. An open closet,

115

jeans and corduroy shirts draped over metal hangers. The jeans looked to be about size forty, give or take.

The clothes smelled worse than the stove. Maybe Stone didn't have a washing machine.

Another door, this one shut, led into a small bathroom with a stall shower. A couple of sports magazines—baseball, mostly—lay on the floor by the toilet.

"Found you at last," Macon said for a joke, and yanked back the mildewed yellow shower curtain.

Empty, of course. Like the whole damn building.

"Come on, goddammit," mumbled Macon, and gave the bathroom door a whack with the back of his hand. "Where are you, man?"

This was no good. After all the grief he'd had just getting to this place. . . .

"Don't know if I'd chance it," that's what the woman—homely little bitch, with a complexion like the surface of the moon—at the snowmobile company had said. "Got a bad storm coming in, and the avalanche danger's real high; so I'm not doing any rentals right now. Maybe you could wait a few . . ."

He'd given her what Nattie always referred to sarcastically as The Look, which had never failed him yet with a woman . . .

Except for one, maybe.

. . . and watched her melt. That trace of a brooding smile, though not enough to spoil the clean line of his jaw, and the way he got his eyes really intense. That's how that magazine photographer had described it. Intense. And this woman, stupid as well as ugly, had started to stammer and blush. Like they all did.

He'd done some winter survival, he told her, saying the word "some" so she'd understand he was being modest. Went to college for a couple of semesters at Fort Lewis over in Durango, and did *some* mountaineering even back then, when he wasn't playing football . . .

At which point she began filling out the rental agreement.

Wait a few days? He'd waited over a year. And he wasn't going to wait even a few more minutes.

He didn't tell the woman that part, of course. But, leaving her lovestruck, he did promise her he'd be all right.

And he had been, but only barely. After a few miles along what in summer was a jeep road, the blizzard had found him. It was good that his story about winter survival experience was true, because what had followed was ten hours in hell. . . .

Ah, but Nattie my love. You're going to make it all worthwhile.

Rick Macon had met Natalie Kemper during his year at Fort Lewis College, right after he returned from Los Angeles—which was something he preferred not to talk about. He was a little older than the other entering freshmen, who were mostly seventeen or eighteen, he was also a football player, and of course, he looked the way he looked. The combination of those three facts made the experience gratifying, at least for a while.

Nattie was the outdoor type, a small, fresh-faced twenty-year-old beauty from nearby Pagosa Springs, who was mostly majoring in skiing and backpacking, and in escaping from her mother, JoAnne. Nattie, whose father had died while she was in high school, had a real problem with JoAnne, who tended to take over any room immediately upon entry. Macon had no such problem with the lady. From Day One—Look One at that chiseled profile, actually—good ol' JoAnne was Rick Macon's biggest fan. He even told her about his time in L.A., though he managed to put his own spin on it.

When Macon inevitably got bored with being the big frog in the very small pond that was Fort Lewis College—and also realized his future lay more in the direction of smiling into camera lenses than getting tackled by big country boys who might eventually do unpleasant things to that profile—he decided to return to Denver, where he'd grown up. He never doubted Nattie would go with him, and, apparently, neither did good ol' JoAnne. And, sure enough, Nattie went along, transferring to the University of Colorado. Given his opinion of himself, it didn't occur to Macon until later—much later—that her move may have been as much to get away from her mother as any romantic longings for Rick Macon.

While Natalie Kemper Macon, now turned serious student, pursued an English degree up at Boulder, Rick Macon—in between modeling assignments and a little bit of TV commercial work—was discovering the world of the hard-core bodybuilding gym. Any place that full of mirrors, on every wall, floor to ceiling, was a natural draw for him, and his physical transformation delighted him. In less than three years he went from a lean but sinewy one hundred and seventy pounder to the unchallenged lord of the gym, still as handsome as ever, but now carrying two hundred and twenty-five pounds of fat-free muscularity on a six-foot, one-inch frame.

Helped along a little, maybe, by the steroids he never bothered to mention to Nattie. And, if they also intensified certain aspects already present in his personality, that wasn't really a problem. At least not for him.

This was about the same time Nattie was finishing a Master's degree in English lit at C.U., a notoriously liberal campus that seemed to be having some unfortunate effects upon her once pliable nature. Nattie, now twenty-four years old and no longer the confused young girl who'd seen any place away from her mother as a better place to be, had somewhere discovered a mind of her own. And the backbone that went with it.

After that, things headed downhill in a hurry.

As his body warmed, Rick Macon realized how hungry he was. The fridge had a large box of stale-looking doughnuts sitting on top, next to a package of Twinkies. He automatically passed both of them by (sugar and cooking grease), and opened the door, where he found a

118

supply of useless processed stuff like franks and bolo-
gna—as well as uncountable stacks of TV dinners in the
large freezer—but also some cheese and a package of
onion bagels. Good carbs, and his rapid-fire metabolism
would burn the fat in the cheese. He fished out a quart
bottle of unsweetened orange juice and carried it all back
into the comm center's main room.

He looked at the room more closely this time. Large
and rectangular, with the old piano at the back and the
woodstove to one side, close to a big phony-leather recliner. A small, shuttered window, high up, on each of
the side walls, and two larger ones at the front. There
were some file cabinets on the far wall, a hot plate and a
Mr. Coffee sitting on top. Some cups up there, too.

The room was warming up. Macon added a large
chunk of oak to the woodstove, then closed it. He took
off the black, one-piece snowmobile coveralls he'd worn
under his parka, and then the Gore-Tex wind suit beneath it. Peeled down to sweat-soaked, insulated underwear and a pair of faded black jeans. With that mirror up
there, he briefly considered coming out of the insulated
top, but decided against it. Stone might still show up, and
besides, the Thinsulate material was sweat-plastered to
him anyway, clinging to every line.

He finger-brushed his long, dark brown hair into
place, and studied the lean, chiseled features of his face.
Then the wedge-shaped bodybuilder's torso that
dropped from his thick shoulders into that famous thirty-
inch waist.

He gave himself an A−, counting off for the temporary lines of fatigue around his eyes, then carried his
snacks over to the file cabinets. He didn't drink coffee, or
anything with caffeine; but there were cups there, and he
wasn't about to drink that o.j. straight from the bottle.

Three of the cups had coffee in them. Macon dipped a
finger into one and found the liquid to be tepid.

Not that long since it had been poured.

"What the hell's going on around here?" he muttered.

119

Because this wasn't acceptable. Not after a year, not when he was finally this close . . .

Not after twelve months of looking, and—worse than that—sucking up to good ol' JoAnne.

I just want to make it right with her, JoAnne. How can I do that if she won't talk to me? If I don't even know where she is?

He wasn't going to let it all go south now. Not now.

I just wish she'd inherited some of your good sense, JoAnne. I mean, she got your face, but, no offense, sometimes I wonder about her head . . .

"That's from her father, God rest his soul," had been good ol' JoAnne's reply, once she got through enjoying the compliment. "Poor man, he didn't have an ounce of common sense either. I mean, look at the way she took up with that Van Zandt. And then what he did to her. I tried to warn her, but no . . ."

Which was when Rick Macon knew he was home free. That good ol' JoAnne was going to tell him.

And she did. All about Nattie's new job with that Boulder-based research foundation. Scut work, JoAnne called it. So far beneath her daughter's aptitudes . . .

And all about Walker Lake.

She told him, finally, everything she knew. It had taken a year, but Macon had kept the faith. His own brand of faith regarding women in general, and JoAnne Kemper in particular.

Just another stupid bitch. And, in this case, possessing all the conviction of the wholly self-deceived.

But now, when his reward for keeping that faith was so near . . .

Marvin Stone was nowhere to be found.

Macon went over for a closer look at the radio set by the front window. It was a big one, modern-looking, which was pretty much the extent of what he knew about the damn things.

Ten-four, good buddy.

"Where are you, Nattie?" he whispered. "Close, I'll bet. I can *feel* you, Nattie . . ."

And, so thinking, he laid the bagels and cheese on the windowsill and pushed the Thinsulate sleeve up over his thickly developed right forearm. Looked at the dense musculature there, which he flexed by making a fist and curling it inward, and then at the scars. Jagged scars, twisted and bone white, angling down toward the sinewy wrist. When he flexed his forearm, the scars stretched in dead white, threaded lines across the muscles.

A pulse began to hammer in the thin skin along his temple, but he didn't notice. His gaze had followed the line of scar tissue, down his forearm to his wrist.

Handcuffs. They'd put handcuffs on him. And that goddamn pencil-neck newspaper photographer had been right there the whole time, of course, because Rick Macon was a well-known face in Denver. Snapping away while they handcuffed him and read him the Miranda, then led him downstairs to the squad car . . .

For everyone to see.

"Nattie my love," he said, and slid down the shirt-sleeve.

Nattie and her dog.

He stuffed the last bagel into his mouth and washed it down with the o.j., poured into a clean cup . . .

And that was when he noticed the coat rack for the first time. And the huge navy blue parka hanging there.

Size forty-eight. Macon could wear a forty-eight, though he had to have everything tapered in for his waist. This coat was shaped like an enormous pear with sleeves.

"Marvin, my man," said Macon. "You went out in this weather without your coat?"

That stain he'd noticed earlier was next to his foot. Drying the color of coffee, probably spilled from one of those cups over on the file cabinet. . . .

What was in those files?

Natalie Kemper was, as it turned out. Just one folder, thin, with the notation GOV'T CABIN 4. And C-6 marked in red ink at the upper left corner.

C-6. What the hell was . . .

"C-6," said Macon, and looked across the room at the

huge topographical map tacked to the wall. Right there next to the woodstove.

The irregular shape of Walker Lake—somewhat like an amoeba swimming north to south—was in the center of the map. Macon saw that letters were the vertical scale, going down the left side, and numbers were the horizontal scale, going across the top. He found letter *C,* then went left to right across the lake to number 6.

Fewer wavy lines in that quadrant, which meant an area that was relatively flat. Like a small plateau, maybe . . .

Nattie. Right there in small, neat print. Red ink. A tiny rectangle, and the printed word "NATTIE."

Rick Macon realized he'd begun to hyperventilate. He stepped away from the map for a moment, looked at nothing out the front window. Just blowing, howling whiteness out there. Howling like the inside of his mind.

His lips formed a word. "Nattie." He never knew it.

After a little while, he stepped back to the map. Calmer now. Able to concentrate.

On a topographical map, the wavy lines were there to indicate levels of altitude, which meant they also indicated degrees of steepness. The closer the lines were together, the steeper the terrain.

On the surface of Walker Lake, the small number 9407 was written. Macon traced the wavy line nearest to Nattie's name and saw the number 11296. Which meant Nattie's cabin sat at an altitude of about eleven thousand three hundred feet above sea level. And nearly two thousand feet higher than the lake.

Two thousand feet wouldn't be that easy this time of year. Not with snow five or six feet deep out there, and getting deeper the higher you went.

Macon checked the straightest approach from the comm center to the cabin, roughly north-northeast. He saw how the lines converged at the narrow end of the lake. . . .

No way. There was a canyon up there, with the name

Empinado written in red. Probably carved by the same running water that had created this narrow basin in the first place. Walker Creek, it said on the map, the creek that had obviously been dammed to form this lake. And, at the upper end of Walker Creek, a box canyon and a couple of cabins with names and the word "Summer" in parentheses. And a mine, Ojo del Plata, with the number 9982 beside it.

That was a dead end up there. A sea of wavy lines indicating a cliff well over a thousand feet high, if the numbers were accurate. Probably some hellacious climbing in the summertime . . .

But not in February. If there was a cabin built above that monster wall, there had to be an easier way in.

And there was. On topo maps, trails were indicated by dotted lines. Macon picked the one nearest Nattie's name on the map and traced it with his finger. It started east, toward the cliff, then turned south, becoming a series of convolutions that mirrored the wavy lines.

Switchbacks. This was a trail that descended from the high plateau in a less steep area. It wound its way south, consistently losing elevation, until it began to follow a creek—Right Hand Creek was the name—which flowed into Walker Lake just a short distance from the comm center.

How far was it up there? Each square on a topo map indicated roughly a mile. Macon counted the trail. About half a mile from here to Right Hand Creek. Then about nine more miles, maybe ten, to the name NATTIE on the map.

Ten miles, and an altitude gain of two thousand feet up to the cabin. In the middle of a blizzard . . .

I guess it all depends, he thought. How badly do I want her?

I could wait here. Wait for the storm to break. Even a storm like this has to have an end.

And what about Marvin Stone? He comes back from

. . . wherever the hell he is, sodomizing mountain goats, whatever. And what do I tell him? How much has *she* told him?

He gets on that goddamn shortwave, gives her a call. Oh, hi, Nattie. Say, your husband's down here looking for you. . . .

Rick Macon went over to the radio set and pulled it away from the wall. He didn't know how to operate the damn thing, but destruction had always required less talent.

He could just leave it alone, slip out quietly right now, but you never knew, did you? She probably had one, too.

The radio had a back on it, that pressed plywood stuff. It came off easily enough. And the handful of circuit board and wiring that connected to the power cord and then probably to a gas-operated generator, that wasn't too tough either.

—

Macon was moving fast now, because he'd crossed a definite line in this place. He took the entire topo map from the wall, even though he'd need only a small part of it. No clues left behind.

He went back to the bedroom and cleaned out the fridge—he even took the doughnuts—then folded everything into a bundle that would fit inside the Yamaha's storage compartment. He dressed again in the outerwear, which he'd left near the woodstove to dry, then took a last look at the room.

Checked himself in the mirror.

When he pushed open the door, the force of the storm took his breath away. Icy air blew into his lungs, and his powerful legs buckled for a moment before the blizzard's fury.

But he went on. Found his snowmobile by the shed, and cleared the drift that had already formed across it. Emptied his reserve fuel into the tank, then located some more inside the shed, which—like everything else around here—was unlocked. Revved his way out of the deep wallow next to the building, and onto the flat by the trees. Headed northeast along the shore of the lake.

Because it all depended, didn't it? On how badly he wanted her.

Chapter Nine

They were nearly three hundred feet down the side of Empinado Canyon when the first of the shots was fired.

"Nattie!" yelled Ben McKee, who was clinging to the base of an ice-crusted basalt pinnacle about eighty feet below her. "Did you hear that?"

His voice, like the echo of the gunshot, was swept away by the wind.

"I heard it." Nattie leaned out from her perch on a narrow ledge. "You just hold me a firm belay down there, bud."

She looked up the cliff, knowing she wouldn't be able to see the top. The storm was strengthening again in its continual ebb and flow, and her range of vision barely covered the distance to where Ben was, his face a pale blur at the edge of a swirling gray-white universe. The snow was like finely ground sand, burning her eyes and blinding her anytime she tried to do more than squint.

A second shot, up there on the rim.

They're not firing at us, Nattie thought. They can't see us any more than we can see them.

Must be a signal of some kind.

She had to get moving again, down to where Ben was wedged into the rocks below. Even with her insulated clothing, the icy wind was cutting her to the bone, and it had to be much colder for him. The windchill was probably minus thirty, and the worst thing they could do was to sit still. At the very least, they were both likely to come out of this with frostbite.

At the very least.

Nattie gave the tubular ice screw an extra twist. There were areas of exposed rock between the sheets of ice along the cliff; but she'd had no pitons in the snowmobile's storage compartment, so the screws would have to do. She rechecked the carabiner which was clipped into the screw's flexible eye. Also the loop of rope running through the 'biner, to be sure that the gate had remained shut. Then she tested the screw with a hard tug before paying out some more of the rope.

This was crazy. Certifiable, in fact. It had been crazy three hundred feet above, up on the canyon rim, and it hadn't gotten any smarter in the interim.

There were correct methods for a technical descent, especially when accompanied by a total novice like Ben McKee. But none of those methods included the concept of *one* set of climbing gear. And, as dangerous a scenario as this produced on dry rock, it was ten . . . hell, a hundred times as deadly on black ice like this, so-named because of its near-invisibility. Look at a surface coated in black ice—especially in overcast conditions where there was no sunlight to create a reflection—and it would appear dry and solid and trustworthy. Until you touched it. . . .

Black ice was the greatest fear of any wintertime climber. When a rock wall you thought you knew like an intimate friend revealed the face of a stranger.

And even the emergency measures Nattie had seen used, generally a set of fixed belays, weren't going to work here because there was simply no time for them.

So she'd improvised. One thing Nattie had learned in the last year, when you can't do anything else, you improvise.

She'd gotten Ben into the rappel harness, a series of straps and webbing that fit securely between his legs and up over his hips; then she'd tied into his figure-eight descender on the front. A tight bowline knot.

He hadn't liked the idea of being lowered down the wall, especially by a woman who weighed probably seventy-five pounds less than he did, but the reverse wasn't an option. Because, after he lowered her, how was *he* going to descend?

So Nattie's improvisation had become a plan. She'd set herself in the rocks at the canyon's edge, the red and blue rope pulled around her hips in a top belay, backstopped by giving it one turn around a ragged old Douglas fir behind her.

And down he'd gone, this man from the city who was utterly terrified of heights. Down into the blinding emptiness of the storm.

Without even the rock face to reach out and touch at first, thanks to that initial overhang. When his body began to twirl slowly at the end of the harness, unavoidable in a hanging descent because of the lateral tension in the fibers of any climbing rope, she'd expected him to start yelling. She was impressed when he didn't.

Whatever else might be true of this guy—and she had no way of knowing what that might be—he didn't lack courage.

"Hey!" he yelled up at her. "You coming down, or what?"

Which still didn't keep him from occasionally being a serious pain in the butt. She leaned out and made a shushing motion toward him.

"Right." He nodded. "You couldn't hear a bomb go off in this damn wind."

"You might be surprised," muttered Nattie, privately pleased that he still had some spirit left, and payed out more rope. The Maxim kernmantle was a fifty-meter length, which meant each leg of the descent could be only half that distance. Each time Ben reached a spot anywhere near twenty-five meters down—about eighty feet—where he could find safe purchase, he simply had to grab whatever was available and hold on. Then Nattie, using a fixed ice screw and carabiner to secure the top, would descend the other half of the rope in a free rappel, down to where Ben was. His superior body weight, attached to the harness on his end, acted as a bottom belay.

Then lower him another twenty-five meters, back-stopped by a new ice screw, rappel down herself, pull the rope free through the carabiner above them, and do it all again. A game of vertical leapfrog down the frozen wall of Empinado Canyon.

It was a ragged, primitive method of descent, conceived in desperation, but it was working so far. Not unlike two kids throwing a rope over a tree limb, then each grabbing one end to counterbalance the other. As long as the heavier kid didn't let go, the lighter one could climb up or down.

Slightly higher stakes here, of course.

Nattie heard a third gunshot from up on the rim. She held out a gloved hand, a caution for silence, to Ben McKee below her.

It had to be a signal. Cleese or one of his goons had found the spot where she and Ben started down the cliff. There'd been a lot of torn snow there at the edge of that first dropoff. It was inevitable it would be spotted.

What would they do now, those four up top, standing at the edge and trying to see down into this gray-white, howling nothingness? Would they give it up? Go back to their downed helicopter, or maybe the Lear, and sit out the storm?

Or continue the pursuit?

That was a stupid thought, except . . .

He won't quit, that's what Ben had said about Cleese. *Not ever. He's relentless.*

Nattie wondered what kind of gear they'd brought with them in the helicopter.

Whatever they'd needed to find a downed airplane, apparently. Whatever they'd needed—and she'd figured out this part with no coaching from the audience—to make sure the occupants of that plane stayed dead.

She didn't know what their reasons were, but she had no doubt about their goal. A goal as yet unachieved, because Ben McKee was still alive.

And so was she. Nattie had no doubt about one more thing. She was part of their problem now, with or without Ben McKee. Which was another, possibly less noble reason for not abandoning him.

How well prepared were they to solve that problem? Prepared enough to descend this cliff in pursuit?

Nattie stood up on the ledge and looked around her, eyes squinted against the blowing snow. In the summertime, the view from here was breathtaking: The high, jagged cliffs across the canyon, shades of white and black and vermillion rust, with the peaks of the high San Juans towering snowcapped above them. Down to the waterfall-filled canyon below the Ojo del Plata mine, where Walker Creek flowed through forests of evergreen and aspen toward flower-filled meadows and the distant midnight blue oval of Walker Lake. Golden eagles riding the thermals and watching for some careless marmot in the talus below, ignoring the humans and their ropes so long as they didn't get too near the nests built into the cliffside.

But that was in the summer. A completely different world from this. Now there was only the ice and the frozen granite and the emptiness below. And the storm.

Nattie brought her end of the rope back between her legs and then around her right hip. Up across her chest, then over her left shoulder and hanging free down her back. Right hand to guide, left hand to brake, and thank God for the friction-pad palms on her gloves.

She hated free rappels, especially in wet weather conditions, but the rappel harness was down there with Ben, where it had to be. At least the crampons, with their razor-sharp edges to dig into the ice, helped a little.

And this was the easy part, really. Much easier than lowering Ben each time. Despite her work-hardened strength, Nattie was beginning to tire some from his dead weight, probably one hundred eighty pounds, on the rope. Without the ice screw to backstop her and take part of that weight, it wouldn't be possible.

She watched him watching her from the base of the pinnacle below, and signaled she was coming down.

There was virtually no chance they could be heard up on the rim—not over the endless roar of the wind—but she decided not to risk it.

She gave another tug on the screw, then leaned out from the rock face. The rope bit into the carabiner and slid with her. Supported her easily. She pushed off the ledge in a short bound, and felt the rope's friction against her inner thigh and across her chest. An additional disadvantage to free rappels was that each bounce down the cliff had to be shorter than if she'd had the harness. About ten feet at a time.

She bounded out again, then twice more, the rope slipping through her gloved fingers. When she was a little past halfway down, she glanced between her legs to where Ben McKee was watching her . . .

Just as he slipped and fell.

She saw his booted foot—that slick, useless cowboy boot—slide off its purchase on the basalt pinnacle. Saw him grab for a better handhold on the icy rock . . .

Too late.

"Oh, shit . . ." His voice was muffled by the storm as he slid off the pinnacle. And went tumbling down the cliff.

Nattie had only a moment to react before her half of the rope jammed tight around her, then began yanking her upward. It was all a matter of leverage, and the weight was on his side of the ice screw.

Nattie locked down her brake hand on the rope, just an instant before she was slammed headfirst into the rock . . .

Thank God for her helmet.

. . . and dragged up the wall. She spun sideways and banged her shoulder so hard it knocked the breath out of her. Felt the rope trying to pull free of her grip . . .

If she turned loose, they were both dead.

. . . and then hit a patch of ice. She bounced up across it, scraping loose a shower of tiny ice shards . . .

And had a glimpse of an outcrop just above. She spun

in the rope and brought her legs up. Slammed her feet against the underside. If it was ice-coated . . .

But it wasn't. It was the bottom of a squared-out over-hang, partially protected from the weather, and the rock was dry. Nattie's cramponed boot heels hit against algae-coated stone, and she felt the jolt all along her spine. The impact tried to pull her off balance sideways, but she fought it.

And came to a stop, upside down in the rope, both feet shoving as hard as she could against the underside of the outcrop, the crampons' teeth scratching furrows in the algae.

The pressure—holding both herself and Ben McKee on the other end of the rope—built along her thighs and back, trying to buckle her legs. But if she let go with her feet, got catapulted the rest of the way up into that ice screw. . . .

Then the pressure eased suddenly. Nattie's legs straightened, and she dropped a few feet below the outcrop. She swung back to normal vertical, her feet sliding down the wall and her head popping back up. Which could only mean Ben had found something to stop his fall.

And he had. Nattie set herself against the wall and looked down between her legs. Ben was barely visible with the snow blowing across him, but she could see the large, diagonal crack in the canyon wall where he'd jammed his feet. As she watched, he pulled himself up into the crack and wedged his body in place. The rope let off some more slack on her side, and she dropped down a foot or so.

"Are you okay?" she yelled down.

"Just dandy." His voice was muffled by the wind. "Just goddamn swell. Let's do that again . . ."

He was saying something else, most of it fairly pro-fane, but Nattie ignored him once she saw he was all right. He'd fallen maybe twenty feet below the pinnacle, and pulled her upward the same distance on her side of the rope, which left her another twenty feet below her original ledge. She could probably climb back to her starting point, but she doubted he could reach his. Or would be interested in trying, now that he was in a secure location. She couldn't blame him for that.

And, since he was now below the halfway point, she no longer had enough rope on her side to reach him. She'd have to rappel down to the nearest safe spot, and then release the rope on her end. Pull it from the other side, back up through the ice screw to free it, then set up a new belay point. Time consuming, and not a lot of fun, but it could be done.

She wished she'd had time to count the ice screws in her bag. When they ran out of carabiners, which was going to happen pretty soon, she'd have to thread the rope through the eye-hole of the screws alone. And if they ran out of those . . .

She'd have to improvise something else, though at the moment she had no idea what that might be.

Ben McKee was silent below her, probably just now fully realizing what had nearly happened to him. He appeared to be well set up in the diagonal crack.

"Coming down," called Nattie, who figured there was no longer much point in worrying about silence. She pushed away from the ice-covered canyon wall.

And dropped down again, into the storm.

"So, what do you think?" asked Eugene Cleese.

The four men were huddled together while the blizzard blew across them. They were looking at the torn snow next to their feet. At the spot where rocks and snow and ice gave way to empty air.

The wind howled over the edge in downdrafts. It tried to pull them forward, and they braced themselves against it. Leaned back toward the sanity of the ridge top.

"Tell you what I think, *esse.*" Arturo Garza's bushy black eyebrows were white, crusted with ice above his wool half mask. "I think those two are major road pizza, down there at the bottom."

Cleese glanced over at Garza. "You think?"

"Gotta be, Gene. Hell, they probably panicked, and—"

"That's a rope blister." Liam Riley pointed to a discolored mark on the trunk of a wind-twisted old fir tree next to them. A narrow line of broken bark.

"Yes." Cleese nodded. "I believe it is."

Riley leaned over and rubbed one gloved finger along the mark. He showed his fingertip to Cleese.

Cleese studied the tree sap on Riley's glove. "Looks fresh," he said.

"Yeah, but come on, Gene. Why would they have a rope?" asked Milton Wallace. "Riding around on a snowmobile in the middle of this ever-shitting blizzard, what would they be doing with a rope?"

"McKee wouldn't," replied Cleese. "But that woman . . ." He looked at Wallace. "What do you think of that woman, Milt?"

The big man lifted a hand to the spot where his cap covered his forehead. "Raised by piranhas would be my guess," he answered. "Or maybe Comanches."

"She seems to be resourceful," agreed Cleese. "She had that four-ten, and she had that snowmobile. Maybe she has a rope, too. Look at those tracks. Somehow or other, they went off the edge here. Down the side."

"One rope for the two of them?" Riley looked doubtful. "On a wall like this? Why would they do it?"

"Hey, *mano,* why'd the coyote cross the road?" Garza shrugged. "'Cause he had his teeth caught in the chicken's ass, that's why."

"Because he had no choice, in other words." Cleese pulled the collar of his orange snowsuit up higher around his head. "Probably an accurate analogy, Artie. They went for the plane, but only after their snowmobile was crippled."

"You saw those empty holsters," said Riley.

Cleese nodded. "Ben probably knew about those guns. But, even so, they were headed *down* the meadow before they started losing oil. Remember that trail we saw on the

134

map? The one that parallels the ridgeline south? I believe they were trying to reach the lake. Maybe they still are."

Riley leaned out toward the rim of the cliff. A wind gust caught him, and he grabbed onto Wallace's big shoulder for support.

"Helluva shortcut." He grinned.

"If we're gonna discuss this any further, how about we get away from that edge." Wallace kicked his way through the snow over toward the old tree. "I don't much like that edge, man."

"¿Como dice, mojado?" said Garza. "What the hell, our pilot don't like heights?"

"Not unless there's a motor involved somewhere," replied Wallace. "You know I'm a flatlander, Artie."

"They were going for the lake." Cleese moved up next to Wallace, and the others followed him. "For that comm center, probably. When the snowmobile got disabled, they went to the plane instead. For the guns. But they're still trying to reach the lake."

"Maybe we should've trashed that radio receiver," said Riley. It was as close to a criticism as he ever got.

"You could be right," replied Cleese. "But I like the way the place looked when we left it. Undisturbed, except for maybe that coffee stain, because you never know who might drop by. Anyway, let's figure Natalie Kemper has a rope. And knows how to use it, since that's no ordinary summertime descent over there. And McKee, maybe there's more to him than I thought. He survived the airplane. He got out of that burning cabin, and now he's taken up technical climbing, it seems. These two could be a challenge after all."

"So we go down after them?" Riley was grinning again. Cleese saw the anticipation there, in the tall man's cold, gray eyes.

An old courtship renewed.

"Not me." Milton Wallace shook his head emphatically. "Huh-uh, brother."

"You think you can get that 'copter airborne again, Milt?" asked Cleese. Being the leader had always meant

135

knowing his people, both their strengths and weaknesses.

The big man's face was covered to the nose with his ski mask, but the relief showed in every line of his body.

"If anyone can, I can," he answered.

"Good enough," said Cleese. "It takes a lot of nerve to put a helicopter up into this storm. Those two have a pretty good head start on us. If they should happen to reach the bottom alive . . ."

"They'll have a welcoming committee waiting when they get there," finished Wallace.

"Hey, what about me, Gene?" asked Garza. "You know I'll try anything once, *parejo,* but . . ."

"But Liam and I are the climbers." Cleese nodded. "Why don't you go with Milt?" He unsnapped the bindings of his snowshoes and handed them to Garza. "We'll meet you two at the bottom."

"Hey, we're outta here right now." Garza attached Cleese's snowshoes to those of Riley, then turned in the direction of Wallace, who was already climbing the ridge. *"Vaminose, el calvo."*

"You better watch your mouth, little man," shot back Wallace, who was sensitive about his baldness. "Else you're gonna be hangin' with Elvis."

Cleese watched them struggle out of sight up through the trees, then turned to Riley, who was already digging out a set of crampons. "You've got everything?" he asked.

Riley pulled a coil of purple and black eleven-millimeter Edelrid rope from his pack. "Brought pitons instead of screws," he replied. "But I'll manage."

"Okay then. Let's rope up."

"I can't feel my toes," said Ben McKee.

He said it lightly, matter-of-fact, but Nattie saw the pain and fatigue in his face. And maybe the beginnings of apathy, that first indicator of returning hypothermia that could switch off the survival instinct like cutting off a light in a dark room.

He'd had a brief burst of energy, probably adrenaline-charged and completely understandable after his near-fatal fall, that had carried him for a while. But it appeared to be about gone now.

Nattie felt an icy touch of foreboding, colder even than the biting wind. If he quit on her now. . . .

They were at the bottom of the sixth leg of their descent, nearly five hundred feet below the rim. With close to a thousand feet still to go, she calculated, but she wasn't going to tell him that. There was no way to see the bottom, or the top either, in this storm, so it might as well be a mile as far as he was concerned.

They'd found a wider ledge than usual, a place where a huge chunk of rock had broken away in some dim past and had created a protective pocket in the canyon wall. They were huddled together, mostly shielded from the wind and blowing snow, with the rope coiled behind them to keep it dry, and Nattie had put an arm around Ben's shoulders without thinking about it much.

"Hungry?" she asked, leaning over to speak into his ear through the red wool cap she'd lent him. Below the cap, the skin of his jaw was dead white. Bone white, with the first tiny threads of gray.

Frostbite, she thought.

"I'm too tired to eat," he mumbled.

Which wasn't going to do at all.

"That's when you need food the most." Nattie dug a couple of cellophane-wrapped squares out of her pack. "See this?" She wiggled one of them in front of his face. "This is the best chocolate brownie you're ever going to hang a lip over. A lady in Pagosa Springs named Patti Stickler makes them, two zillion calories per bite, guaranteed. I can gain weight just sniffing the shrink-wrap."

"Wouldn't hurt you if you did." He looked back at her, eyes still vague.

"There are two schools of thought on that subject," she replied, which briefly opened an old wound . . .

Did you weigh this morning, Nattie?

. . . but that was okay. Anything to get him going.

She'd stand up on the ledge and strip if that's what it took.

He'd gone back to staring ahead. Out into the blank, gray-white distance beyond the ledge. She could see him starting to fade, right before her eyes.

And they still had nearly a thousand feet to go.

You could leave him here, Nattie. Take the harness off him. Rappel on down by yourself . . .

Shut up. Shut up, you selfish bastard.

Sometimes selfish isn't so bad, Nattie my love. This guy's toast, and you know it.

"No!" she said aloud, and was surprised how the sound cut through the wind.

"Say something?" Ben leaned into her, like a worn-out child in his mother's arms.

"I can't feel my toes," he muttered again.

Those western boots, from the dead pilot in the equally dead airplane. They were too small, cutting off the circulation. And in this cold . . .

Something had to be done, and right now.

"Hey," said Nattie. "Can you feel this?"

And she kissed him, squarely on the mouth.

It started out pretty grim. His lips were icy and rough-scabbed. Unresponsive. But she stayed with it, and after a few more moments things became different. The kiss itself became different . . .

Which wasn't part of the plan. She pulled back from him, fighting an eerie sense of confusion.

And found him looking at her with the faintest edge of a smile. He appeared somewhat livelier than before.

"What was that for?" he asked.

"Got your attention, didn't it?" She was fairly sure her face was too wind-roughened right then to show the blush she felt warming it. "Now, are you going to eat this damned chocolate, or do I feed it to you rectally?"

He looked at her, then at the brownie in her hand. "You're a hard woman," he said.

She broke off a piece, stiff and crumbly from the cold. "Take a bite," she ordered.

"It's frozen. It'll break my teeth."

"What a baby. Take small bites. It'll warm up in your mouth."

"Melts in my mouth, not in my hands." He began to chew slowly.

"I guess that must be some of that famous urban humor I've heard about," she replied, but she was glad to see him working on the chocolate. A tiny bit of color was returning to his pale face.

"Small bites," she said again, and went to work on her own snack. "I think you're in the middle of a comeback, bud."

"Maybe another kiss," he said.

"Just eat the damned brownie." She purposely glanced away from him, because this time she was definitely blushing. "And don't push your luck. It's a long way down."

Bad choice of words, she realized as soon as she said it. She felt his body tense against her.

"I haven't been watching." His voice changed, lost its bantering tone. "Ever since . . . I haven't been able to."

"Then don't." She looked back at him again. "And don't worry about it. It scares the hell out of me, too. Anyone who isn't scared by what we're doing, they won't be in the gene pool for long, I promise you that. The main thing is you're doing it, Ben. You're getting it done, scared or not."

"Mountain Man McKee," he said. "But I still can't feel my feet."

"That's because those boots . . ."

Then she saw the smile, and remembered that was when she'd kissed him last time.

"Nice try." She nodded. "Wiggle your toes."

"How will I know if I'm wiggling them if I can't—"

"Do it anyway. You didn't think you could eat that chocolate, either, and I notice it's gone now. So wiggle your toes. Wiggle them on faith."

"Faith." Ben glanced up at the logo on the front of her

climbing helmet. "All Empty Roads Require Faith To Travel," he read. "You believe that?"

"As much as I believe anything."

He glanced past her, toward the end of the ledge. "This road's emptier than most," he said.

"And it isn't traveled yet," she replied. "Not by a long shot. Are you ready to get started again?"

She saw the fear return, flit across his face for a moment, to be replaced by something else. More like a patient kind of dread.

"Can't stay here, I guess." He struggled to his feet, and she rose with him. Outside the relative shelter of the small alcove, they felt the storm again. Still there, still brutal.

Still waiting.

Nattie uncoiled the rope, then began twisting another tubular screw into the ice.

Chapter Ten

Battered by the blizzard's gale-force winds, Eugene Cleese went down his rope to the left of and slightly below Liam Riley. The younger man was an expert at rappeling from his Special Forces days, pushing away from the canyon wall in long, graceful bounds. Three, four at most, and he'd reach the mid-point of his line. Then he'd set up in that distinctive half-comma position against the cliff, his crampons digging their razor-sharp teeth into the ice, while he found a bare spot to drive a piton and tie off with a carabiner. Then he'd tug his rope down from the 'biner above, and do it all again.

He was very good, but so was Cleese. Their training had the same source, after all.

Frequently they spotted where someone—probably the woman—had recently set ice screws, about seventy or eighty feet at a pitch. And, on those occasions, Cleese used her screws for his belay, enabling him to save the ones in his own bag.

He was willing to put his life into her hands in that way. He'd developed a large amount of respect for her already.

Lucky Ben. He could have come down anywhere in that plane.

Cleese bounded away from the frozen cliff face on another descent. He was enjoying this—the steady pull of the rope against his rappel harness, the guiding and braking action of his hands, the quick impact of each bounce

141

on his flexed thigh muscles. It was also doing a good job of keeping him warm.

He didn't feel old. Didn't feel a few months from being sixty-two. Of course, he didn't exactly feel young, either. He remembered that well enough, and this wasn't the same.

He felt . . . eternal.

And it was better than youth in one way. If he was young, he wouldn't have Genie. Seeing her nearly every day, watching her grow up, something he'd missed with his own daughter because of Ruth. When she found out about Machtel, about what he did for Machtel, leaving hadn't been enough for Ruth. "Stay away from Kaydra," she'd warned. "Don't come near her, or me. Not a word, not a letter, not a phone call, unless you want me to place a phone call of my own . . ."

And so, by mutual agreement, he'd lost his daughter. Kaydra had grown up a stranger to him. Cleese didn't know what Ruth told her about him during those years, harsh things beyond doubt, but apparently they hadn't included that one item. Ruth had taken the enormous cash settlement, and then kept her end of the bargain. There were no phone calls—on either side.

And then Ruth was gone, and with her gone Cleese made an awkward kind of peace with Kaydra, who was divorced and pregnant and needing someone badly. And ready for whatever uneasy truce she and her father could attain after all the years.

Just in time, as it turned out. Just in time for Genie, who was waiting impatiently for him now, back there where it was golden and blue and warm. Waiting for him to be done with this cold, gray-white place, and to come back to her.

Safe again. Both of them.

Cleese had a glimpse of Riley stopping on the rope. He did the same, locking down his brake hand and gliding in toward the canyon wall to absorb the bounce. When he stopped, he noticed the storm more. It beat on him, cold and gray-white. Tried to push him sideways across the ice.

He glanced over and saw Riley about thirty feet away, looking back at him. The tall man raised a gloved hand, one finger, then another, and pointed downward.

Cleese leaned out and looked over one shoulder. Down into the empty, wind-whipped depths . . .

Except it wasn't completely empty now. Far below, Cleese saw a brief flash of color.

Red, like the cap Ben McKee had worn at the cabin.

Cleese squinted for a better look. He took great pride that at his age, he didn't need glasses, but few people's eyes were as sharp as Riley's. The man had held up *two* fingers.

Then Cleese saw a second figure, closer but partially shielded by an outcrop. The woman.

They were down there, descending this sheer wall of ice and stone with one rope. Lower with half of it, then rappel the other half. Cleese's smile was as much admiration as anything else. Natalie Kemper. She was . . .

Remarkable, really. The kind of woman Genie would be someday.

But Cleese's admiration had nothing to do with the task at hand, or its inevitable outcome. It was Natalie Kemper's misfortune to be in the wrong place at the wrong time, as much of a threat now to Genie as Ben McKee was.

Which was regrettable, but . . .

Life and death, they're meaningless, boy.

Cleese estimated the pair to be almost two hundred feet below him, at the extreme edge of vision in this blizzard. A bit beyond it, actually, since he kept losing sight of them.

They were descending in the fastest way possible, given the limitations of their gear. Unhampered by such limitations, Cleese and Riley would gain steadily.

An hour, maybe less.

And there would be no need for guns, if it was done right. After those two fell, their bodies might not be found until spring, and it would be *much* better if those bodies contained no bullet holes. Much neater.

Once again Cleese had to smile, the way things sometimes worked out.

But it would have to be done right, which meant silence. Cleese looked over at Riley and raised his hand, fingers held flat across his mouth. Riley nodded.

They continued to descend.

By the time he passed that same deadfall of trees—sticking up out of the snow along a steep ridge—for the fourth time, Rick Macon began to deal with the possibility he wasn't going to find the cutoff for Right Hand Creek. Or the trail leading up the mountain to Nattie's cabin.

No matter how badly he wanted her.

He dealt with it as he had always dealt with the disappointments in his life. First with anger, and then with either cleverness or violence. In this case, violence, since cleverness wasn't getting the job done at the moment. He raised a gloved hand and slammed it down hard onto the flimsy front panel of the rented snowmobile. Left a crater there the size of a softball, with a smaller dimple in the shape of his college ring.

Which made him feel a little better, as hitting something—or someone—usually did, but he knew it was only temporary.

He should have realized how the deep snow would alter the landmarks of the terrain around him. Right Hand Creek was long since frozen over and buried, probably four or five feet deep. So was the spot where it emptied into Walker Lake, and likewise the place where it emerged from the trees up on that ridge. There were intermittent gaps all along there. Any of them could be the creek.

If he couldn't find Right Hand Creek, he couldn't find the trail that ascended alongside it. And, without the trail, there was no way to climb through two thousand vertical feet of heavily forested slopes and reach that plateau on the map.

Where Nattie was.

Macon wiped a glove across his snowmobile glasses to clear them, then looked around him. He was near the right edge of a vast white bowl, bounded on this side by a wall of evergreens rising up into the blindness of the storm. Out there on his left was the frozen lake, distinguishable only because of its smooth snow cover. Ahead of him, the bowl began to narrow and steepen, which meant that box canyon was up there somewhere. A dead end.

Behind him was the lower, rounder portion of the lake. Also the comm center.

Rick Macon had never been one to handle defeat well—not as a minor star in Denver high school football, not as a mostly unsuccessful TV actor during a stay in Los Angeles that ended abortively one night when a strip-joint waitress threw a drink in his face and was subsequently found outside beaten half to death but unwilling to identify her assailant, and not several years later as the loser in a bitter Denver divorce case centering on physical and emotional abuse. His unrelenting stubbornness along those lines was why he'd driven past this particular deadfall three more times after he first realized it wasn't the route to Right Hand Creek. But his fuel gauge was already down by a quarter, and his watch told him it was nearly three P.M. This time of year, with this weather, it would almost certainly be dark before six, and he'd already spent one night too many on the back of this goddamn machine.

He wasn't aware he was still hitting the panel, steady punches that continued to dent the thin surface. His hands were too cold to feel the impact anyway.

He was getting very angry.

He couldn't reach Nattie's cabin on a snowmobile; that conclusion had finally become inescapable. Not on this day. Not in this storm. She was up there above that canyon, just a few miles away, after all this time, and she might as well be in goddamn Nicaragua, because he couldn't reach her . . .

Which was when he heard the helicopter. Up ahead somewhere, it sounded like, though the wind made any pinpoint locating impossible. Somewhere near the upper end of the lake.

A helicopter. What if . . .

Of course. It made sense. That was why Marvin Stone was missing from his post. With a blizzard this bad, they must be evacuating people down to safety. All those little squares and printed names on the map, those people were being brought down by chopper.

Including Nattie.

What a joke that would've been. Hours of struggling up to that cabin, only to find it empty. No Nattie, probably not even her goddamn dog.

If she wasn't with this particular group, she'd be with another. All Macon had to do was go back to the comm center . . .

Which created a problem. A couple of them, in fact.

One problem was that he'd left the place a bit roughed-up. The torn-down map, missing food, the wrecked radio receiver.

Hey, it was like that when I got here this morning. An unlocked door, anyone could come in, right? It's a real shame that the mountains have gotten just as bad as the cities nowadays. Can't go off and leave your door open, not unless you want to hang a big sign on it. Welcome, Vandals . . .

The first problem could be handled.

The second was more serious. She walks in the door, sees him standing there, then what? With all those other people around, maybe including some search-and-rescue types . . .

And she starts screaming bloody murder, that's what.

Hey, folks, it's all right. She's my wife, see, and she's had some, uh, emotional problems. She was under a doctor's care 'til she just took off one night . . .

Macon was less pleased with his second solution.

146

Chances were those people knew Nattie, so who would they believe? Maybe her husband—if he was as calm as she was hysterical—but maybe not.

Search-and-rescue people were frequently deputized, and carried guns. Rick Macon had no intention of winding up in a pair of handcuffs. Not again.

His entire plan had been built around finding Nattie alone, out here in the boonies in some isolated cabin.

If he could reach her cabin now, he could wait there for her. And, after the storm cleared, when they flew her back home . . .

Hi there, Nattie my love. Surprised to see me?

But he couldn't reach her cabin, which meant it was time to come up with Plan B.

The helicopter sounds were moving away from him, farther up the canyon.

He had to return to the comm center; that much was evident. Maybe to that wooden shed where he'd found the spare gasoline. From there he could watch, see who unloaded each trip. Maybe she wouldn't even show up. If not, he could wander in after a while, the way he'd originally planned. *I wonder if you could help me out. I'm trying to locate someone named Natalie Kemper.*

And if she did show up?

Look for the opportunity to get her alone. Create that opportunity if necessary. He hadn't come all this way, after all this time searching, to fail.

Forever, Nattie . . . That's what he told her once, and it was still true. Now, more than ever.

Forever . . .

He revved the Yamaha's engine, put the vehicle into a long, sweeping arc below the deadfall of trees, and headed back toward the comm center.

"Este nieve demontre," grumbled Arturo Garza, and grabbed on as the helicopter shook its way forward against the headwind. *"Se va a caer, yo se que . . ."*

"What the hell are you bitching about?" Milton Wal-

147

lace fought the cyclic control stick, his feet simultaneously working the yaw pedals to steer away from the cliff on their right. "You gotta be bitching, do it in English, dammit!"

He got stabilized for a moment, then felt the 'copter's tail swing out on him again. Felt the strengthening torque that was nothing but Bad News with capital letters.

"Paso por aqui Arturo Garza. El vato pobrecito, prisionero de sus propias trampas . . ."

"Goddammit, Artie!" Wallace cut his eyes away from the erratically bouncing manifold pressure gauge. "What . . ."

"What I said is we're doomed, *pendejo.*" Garza bounced forward against his safety strap, then back as the helicopter lurched again. "Down the tubes, *comprende?* Circling the drain. Tits up and taking on water . . ."

"We're not dead yet," snarled Wallace, and manhandled the stick some more. "I've seen it nearly as bad as this along the Sierras in the summertime. Except that was updrafts . . ."

"Now there's a comfort." Garza tried to find something to grab that didn't look like controls. " 'Oh, sure. Gene', he says. 'I can fly a chopper in a blizzard. No problemo' . . ."

"Keep your damn hands away from the stick!"

"And good ol' Artie, I.Q. like a house plant, he goes along for the ride. *¿Por qué no?*"

The nose dropped, and Garza was thrown forward again. *"¡Hijo de la chingada!"* he screamed, and hung on to the seat frame.

The LongRanger 206L3 had a five-hundred-horsepower Allison turboshaft engine, specifically modified for high altitude. But no amount of modification could prepare it for a storm like this. Wallace kept after it, alternating the pitch angle and the rotor rpm, but he couldn't prevent the increasing torque. Only the small vertical tail rotor could do that, and it was no match for the fury of the wind that was smashing it broadside.

It was only a matter of time before the escalating torque put the small craft into an irreversible spin, or possibly shook it apart in midair.

Yeah, Gene. Wallace gave a snort that was more anger directed at himself than fear. Yeah, I can fly through this storm. If anyone can, I can.

But this was still a helluva lot better than trying to climb down the side of that ice-coated canyon wall, wasn't it? Better than hanging in those ropes. . . .

This was no country for an up-and-coming Sonoma Valley businessman. Or viticulturist, he reminded himself. Right about now he should be sitting at his desk in front of that big window that overlooked the volcanic Mayacama hills to the east, sampling a glass of the new Merlot and calculating the effect of the unexpectedly heavy winter rain on the harvest that would finally see the Gold Hill label financially independent. If he hadn't needed a quick cash flow for more fermentation tanks and replanting one hillside devastated last summer by phylloxera parasites . . .

And . . . come on, admit it. The chance to team with Eugene Cleese again. Cleese, whose specialized needs, and his willingness to pay top dollar to have those needs satisfied, had over the years transformed an old compatriot from a debt-plagued airplane mechanic into one big payday away from becoming landed gentry like that film guy Coppola, whose vineyards were just over the ridge there in the *real* high-rent district, the Napa.

But this would be his last trip. His last job. That was a promise he'd made himself. Milton Wallace could be as tough as he had to be, because business was business after all, but he knew he lacked something that was present in Cleese and Liam Riley. Something . . . as much hot as it was cold, if that made any sense. It had always been there in Riley, even back in Saigon, due to the fact that Riley was just plain nuts. The king of the adrenaline junkies, of the death wish. Cleese, on the other hand, never allowed that *hot* part to get the better of his good sense, which was what kept Wallace coming back. He would never have worked with Liam Riley alone.

Or Artie Garza either, speaking of the thermostat-impaired. Imagine Garza and Riley, off by themselves somewhere without Cleese's firm control, and with other living things in the vicinity . . .

Now there was a scary notion. A helluva lot scarier than flying this helicopter into the teeth of a blizzard, if you stopped to think about it.

Wallace ignored Garza, who was still bitching away in that East L.A. hybrid of Spanish and Tex-Mex, and tried to find the cliff on his right. Instant death over there, even the slightest touch, and that was the way the vertical wind shear was forcing him. Up ahead, things seemed to be narrowing.

"Nearly there, Artie." Wallace lowered the collective pitch lever to decrease the pitch angle and therefore their forward speed, and with it felt the dampening effect of the Noda-matic. "Hang on, I'm going to bring . . ."

The tail rotor finally gave it up. The copter began to spin.

"God almighty! Going down, Artie . . ."

"*¡Mierda . . . !*"

The helicopter dropped into the storm.

Ben McKee saw movement above Nattie. Or thought he did.

He shifted a little to one side, trying to get a better angle, but when he did that he started to slide.

"What the hell . . . ?" Nattie's voice drifted down to him. "Hold still down there!"

This was the tenth leg of their descent, if Ben's count was correct. Or maybe the eleventh . . .

Hard to be sure. Hard to focus, he was so damned cold.

. . . and it was one of their worst. This had happened a couple of times before, when he'd reached the rope's midpoint, only to find nothing there except a stretch of sheer, ice-coated canyon wall. No ledge, no pinnacle, nothing to support him. When that happened, he could only grab on—the rock or the sharp shards of ice, whatever—and let his weight, like a sack of potatoes dangling from the rafters, act as a counterbalance for Nattie while she rappeled down to him. Then, without any hand or footholds, she'd have to insert a screw—they'd long since run out of carabiners—attach Ben's figure eight to it, release her own grip on the climbing rope, and hold on to him while he pulled the rope free from its rappel point above. During these moments of improvised, high-wall gymnastics, they were at their most vulnerable, hanging above the abyss without the support of the rope.

At least this one wasn't quite as bad as the other two times. Ben had found a place to wedge his feet between these rock abutments, and even a ragged, icy crack for one handhold. It kept him from swinging around so much, something that usually resulted in Nattie being yanked back up her side of the rope.

She was about halfway down now. When she reached him, he'd show her the foothold. Also ask her if she'd heard that noise a few minutes earlier. Just for a moment there it had sounded one helluva lot like a helicopter . . .

Which, fortunately for them, was impossible. No way Cleese could've gotten that chopper back up in this worsening storm. Whatever the sound had been, it was gone now anyway. Probably just a bad case of frozen eardrums. . . .

Ben glanced down between his legs, something he'd started doing again in spite of the memory of his earlier fall and the stomach-hollow, breath-grabbing terror it caused. Looking for the bottom, hoping for it . . .

And saw a slope below him. Maybe twenty feet away.

It wasn't much of a slope, steep as hell and covered in ice and oddly colored rock, angling downward for perhaps a hundred feet or so before another dropoff. Another cliff.

But it was something. A rare section of this godforgotten canyon wall that wasn't totally sheer. Maybe there was a place in those rocks to stop and rest.

He looked back up at Nattie, only a short distance away now. He saw her watching him as she descended, her face pale but determined, the snow blowing laterally across her.

And then he looked past her, up the cliff . . .

To where the two figures were dropping down onto them, out of the storm. To where the figure in orange was reaching the ice screw. And the rope.

Ben saw the knife, glittering brighter than the ice itself.

"Nattie!" he yelled. "Look out!"

He saw her eyes widen. Saw her look back above her head. Saw her fumbling for her jacket pocket with one hand.

He saw Cleese, suspended there on the cliff, and he saw the quick slashing motion of one orange-clad arm.

He saw Nattie's hand pull free of the jacket pocket, and the dark shape of the pistol . . .

Just as the climbing rope was cut.

Ben felt the rope's pressure go slack against his rappel harness, and realized he was holding himself now, supported only by his hand and foothold. He saw Nattie up there above him, dropping the gun as she fell, grabbing for the cliff.

But there was nothing to grab.

The pistol flashed past Ben, narrowly missing his head. Nattie fell past him . . .

And, in that same stretching, expanding moment of time, he did something very strange. He reached out instinctively with one arm and grabbed her.

Held her, for only an instant before her plummeting weight tore loose his grip on the rock.

They fell together, forever it seemed, but really only another of those elastic, timeless moments. Then they hit the slope with a force that drove the air from Ben's lungs.

And tumbled, tangled in each other and the remnants of the rope, over rocks and ice that were a series of

152

numbing blows all along Ben's back and legs. He felt something wet, realized it was blood—somebody's blood—at the same time he heard Nattie's voice.

"Shit!" she yelled, and was grabbing for something . . .

Then her hand came up, holding one of her ice axes. She took a wild swing, and Ben felt the impact through her body. He locked an arm around her . . .

Just before they swung wide in a sweeping pendulum arc. And slid to a stop.

After a moment of absolute silence, Ben heard his heart slamming his rib cage. Then he could hear the storm again. Feel it, roaring across them.

Still alive. Two falls down this god-awful, never-ending cliff, and he was still alive.

For the moment, at least.

He raised his head and saw they were lying on an icy, rock-strewn slope below the sheer cliff. Above them, he saw gouges torn from that slope, rocks broken free and starting to slide their way. And dark streaks on the ice.

Nattie was holding on to the ax with both hands, her body splayed face downward, legs dangling below. Ben was entangled with her, one arm beneath her body and his other hand holding a section of the rope that was still twisted along her back.

She said something then, but he couldn't hear it.

He sneaked a quick look beneath his free arm. The slope below them continued the same, but only for another twenty feet or so. At the end of it was the overhang he'd seen earlier. The continuation of the cliff.

They'd tumbled most of the length of the steep slope before Nattie buried the ax full-depth into a mixture of ice and that same odd-colored shale. Another five seconds, another twenty feet . . .

Lord God.

Ben grabbed on to a protruding outcrop of rock—saw both his hands were bleeding—and pulled himself up a little. Tried to get his bearings. After a few seconds, Nattie raised her head and looked at him. Her face was bone white below her battered climbing helmet, and her green eyes were dazed.

"Gotta move," she said, and he read her lips more than heard her. "They're coming, dammit. We've gotta move . . ."

"Where?" He pulled himself to a seated position on the outcrop and looked around. The slope was on either side of them, the cliff was above, the overhang was below.

Laterally. The only direction they could move was laterally across the slope.

Nattie dragged herself up the haft of the ax. "Go rock to rock," she was saying, and Ben saw she was half-conscious. "Look for an opening."

"What . . . ?"

"These are tailings. Mine tailings. There'll be—"

A gouge exploded out of the ice above her head, followed a moment later by a shrill whine of noise.

"They're shooting!" Nattie tried to dig in with her crampons. "They're shooting . . ."

Just as the tip of a rock shattered to her left. An exploding spray of granite shrapnel, another ricochet of sound.

"Jesus Christ!" Ben grabbed Nattie's arm and began pulling her sideways across the ice as more shots whizzed past them. They were sitting ducks out on this slope. Only the force of the wind, and its effect on the men above trying to fire downward from a moving, hanging position, had saved them so far.

Look for an opening, she'd said.

Ben lunged from rock to rock, still pulling on Nattie's arm. Some of the stones broke free under his weight, and he kept sliding. In spite of his best effort, they were moving at an angle, to the right but also downward. And there wasn't much room below them to spare. Maybe fifteen feet now above the overhang.

Ricochet from the bullets was whizzing all around them, and Ben felt a chip of something—ice or rock or shell fragment—strike his cheek. His skin was so numb there was no pain, but he knew he was bleeding again.

"Up there!" yelled Nattie from behind him. "Look up there!"

Ben glanced back, then followed the line of her pointing finger. Up the slope, but farther off to the right, at the base of the cliff. A jagged crevice, barely visible through the storm.

"Climb for it!" She pulled free and went past him, both hands and feet scrabbling for purchase. He went with her.

Later, Ben McKee had little memory of the climb up that ice-covered slope, the wind howling over him, the snow blinding him, and the whine of gunfire all around him. All he knew was that he sighted in on Nattie Kemper's legs just ahead, and he climbed harder and faster than he would have ever imagined was possible.

They reached the base of the cliff as the shooting stopped, and Ben realized their angle had put them momentarily out of the line of fire. He saw the crevice was considerably larger than it had looked from below. He also saw that it was man-made.

He followed Nattie inside.

Chapter Eleven

At twelve P.M., Mountain Standard Time, the National Weather Service updated its Winter Storm Warning for the San Juan Mountains of southwestern Colorado. The storm warning was extended, this time until midnight. In addition to the shut-down of mountain passes, highway closings were now included at lower elevations. Also the continued cancellation of public school classes and most non-essential government functions.

In towns like Pagosa Springs, Durango, Telluride, and Ouray, grocery stores sold out of staple products as weather-wise locals stocked up in preparation for being snowed in. Most of the adults—other than some liberated schoolteachers—found the situation less enjoyable than the children, who maxed-out their second school holiday in a row by either hauling sleds and inner tubes up the nearest slope, or overdosing on daytime TV.

Until a little past two P.M., when the main Public Service of Colorado feedline from Montrose went down, and the entire region lost electrical power, halting several search-and-rescue operations before they could get mobilized.

Including one that centered on a faint ELT signal from the high mountains east of Telluride. . . .

"Okay, there were these two hunters." Arturo Garza leaned forward and twisted gingerly side to side. "Rich

156

Anglos, hired a chopper to carry them into some primo elk country."

He rotated his arms—neither one broken, apparently—and released his safety belt, which dropped him sideways across the ruined cockpit. He slid down against Milton Wallace.

"Get your fat little ass offa me," said Wallace.

"So the chopper pilot reminds these two Anglos, before he flies off and leaves them. One elk, *tu ves?* This bird can carry the three of us and one elk."

"Pilot was a Mexican, I take it." Wallace wiped a trickle of blood off his upper lip. Between his nose and his buckshot-pimpled forehead, he was beginning to look the worse for wear.

"Desde luego," Garza nodded. "Of course. This is my story, isn't it?" He pushed with one booted foot against a shattered plexiglass panel. "So, a few days later the pilot comes back, finds those two *mamalones* with three elk. They say, 'Last year we paid you a hundred extra to haul three, remember?' Pilot tells 'em this year it's two hundred extra."

Wallace got his legs free. Began to rummage behind the mangled seat for his gear.

"So the chopper takes off, right?" Garza fished his mini-Ruger from out of the scattered equipment beneath him, and checked its clip. "Weaving around with all that extra weight, goes a little way and then crashes into some trees."

"Evergreens, no doubt." Wallace reached up to slap at a broken spruce limb swaying above his head.

"First Anglo climbs out of the wreckage, all beat to shit, says to the pilot, 'Where the hell are we?' Pilot crawls out, takes a look around and says, 'About a hundred yards from where we crashed last year, bro.' "

Wallace started to laugh, then touched his ribs and winced. "This story got a moral to it, Artie?"

Garza shrugged. "Only that there are some real slow learners out there, *parejo.* In here, too, maybe."

"Well, we're alive at any rate." Wallace helped Garza

kick the plexiglass panel loose from its metal supports. "And we're not in too bad a shape, all things considered. And we're at the bottom of that damn cliff, without having to climb down a rope to get here. Count your blessings, Artie."

"*Uno, dos* . . . I think what I better count is my fingers and toes, man. Damn good thing that C-4 wasn't packed with the detonators. There's a lot of bang back there." Garza got snapped into his snowshoes, then led with his feet. He pushed through, and tumbled forward into broken branches and torn snow.

Snow everywhere. *Mucha nieve, verdad?* In Artie Garza's neighborhood, a section of southeast Los Angeles squeezed in between the Compton homeboys—where wearing blue when you should have on red (or vice versa) could get you a quick ave from the priest—and those *pinche cabrones* from Whittier on the other side of the freeway who were just as bad, snow was hardly ever seen. At least not the kind that fell from the sky.

Plenty of the other kind, of course, and the money that came with it, if you had the *cojones* to stand up and be a man.

Machismo grande, that was what Garza's widower father called it, with just a fine edge of contempt in his voice. Children playing at being men—*hombres mucho*—who had no idea what it really took to be a man.

But what did he know? He was sweeping out the elementary school and swamping the toilets down at the bus station, the last Artie Garza saw of him. Probably still there, working his ass off at two jobs, confessing to the priest once a week how his greatest sin was being ashamed of his son the criminal . . .

Say ten Hail Marys, Joberto, and perform a good act of contrition.

. . . and then going home to sit on his threadbare couch and drink Coronas by the six-pack and fall asleep watching TV until it was time to get up and do it all over again.

Joberto Garza had given his son the choice when Arturo was thirteen—ten years ago—and first beginning to gangbang with Los Lobos del Valle. "Make some major changes in your life, *pedoro*, or don't let the door smack you in your *culo* on the way out."

Which was when Artie Garza moved in with his maternal grandmother, who lived over near La Habra and was widely believed to be a *curandera*, and subsequently avoided like the plague (or maybe La Migra) by her superstitious neighbors. Oddly enough, having a witch for a relative only enhanced Garza's position with Los Lobos.

He rarely saw his father after that.

And, as was often the case, little things led to bigger things over the next few years, and Artie Garza's reputation as a real balls-to-the-wall stand-up type expanded. It was shortly after he did some work on a free-lance journalist who was irritating the wrong people at a company called Machtel, Limited—something that could have been very messy, but ended up on the Pomona police blotter as an accidental death involving DUI—that Garza became better acquainted with a huge, balding redneck named Milton Wallace. And then, having apparently said and done the right things, he was introduced to Eugene Cleese. At which point, Garza—his gangbanging days behind him—began to travel and see the world . . .

Many parts of which, evidently, were a lot snowier than Compton and La Habra.

Wallace tossed out their packs, then followed Artie Garza through the shattered plexiglass of the cockpit. Both men stumbled away from the helicopter.

Or what was left of it. The little aircraft had shattered across the remains of several trees. It was broken into two major pieces, just behind the cockpit, with the rotor foil and some other smaller debris scattered around in a rough semicircle.

The trees themselves were in even worse shape than the helicopter. Before it snapped at its base, the main rotor had sheared off the branches coming in. Then the impact

159

of the fuselage had scalped everything else above trunk level.

Garza looked at the wreckage. He knew he was still alive at this point mostly because of Wallace's uncanny skill as a pilot, but he wasn't about to say so.

Keeping ol' Milt humble was part of Garza's job.

"Lucky for us, hitting those trees instead of rocks." Wallace led the way downslope. "And the deep snow, too."

"Where the hell are we?" Garza was trying to stay in the larger man's wake.

"About a hundred yards from where we crashed last year, bro," replied Wallace.

"No, really."

"We're at the head of that canyon." Wallace moved forward, and was harder to hear now as they emerged from the trees into the full force of the storm. "Box end's up that way, so we should be nearly below where those two started down the cliff. Quarter of a mile, maybe less. You ready?"

"*¿Estoy listo?*" snorted Garza. "Hey, bang on, bro. Us East L.A. boys, we're born ready."

The two men slogged ahead in silence for a while, struggling through snow that varied from thigh- to waist-deep, even with the snowshoes. Carrying full packs didn't help much, but there was no point in leaving food and gear in the ruined helicopter. After a few more minutes, Wallace stopped.

"What's that up there?" he asked.

"I'm not sure." Garza leaned out from behind the big man for a better look. He saw something ahead, next to the canyon wall, that was darker than the surrounding rock. Regular lines . . .

"Some kind of an entrance," he said. "Could be a mine. I hear they got lots of old mines in this country."

They headed toward it.

* * *

"I think we're pretty far ahead of them, but we still need to keep moving." Nattie held her stump of candle higher and stepped around a broken coal-oil lantern lying in the middle of the muddy passageway. If they could only find one of those that worked.

She shrugged off another wave of dizziness and held the candle in front of her to keep the darkness at bay. The last place, the *very* last place she wanted to be was in this mine . . .

The blackness . . .

. . . but it had saved their lives, in a couple of ways. Something she hadn't told Ben McKee was that her supply of ice screws was almost gone.

"You okay to go a little farther?" She spoke back over her shoulder. "We'll stop in a few more minutes."

"That's what you said a few minutes ago." Ben's voice was a hollow echo behind her. "You know those adventure movies, Indiana Jones, stuff like that, where the good guys are running for their lives from bloodthirsty villains?"

"What about them?"

"You ever notice, in those movies, how nobody ever has to stop and take a pee?"

She looked back at him, outlined in a flickering silhouette by his own candle.

"I think my plumbing's finally thawed out," he said, and turned into one of the numerous little side tunnels.

"Why don't I just wait for you?" Nattie crossed her arms. "You take your time, bud."

"Name's not bud." His voice echoed back to her. "Name's Ben."

"Yeah, yeah." She stood next to one of the damp, musty-smelling walls and listened to the steady drip of water. They'd gone deep enough now that the storm outside was only a faint background sound. Soon they'd lose it altogether.

To Nattie, escaping the noise of the blizzard—that nonstop deafening scream in her ears—was nearly as

161

welcome as getting away from the snow and the cold. If it wasn't for this darkness. . . .

She spotted another tiny piece of guttered candle and scooped it up to go in her pocket with about half a dozen others. They already had more than they'd need, but every one they found was one less for Cleese and his pal . . .

Who were back there somewhere in the dark, as sure as hell and devils. And Nattie was continuing to wonder where the other two men were. If they didn't climb down the cliff. . . .

"Everything come out okay?" she asked, when Ben McKee reappeared from the side tunnel. He was carrying another broken lantern, leaking coal oil down onto the floor.

"Lots of junk in here," he said, and laid the lantern aside.

"Lucky for us, yeah," replied Nattie, nodding toward the candle she held. "The Ojo del Plata is spelunker heaven during the summer. The National Forest Service puts up those iron-bar safety barriers everywhere, 'til all the entrances look like the county jail, but people just crawl over them and around them in spite of the warning signs. I've been down by the main entrance myself, but I had no idea the mine extended this high."

"Lucky for us it did."

"Thank God it did. And also for that mill-tailings slope out there to break up the cliff. We were pretty much at the end of our rope, no pun intended."

Ahead of Nattie, the dark passageway continued in a straight line, periodically reinforced by sagging timbers. Not much imagination to these old hardrock mines, but there was bound to be a vertical shaft before much longer. Some way down to ground level. Otherwise, all this spelunker debris wouldn't be up here. Speaking of which . . .

Unless they came down the canyon wall incredibly well prepared, Cleese and the other man should be stumbling around in the dark right now. From the very first piece

162

of candle she'd found, only a few yards inside the entrance, Nattie had been picking up every one. The single greatest advantage inside this huge, multilevel catacomb had to be the ability to see where you were going.

They were probably far enough ahead by now.

"You ready to take a break?" she asked.

"Me?" Ben's voice was ragged with fatigue. "Oh, hell no. I thought we'd jog for a while. Maybe do a few pushups . . ."

Nattie found a relatively dry spot on one side of the narrow tunnel and sat down. It wasn't until she leaned back against the wall and let her legs relax that she realized how exhausted she was. The large muscles in her thighs kept quivering, trying to cramp.

Ben McKee was a heavy load, in more ways than one.

She flashed for an instant on awakening that morning in her own bed—gone now with her other possessions destroyed in the fire—to find him staring at her . . .

Where'd you get that scar?

. . . about a million years ago.

Or more like nine hours. According to her trusty old Timex, which had clearly taken a licking and kept on ticking, it was just past three. Sixteen hours since she first looked up and saw the lights of that little jet passing above her cabin . . .

To change her life.

Ben settled across from her, a dim figure in the twilight of their two candles. He was prying off one of the dead pilot's boots, and then flexing his toes inside an expensive-looking sock. Maybe he'd beat frostbite after all, though he was still a prime candidate for the residual effects of hypothermia.

Assuming either of them lived that long.

"Wet in here, isn't it?" He went to work on his other foot.

"That's snowmelt, trickling down inside the rock," she replied, then lowered her voice when she heard it echo. No point in giving any help to their pursuers, especially since they'd already passed several side tunnels. Maybe those two would take a wrong turn in the dark. Wander off forever, like Injun Joe in *Tom Sawyer*.

"Must be a lot warmer in here," said Ben. "It sure as hell wasn't melting outside."

"It is warmer, which could eventually create some problems for us. All these old mines are porous as a sponge, and the water has to go somewhere."

"The Ojo del . . . what did you call it?"

"Ojo del Plata," finished Nattie. "Eye of Silver."

"This was a silver mine?"

"At one time, yeah, though there are a lot of stories about where that name came from. The mine played out in the Twenties, I guess; then they came back in and dredged it for the last of the minerals about ten years ago. It made Hiram Walker a millionaire. Also his children and grandchildren.

"Walker Lake," said Ben.

"And Walker Creek." Nattie nodded. "Walker Canyon, too, 'til some of the slave labor ol' Hiram imported from Mexico started calling it Empinado instead. Means steep."

"No shit," replied Ben.

Nattie smiled faintly. Her headache was getting better now. When she looked, she saw only one shadowy Ben McKee instead of two, or maybe three.

If necessary, aim at the middle one, she decided.

"It was Hiram's grandkids who ruined this place," she continued. "About ten years ago they brought in a reclamation company to dredge it out and then leach mine the quartz with cyanide. A profitable process, but a nasty one, not only for the mine itself, but also for the creek and the lake down below."

"Cyanide? That water's poisonous?"

"Not according to the EPA. But I've never eaten any fish taken from there, and I don't plan to."

"I'll tell you something." He placed one hand on his midsection. "Fish sounds pretty good to me right now. Even poisoned."

"I think blackened's probably more your style. Isn't

that how they serve it at Spago? Or am I hopelessly behind the trends again? Promise you won't tell Todd and Heather . . ."

"Damn." Ben shook his head. "You never give an inch, do you?"

"Not a millimeter, even." She studied him in the candlelight. "But maybe I should. You saved my life out there."

"No, I . . ."

"Sure you did. When you reached out and grabbed me, it slowed my fall."

"For about one second, maybe."

"Long enough to make a difference. At the very least, I'd've been knocked cold when I hit that slope. Which means I wouldn't have pulled out my ice ax . . ."

"And over the side we'd've gone. Good point. But I think it was that helmet that really saved you. Did you notice the crack down the center?"

Nattie removed her battered helmet. "I see what you mean," she replied. "But I owe you anyway. Which is why I've let you slide up to now on the explanation you owe me."

"I'm really tired, Nattie . . ."

"So make it brief." His words shot a quick flare of anger through her. "Give me the Cliff Notes version, because I'm tired, too, from lowering you all the way down that cliff, among other things. I also have a home that's been destroyed, a dog that's been killed, and several of your pals around here somewhere, looking to kill me, too, just because I'm with you. By my own conservative count, I've saved your yuppie butt four times already, which still leaves you three in the hole. So I think it's time for you to talk and me to listen."

She dug another cellophane-wrapped brownie out of her pack and tossed it toward him, maybe a little harder than she'd intended. Or maybe not.

"Chew on that to keep up your strength," she snapped. "Pretend you're eating herbed mushrooms on

165

toast with a bunch of your buds who gather monthly to discuss Proust—"

"A Big Mac would do, actually." He'd reached up and caught the brownie, which was a good sign. Poor hand-eye coordination was an indicator of hypothermia.

"Whatever," said Nattie. "And don't change the subject. As the King of Hearts said to Alice, begin at the beginning and go 'til you come to the end. Then stop."

"English majors. Jeez." Ben began to unwrap the cellophane, and even in the flickering candlelight Nattie could see his fingers trembling.

Exhaustion, or something more?

Her own head was still a little vague from her impact with that rock-strewn slope. Still a little dizzy . . .

I think you may have yourself a concussion, Nattie my love . . .

. . . but she made herself stay alert. It probably wasn't a concussion, anyway, thanks to her old helmet. Her headache was fading too easily for that.

"Okay," said Ben, after slowly unwrapping the chocolate . . .

Still stalling for time?

. . . and biting off one corner. "It isn't really that complicated."

"That's what my first steady boyfriend told me," said Nattie. "As I recall, he was wanting to show me how a condom works."

"You want to hear this, or not?"

"You know I do. Just keep in mind that my legs are *still* crossed."

"I believe that." He smiled faintly. "Okay, how much do you know about computers?"

"Probably as much as you know about rappeling. I can work a word processor well enough, and I could maybe do a spreadsheet if someone held a gun to my—"

She frowned. "Sorry. Bad choice of words."

Ben broke off another piece of chocolate. "I work . . . or I did work, for a company called Machtel, Limited. Ever hear of it?"

"Nope. Limited to what?"

"Not much, as it turns out. They're a multinational corporation, based in Southern California, that specializes in computerized commodities trading. I was one of their wonks . . ."

"Excuse me?"

He smiled again. "Numbers crunchers. Computer nerds. You know, the guys with the taped-up glasses and a pocket protector?"

Ben McKee didn't strike Nattie as nerdlike, computer or otherwise, but she let it pass. Kept her mouth shut and listened.

"Anyway, one day I was running some numbers, and tapped into the wrong access file. Just a stupid mistake, and I was about to punch in Escape . . . God, I wish I had."

"Why's that?"

"Because just before I hit that key, I realized what I was looking at, which was Caribbean bank records. From the Cayman Islands, to be a little more specific. How much do you know about the illegal transfer of funds?"

"I know it's called laundering."

"In some cases, yeah. The most important thing is the interest off the original capital, because that's the easiest part to wash. What you do is spread that interest income around to various offshore banks, then invest it from time to time in either dummy corporations—what they call paper companies—or in legitimate ventures on the mainland. Real estate's pretty popular right now, for example. Places like Vail and Aspen . . ."

"I returned from Aspen once," deadpanned Nattie. "Which is the only thing to do if you find yourself there."

As usual, her tolerance for being danced around was low. She was ready for him to get to the point.

"Of course, the original principle has to be moved from time to time, also," he went on. "Usually by wire transfers, at which point it's reinvested until it comes clean, too. Anyway . . ."

"Anyway," she prompted.

"To make a long story short, what I was looking at on that computer screen put the business affairs of Machtel in a very different light, you might say."

"So what did you do?"

"What did I do? I hit that damn Escape button, that's what I did. And hoped like hell that was the end of it."

"But it wasn't," said Nattie.

"Not by a long shot." Ben's voice was beginning to slur with fatigue. "Because a few days later I was contacted by the IRS . . ."

"Internal Revenue?"

"Yep. Interestingly enough, one of the simpler ways to nail that sort of scam is on income tax evasion, since any returns are pretty much de facto fraudulent. Only problem is, those offshore banks won't give the IRS the time of day, let alone a peek at their records."

Nattie studied him in the faint light. "How did the IRS know to contact you?" she asked. "How did they know what you'd found?"

He shrugged. Looked away down the tunnel. "They're the IRS. They know everything, right? They probably know what brand of tea you buy, and when you last went to the dentist."

"Uh-huh." Nattie's internal lie detector was beeping again. She'd thought once before it was to Ben McKee's credit that he was a poor liar. Now she wasn't so certain.

"So what did they want?" she asked.

"They wanted me to go to New York to talk to some supervisor there. Maybe to Washington later, if what I said checked out. They said they had an unregistered private plane, and that nobody would know."

"Then the Lear's their plane? And those two men, Landry and . . . whatzizname . . ."

"Taliferro. Bill Taliferro."

"Yeah. That's why they had guns. So who's Cleese?"

"Eugene Cleese." Ben's expression was bleak. "The story is Machtel recruited him straight out of the military, where he was involved in some of that no see-um,

168

no talk-um stuff across the border in Laos during the Vietnam War. Now he's what they call a troubleshooter. Interesting euphemism, wouldn't you say? The feds've been trying without any luck for years to get something on him. It was Cleese who fixed the plane . . . somehow or other. Had to be. I realized that for certain when he showed up at your cabin."

"But . . . how did he know what you were up to? Or which plane you'd be on?"

"Who knows?" He evaded her eyes again. "He's Cleese, for God's sake. He finds out things. He and the IRS are flip sides of the same coin."

"So he fixed the jet, somehow or other. Then when he found out it wasn't destroyed . . ."

"That damn crash beacon, probably."

". . . he came up here to finish the job." Nattie felt a chill that had nothing to do with her damp clothes. "Jesus . . ."

She glanced over at Ben McKee, who was lying back against the wall. His eyes had closed.

"Who's Shelley?" she asked softly, mostly to give him the opportunity for one more lie.

But his eyes didn't open.

Chapter Twelve

The cone of light was fitful, flickering, good for perhaps a hundred feet before it faded out each time.

"Better stop," said Eugene Cleese, and cupped one hand over the flame. It dimmed while he watched it.

"Here," said Liam Riley, and held up the broken lantern again. Cleese used his thin-bladed Buckmaster knife to slice off the frizzed piece of climbing rope, then immersed the new end in the coal oil. Soaked it for about three inches down.

"Okay." He nodded, and moved his hand while Riley flicked his lighter against the rope. The oily end flared into a blue-green flame, and a thick odor that reminded Cleese of summer night revival meetings in his father's church. Black smoke curled up around his head.

"Pretty smart," said Riley.

"I know someone who watches *MacGyver,*" replied Cleese, and peeled back the wrapper on a high-calorie energy bar.

They moved along the tunnel, narrow and barely higher than Riley's head. Cleese estimated they'd come at least a hundred yards from the crevice on the cliff. Maybe a little more.

Those other two, they must have a better light source. Otherwise they'd have caught them by now. Cleese wasn't surprised. He was past being surprised by anything concerning Natalie Kemper.

He pictured her again, down below him as he cut her

rope. Most people, male or female, would have been screaming their heads off. Natalie Kemper was looking up at him, pulling that gun, even as she fell.

She had green eyes. Like Genie.

He *had* been surprised at Ben McKee, though. Turning loose to grab her like that. Falling with her to the slope below.

Not much like Shelley's previous protégé, the late Will Carter, whose passing had not been a dignified one. It was beginning to appear that McKee was nothing like Carter at all . . .

Except where it came to Shelley.

Maybe it was this woman, Natalie Kemper, who'd made the difference in McKee. Cleese could still see her driving that ice ax as they tumbled down the slope. Maybe she was the one who'd put the steel into Ben McKee's backbone.

In any case, it complicated things, and Cleese automatically loathed complications.

He wondered if she'd known all along about that crevice, the upper entrance into this mine, or whether that was just luck. Either way, without it this business would already be concluded.

And he'd be on his way out of this place.

Cleese glanced at his jury-rigged torch and saw he had perhaps another couple of minutes left on it. He was well aware that whoever carried it would be a walking target if those two were waiting for them up ahead.

The woman had dropped her gun down the cliff, but there'd been *two* empty holsters on board that plane.

Cleese slowed when he approached another intersecting tunnel, smaller than the one he and Riley were following. If Natalie Kemper knew her way around in here, she and McKee could have already branched off somewhere . . .

Except that ever so often Cleese kept seeing smudged spots along the passageway's muddy floor. In this wet, continually dripping environment, it was impossible to tell if the marks were fresh. He was simply going to have to trust that they were.

As he had at each intersection, Cleese stopped and shined his light into the side tunnel. And, as always, he heard Riley step out from behind him to point the barrel of his compact Steyr TMP machine pistol down the passageway.

It was empty, like the others had been. No marks on the muddy floor. Riley lowered his weapon.

Cleese, no fan of these various Uzi clones, was carrying only his Glock Seventeen. The weather had rendered his Mauser rifle useless, at least for the moment, and he'd left it in the helicopter. He did wish now he'd brought along the shotgun. Cumbersome on the rope, but it would have been very effective in a place like this. Tight quarters, pull up and shoot, with that double-ought load absolutely murderous at close range. It was in the 'copter, too.

Which caused Cleese to think about Garza and Wallace, and the sound he'd heard out on the cliff just before he reached Natalie Kemper's rope. The sound of rotor blades.

By now the helicopter was probably on the ground again, somewhere in the canyon bottom near the entrance to this mine. Just like Wallace had promised.

Sheer dependability had always been Milton Wallace's trademark, ever since Cleese first found him, up to his elbows in engine grease under the cowling of a big double-rotor Huey slick outside one of those *xol dao*—beans and rice—villages on the DMZ. If it had an engine, Wallace could fix it, no problem. And if he could fix it, he could fly it.

He was the perfect brake for Artie Garza's runaway temperament, which was why Cleese usually made a point of pairing them. Low key by nature, all business all the time, whatever Wallace lacked of Riley's and Garza's spontaneous fire he made up for in precision. Cleese didn't know much about the big man's private life, either before or after Vietnam—Wallace preferred it that way—but he'd have bet old steady Milt was the only one

172

among them whose personality hadn't been twisted off-line by the events of his youth.

Which was much more than could be said of Liam Riley and Artie Garza. Cleese knew their histories quite well, and what those histories had produced . . .

Just as he knew his own.

Cleese held his homemade torch a little higher, trying to extend the range of his vision. This main passageway couldn't go on forever. There had to be some means of descent somewhere ahead. Maybe the two he and Riley were following had already found it.

He moved on past the side tunnel. More smudges in the floor now, though it was hard to tell because his light was beginning to fail again.

Ben McKee opened his eyes only after Nattie closed hers. Feigning sleep wasn't something he'd wanted to do, but it had seemed the easiest way to stop her questions.

He wondered how much of his story she believed.

Shelley, you cold-minded bitch, he thought, not for the first time. What have you gotten me into?

Me? He heard her voice in his head, cool and light, with that ever-present undercurrent of laughter. *Moi? Who got whom into what, Benjamin? Maybe you'd better think about that before you start pointing any fingers.*

He saw her for a moment, long and lean, with that short-clipped black hair above dark, piercing eyes. One of those upper lips that formed a Cupid's bow. Not a beauty in the way Nattie Kemper was, but not someone who slipped easily from your mind either.

For just one moment he wondered what she'd looked like once Cleese finished with her; then he shelved that thought so hard he could almost hear it rattle.

"You and I, we're like the old joke about ham and eggs, Benjamin," she'd told him that night. *"The pig is committed, whereas the chicken's only involved . . ."*

Until yesterday, when Eugene Cleese gave her a different view of breakfast.

Cleese had broken her down, of course. Even tough, cold-minded Shelley Gallatin was no match for Cleese. But she'd obviously held one thing back, right to the end. She hadn't told him about the disk. Because if Cleese knew about the disk . . .

Everything that followed would have proceeded very differently, wouldn't it?

Ben looked across the dim passageway at the woman leaning against the wall over there. Nattie wasn't pretending to sleep, not with those small twitches that moved her arms and legs, and not with the faint sounds she was making.

An unpleasant dream, apparently.

Watching her like that, shadowed by faint candlelight, the constant dripping of water all around them, Ben was reminded of another time he'd watched someone sleep.

It was a rainy Oregon night that time, a day or two after he'd brought his father home from the hospital. Galen McKee had stood the exploratory surgery well— surgery Ben had paid for since his parents had no medical insurance—and Ben had stayed on for a few days, even as much as the tiny rental house depressed him . . .

Too poor to paint and too proud to whitewash, was how Galen described the situation.

. . . and as much as he wanted to get into his car and just point it south along the coast.

Galen, who was on a stiff dose of pain medication, had fallen asleep in his old chair under a down comforter. And Ben's mother, Marie, worn out by tension, was also asleep, sitting on the couch. Ben had been reading something—a paperback thriller by Robert McCammon, maybe—in a chair across from them.

After a while, he put down his book and listened to the rain hitting the roof above his head. Watched it slide down the dark glass of a window behind the couch.

Ben watched his parents sleep. He watched Galen's shallow breathing that barely moved the comforter above his frayed corduroy robe. He looked at loose, chafed-from-the-razor skin on his father's neck, and at how thin Galen's hair was getting there on his forehead. At the sags and furrows accrued like compounding interest by sixty years of life. By over forty years of hard physical labor, working to make someone else rich. Someone who wouldn't even carry Major Medical for employees like Galen McKee.

Marie had slid sideways a little on the couch. Ben remembered when she'd been slim and still pretty, with her bright smile and brighter blue eyes—her legacy to her son. She rarely smiled anymore, and her eyes were often worried and confused. She'd put on weight, a lot of it, in the past few years. Now she was kind of . . . shapeless, maybe, in her matching robe.

Ben watched her glasses slide down and stop at that spot where her nose tilted. Without awakening, she reached up and removed the glasses. Let them drop into her ample lap.

If anything happened to Galen, she'd be lost. Ben had watched her earlier when she pulled the comforter up on her sleeping husband's chest, and then lightly touched his cheek. A gentle gesture, something from the heart of what people needed from each other.

This prostate surgery, despite its hopeful outcome, had been harder on her than on her husband, in the ways that counted most.

Ben watched his parents sleep that night, and listened to the rain on their roof. He saw them, in his mind's eye, as they'd once been, and he saw them as they'd become. And behind the emotion he felt at first—tenderness and love, and more than a little sadness at how life moves on without a backward glance at the scar tissue it leaves behind—there was another emotion that rose up inside him.

Fear.

Not me, he'd thought, that fear suddenly grown large and smothering. This won't be me, old and nearly broke and having to depend on my only child to keep a rented roof over my head and find a doctor who won't look down his manicured nose at doing the surgery that may keep me around awhile longer.

Not me.

Ben's emotions were love and fear that night, almost five years ago, and there was something else that happened, too. A decision was made. Not as tough as he thought it would be.

Two years later, he'd bought his parents the first home they ever owned. They were living in it now, and his mother's eyes were no longer so worried and confused. A brighter blue again.

But then, everything's a trade-off, isn't it? You make choices every moment of your life. Even doing nothing at all is a choice.

Ben realized he was beginning to fade, along with the tiny candle stubs in the dark passageway. No faking it this time. Probably he should light a couple more, but he was so damned tired. . . .

Across from him, Nattie was crying in her sleep. Like the night before in her cabin. Whispering along with it, something that sounded like the word *no*. Ben McKee's last conscious thought was to wonder why her dreams scared her so much.

Still half-conscious, Nattie tries to dodge the next blow. But Rick is too quick for her.

He's good with his fists.

She feels the impact lift and turn her. Feels the skin rip beneath his big college ring and then peel back in a bloody spray. As she spins toward the floor, she has a momentary glimpse of George Van Zandt lying motionless in the bathroom doorway, his skin whiter than the towel still knotted around his waist. Dead white, except for the spreading stain beneath his head. . . .

Then she hits the floor, feels the bones grind in her already broken nose. Rolls over and sees him through one eye not yet swollen shut. Sees that he's smiling. . . .

"Nattie my love," he's saying. And smiling.

And that's when she knows he's going to kill her this time.

He locks one hand in her long hair and raises her head. Drops to his knee next to her. She tries to lift her arms to protect her face, but they're too heavy and stiff and slow.

She sees his hand, closed in a fist, but she's also hearing something now. Some noise. . . .

She sees the fist, and the big college ring, and she sees his smile. The . . . madness there, finally broken free. Finally loose, out of its cage behind that smile.

She closes her remaining eye.

Now I lay me down to sleep . . .

Isn't that funny? Where did that come from?

. . . I pray the Lord my soul to keep . . .

"Nattie," he's whispering to her. "Nattie my love."

. . . if I should die . . .

Then there's that sound again, only closer now. Furious now. And someone's . . . screaming?

Her head hits the carpet, and her eye opens. Through a bloody, half-blind haze she sees Rick falling backward away from her. Beating with one hand at the small dog that's tearing at his other arm.

It's Rick who's screaming.

That dog. The puppy she got from the pound only a month before. So small, and still so skinny. Holding on and tearing at Rick's forearm. Growling and crying out in pain at the same time . . .

The sound she heard.

. . . but not letting go. And there's another sound now. Over there somewhere, pounding on the door as everything goes black. . . .

Nattie awoke into blackness.

"Ogod," she was whispering, down in her throat. "Ogod, ogod . . ."

She felt the tears, wet and warm on her face.

The blackness . . .

Then she remembered where she was. Fumbled in her

parka for the little box of waterproof matches. She felt for the stump of candle, couldn't find it . . .

Ogod. *The blackness* . . .

. . . and grabbed another from the ones in her pocket. She lit it with hands that shook so badly the flame danced in the windless air before her eyes.

Then the tunnel was there, coming into her view out of the serrated edge of the shadows. Crumbling, rock-imbedded walls and splintered timbers. Dripping water that broke the silence, along with the drumbeat of her heart.

The heavy odor of mildew and decay.

Ben McKee was slumped across from her, his candle also burned out. Another sound in the near-darkness was his heavy, congested breathing as he slept.

Nattie held the candle in front of her while the dream slowly dissipated into the dark margins of her mind. She leaned back against the wall and waited for her pounding heart to slow down while she watched the light. Tried to draw it into her. . . .

That had been her worst fear, before they removed the bandages. Not the scars, she could deal with that. But if she couldn't see, if she was blind. . . .

Those days and nights in the hospital, indistinguishable behind the bandages that covered her eyes. And the fear, growing beyond all rational thought with each passing hour. There in the prison of her blackness. . . .

Damage to the zygomatic arch and sphenoid, both eyes, she'd heard that much. The kind of hushed, end-of-the-bed whispers that weren't supposed to penetrate her floating Percoden cloud, but they had. It was always delicate, working around the eyes like that. . . .

Nattie realized her free hand was on her face. Touching the skin next to her eyes, then down toward the scar beneath her lip.

"Where'd you get that scar?" Ben McKee had asked.

There were visible scars, she thought for the second time that day, and there were invisible ones. It was amazing, considering how she'd looked when the police battered their way into her Denver apartment that night—and later took those incredible, awful photographs that became State's Exhibits five through nineteen—that she now had only this one *visible* scar.

And that she could see, twenty-twenty in her right eye, nearly as good in her left. Only the occasional headache when she read for too long at a time.

If it hadn't been for Jack, that skinny little pound mutt. . . .

Nattie was crying again, but it was okay this time because she wasn't crying for herself.

Little Jack the Wonder Spaniel. He'd had six broken ribs, but the cop said he wouldn't let go of Rick's torn, bloody forearm until they bodily pulled him loose.

He'd saved her life that night. And again today. . . .

Her husband, being Rick, had naturally concentrated on Nattie's face. That was what had always gathered her the most compliments, and besides it was the kind of fear he understood himself on a personal, gut level.

Handsome Rick. Egocentric as a cat.

But thanks to the considerable skills, over the period of a year, of a Denver surgical team headed by Dr. Lawrence Gilly, Nattie had her eyesight, and only this one small, jagged scar below her lip where her teeth had ripped completely through to the outside.

George Van Zandt should have been so lucky.

Unless Rick finds me again. That thought rose out of somewhere, up out of the blackness of this tunnel maybe, actually kind of ludicrous considering her current situation. But there it was anyway.

Unless he finds me again. Then George will seem like the lucky one.

Nattie looked over at Ben McKee and saw he was awake. He started coughing, and struggled up onto one elbow. Looked around at the dim, dripping passageway as though he'd never seen it before.

"Are there bats in here?" he asked. His voice was hoarse.

179

Nattie had to laugh, she couldn't help it, and immediately felt better.

"This is the middle of winter," she said. "All the bats are down in Central America working on their tans."

"Bats migrate?" He coughed some more.

"What did you think, they fly over to Neiman-Marcus and buy little fur coats?"

He shrugged. "I figured they hibernate. Or something."

"Bears hibernate . . ."

"Bears?" He looked around again.

". . . and bats migrate south, which is what we need to be doing about now. Are you okay to travel some more?"

Ben reached down to rub his socked feet. "I think so. At least I can feel my toes again. They itch."

"That's frostbite, but it's also a good sign." Nattie pushed up onto her own feet. "Maybe you'll save some of them after all."

"Some of them?"

"The big one and the pinkie, that's all you need for balance."

"Marvelous." He looked at her. "So now we know how I am. Toeless Joe Jackson. How are you?"

She paused in the middle of collecting her gear.

"Me?" she asked.

"You. You were crying in your sleep."

"Yeah, right." She looked away from him.

"Except you were. Woke me up. You were crying, and you mumbled something about blackness . . ."

"Remember what you said this morning about hallucinations?"

"You never did tell me, did you?" He studied her. "What a woman like you is doing holed up in these mountains."

"A woman like me, huh? Who writes your dialogue, Jackie Collins?"

"Evading again . . ."

"Well, you'd know all about that, wouldn't you?" Nattie slung her tied-off crampons over one shoulder.

180

"Me?" His blue eyes were wide. "I'm the one spilled my guts a little while ago, remember?"

"Uh-huh. Let's just say we both have our secrets, okay? Leave it at that."

And at least I don't lie about mine, she added mentally.

"Better get your boots on," she said aloud. "It's—" she held the candle near her watch—"nearly four o'clock. Your pals were probably gaining on us the whole time we were asleep."

Ben hooked his index fingers around the pull-straps of one water-stained boot and pushed his foot into it.

"This damn thing's shrunk," he muttered.

"Maybe. Cowhide'll do that when it gets wet. Your foot's probably swollen, too."

He pushed harder, pulling on the straps at the same time. Finally the boot slid on.

"Comfy?" asked Nattie.

"About like a tourniquet." He started on the other boot.

"I don't doubt it, but for now they beat going barefoot." Nattie lit a second candle, the one she couldn't find earlier, from her first. "Maybe we'll find a shoe store down on the main level."

"That, and a MacDonald's, I hope." Ben got to his feet, limping slightly, and took the second candle from her. They gathered the rest of their gear, including the candle he'd carried earlier, and started along the passageway.

"It's getting wetter," said Ben.

He was right. The tunnel had widened some—a hopeful sign—and Nattie began to see the cross-timber supports overhead more frequently, but the floor was undeniably getting muddier. They were splashing through occasional pools of standing water now, though most of them were still only a few inches deep.

All this water would be following gravity, seeking its lowest level here in the mine. . . .

"Wo." Ben stopped behind her. "What the hell is that?"

Nattie looked around. "What?"

"Up there." He pointed past her. "I saw something. Looked like little red eyes . . . Don't start laughing again, dammit."

She didn't, but she had to smile. "Probably rats," she said. "This *is* a mine, McKee."

"I thought you said they migrated in the winter."

"Rats? Where would they go? Club Med? I was talking about bats."

"Six of one, what the hell. You got your aviators, and you got your foot soldiers . . ."

"Any sheltered place in the high mountains has rats during the winter. I had them in my . . ."

She felt a sudden tightness in her throat. I had them in my cabin, she'd been about to say. The ones Jack didn't catch . . .

"They don't eat much," she said instead. "Tiny little bites. You did put those boots on, I guess. Anyway, you're the city boy, remember? All that bold talk about tenement rats, these are just their country cousins."

He mumbled something she didn't get all of. Something about the women he'd known having the good sense to be scared of mice.

"Rats, not mice," she replied. "Just think of Mickey on steroids."

Which, as quickly as it was out of her mouth, conjured another of those uncomfortable intersections of memory.

Rick had never realized she was onto him. And she, a different Nattie in those days, had never mentioned the small blue Dianabol tablets or the needles and the vials.

To him, or to her mother.

Ahead of them, the tunnel continued to gradually widen. There was some kind of junction. . . .

She felt Ben's hand close over her shoulder. A powerful grip that stopped her between steps.

"What . . . ?"

Then he pulled her back against him, his other hand

182

over her mouth. She smelled the wet leather of his glove.

"Listen," he whispered against her ear.

Nattie realized two things simultaneously. The first was that he'd been teasing her before, pretending to be startled by the rats. His manner was completely different now. This time he *was* startled.

The second was that she heard something, too. Back behind them, along the dark passageway. Just a whisper of sound.

Ben reached around her and pinched off the flame of her candle, then did the same with his own. The tunnel went black, totally black, the stifling, suffocating black . . .

Of blindness.

Nattie felt her heart lurch upward toward her throat. The inside of her mouth suddenly tasted like old iron.

The blackness . . .

"Listen," whispered Ben, but she couldn't. Couldn't listen, couldn't move, couldn't even think because she couldn't see. The blackness pressed against her like bandages across her eyes. Like blindness. And she knew that soon, *very* soon, she was going to lose this steely grip she was holding on silence.

Start crying, maybe. Or screaming. The beast was no longer just in her mind. Now it was leaving footprints.

"You hear that?" Ben whispered next to her ear, his hand still over her mouth, and she grabbed his wrist. Held on to it like she was holding on to her silence.

"Somebody's moving back there," he said.

They were coming. Cleese and the other one. Like the beast escaped from her mind, they were coming. Along that coal black, blind black passageway. Carrying death with them.

And she couldn't move.

What's wrong, Nattie my love? Scared of the dark?

Don't do this. Don't freeze up now . . .

"Come on," whispered Ben, and moved her forward. She stuck out her right hand, felt the wet tunnel wall. Took a step—the hardest step—and then another.

"Look," she heard him say, and felt him turn her.

Back behind them, at a distance she could only estimate, Nattie saw a tiny flicker of light come into view. Moving slowly, as slowly as she and Ben were.

"They didn't see us," he murmured. "They'd've killed their light if they had."

And it was that tiny light, so far away, that broke through the ice of Nattie's paralysis. She wasn't blind. She wasn't trapped in the blackness. She could see that light.

She moved Ben's hand away from her mouth. "There's something up ahead," she whispered. "A junction of tunnels. I think it may be the vertical shaft down to the main level."

The loudest sound around them now was the steady drip of falling water. They inched forward in the darkness, feeling their way, and Nattie kept glancing back from time to time, looking at the tiny light. The killers' light.

It was a strange place to find comfort.

Then she lost the wall with her right hand, stretched out to reach farther that way, and felt her boot bump against something hard. She crouched down and found a raised, smooth surface.

"It's an iron rail," she whispered to Ben. "For an ore car."

And she heard the faintest echo, even from that whisper, that told her the side wall was gone. This had to be the convergence for this level, which meant the vertical shaft was close by. Did it still have its lift intact? And was that lift still working?

There would be support timbers for the lift cables, double reinforced below the bullwheel and probably four or five feet apart. Extending, three-sided, out from a rock wall ahead that would also be the back wall of the shaft. Two of the sides would have extra lateral supports, a waist-high barrier of lumber nailed in for safety. And there would be a detachable gate on the front.

Nattie moved forward, and her blind, sweeping right

hand touched something rough and splintery. One of the support timbers for the shaft. Since she felt no gate in front of her, she played it safe. Stepped to her left . . .

And off into nothing.

Chapter Thirteen

Rick Macon waited for nearly two hours in the window-less wooden shed behind the Walker Lake communication center. He kept watch out a small side door while the light—such as it was—faded toward a gray-white dusk. The wind increased, and the snow continued to fly past in hard lateral sheets until he could barely see the main building fifty feet away. The cold air inside the shed penetrated beneath his polyurethane outerwear and then his neoprene long handles. Right down to the bone.

No helicopter arrived.

Macon walked up and down the dirt-floored length of the small building. He stamped his feet and slapped his sides with his arms, and he thought about the woodstove in the comm center. Burned down to ash again by now, but he could get it going . . .

If he went inside.

She wasn't going to show up now. It didn't matter what the crisis might be, that goddamn helicopter wasn't going to be flying after dark in this storm. They'd probably shut down not long after he heard them, were probably spending the night at whichever cabin they'd reached at that point. They'd wait there for morning.

And, in the meantime, there was a perfectly good shelter no more than fifty feet from this shed, going to waste because there was nobody inside it to stoke up the fire and then sit back in that rump-sprung old recliner next to it.

Get the place warm, relax and eat a bite . . . or maybe several bites. Get some sleep.

How long had it been now since he'd slept?

Set that mental alarm clock that never failed him—simply a matter of self-discipline—for about six A.M., and then come back out here. Continue the rest of it as already planned.

Macon tried to remember how much wood he'd seen inside, there by the stove. It was going to take a pretty good fire to warm that place up again.

He went over to the big stack of aspen and scrub oak that was laid out in cord lengths along the shed's back wall behind a pair of snowmobiles. An armful of aspen to begin with. It might take more than one trip.

He wondered where Nattie was tonight. Still in her cabin, or with the others in the chopper? Thinking of her made him smile. He flexed his big hands into fists, then opened them to start gathering split aspen logs off the far end of the stack.

He wondered what she'd do if she knew. . . .

Macon stopped, his arms half-full of wood, and looked down at a pair of glasses sticking out from behind the last layer of aspen. Little round glasses with gold rims.

Next to a hand, palm-up and gray in color. Fingers curled slightly inward. . . .

"No . . . shit," said Macon.

"I don't much like this place, bro." Arturo Garza looked around him, then at the lift platform. "Wonder how you operate that sucker?"

"You're asking me?" Milton Wallace came back down one of the side tunnels, sloshing through ankle-deep icy water as he walked. The farther back from the mine entrance they went, the warmer it got—though warmer was a relative term in this case. Warm enough at least to replace ice with flowing water. A lot of it, apparently, back down that one tunnel where Wallace had heard the roaring sound like an open fire hydrant.

"Hey, you're the mechanical genius, *esse*," replied Garza. "Captain Whirlybird."

He stepped onto the open-fronted wooden platform and studied the greasy old cables that extended upward from it.

"Looks like a hand crank to me," he said. "Some kind of pulley. You just pump yourself right to the top."

Wallace chewed on a candy bar while he peered up the shaft. After about the first twenty or thirty feet, it disappeared into absolute darkness.

"Doesn't make any difference, Artie," he answered. "We got no reason to go up there anyway."

Wallace knew Garza wouldn't mind hearing that. The ordinarily fearless little gangbanger had been raised by a crazy old grandmother believed to be a witch by half the barrio, and he was highly superstitious. This mine, with its shadows and echoes, wasn't Artie Garza's type of place.

"That suits me, man." Garza looked relieved. "I don't much—"

The sound echoed down onto them. And then the rocks.

"Shit! Look out, Artie!" Wallace dove sideways, splashing into mud and icy water. Garza was right behind him.

Small rocks rained down onto the platform, bouncing off wood and stone. Then something else, glittering and reflecting light, ricocheted past Garza's head.

"*¡Mierda!*" he gasped, and raised a hand to shield his face. "*Chinga el diablo . . .*"

Then the rock shower stopped, as suddenly as it began. But there was still some sound. . . .

"What the hell was that?" Wallace crawled to his feet. The front of his white snowsuit was covered with mud.

"*No se,*" replied Garza. He stepped cautiously toward the platform. Looked down at the pair of razor-edged

188

crampons that lay in the mud by his feet, tangled in a coil of climbing rope.

And heard it again, from up there somewhere in the blackness of that vertical shaft. Someone's voice, far off . . .

"Nattie," said the voice.

Garza looked over at Wallace. "You hear that?" he asked.

"I heard it." Wallace stepped onto the platform and kicked some of the rocks off the edge.

"Darker than a mole's ass up there, home." Garza frowned up into the shaft. "I guess we're going, huh?"

"I guess." Wallace reached for the hand crank. "And we're taking turns on this mother. Keep that in mind."

"*¿Cómo no, viejo?*" Garza checked the clip on his Ruger. "Wouldn't have it any other way."

"Nattie?"

Ben McKee was lying on his stomach, with his head and shoulders extending out over a deeper blackness that had to be an empty shaft. Wet, warming air rose past his face, carrying with it the odor of mildew and greasy metal.

"Nattie?" he whispered again, then glanced over his shoulder. That light back there, down the corridor some-where, it was gone.

They heard us, he thought. They'll come on in the dark now.

One moment she'd been there, right in front of him, his hand on her back. Then one step forward, and she was gone. A soft *whoosh* of sound, a startled indrawn breath . . .

Even then she hadn't screamed.

. . . and she was gone.

Ben had heard the sounds of falling, just ahead of him. Rocks breaking free, something striking and echoing below. He'd dropped to his knees and crawled forward, until one hand reached out and found nothing there. Empty space.

This had to be the vertical shaft she'd mentioned earlier. The one leading down to the main level of the mine. How far down? Five hundred feet?

She was gone.

Ben felt a burning sensation behind his eyes, and a cold, bitter lump of . . . what? grief? crowding into his throat. Nattie . . .

It wasn't an emotion he'd had experience with recently, at least not until the last six months. Both his parents were doing much better now, settled into a home of their own, and as for him . . . well, he'd adapted, hadn't he?

Not a sad story anywhere. Not until six months ago when this nightmare began. Carter and then Shelley . . .

And now Nattie Kemper, who never asked to be here. Who had nothing to do with any of this. Ben felt the burning behind his eyes sharpen, trying to form tears.

Get a grip, stupid. He shook his head to clear it. This isn't the time. Not with those other two, Cleese and his goon, right back there behind you. Creeping closer right now. *Right now.*

But he was thinking of Nattie, not of them. Thinking about that smart mouth of hers, all attitude, at least on the surface.

And about that kiss. . . .

"Dammit," he mumbled, and was just starting to take the thirty-eight out of his coat pocket when he heard a faint noise from below.

The sound of movement. Creaking . . .

"Nattie?" he whispered again, realizing as he said it how stupid it was.

"Ben!" The voice was a soft hiss. And it was part of that other noise. "Ben, down here!"

Good God, she was alive . . .

And moving away, by the sound of her voice.

"Nattie?"

"Reach out with your hand." Her voice continued to diminish. "Can you feel it?"

Ben stretched forward, almost to the point of losing the counterbalance provided by his lower body. He made wide, sweeping arcs in the darkness with one arm.

"No," he whispered. "Feel what?"

"Then, you'll have to jump for it. The cables. They're out there, Ben. Trust me . . ."

Jump for it?

Jesus Christ, jump for it? Stand up in this absolute, utter blackness. Find the edge of this bottomless pit with one foot. Then jump, out into . . . *nothing,* trusting that there were cables out there somewhere. And if he missed them. . . .

The creaking sound continued.

"The cables are moving, Ben." Her voice was fading into distance. "Be sure you get on the one that's descending."

Moving? Why were the cables moving? Unless . . .

Someone was coming up from below.

Ben stood up. He slid his right foot forward, felt the boot tip hook over the edge of the shaft; then he stopped. Frozen, paralyzed by his own fear.

He saw himself looking down into the pit, and it was no longer dark. Just that terrible, yawning depth below reaching up for him. He saw himself falling . . .

Like that little boy, ten years old again, looking down the wing of the airplane toward the earth so far below.

I can't do this. I can't!

But that one particular spot, high on his back, was beginning to twitch. The spot where his shoulders met his neck, centered on the spine.

The exact spot, Shelley had finally confessed, where the blade entered Will Carter.

Cleese. Cleese was right behind. Back there in the dark, and getting closer every moment.

And the pit was right in front. With two cables out there somewhere, moving, because someone was coming up from below.

191

"Jump for it," Nattie had said. She was down there, too, somewhere in that darkness. "Jump for it. Trust me . . ."

"Oh, shit," moaned Ben. "Oh, holy sh . . ."

He jumped.

The platform bucked and slung Wallace sideways against a rail, then began ascending again.

"Aw man, I knew it." Garza was cranking now, and everything—the platform, everything—suddenly got heavier. "Goddamn thing's breaking."

"No." Wallace put one hand up on the spot where the ascending cable yoked together. "No, it's not breaking, but there's some kind of drag on it, all right. Let me crank for a while."

"You got it." Garza held on to the rusted handle until the larger man took over—just a movement of shadow in the darkness that deepened as they ascended.

"All right," said Wallace, after a moment. "It's gone. Whatever was dragging."

The voices were still there, two of them in the blackness somewhere overhead. But now, up inside the shaft itself, everything was echoes. Impossible to make out. Spooky sounds that for some reason made Garza think about his grandmother, and her stories of La Llorona, the Wailing Woman who came in the darkness to carry away the souls of frightened children.

Garza could no longer see Wallace. He could no longer see anything. So he stood in the center of the platform and held his assault pistol pointed upward. It was mainly his memory of the falling rocks from before that kept his finger off the trigger.

"I really don't like this, man," he muttered.

They continued to ascend.

Nattie hung on to the cable as she slowly descended. Wrapped her legs more tightly. The cable's surface was greasy, the only thing that had prevented her gloves—and her hands—from shredding to ribbons when she'd grabbed it . . .

While falling blind, falling to her death.

Her heartbeat was finally slowing a little, which was possibly a bit ridiculous considering her circumstances, but this action—this desperate fight to hold on to the moving cable—was keeping her mind off the utter blackness of the shaft.

Her gloves were gumming up with grease, and she slipped again. Slid down a foot or so. This wasn't going to work much longer. Even if she held on, she wasn't that far above the lift ascending from below her. Every foot she dropped down was a foot it rose.

And she'd already heard the voices down there.

There was a chance, of course, that they weren't Cleese's other two men. That they were innocent bystanders who just happened to be in this mine in the middle of a blizzard.

Right . . .

She wondered if Ben McKee had jumped for the cable. If he had, he'd caught it, based on the empirical evidence that he hadn't gone tumbling past her. She'd have at least heard that, or felt the impact when he knocked her loose as well. So, he was either on this same cable, also descending somewhere above her, or . . .

Or he hadn't jumped at all. He was so terrified of heights, he might've decided to stay up there with that pistol. Take his chances with Cleese.

If so, she'd be hearing about it before long.

A third possibility was that he'd jumped, but grabbed the *ascending* cable, then froze, too scared to switch over. In that case, he'd get carried up into the huge, revolving bullwheel at the top of the shaft.

She'd hear about that, too, if it happened.

She slipped some more. The entire front of her parka was slick with grease now. So were her jeans. She was dropping much faster than the cable, kind of a controlled slide.

Down toward the lift. And the men on the lift.

She had to be passing other levels. Other passageways that fed this same shaft. It would be worth jumping for one of them, if only she could see them.

And then she could.

Down there below her. The faintest kind of *milky* light, then the outline of something. Straight lines . . .

Support timbers, becoming visible below her. It was another of those convergences. Another level of tunnels.

The illumination was coming from off to one side, shimmering and so faint that everything was only a series of silhouettes. Depth perception was impossible. Those supports might be farther away than they looked.

But there was no choice.

Nattie pulled off one glove with her teeth—the gagging taste of lube grease in her mouth—then the other. Her bare hands dug into the slick cable, stopping her slide for a moment.

Then she pulled up her legs, braced her booted feet against the cable, and shoved sideways. Out into the milky light . . .

And slammed into one of the lateral supports, so hard she bit through her tongue. She wrapped her arms around the rotting beam, felt the splinters tear her hands. Hooked one leg over the support and pulled hard.

Over the edge and onto the tunnel floor.

She rolled away from the shaft and up onto her knees. There was just enough light to see the splinters imbedded in her fingers. Dark and stained, with grease or blood or both.

Nattie looked over the edge into darkness, even blacker down there now—if that was possible—because of the faint light behind her. Wherever the lift was, it hadn't yet come into view. Maybe there was still time.

She looked upward—just as dark up there—to where the cable continued to descend.

"Ben?" she called.

*　*　*

194

Cleese heard the sound coming up the shaft.

"Ben . . . ?"

It was Natalie Kemper's voice, little more than echoes. From far below.

He glanced over at Riley, lit by the stump of candle they'd found at the edge.

"Nine lives." Riley flashed his wolf's grin.

"I think she's used about seven of them," replied Cleese.

"Ben . . . ?"

Cleese leaned out, toward where the two cables were moving in the center of the shaft.

"Nattie?" he yelled down, remembering that was what Marvin Stone had called her. "Where are you, Nattie?"

There was the echo of his voice, then silence.

"Nattie?" He tried again. "Where are you?"

Silence.

"Think they have a code?" asked Riley.

"I doubt it. They haven't known each other . . ."

". . . down the cable, Ben! Hurry . . ."

". . . long enough," finished Cleese, then leaned out again. "I'm caught in the cable, Nattie! Where are you?"

". . . some kind of light down . . ."

"Shut up!" Another voice rose out of the shaft. "It's not me! It's Cleese!"

"Ben, Ben," murmured Cleese. "Ah, well." He leaned forward. "Okay, Ben," he called out. "Where are *you?*"

". . . straight to hell, you sonofabitch!" The reply was all shrill echoes.

"The lift's coming up, and they're not on it." Riley leaned out over the edge. "You heard what she said about the cable."

"So it must be our people on the lift." Cleese nodded. "That, or some marooned summer tourists." He cupped his hands. "Milt! Artie! If you can hear me . . ."

He waited a few moments for the echoes to subside.

"They're coming down to you on the cable!" he yelled, then waited again. "Look for a place where there's some light!"

He stepped back from the edge.

"Now what?" asked Riley.

"I think we should wait a few minutes." Cleese dug another energy bar out of his pocket. "And see what happens."

Nattie could see movement below, down there in the blackness of the shaft. It was the lift, gradually ascending toward her.

She looked upward, straining to see Ben McKee on the cable, but saw only darkness. In another minute, two at the outside, the lift would be here. She couldn't stay.

"Look for the light," Cleese had yelled.

How could she be so stupid? *Stupid.* The voice had come down the shaft, distorted by echoes, and she'd hesitated to answer at first because it didn't sound right. But only for a moment, then the rush of relief that he was alive after all had overcome her good sense, and she'd yelled out like an idiot.

Stupid.

Now they knew where to look. Look for the light.

But Ben had yelled, too. And he *was* alive. Had he heard what she said about hurrying? About sliding down the cable? Did he understand the reason why?

He probably did by now. Maybe he'd jumped off at another level, into another tunnel somewhere above . . .

Into pitch darkness, scared to death of heights?

The lift was still coming, creaking up the cable from below. When it drew level, she'd be a sitting duck in this faint light. She had to run now, seek the blackness that was her own particular horror. Find it, and hide.

Run for it, Nattie. I wouldn't want someone to hurt you. Someone else . . .

The lift was coming. Nattie looked around her at the confluence of three tunnels. They were dark, except for that one, nearly dark itself. But not quite. What was that light?

The light drew her.

Movement above her. Nattie spun, grabbing for the single ice ax still in her accessory belt . . .

As Ben McKee came sliding down the cable.

He saw her and tried to stop, but he was moving fast, covered in grease.

Jump! she thought, but kept her silence and ran toward the edge of the pit . . .

Just as he did jump. He flew out at an awkward angle, without the kind of momentum she'd gained with her feet. Down the shaft. . . .

But he was taller. His arms and legs were longer. He stretched wildly with one arm, his mouth open in a noiseless scream, and his arm hooked the rotting support timber.

It cracked. Collapsed outward . . .

Just as Nattie grabbed Ben's arm, as greasy as hers were, and pulled. A moment of clawing, sliding counterbalance on the edge, then they fell back together on the floor.

She held on to him, arms around him for another moment, his heart pounding against her own.

"The lift," she whispered, her mouth against his ear. "They're coming . . ."

He pulled her to her feet, and they ran down one of the tunnels. It may not have been the smartest choice available, but they didn't hesitate.

They ran toward the light.

Chapter Fourteen

"Dios mi . . ." Arturo Garza's mouth had fallen open. "What the hell *is* that, Gene?"

Eugene Cleese studied the shimmering light from one of the three passageways in front of them. It was so faint it wouldn't have even been noticeable in some place less dark, just enough to create a dim sort of twilight.

It seemed to *flow*.

"I think it's from outside, Artie," he finally answered, and finished re-coiling one of the climbing ropes he and Liam Riley had used to descend the shaft to this level where Garza and Milton Wallace had stopped. "That tunnel probably has a borehole through the canyon wall, like the one Liam and I came in on."

Garza didn't look convinced. "That's some funny-looking light, bro," he muttered.

Cleese glanced at the fluorescent dial of his watch. Ten minutes before five. "It's getting on toward evening out there," he said. "The light changes near dusk in these high mountains."

"You think that's the way they went?" Wallace was poking around the muddy floor, hunting for a candle stub like the ones Cleese and Riley held.

Cleese looked at the other two tunnels that branched off this confluence. Utter blackness down each one.

"Could be," he replied, but he was thinking something else. Considering what he'd already learned about Natalie Kemper.

"That's what I think," said Riley. "By now they're back out on the cliff, like before."

"They no longer have their rope, remember." Cleese tilted his candle in Riley's direction. "Or those crampons. They tumbled down the shaft onto Artie."

"Damn near sliced off my head." Garza nodded.

"That was only half the rope they lost," replied Riley. "They still have the other half, and that's about seventy or eighty feet, from what I could see."

"True." Cleese considered it. "We're what, two or three hundred feet above ground level? Milt, did you see any other way down on the inside?"

Wallace shook his head. "Just this one vertical shaft." He nodded toward the lift platform behind them. "But I didn't go very far back into the side tunnels. Way too much water, and there didn't seem to be any need at the time."

"What about you, Artie?"

"I didn't look." Garza shrugged. "This whole damn place's spooky, Gene. *Sombras y brujas,* y'know?"

"Oogedy-boogedy." Wallace grinned, to which Garza responded with a raised middle finger. Wallace had been a bit abashed at first, describing the helicopter crash to Cleese, but his spirits had apparently improved.

"Okay," said Cleese. "Then, we'll have to assume, for now, this shaft's the only inside access to the ground. Which means we can't just go off and leave it if there's any chance they might double back on us. Artie, why don't you take the lift on down? Is there someplace down there at the mine entrance where you can see both the cliff and this shaft?"

"Should be."

"Good. That way, if Liam's right about them being back on the wall, they'll climb down right on top of you. And you can also see them if they sneak onto the cables again."

Cleese turned to Riley and Wallace. "The three of us should probably split up."

Riley smiled. "I still think they went for the light. Running scared."

"Okay." Cleese doubted that, since he hadn't seen anything panic Natalie Kemper yet. He had a very strong mental picture of her and McKee, hiding just out of sight up one of those black tunnels, listening and waiting for him and his men to vacate this area by the shaft. The old open-the-window-and-then-hide-in-the-closet trick.

Question was, which tunnel? The two remaining passageways were a toss-up. Fifty-fifty.

"Milt?" he said. "Which one?"

Wallace had found a muddy stub of candle and was lighting it. "Whichever." He shrugged.

"Okay, I'll take . . ." The one on the far left looked smaller, less promising, so conversely . . . "I'll take the one on the left. We all need to check the floor as we go along. Liam and I were able to track them in the mud before. If any of us go for a while and don't see any marks, we're most likely in the wrong tunnel."

Unless you're listening right now, Natalie, he thought.

"And there's something else we need to remember," he added. "They probably still have at least one of those guns from the plane. Let's don't walk into any ambushes."

"And you watch out for those spooks and witches, Artie." Wallace apparently understood more Spanish than he admitted. "Down there all by yourself."

"Just don't be poking that bald white head of yours around the corner without yelling first, *vato.*" Garza stepped onto the lift platform. "It's already got enough lead in it for one day."

As he began lowering into the shaft, Garza watched Cleese and Wallace fade into points of candle-flame down the two dark tunnels. Riley went along the third passageway, following the strange milky light.

Garza watched him go. A weird dude, that Riley. Speaking of spooky . . .

* * *

200

Liam Riley was sixteen years old when he committed his first murder, but, unlike Arturo Garza, it had nothing to do with gangs.

More to do with families. At least at first.

The area off West Broadway in Boston was commonly referred to as South Shanty, or just Southie, because of the squeezed-in families of Irish immigrants who lived there. It made no difference to outsiders what any of them had been back in Ireland.

But it made a big difference to them.

The Quinns, who lived downstairs from the Rileys, came from County Mayo, where they'd been prosperous landowners until the summer their huge flock of sheep was decimated by anthrax. They were left with barely enough money to emigrate on the promise of a job in Boston.

The Rileys—on the other hand—were simply Protestant trash from the slums along Shankill Road in West Belfast. The kind of people a Quinn might flip a shilling on the street, but would never be found talking to. Or living downstairs from.

To most of proper Boston, people like the Rileys and Quinns were exactly the same. Shanty immigrants. Neither the Rileys nor the Quinns, however, saw it that way. They hated each other as only Irish Catholics and Irish Protestants could hate each other. As only the equally dispossessed, who were once light-years apart socially but now shared the same level—the bottom level—could hate each other.

Liam Riley was the youngest of three boys, and he generally caught it coming and going. From his brothers, who enjoyed dangling him from the tenement roofs along D Street by his feet until he smiled and convinced them he liked it—at which point they quit in disgust—to the two older Quinns downstairs, who made a point of ambushing young Liam every time he came outside. He said he liked that, too, though it usually failed to have the same effect.

What none of them realized was when Liam said he

201

liked it, he was telling the truth. What began as fear had mysteriously transmuted into something else along the way. A survival mechanism gone ballistic, turned into something he had no name for himself . . .

The term adrenaline rush being somewhat beyond him in those days.

. . . but which he knew he liked. And the more he sought it out, the less interested the street bullies became in providing it for him. Mostly because, as Liam Riley grew, the process had started becoming much more painful for them than for him.

He was crazy, according to the people around Southie. Look at that smile, stretched there like an open wound below eyes the color of ashes. One of these days he was going to do something . . .

Crazy.

He took to hanging around near Saint Peter's and Saint Paul's, where there was always some big Catholic kid ready to mix it up with a skinny little Belfast Orangeman. The trick was to run until all of the big kid's reinforcements had been outdistanced. Then into an alley, where he'd suddenly stop . . .

And change that kid's day for him.

So he grew, thin as a rail, but six feet, four inches tall by the time he was sixteen, by which time also very few young men of either religious persuasion were willing to chase Liam Riley anywhere. That tall, skinny kid, always smiling . . .

And he was smiling that rainy afternoon when he found himself outside a warehouse near Liffey's saloon, and looking up the ramp at Roger Quinn, youngest heir of the Mullraney Quinns. When young Roger saw Liam, he naturally ran as if the Banshee were after him.

Into the warehouse, a poor tactical move on his part.

Because Liam Riley not only changed Roger Quinn's day for him; he also changed the boy's life. By ending it.

Even many years—and lives—later, he wasn't certain exactly how it happened. The memory was a beautiful one, involving the high and mighty Quinns as it did, but a fuzzy one where it came to details.

Something he never forgot, though, was how he felt when it was done. How he walked down Salisbury Beach, that grin from ear to ear, and how he spent his last dollar on a ragged bouquet of flowers which he carried home to his mother—who took one look at his grinning face and locked herself in the bathroom until he was gone.

After that, it became necessary to leave for a while. He lied about his age, and was in Saigon within six months, where he eventually met an interesting man, a Special Forces officer named Eugene Cleese, who turned out to be the nearest thing Liam Riley had ever seen to someone as scary as he was himself. After serving three tours, and then spending some time in his family's ancestral haunts along Shankill Road in Belfast, he returned to the states, and finally to a more upscale section of Boston out near Cambridge.

Many things amused Liam Riley, but not many surprised him. So it was no surprise when, a number of years later, he was contacted by Eugene Cleese.

Cleese, it seemed, was still as interesting as Riley remembered.

"God almighty," murmured Ben McKee.

Nattie just stared.

The smallest pools of water began directly below her feet, where the tunnel expanded into a cave. Then more water, water everywhere, dripping, flowing, pouring, down and away from her.

"Did you know there was anything like this in here?" asked Ben.

"I heard some stories." She shrugged. "I told you all that water had to go somewhere, remember? But there are stories about any old mine, especially one this large."

They were standing on the last piece of level floor, at the edge of where it crumbled and fell away to a long, rocky slope that held more pools of water. Water trickled down from the ceiling above them, from out of the tunnel behind them, and especially from the far wall, about one hundred feet away, which dominated the entire chamber.

A wall of sheer, glittering ice. Flowing, shimmering, in its own milky white illumination.

"That's where the light's coming from." Nattie nodded. "From the outside, through those cracks in the cliff."

The milky light was continuing to fade, like the last stages of dusk, but Nattie could see where the little cave sloped away below them. The water followed gravity, filling pools that fed lower pools surrounded by slick-looking rock.

"You can see what probably happened." She pointed above Ben's head, at the last of the support beams. "They were just tunneling along when they broke through into here. I imagine it was the end of the mining for that day."

"I guess," said Ben.

"We'd better keep moving." Nattie looked back down the dark tunnel. "While we're still in the lead."

"Keep moving where?" Ben looked around him. "Do we try to get back out on the cliff?"

She shook her head. "You notice there's no wind? That's 'cause the ice has those cracks sealed tight. It's melting and flowing in here where it's warmer, but it's frozen solid on the outside, probably at least eight or ten feet thick. We'd never break through it, even if we still had the crampons to climb up there and try. We'll just have to follow this cave on down. See where it goes. At least it's headed in the right direction."

There was a small dropoff down onto the steep incline below the tunnel floor. Nattie hopped over the edge, using the rocks as stairsteps.

"These things are slick," she warned. "Watch where you step in those Texas clodhoppers. They have leather soles."

Ben scrambled down behind her, and they began to descend. The slope was a mixture of rock and a chalky, gray-tinged dirt that had turned to a pastey mud near the pools.

"Something stinks." Ben curled his nose.

Nattie smiled. "You remember you asked me about bats?" she said.

"Yeah?"

"Looks like they use this place for their colony during the summer, when those cracks to the outside are open. That's bat guano you're stepping in."

"Great," he mumbled.

"Just try not to trip." She led the way past another of the pools of water. The slope on either side of it was steepening a little more—the whole chamber reminded Nattie of the shape of a funnel—but the footing remained solid. From time to time she looked back up the incline toward the mine tunnel opening. They might have to dive for cover fast, right into the guano, but not yet. There was nobody in sight. Yet.

"Why's the water that milky color?" asked Ben. "The ice, too."

Nattie shrugged. "Maybe algae. There are some places where it turns water red . . ."

"The Red Sea."

"Clever man. Or it might just be from feeding through all this limestone, which turns the water acidic. That's how it creates a cave like this in the first place. Eats its way right through."

As they continued to descend, more than one hundred feet below the tunnel now, the pools grew larger, spilling over into small waterfalls. The sound echoed all around them, a hollow roar that made it difficult to hear each other.

Or anything above them.

Nattie stopped for a moment, one foot braced on a wet rock, and looked back again. A herd of buffalo could be charging down the hill, and you'd never hear it with this. . . .

The man was standing at the edge of the tunnel up

there, watching them. When she looked up at him, he waved.

And hopped down onto the rocks beneath him.

Liam Riley had been watching the two people below him for a while, watching them pick their way down the steep slope of this oddly lit, water-filled cave. Climbing down the side in the fading milky light. At first, he'd considered calling out to them, but decided it would be more fun to wait until the woman turned back for another look. When she did, he waved at her.

She and Ben McKee immediately went to ground, of course, diving for cover, which was okay. Now they knew he was here. Now they'd have some time to think about it, and to prepare.

Riley descended the slope, rock to rock. He figured those two had at least one gun, maybe more, and he knew his white snowsuit would make a tempting target in the twilight. That was okay, too.

Cut it close. Out near the edge. If you didn't cut it close, what was the point?

He kind of hoped they'd wait to start shooting, though. Until he was nearer. If they were smart, they'd wait. Improve their chances at point-blank range, where Liam Riley's quickness would become the difference between life and death.

He felt his heartbeat accelerate as the adrenaline kicked in. A rush hotter and higher than any drug could provide. The ultimate definition of life itself.

When McKee started shooting, Cleese and Wallace would hear it, of course. They'd come running, but it would already be finished by then. That might disappoint Gene some, but he'd get over it. It was his own fault for choosing the wrong tunnel.

Riley jumped to the cover of another rock. So very quick. There were only the quick and the dead, after all.

Roger Quinn discovered that fact one day, a long time ago. These two were about to do the same.

"He waved." Nattie estimated the tall man's distance at somewhat over a hundred feet. "He could have been sneaking down on us, but he just stood there. And he *waved* . . ."

For some reason that fact chilled her more than the man's mere presence.

"We have to keep moving." Ben peeked around the rock. "You first. I'll cover you."

"With that?" She looked at the thirty-eight he was holding. "I thought you said you have to be close with one of those."

"If I shoot at him, he'll duck," replied Ben. "At least I think he will. Now get going."

Nattie glanced back once, saw the tall man dart, gracefully and so incredibly swift, to the cover of a lower rock before Ben could aim at him.

Oh, sweet God, she thought, and then moved, low and scuttling, down toward a jagged abutment near another pool. Her tongue hurt where she'd bitten it, and she realized her headache was returning.

And she was so damned tired.

She reached the lichen-streaked abutment, probably thirty feet down the steep slope from where Ben was, and ducked beneath it. All around her, the milky light continued to fade with the waning of the day outside the ice wall.

There was another waterfall, much larger now, on her right. It cascaded past her, spraying her with its mist, then down . . .

To a giant pool fifty feet below. A pool that filled the narrow bottom of the cave, at the spot where the rocky slope and ice wall finally converged. Water poured down into the pool from every side, splashing and frothing on a turbulent surface that seemed to capture and reflect all the dim light in the entire chamber. Glimmering up toward her like . . .

A monstrous eye.

Ojo del Plata, Nattie thought. The Eye of Silver.

End of the line, Nattie my love. Off the bus . . .

"He's one confident bastard." Ben McKee slid in beside her, his voice muffled by the waterfall's roar. "He must know we have a gun, though, 'cause he's taking his sweet time . . ."

Ben looked at her, then down at the pool.

"Jesus," he said. "What is this?"

"It's a dead end," Nattie answered. "We've reached the bottom of the cave."

"There's gotta be another tunnel . . ."

"But there's not. This is it. How many bullets do you have in that thing?"

Ben snapped open the revolving cylinder. "Full," he said. "Five shots."

"Oh, that's just swell," Nattie muttered. "Five shots? Why didn't those guys carry something useful? I thought feds always carried machine guns."

"Not when they're flying around in airplanes, I guess." Ben moved up into a mossy crack in the abutment and peered over. "He's still coming. Maybe a hundred feet or so. If we stay behind this rock, he can't flank us at least. It's too narrow down here."

"What about the others?" Nattie tugged her remaining ice ax out of her belt . . .

For all the good it'd do her against assault pistols.

. . . and slid over to the other side of the rock. "Cleese and those other two," she continued. "They can't be far behind this character. And when they get here . . ."

"I don't understand something," Ben said.

"Oh, really?" Nattie looked over at him. "God, I'm sorry to hear that, McKee. I don't understand *any . . .*"

"That water." Ben was looking down at the huge pool below them. "It's pouring in from everywhere, but it's not getting any deeper. That doesn't . . ."

Funnel.

". . . make any sense."

The whole chamber reminded Nattie of the shape of a funnel. . . .

208

"My God," she whispered. "It's running through."

"What did you say?"

She reached over and grabbed his arm. "The water. It's running through; that's why it isn't getting deeper. The bottom of this cave is open, probably eroded away by the acidic content of the water over the years. Don't you see? It's running on through to . . . somewhere."

He stared at her. "Forget it." He shook his head "No way, Nattie. No way in hell . . ."

"That's what you said before. Up on the rim."

"I meant it then, and I mean it now." Ben raised up to check the tall man's progress toward them. "You don't know where that water's going, do you? Like maybe someplace where there's no air. We'd drown like rats."

"Rats rarely drown," said Nattie. "Except in clichés. Besides, it's like I said up on the rim. What's our choice?"

"This time we have a choice." Ben held up the pistol. "That asshole gets close enough, I'll put a bullet in him."

"I thought you said you don't know much about guns."

"What's to know? Here's the trigger, and there's the barrel. You just pretend you're pointing your finger . . ."

"Says who? Magnum PI? You have five shots in that little snub-nose popgun, and there are four of them. And the other three'll be here as soon as they hear the fireworks, if not sooner. I don't know about you, but I didn't climb down that cliff and then fall down a mine shaft to end up trapped like this. Not when there's another way out."

He glared right back at her, his jaw set in a stubborn line.

"Ben . . ." She tried again. "Don't you see? That water is the only *real* chance we have."

He looked back up the steep slope.

"Ben . . ."

"Go ahead," he said, not looking at her. "I'll cover you."

"And then you'll be right behind me. Say it."

"Go on."

"Say it, damn you!"

"Okay." He cocked back the hammer of the pistol.

"If you're lying to me . . ."

"Me?" he said, and smiled at her in the near-darkness. It was that same smile she remembered from before all this, from that morning in the cabin.

A lifetime ago.

Nattie wanted to say something, but she wasn't sure what. So she said nothing and crawled away from him down through the rocks. It got wetter as she descended, and steeper, too. Slick, moss-covered stone and the waterfall pounding down beside her. Spray from the pool below was splashing into her face now.

The Eye of Silver, the only light left in the chamber, boiling up and thrashing against its sides. Twenty feet below her. Fifteen . . .

Then the sound of the first gunshot, booming in the small cave, louder than the water, echoed around her.

Ogod . . .

Nattie jumped.

Hitting the water was like a hammer blow against her body, so cold she lost her breath. She went under, then surfaced in a flurry of flailing arms and legs, and felt it pulling at her. The current. . . .

She looked back up, toward the rocky outcrop where Ben was, but it was all blackness up there now. There was nothing but the milky silver light around her, and the inexorable force of the current.

She filled her lungs with air just before it pulled her under.

"You've been a lot of trouble, haven't you, Ben?" The voice came from the darkness somewhere above Ben McKee, maybe a little to his right. What sounded like a New England accent. "I think you've got Gene aggravated."

"Gene can eat shit and die," Ben said, and then moved

210

in the opposite direction. Nearer the waterfall. He had three shots left, and he knew he hadn't hit anything at all, except maybe some rocks.

"I'll tell him you said so." The other man had moved, too.

"You won't be telling him anything." Ben hoped his voice sounded more assured than he felt.

No reply.

He shifted some more, nearly under the falls now. The icy water drenched him, and he felt himself slip on the rocks. Steeper over here. He lost one foothold and grabbed with the hand holding the gun. Nearly dropped it.

The water was all over him now, trying to knock him loose from the slope. Maybe he could get under it. Under the falls. . . .

When the tall man's body hit him, he thought at first it was still the water. Then a long, thin arm snaked around his neck. Yanked him loose from his grip.

They tumbled down the side, glancing off slick, moss-covered boulders. The waterfall carried them with it, cartwheeling them as they fell.

The man was thin, but he was extremely strong. The pressure tightened around Ben's neck, and everything turned to whirling white dots in front of his eyes.

He struck out blindly, wildly, with the butt of the pistol. Hit something hard, and felt a tremor along the man's muscular arm. Swung the gun again . . .

Just as they both tumbled into the pool.

The water was so cold that Ben felt, for an instant, that his flesh was on fire. Absolute cold or absolute heat, and the body's perceptions go haywire.

Then he surfaced, and realized the arm no longer encircled his neck. Everything was silver, all around him, ice-cold and so silver and bright it hurt his eyes.

Across from him, six feet away, the tall man's head broke the surface. He looked at Ben and smiled, a glittering wolflike smile, then lunged for him.

They both went under, down into the churning water

211

and milky light. The current had them, pulled them sideways as they fought it and each other. Ben tried to swing the pistol again, but his hand caught in the loose gun harness around the other man's shoulder. Ben pulled on the web sling and jabbed his fingers toward the grinning face. Missed, because the force of the current yanked him loose.

His body corkscrewed in the direction of that irresistibly powerful pull. Over and over and twisting downward toward what he only glimpsed as an uneven series of rips in the bottom. A jagged rock tore at his coat, snagged him for an instant, then the current pulled him free. Down into darkness.

Nattie, I hope to God you're right, was the thought he had, just before the milky light disappeared.

He also wondered how long he could hold his breath.

Chapter Fifteen

Rick Macon had never seen a dead body before.

Oh, at a funeral, of course, like anyone else. But that wasn't the same. Those bodies—his grandmother, a cousin who had died at eighteen of Hodgkins, and so forth—those bodies were like department store mannequins. All combed hair and cosmetics, suits or dresses. Placid faces.

That thing out there in the shed—Marvin Stone, it had to be—*that* was a dead body.

What was it doing there?

Macon wanted to go out to the shed and look at it some more.

Better not. He was already walking around on some pretty thin ice, so to speak. He was going to have to be very careful.

He padded over to the woodstove in his sock feet, and fed in some more aspen and scrub oak. The main room of the Walker Lake communication center was warming up nicely now, and so was Macon. He peeled down to his black, sweat-stained long-handle top and jeans. Gave himself one of those this-is-purely-by-accident glances in the mirror above the player piano.

Which reminded him to close the window shades in the room, since it was getting dark outside. He'd been in his Denver condo one night, checking himself out in the mirror over the fireplace, and the next day that smartass bitch Mona Ferguson started ragging him about it out at the pool. "Gonna stand around drooling over yourself, better close your drapes, pretty boy. A lighted room at night with the curtains open, that's better than television . . ."

For some reason, The Look never had much effect on Mona Ferguson. Probably a lez.

Macon closed the last of the shades, which was the window overlooking the snowmobile shed behind the main building. Invisible now, hidden beyond that blowing, gray-white shroud of night and the blizzard. That shed . . .

Where Marvin Stone lay behind the woodpile. Pretty much gray himself, speaking of shrouds, skin the color of putty. With those opaque, half-open eyes and an expression on his face that might be described as mild surprise.

And a small horizontal gash across the back of his neck, right above the line of his shoulders. Some kind of knife probably, a narrow blade. Right in through the spinal cord.

There was a little blood, but not a lot. Macon glanced over at the stain he'd noticed earlier, on the carpet next to the shortwave radio. He'd assumed it was spilled coffee . . .

And it probably was. Whoever clipped Stone's cord for him was very precise. Not the type to tolerate something as sloppy as blood on the floor.

What the hell was going on here? Helicopter sounds, but no helicopter, a deserted communication center in the middle of a blizzard, a body hidden behind a pile of firewood out in the shed. . . .

Macon *really* wanted to go out and take another look at the body. Maybe there were some answers he'd missed the first time.

But that was just an excuse, wasn't it?

There was something about the body that drew him. The face of Death, maybe. Capital D. Those glazed eyes, and whatever it was they'd seen, right at the very end . . .

Nattie had closed her eyes. That time. He'd felt cheated.

214

. . . right at the very moment. Maybe Capital-D Death had left an imprint, like the trace on a photographic plate.

Macon realized he'd taken a half-step toward the front door. He made himself stop.

Better not. That thin ice, after all.

He was alone here, in the middle of this storm, with a body. And not just some grab-your-chest-and-drop-dead-on-the-floor body. Not at all. This was the body of an obvious murder victim. He was also alone here with a pillaged government building and a trashed shortwave radio. None of this was going to look good.

Especially not for someone with a criminal record. Assault With Intent.

No jail time, of course. Not after he'd shown that bleeding-heart judge some of his best acting—*Visualize, Rick. Visualize remorse*—since he left L.A. Probation instead, and counseling, and all that other related bull-shit. And having the former mother-in-law as his staunchest advocate didn't hurt either.

But that might not cut much ice if the local Deputy Dawgs found him—a Violent Crimes offender. Sweet Nattie would be screaming *that* fact to high heaven if she was with them . . .

Can I get a witnessss . . .

. . . sitting here alone with this undeniable violence all around him.

This was not good.

His best bet was to leave. Out the door, onto that snowmobile and back to Ouray, nobody the wiser . . .

I guess you were right, folks. You can't make it to Walker Lake in this weather.

Except he couldn't leave. Not now. Not after dark in this goddamn storm. He'd made it the night before, but he'd been fresh then. Well rested and full of food. And the blizzard had gotten worse since then, if such a thing was possible.

Better stay here, tonight at least, inside this warm,

sheltered building with its bed and its food supply. No-body would be arriving tonight.

Take some time to ponder several very intriguing questions. First question, what's going on around here? Second question, who killed Fat Marvin? Third question, does it have anything to do with Nattie?

Fourth question, is there some way all this can serve a useful purpose?

That fourth question was the one with the most potential. It would require some thought.

Rick Macon walked over to add more firewood to the stove. And, since the shades were down anyway, he went ahead and took off his long-handle top.

Nattie stopped swimming when she felt her feet strike bottom. She stood up, and found herself waist-deep.

In the blackness behind her, water continued to roar out of the cracks in the rock. The pressure, like a firehose, had quite literally spat her into the icy depths of this pool.

She began to wade forward, toward a grayness that wasn't so much light as it was a lesser degree of darkness than what lay behind. She was no longer cold, too numb from this liquid ice to feel anything at the moment. But she knew she would, and soon. The weight of her water-soaked clothing pulled down on her, and she was already missing those grease-gummed gloves she'd lost earlier.

It had been a nightmare descent, down through the blackness. The high-ticket ride at *Water World From Hell*. Banging against rocks she couldn't see, being spun like a top by the spiraling force of the current, snagging her clothes and her last bit of climbing rope until it had yanked loose from her.

Holding her breath as long as she could. . . .

How long was that? No way to tell, not in that icy, dead black, body-hurtling environment. It could have been ten seconds. It could have been ten minutes, though of course that was impossible.

But it had seemed that long.

She wasn't even certain when she'd tumbled into this pool. Just that she'd felt her body stop spinning, and then she'd raised her head thinking that was fresh, cold air on her face, but not certain. And it was.

The light ahead—or more accurately, the lesser darkness—had to be coming from outside the mine. As her numbed senses continued to clear, she could smell it. It smelled different from the musty tunnels, the faint scent of snow that people said you couldn't really smell, but you could.

The pool gradually grew more shallow. Knee-deep now. Nattie slogged forward until her booted feet dug into mud. Then up a slight incline to a rocky shelf.

She sat down, legs trembling noticeably, and took off her cracked climbing helmet. Thank God she'd kept it on, because she'd hit several rocks with her head during that awful passage. In the faint gray, the white helmet was an indistinct blob. She ran her fingers across the hand-printed logo she couldn't see, and imagined she could trace the letters like Braille.

Empty roads, all right. What was that Ben McKee had said? "This one's emptier than most . . ."

"And it isn't traveled yet," she'd replied.

She thought about the gunshots, up there in the cave. Had he stayed behind, preferring to take his chances? There was no way to know for certain, not unless . . .

"Nattie?"

. . . unless he came wading up out of that black tunnel behind her. And she couldn't wait very. . . .

"Nattie, where are you?"

She spun around, only certain she'd actually heard him the second time.

"Ben?"

And then he did come, wading toward her, a moving silhouette in the dark.

She rose to her feet, just as he climbed onto the rocky shelf. She threw her arms around him, felt his arms encircle her.

They stayed like that for a while.

"You're bleeding again," she murmured, and touched his face. "I heard shots . . ."

"Never laid a glove on me." His voice was hoarse. "But I hit every rock there was on my way through. Now I know what clothes feel like on the spin cycle."

"Where is he?" Nattie looked back into the darkness, back toward that roar of sound.

"I don't know. I kept listening for him while I waded out . . ."

"He could be right next to us, and we'd never hear him over the noise of that water. We'd better get moving."

"Where are we?"

"I'm not sure." Nattie bent to retrieve her climbing helmet. "But I think we're on ground level. One of the lower tunnels. There was still some light when I first got here, but it's about gone now."

They began walking. At first Nattie looked back over her shoulder every few steps, but finally she gave it up. Even if he was back there, the tall man, he'd be invisible in this blackness.

"Do you still have the gun?" she asked.

"No. I lost it somewhere under water."

No gun. And her remaining ice ax was gone, too. No weapons, not even the rope or her rappel gear. All gone, except for her helmet and a little box of waterproof matches.

They hurried along the dark tunnel, their teeth chattering now from the icy weight of their wet clothes. They waded mud and navigated by touch, toward what once may have been the light.

Eugene Cleese climbed across a rocky abutment next to a waterfall. Below him, a huge pool lay in a milky, glimmering reflection of candlelight.

"So, where'd they go?" Milton Wallace was just behind him, speaking up to be heard above the roar of the falls. "Those gunshots came from in here. They had to."

Cleese nodded, and looked around. Held his candle high to illuminate a chamber gone nearly black.

"This is the bottom of the cave, Milt," he said. "Looks like a dead end to me, unless "

He began to work his way down across the slick, wet rocks toward the pool.

"Unless what?" Wallace followed him, his HK assault pistol at the ready.

"Unless they went through there." Cleese pointed at the seething surface beneath him. "That water goes somewhere, maybe on down to that bottom tunnel you mentioned. The one you waded back into."

He leaned forward at the lip of the pool, bracing himself on a mossy spur that overhung the edge.

"See something?" asked Wallace.

"Something." Cleese began unzipping his orange snowsuit. "Milt, why don't you take one end of this rope and hook it over that big rock up there. I'm going to need you to hold it tight."

"You're going in that water?"

"Just for a quick look." Cleese peeled out of his insulated underwear, then tied the other end of the climbing rope around his waist in a snug bowline knot. "I'll need you to feed me some slack, but not very much."

"Dammit, Gene . . ."

Cleese clambered into the icy water, his knife scabbard in one hand. "I'm counting on you, Milt," he said.

He took a couple of deep breaths, and then dove under. An instant later, the current took him. Pulled him down . . .

To where the body hung, a dark silhouette flailing back and forth in the maelstrom, halfway into the deeper blackness of a jagged hole at the bottom of the pool.

Liam Riley was caught by the web harness of his Steyr, which had apparently encircled his neck when he tried to twist out of it. His body danced in the water's flow, in and out of the hole beneath him. Legs in, and the harness tightened around his neck. Legs popping back up, and the webbing loosened slightly.

But not enough to unhook the harness. There was no way to pull him free of the current.

It looked like Riley's eyes were open, though it was too dark beneath the water to really tell, and Cleese imagined the man's lips parted in that lupine smile. One of his hands was tangled in the harness, and his other arm waved up and down with the current. A friendly sort of motion.

Eugene Cleese never swore, not even the mildest oath, not since that so-long-ago day when his Baptist preacher father fixed that. Oh, the Reverend Eugene Cleese, Sr., fixed Little Gene's wagon for him that day, all right. A dose of lye soap that left blisters inside the six-year-old boy's mouth for a week of sheer agony. And since then, he never swore. But this. . . .

He pulled the Buckmaster from its scabbard and cut through the web harness around Riley's neck. In the next moment, the body was gone, carried by the relentless current down into the black hole beneath it.

Cleese sheathed the knife and began to pull himself back along the rope. He was very cold and nearly out of air. And, for the first time in a long time, he was getting tired.

"See him?" whispered Ben McKee.

Nattie wasn't sure. She rubbed her eyes, still burning from the icy, mineralized water, and stared harder.

Maybe . . . over there by the entrance, silhouetted against a gray-white backdrop of blowing snow. Maybe.

It made sense. Cleese had three men with him. The tall one had pursued them into the cave . . .

Might still be behind them somewhere down this black tunnel.

. . . which would leave two others he could deploy. This was a logical spot for one of them.

The silhouette moved.

"Told you," whispered Ben.

The figure shifted slightly again. Whichever of the

other two it was, he was certain to be well armed. And he had the mine entrance blocked.

Now what?

A set of choices, all of them poor. One was to stay here, still soaking wet, with that icy wind blowing in from outside. Gradually freeze into unconsciousness, unless the tall man came walking up behind them first.

A second was to try for one of the other bottom tunnels. See where it lead . . .

Which was probably nowhere. Back into the dark again.

A third was to sneak over to the lift platform, about fifty feet away. If they could crank themselves up into the shaft before that goon by the entrance heard them—a faint possibility with the noise of the storm all around him—maybe they could reach one of the levels above. Find a relatively dry place . . .

Yeah, right.

. . . to hide until they thawed a little.

The fourth was to jump the guy at the entrance. Which of course was the only *real* choice. It was just a matter of figuring. . . .

"Artie!" The sound echoed down across Nattie. Only Ben's arm around her waist kept her from leaping out into the corridor.

"Artie!" Louder this time. Coming from the vertical shaft.

"I'll be damned," whispered Nattie.

"What?" asked Ben.

"Cleese and that other guy, they're stuck up there unless they want to shinny down the cables like we did." Nattie pointed at the lift platform.

"Garza!" Two voices now, in a near-unison of ragged echoes.

"When they sent ol' Artie down here to stand guard, he rode the lift," whispered Nattie. "It's hand operated. It has to be cranked down, or up."

"So . . ." Ben leaned in closer to her. "He'll have to go up for them . . ."

"Artie!"

The figure by the entrance was moving toward them now.

"If we jump him when he goes by," said Nattie, "we could get his gun."

"We could also end up looking like that last scene from *Bonnie and Clyde.*" Ben pulled her farther back into the tunnel. "Remember those weapons they're carrying? Uzis or whatever they are. Let him go on up the lift, and we can walk right out of here."

"Arturo!" The voice was Cleese's this time, and it sounded considerably closer.

It appeared the man—short and stocky from his silhouette—hadn't been sure before, possibly because of the wind's noise by the entrance. Now he was hurrying over to the vertical shaft.

"Gene?" he yelled.

". . . see anything?" The response was distorted by echoes.

The figure made a slow three-sixty, weapon raised, and Ben pulled Nattie lower.

"Nothing. What's going on?"

". . . ley's dead! I'm coming down!"

"Dead," Nattie whispered, and squeezed Ben's arm.

"Hideputa," the man muttered. Then he yelled, "You want me to come up?"

"No! . . . using the climbing gear. You stay there . . ."

"Damn," whispered Nattie. She'd forgotten Cleese had a rope.

". . . your eyes open! They may be down there . . ."

"He's already part way down." Ben pushed Nattie ahead of him. "We can't wait any longer."

She hurried toward the entrance, felt her frozen joints creak as she tried to run. It was up there, just ahead. . . .

It felt like she was swimming again. Everything in slow motion. She focused on the opening, where the snow was blowing past like a curtain of lace.

Nearly there. . . .

"Hey!" A voice from behind her.

"Run!" yelled Ben.

"*¡Cabrones! Vengan . . . !*"

Then a chunk of wall exploded, off to her right, spraying her with tiny bits of rock, followed by a chattering echo of sound. Nattie lowered her head and ran faster, just as mud kicked up next to her feet. The sound was all around her . . .

Then it was gone, drowned out by the scream of the wind. She was outside.

Instinctively she spun toward her left, ran along an elevated handcar trestle, its cross-ties broken and rotted. The storm howled down over her again, its fury unabated by the hours they'd spent inside the mine.

Except now it was night. And the wind buffeting her head and her clothing was colder than even the pool of water had been.

Nattie glanced back once, glimpsed Ben McKee close behind her, then jumped from the trestle. Down into deep snow ten feet below that swallowed her whole.

Ben landed next to her, and they floundered to their feet and struggled beneath the sagging tracks.

The blizzard blew across them, combining snow from the air with more snow its wind was pulling up from the surface. Nattie was blinded until she turned her head away. She and Ben crawled farther back beneath the old support timbers.

Movement above them. She couldn't hear it, couldn't hear anything over the wind, but she felt the supports moving next to her. She shielded her eyes and looked up through the broken cross-ties above her head.

Someone was up there, walking along the trestle. She saw a shape, windblown, stopping directly above them. Next to a broken section of track.

If he looked down. . . .

Nattie held her breath. Saw the outline of the man's head moving side to side. Then down.

She felt her heart lurch. Felt Ben stiffen next to her.

223

Then the man looked up again, stepped carefully around the broken ties, and moved on.

He can't see us, she realized. He can't see anything, not in this darkness. Not in this storm.

But the others . . . Cleese said someone was dead—maybe the tall man?—but he and at least one other would be down soon. Cleese was good on the ropes.

There were still three of them.

The figure on the trestle was coming past again. Nattie thought she heard him say something, but the wind took his voice away. He stepped around the broken ties and moved out of her sightline. Back toward the mine.

She prodded Ben with her hand against his shoulder. Pointed into the blowing darkness, and pushed him again.

In the direction of snow-buried Walker Creek, although he probably didn't know that. And, by extension, in the direction of the lake and the comm center.

How far away? Four miles, maybe five?

They weren't going to make four miles in this storm. Not in these wet clothes, dead-tired and half-frozen, with nothing to eat since breakfast except chocolate brownies. And especially not in the middle of the night. They had to find . . .

"Shelter," said Nattie, and stopped in her tracks, halfway out from under the trestle.

Ben turned and looked at her. He held up his hands in a silent question . . .

That she had an answer for. Just like that, because she'd remembered Marilyn and John Whittaker. And the Thomas brothers. Summer people from Texas who had the two cabins less than a mile down Walker Creek.

The cabins had almost certainly been winterized and boarded up tight, but that wouldn't be much of a problem. Not after what she and Ben had already been through. Anyone could break into a summer cabin if they wanted to badly enough.

Another vicious wind gust hit Nattie, spraying snow

224

across her, and she realized she'd stopped shivering. A very bad sign.

It was going to be a race against time now.

She pushed Ben forward, her bare hands already like blocks of wood, and pointed to show him the direction. He was considerably larger than she, so it was better for him to break trail through this deep snow. For as long as he could, at least.

They left the partial shelter of the trestle, detouring around the old, snow-buried cyanide leach pads, and worked their way toward the black outline of some evergreens beneath the canyon wall. Nattie only looked back once, and by then she could no longer see the mine. Just blowing snow and swirling darkness. She was well aware they were leaving a wide trail anyone could follow, but there was no help for that now. Maybe up in the trees. . . .

It was about fifteen minutes later when they came upon the wallowed-out tracks in the snow. And ten more before they found the wrecked helicopter.

Chapter Sixteen

Eugene Cleese stood at the entrance to the abandoned mine and watched the snow blow past outside. It was full dark now, a few minutes after six o'clock. Impossibly, the blizzard appeared to be escalating again.

Gray-white darkness out there, propelled by that howling wind. Cold colors. The colors of death.

Cleese felt a smothering sort of fatigue pulling at him. The uncommon feeling of being bone-tired. Not old, of course. Not at all. Just a little tired.

He turned when Milton Wallace walked up beside him.

"Did you find him?" asked Cleese.

Wallace shook his head. "It was like you said, Gene. It's all flooded out back there, all that goddamn water coming down through the wall. That whole end of the tunnel's under water. Maybe in the morning, when there's more light . . ."

"Maybe." Cleese nodded.

"I did find some tracks in the mud. Looks like that's how they got through, all right."

"Remarkable." Cleese watched the snow.

"It's my fault, Gene." Arturo Garza looked over from where he was boiling water for their freeze-dried packets of food. "I'll take the hit for this one. I let them get past me."

Privately, Cleese agreed with him. Someone like Liam Riley would never have allowed it to break down like that. But a good leader always knew when to temper

226

criticism with support. This business was far from over.

"There was no way for you to anticipate what happened," he said, which was at least partly true. "You were trying to watch the lift shaft, and keep an eye on the wall outside. You had no reason to think they might come out of a side tunnel."

Wallace stood silent behind Cleese. Looked out at the storm.

"It was still my fault." Garza pushed the bobbing plastic packets under the water. "But it won't happen again, *parejo. Es cosa de pundonor.*"

"So," said Wallace. "When do we go after them?"

"Not tonight. It would be stupid for us to try it."

"They did." Wallace nodded in the direction of the trestle, invisible now in the blowing darkness.

"They had no choice," answered Cleese. "We do. We'll pick it up at dawn. We know where they're headed, not that they'll ever get there. Not in this storm. Anyway, the trail they're leaving in the snow will still be there at first light. My guess is, when we find them it'll just be a matter of confirmation. Neater that way, too."

There was more, but he didn't say it. How he was too tired to go out in the blizzard again. Not tonight.

He stared into the dark until Wallace walked away, back over to where Garza crouched by the fire.

It was time to factor everything by three now, instead of four. Unfortunate because Liam Riley had been Cleese's best man. The best he'd ever worked with, in fact. But Riley had always pursued death, ever since Cleese first saw him—a tall, gangly teenager with predator's eyes, standing outside a whorehouse in Saigon. Through the years Riley had courted death like a beautiful woman, plied her with the kind of gifts she'd like the most. Given that, it was inevitable that one day she'd finally turn toward him and smile.

Riley had been like Cleese's father in that one small way. Both had held life cheap.

Except, for the Reverend Eugene Cleese, Sr., death was equally meaningless. "This is just the way station, boy," he'd said. "We're all passengers in the way station, waiting to board Eternity. It's only what we do while we're waiting that counts."

When Cleese remembered his father—and tasted the burning agony of lye soap in his mouth, which *always* accompanied the memory—he usually thought of the Glorious Ascension Baptist Church in Newlinburgh, Kentucky. And the Reverend Eugene Cleese, Sr., up there in the pulpit, thick gray hair swept back above a lofty forehead, pearly beads of sweat rolling down his lean, handsome face.

Are you washed . . . ? Are you washed . . . ? Are you washed in the blood of The Lamb . . . ?

"Life and death here in the way station, they're meaningless, boy." That was how the Reverend Eugene Cleese, Sr., explained his use of the leather strap when Little Gene—home from the first in a series of military schools—made the mistake of crying at his mother's grave. "She's the Lord Jesus God's handmaiden now, boy. Gone to serve him, and what could be more joyous than that? Don't let me see you crying again, boy."

And Cleese never did . . .

Life and death, they're meaningless.

. . . until that day he held Genie, tiny and beautiful and so completely *his,* in his arms.

By then it was much too late, of course, for most things. But not for Genie.

Cleese wondered what Liam Riley might be having to say to the Reverend Eugene Cleese, Sr., right about now. He had little doubt they were in the same place.

Cleese started walking back to the fire. In some sort of natural progression he didn't question, he found his thinking had switched to Natalie Kemper.

She didn't act from panic, except for—maybe—that flight into the lighted cave. And even that could have been calculated if she knew about the pool.

But this time she'd had no choice. Take the storm or fight it out in the mine, so she'd taken the storm. She and McKee would die out there tonight.

Unless. . . .

Cleese stopped in mid-stride and felt a hot flush creep up his neck. For the second time in less than an hour, he felt the overwhelming urge to swear . .

Because he'd forgotten about the helicopter.

Nattie used the shotgun butt to snap off the small lock that held the wooden shutters in place. Then she pulled the shutters back and broke a windowpane.

She'd selected a window in back, where snow-laden spruce trees hid that side of the cabin from view.

She bent down to unsnap the nylon bindings of the snowshoes—*her* snowshoes now—and placed one booted foot into Ben McKee's interlocked fingers. He boosted her up, and she reached inside the broken pane to unlatch the window and slide it up. Hooked her hip over the sill, and stepped into the dark room.

By the time Ben followed her, tossing the Mauser rifle in ahead of him, she'd managed to locate the kitchen cabinets. As in most mountain cabins, a handful of tall, tapered candles were stacked next to a box of matches.

"Pretty cozy." Ben pulled the shutters closed, then let down the window. He turned to look around while Nattie lit another of the candles, and she saw his movements were hesitant and slow, those of a man half-dead on his feet.

"Beats our previous accommodations, I'll say that," replied Nattie, and thought to herself, I got him inside just in time.

Though far from ornate, the cabin was somewhat larger than hers had been. Two stories tall, with a main room on the lower floor that included a kitchen, and a half bar as a room divider. A sturdy old naugahyde-covered couch and several unmatched chairs were clustered around a scarred coffee table, and the far wall was dominated by a huge rock fireplace.

"You can tell they're summer people." Nattie nodded in that direction. "They have a fireplace instead of a woodstove. Those things are nearly useless in really cold country. Most of the heat goes up the chimney.''

"I'd be willing to give it a chance," said Ben. In the comparative warmth of the unheated room, snow and ice were beginning to melt and drip off him.

"Me, too, but we can't. Guys like Cleese don't miss much when they're interested, so this place has to look deserted. That way, if they're tailing us, they'll probably hit that other cabin first, and we'll have some warning at least."

A gust of wind whistled through the broken window-pane behind Ben. Rattled the shutters against the glass.

"Why don't you see if you can stuff a towel or some-thing in that hole," said Nattie, continuing to rub feeling back into her numb fingers. "I'm going to look upstairs."

The candle lit her way up a narrow, enclosed staircase to an equally claustrophobic hallway, made even spookier by the sounds of the storm battering the walls outside. There were four doors up there. One opened on a small bathroom with a single lavatory, toilet, and tub. Two of the others led into bedrooms, sparsely furnished with a bed and chest of drawers.

Nattie looked around in the flickering candlelight. Now that she was thawing some, the waves of fatigue were hitting her harder, trying to buckle her knees. Some food would help, and something to drink, though she wasn't really thirsty—which could be deceiving when the body's core temperature was low. As much as anything else, they both needed to get rehydrated.

She'd been told that the Thomas brothers—despite their money and matching private planes—weren't big on amenities, and she saw it was true. This place was a basic hunting and fishing cabin, skillfully built but without much glitz to it.

Hunting . . .

Nattie opened the fourth door, out in the hallway. It was a closet, with a clothes rack across the top.

She went to the head of the stairs. "Hey, Ben," she said, starting down. "There's a closet up here with hunting clothes in it. All that heavy-duty insulated stuff. Why don't you get into something dry, and I'll look for food."

"I hear that," he replied, and shuffled past her up the stairs, carrying a candle of his own.

In the small kitchen, Nattie found a step-in pantry above a bolted trapdoor that probably led down into the crawl space. The pantry shelves held stacks of canned goods and several containers of bottled water, only half-filled to protect against bursting if they froze.

Dinty Moore stew. She took out a can with that distinctive oversized thumbprint on top. In her previous life, she and Rick had known a climber from down near Durango named Don Magill, who claimed he could ride out the Apocalypse with a can opener and a couple cases of Dinty Moore.

Can opener. She rummaged through a drawer beneath the cabinets and found one. Some knives, too.

"We're all set for dinner, bud," she mumbled. "Unless you like your food hot. At this point, my guess is you'll take it any way you can get it."

She was prying the lid off the stew, bothered some by the tiny bits of splinter still imbedded in her newly sensitive fingertips, when Ben came back down the stairs. Both Jeff and Harry Thomas were big men, especially Harry, so the hunting clothes fit Ben well. Insulated pants and coat in a camouflage pattern, over a thick down vest and a flannel shirt. A pair of lace-up Sorel boots.

He'd apparently found the bathroom and towel dried his wet head, then brushed his dark hair into a semblance of order.

"You look a lot better," she said, which he did if you discounted the gray patches of frostbite on his face and the fatigue in his eyes. "Those clothes are a good fit."

"You can see them?" He glanced downward at his camouflage gear, then back at her with a slight grin. "I thought I was supposed to be invisible."

"But seriously, folks." Nattie nodded. "More of that delightful urban humor, I guess."

Actually, she was glad to hear any joke from him, even a lame one. And he *did* look a lot better. It seemed she was constantly underestimating his powers of recuperation.

He's a survivor, she thought. I was wrong about that, as it's turned out.

And about what else?

"So, how do you like your stew, sir?" she asked, putting the thought aside. "We've got cold, with stale crackers, or we've got cold, with pork and beans. Also cold. This place has a gas stove and refrigerator, which means there's a propane tank somewhere outside, but it's been winterized. Everything is shut down so it doesn't freeze and burst."

"Can I have cold, with stale crackers *and* pork and beans?"

"You're a wild man." Nattie opened the second can, then handed Ben a spoon from the drawer. "Take a bottle of that water while you're at it, and drink it all. You're bound to be dehydrated."

"Water?" He made a face, then went over to the apartment-sized refrigerator and opened the door. It was empty, except for a six-pack ring of beer. There were three cans left.

"Busch," said Ben, and grinned at her. "Kinda gives that 'Come To The Mountains' promo a whole new meaning, huh? I've always heard you should drink elegant booze at room temperature."

"Which in this case is about forty degrees, even if it does feel like a sauna compared to outside." Nattie's shivering reflex was finally kicking in, and she felt the hard edge of a chill along her spine. "You go ahead and eat. I'm going to check out that bathroom again."

"There'd be no need if this was *Indiana Jones*," he reminded her, and carried his food to the coffee table.

"You drink that water," she told him as she started up the stairs. "All of it. Taking in fluids is one of the quickest ways to get your core temperature back up to normal."

"Hey, last time I checked, beer was fluid . . ."

232

"It's also alcohol, and don't give me that old line about antifreeze. Drink the water."

Upstairs, Nattie found some more clothes, including insulated underwear, and changed. Her own stuff was excellent, expensive and designed for weather like this, but it was soaked through from her swim. All the clothes she found were too large—evidently Jeff and Harry weren't very keen on bringing along the womenfolk—but at least they were dry.

She took off the green wool cap she'd worn beneath her climbing helmet, and then untied her long hair. The colorful little red ribbon was just a wet rag now, and she touched tiny shards of ice all along her scalp that started her shivering again. She found a towel and rough dried her hair, then a comb—one of those old black Ace combs with larger teeth at one end—and tried not to think about where it had been. She got her still-damp hair at least going in the right direction while she listened to the storm hammer away at the shuttered windows above the bed.

Hey, all you need now is mascara and blush. That thought intruded on her, and she stopped in mid-comb. Maybe some lipstick . . .

Very chic there, Nattie my love. Is that the natural look, or what?

Why was she doing this?

Because you have to get that ice away from your scalp, that's why. That's the only reason you need.

She continued to comb her hair.

Being alone does funny things to the mind, she decided, and realized she was thinking about Ben McKee at the same time. Being alone puts its own particular spin on your perceptions, until they begin to whirl just a little bit off-center . . .

And all kinds of weird stuff begins to seem sensible.

Like a night in this frozen cabin with a stranger. One of *those* kinds of nights. While the worst blizzard in a decade pounds away outside, and three stone-cold murderers follow close behind.

All that romance novel bullshit, in other words.

Nattie put the comb back on Jeff/Harry's dresser and zipped the insulated parka higher around her neck; then she went out into the shadowy, candlelit hallway and down the stairs.

Ben looked at her from the couch. "Are you up there?" he asked. "I can't see you."

Nattie glanced down at her own camouflage-patterned clothing.

"Give it up, McKee," she said, but felt the edge of a grin anyway. After all this time, this long, terrible day, this would be their first chance to really talk to each other. "Did you eat everything in the place?"

"Close. But I did leave you a couple cans of Spam, and some of those little sardines."

"Thanks loads." Nattie used the attached key to open the Spam, then carried it to a chair near the fireplace. "You could toss me that beer," she added.

"It's the last one," he said. "And don't give me that old line about antifreeze."

He tossed it over anyway.

"Chivalry lives." Nattie popped the top. "Spam and beer. You're one helluva date, you know that?" She used a kitchen knife to slice off a chunk of the salty meat. "You could've at least brought along some complimentary peanuts from the plane."

"I guess Landry wasn't much of a stewardess . . ." Ben began, then stopped.

Way to go, Nattie, she thought.

"What time is it?" he asked, after a silence that probably seemed longer than it was.

She looked at her Timex. Still ticking. "Eight o'clock," she answered. "Ten minutes 'til. Quite a day, huh?"

"Like *Hamlet* without the slow parts." Ben's face was bleak, and Nattie inwardly cursed herself for mentioning the plane. "How long 'til they catch up with us again?"

"I think you're giving them too much credit," she said.

"Cleese?" He looked at her.

"Even Cleese. He isn't Superman, Ben. Don't forget

they're on foot now, just like we are. And we have their snowshoes, at least two pair of them. Or do you think Cleese just glides along on top of the snow like a vampire?"

He shrugged.

"And we also have their guns. The shotgun and the rifle. Those assault pistols can't match that Mauser out in the open. It's good for half a mile with that scope."

"I've never fired a rifle, except those twenty-twos they have at carnivals. How about you?"

"Well . . . not a rifle like that, no. But I'll bet I can look through a scope and . . ."

"A gun like that's no good in this kind of weather, anyway. You let them get close enough so you can see them, they're close enough for those Uzis. Or whatever the hell they are. That's why Cleese left the damn thing in the helicopter."

"Maybe so." Nattie felt a brief surge of irritation. "But that shotgun'll do the job up close . . ."

"Have you ever fired one that size?"

"No. Hell, no. Why would I go around with a ten-gauge shotgun? Or a high-powered rifle, for that matter?"

"I don't know." He shrugged again. "You're the queen of the wilderness, aren't you?"

"And you're the prince of the city, I suppose."

He smiled at that, and her anger disappeared. As though it had never existed.

"A deadly pair, aren't we?" He grinned.

"Hey, it could be a lot worse." Nattie washed down some more Spam with a swallow of beer. "Think about it. When you were getting exploded out of my cabin, and strafed on my snowmobile . . ."

"Scared shitless by Laura the Lion," he added.

"Right. And that's not to mention roping down a thousand-foot cliff, fleeing for your life along a dark tunnel and swinging like Tarzan in a mine shaft . . ."

"I get your point."

". . . and then swimming through that hole." Nattie

235

pointed her knife at him. "When you were doing all that, did you ever believe we'd finish the day in luxurious digs like this?" She made a sweeping gesture around her. "Sitting here in warm, dry clothes, pigging out on exotic cuisine?"

"I didn't believe we'd finish the day period, to tell the truth," he replied, and she saw him shivering. Which finalized a decision she'd been waffling over in her mind. Whatever advantage the darkness might provide, there was no way Ben McKee could make the final push for the comm center tonight.

She wasn't sure she could, either.

"Dry clothes, maybe," he added. "I'm not so sure about the warm part."

"At least you're shivering again," she said. "So am I. That's a good sign. Means our bodies are trying to manufacture heat."

"I remember that tub of yours, last night."

"God, don't remind me." Nattie finished off the second can of Spam, but decided she wasn't yet starved to the point of eating sardines. "This food'll help a lot, and so will the liquid, but what we need more than anything right now is to get some rest. There are a couple of beds upstairs."

"A couple? Last night . . ."

"Last night I had one bed." Nattie's face was still cold, and her sudden blush felt a bit like a sunburn. "And, besides, you were pretty harmless then."

"I'm harmless now," he replied. "I mean, look at me. Knocked out of the sky, half-frozen, hauled to hell-and-gone by some mysterious mountain momma . . ."

"Mountain momma?"

"You don't remember John Denver? I think he has a cabin right down this creek somewhere. The point is, I'm probably in worse shape now than I was last night. And being in an ice-cold bed by myself in an unheated cabin in the middle of a blizzard . . ."

"Okay, already." Nattie held up both hands, palms out, in mock surrender. "You're probably right. The

236

body heat from both of us in the same bed *would* get our temperature back up to normal . . ."

"At least."

". . . more quickly. But I'm planning to bring this knife along with me, McKee. You might keep that in mind."

"So, what happened to Bob?"

"Huh?" The sound of his voice made Nattie flinch. There in the darkness, with the wind howling outside the window, Ben McKee sounded inches away, rather than on the far side of the bed.

"Bob." His hand touched her arm, and she realized he *was* inches away. "Isn't that what you said you call your long johns? When there's nobody around?"

"Good God." She tried for a laugh, but her throat was too tight, sealing up her voice into a hoarse whisper. "Don't you ever forget anything?"

"It's a curse." He shifted, and she could feel him now. The warmth from his body alongside hers. "Anyway, these aren't the same ones, are they?"

"Camouflage underwear," she said. "If it was light, you couldn't see me."

"Have to operate by touch, I suppose." His hand moved from her arm, across her stomach.

"Dammit, Ben . . ." This was ridiculous. The way her heart was pounding her chest so hard it hurt. Quite physically hurt.

She was a grown woman, dammit. Not some scared little virgin. But here, in the dark . . .

Big hands. Touching her . . .

Curling around her waist, turning her toward him.

"Remember when you kissed me?" he said, and he was so close she could smell the warm edge of beer on his breath. "Out there on the cliff?"

"You were ready to give up." She put her hand on his chest to push him away, but she didn't. "To quit. I just did that—"

"To get my attention. I know. Well, you got it."

He kissed her then.

She stiffened at first, her mind a swirling sea of memories. Bad memories that rose up like dragons from . . .

This darkness.

But she kissed him back anyway. Because she had to try. At least try.

She had to begin again. Somewhere.

Her hands went from his chest, moved up around his shoulders to lock behind his neck, and he pulled her closer as the kiss lengthened and deepened. Tasting each other. His body was against her, full length, one leg sliding between her legs . . .

Nattie my love . . .

. . . and she felt his hands pushing up her long-handle top . . .

Forever, Nattie . . .

. . . and onto her breasts. Big hands . . .

"No," she whispered.

Saw his grin as he raised his big fist.

"No." She began to pull away.

Touching her . . .

"No! Let go of me!"

Her own hands were fists now, and she swung them wildly. Hit him on the shoulder, then somewhere in the face.

"Nattie? What the hell . . ."

Saw the big college ring, dripping blood.

"No!"

"Nattie . . ."

He's going to kill me this time.

". . . what's wrong?"

And then she was away from him, kicking out with both feet, hitting him with both fists. Pulling down her shirt top as she scrambled out of the bed . . .

And onto the ice-cold floor.

"Ogod." Nattie raised a trembling hand to her face. Felt the tears there. "Oh, sweet God . . ."

There was the sulphur odor of a match, and she saw the candle's glow turn the room to twilight. And she saw

238

Ben McKee, sitting up in the bed and staring at her. His eyes were wide, and his forehead was bleeding again.

"Jesus Christ, Nattie," he said. "What's going on?"

"I . . ." She wanted to answer, but she couldn't. Couldn't get the words past the aching lump in her throat. Because . . .

He's not Rick.

"Listen." Ben wiped a trickle of blood with his sleeve. "Listen, I'm sorry, Nattie. I guess I misunderstood what was happening here. I'm sorry if I scared you."

"No, you don't . . ."

Understand.

"It won't happen again, okay? Look, Nattie, I owe you my life, ten times over. I know that. If it wasn't for you, I'd be dead. And if it wasn't for me, you'd be up there in your cabin right now, warm and safe and going on with your life . . ."

"Ben, you don't . . ."

"I know I mouth off a lot, but I also know what I owe you. And I would never do anything . . . I just misunderstood."

She felt the tears, down onto her mouth. Onto that small scar below her lip. . . .

He's not Rick.

"Come on, get back into bed. It's freezing in this room, for God's sake."

She felt herself shivering, gooseflesh along her ribs. She climbed back into the bed.

Ben started to pinch out the candle flame, then appeared to change his mind. "Good night, Nattie," he said.

How did he know . . . ?

He turned on his side, away from her. And after a while, Nattie heard his breathing deepen into sleep.

She lay there in the dim light, and she listened to the storm batter the outside walls of the cabin; but the hard knot of tension inside her refused to ease. Her mind began to replay the events of this long, incredibly brutal day. She thought about her own cabin, gone now. About

239

Jack . . . sweet little Jackie, who'd loved her more than his own life. Gone from her, and buried beneath the snow up there on the mountain.

About George Van Zandt, who'd loved her, too, even though she'd never been able to return his feelings. But he'd held her the best he could, against the dark night and her fears, and he'd very nearly died for it.

Where was George now? Fort Lauderdale, the last she heard. As far away from Rick . . . and from her, as he could get.

Gone from her, too.

The wind screamed at her from outside, and it was the sound of emptiness. Of loss . . .

Of loneliness. A life alone. Always afraid, and always fighting her solitary war against that fear. Conquering it in small, hesitant steps. Alone.

You fall down, pick yourself up, Nattie. You get knocked down, pick yourself up again.

And go on. Alone.

Ben's breathing was even and slow, there on the far side of the bed. It was a warm sound. It drew her. . . .

This man's not Rick, and he's not George either. Who he is exactly isn't clear . . .

But he left the candle burning, didn't he? He didn't leave her alone in the dark.

His shoulder was warm when she touched it.

"Huh . . . ?" He jerked awake reflexively. "Nattie? What is it? Are they . . . ?"

"No," she said. "They're not. Are you awake now?"

"Yeah. Are you . . . okay?"

"No," she answered. "I'm not. But I'm going to be, and you can help me. I want . . . I need to tell you a story."

She awoke in the dim grayness before dawn, her eyes swollen and grainy, and the candle burned down to a waxy stub. Outside, the wind seemed to have weakened a little.

Ben McKee lay on his back. His arm, which had been around her the last she remembered, was across the pillow.

She'd talked and talked, until her throat was sore and her voice hoarse. All the things . . . *everything* she'd never said out loud. About Rick and George, even about her mother. And her father.

She'd told it all to this . . . stranger. This man who'd held her and listened . . .

. . . and told her nothing in return. But, oddly enough, that was okay. Because what she'd needed was someone to listen.

She slid over next to him and studied him in the faint beginnings of morning. Square-jawed, not quite handsome . . .

He's not Rick.

. . . but close enough. She looked at the bruises on his forehead and cheekbone, the scabbed-over cuts near one eye.

And then he opened that eye. Both of them. Blue eyes. . . .

She leaned down and kissed him. Did a very thorough job of it, in fact. And felt something dark . . .

Black.

. . . and heavy fly away from her.

Like an epiphany, of sorts. The final realization that what had once happened to her had happened, and it was not going to change no matter where she hid. But she could go on anyway, maybe with this man, maybe without him, but she could go on.

And would.

"About that knife . . ." he said.

"Gone," she replied. "You could search me."

"I could, huh?"

"I insist." She kissed him again. "You remember what you asked me about my birthmark?"

"Right next to your Born To Raise Hell tattoo, I believe."

"That's the one. You want to see it again?"

241

"Oh, yeah."

And she pulled him up onto her, both of them shedding clothes as they went, her hands as busy as his, and thought to herself that maybe she'd never really given it a fair chance.

All this romance novel bullshit.

Thursday Morning

BLACK ICE

Betrayal's touch is colder than ice
—Benjamin Howard

Chapter Seventeen

At six A.M., the Winter Storm Warning for southwestern Colorado was downgraded to a Blowing and Drifting Snow Advisory, put into effect because of gale-force winds still riding the backside of the departing low pressure area. Extremely poor visibility due to ground blizzards was expected in the early morning, with skies beginning to clear toward noon.

At the lower elevations, county plows finally began to show some progress on the roads, and people started digging themselves out of snow-buried houses and driveways. This dangerous combination of exertion and a continuing below zero windchill factor created the potential for heart attack among sedentary people suddenly pushing themselves too hard.

After eighteen hours, Public Service of Colorado came back on line at seven-thirty, returning electrical power to the region. And, as communications recommenced, various search-and-rescue operations moved into high gear. There were at least a half-dozen situations—ranging from missing motorists to an ELT crash beacon—to be investigated, and it was estimated the Flight For Life helicopters would be in the air before noon.

If the wind would allow it.

* * *

. . . they each raise an arm, arced outward and oddly double-jointed at the elbow. The index finger is extended, the other fingers hanging below like pale gray lace . . .

Swim out with me, Gramp . . .

. . . and the finger points toward the ocean. Toward the child who's disappearing beneath the water . . .

Gramp! Help me!

. . . the water that's a boiling gray-white, and so cold . . .

"Genie!" Eugene Cleese bolted upright, his heart slamming against his breastbone. "Ge . . ."

Faint light was all around him, and the sound of the wind. A sharp pain knifed into his back, down near his hips.

"Gene?" Milton Wallace was looking at him from a spot near the opposite wall. "You okay, man?"

Wallace and Arturo Garza were squatted by a fire, rekindled with scrap lumber on top of the ashes from the night before. Wallace was stirring freeze-dried packets of oatmeal and soup in flame-retardant pouches of boiling water.

Cleese felt a blush burn along his cheekbones, but he managed a smile. "I'm fine, Milt. Thanks." He made an elaborate stretching motion, arms over his head. "How long have you two been up?"

They glanced at each other. "Just a few minutes," answered Garza. "Thought we'd let you sleep 'til the grub was on."

Because you're old. Cleese heard words that were unsaid. *Because you're a tired old man, and you need your rest.*

Cleese was always the first up in the morning, the one to wake the others. *Always.*

"Bad dream?" asked Wallace. Despite his frequent grumpiness, he was the mother hen of the group.

"I don't remember," lied Cleese. He glanced at his watch and saw it was past six. "How's the weather?"

"Getting better." All the cooking gear was made to be collapsible, and Garza poured hot water into his fold-out plastic cup, then fed in dehydrated soup mix. "The wind's still howling like a sonofabitch, but it's nearly stopped snowing."

"Looks like we may have a little visibility for a change," added Wallace.

And so will they, thought Cleese. If they found the 'copter. If they found that thirty-caliber Mauser with its calibrated scope in the 'copter.

If they're still alive.

He got up from where he'd been lying in a scooped-out hollow by the rock wall, and the pain in his lower back radiated down his left leg. A burning ache that centered in the hip. He walked toward the fire and concentrated on not limping.

That's what a full day in a blizzard will do for you. Snowshoeing through deep drifts, rappeling a thousand feet down a cliff, swimming beneath icy water, then sleeping on rock-hard ground in temperatures just a little above zero.

That's what it'll do for you . . . when you're sixty-one years old. Sixty-two, come April.

"You should've gotten me up." Cleese made sure he said it mildly. "One way or another, this is going to be a long day."

Wallace looked embarrassed. "I was just about to," he replied, and focused intently on his packet of oatmeal.

Cleese took the cup of soup Garza offered. "It'll be full light out there before long," he said, and sipped the hot mixture. Felt its warmth go all the way down. "We have to get moving. When this storm finally clears, there'll be people around. We need to be done and out of here."

"What about Riley?" asked Garza.

No traces. When possible, you leave no traces. Certainly not an unidentified body—neither Riley nor any of them carried I.D.—in a place where it wasn't supposed to be. But . . .

"We'll have to come back for him," answered Cleese. "If we find those two like I think we will, which is frozen dead down the canyon a mile or two, then we'll have plenty of time to come back here and take care of Liam."

In an unmarked grave, somewhere back in the mine—since outside in the snow was out of the question—where summer rockhounds and spelunkers wouldn't find him. Liam Riley would like that. A Boston shanty-Irish ghost for this old Colorado mine.

Of course, there was also the helicopter. . . .

Cleese was feeling better as the hot soup hit bottom. He wanted to walk around some, flex that hip and leg, but he wasn't going to do it with Wallace and Garza watching him. He'd gone on a number of jobs with both of them over the years, and he was pretty sure they'd never thought of him as capable of ageing.

So he winked reassuringly at Wallace, and the big man grinned out of a face that was a wreck. His broad nose was swollen even wider, and those buckshot pimples all across his balding forehead were beginning to look infected.

Like that dog bite on Artie Garza's wrist.

Not a good trip so far. But it was the bottom line where that would be decided.

Garza, always a quick eater, dipped his cup in the hot water, then folded it into a flat disc. "Rockin' on ready, bro," he said, and put the cup in his pocket. "Let's do it."

"You ready, Gene?" Wallace rose more slowly to his full six-four. He was studying Cleese without appearing to.

"As I'll ever be." Cleese smiled, and finished his oatmeal. "I think we should head for the helicopter first. If they did stumble onto it, we could have some new problems to deal with. If not, I still need to get my snowshoes."

"That's some deep snow out there." Wallace nodded.

"That's why you get to break trail for the rest of us, *mojado grande,*" said Garza to Wallace. "That wide-ride ass of yours clears a road like a snowplow."

"Hey, snowplow this, Artie," growled Wallace, and grabbed his crotch. Cleese was glad to see the big man break into a real grin for a change.

And Wallace's spirits would be even better by the time they reached the helicopter because, snowshoes or not, Cleese intended to lead the way. He'd be the one to break the trail, and if those bodies were out there, he'd be the first upon them. Like always. Because that was what the leader was supposed to do, whether it was a southeast Asian jungle or some high-rent California beach house. Or these cold, gray-white mountains.

And because he was Eugene Cleese.

Nattie couldn't get the can opener to work.

"Come on, dammit," she muttered, and listened for a moment to the wind howling past the corners of the cabin. It made for a creepy kind of emptiness, alone down here on the lower floor, and she'd been spooked a couple of times already by faint noises from the direction of the pantry.

It's just the wind, Nattie, she reminded herself. Unless Cleese and his pals have mastered a new disguise as sardines and Spam.

Of course, she was already jumpy, anyway. Which was probably the reason . . .

The reason the can opener wouldn't work. It kept slipping off the edge, gouging holes in the top of the Dinty Moore can instead of turning. And the reason it kept slipping off the edge was because Nattie's hands were trembling. And not from the cold.

"Dammit to hell," she decided.

And glanced at the staircase, where Ben McKee was likely to be descending any minute now.

She'd been like that ever since she awoke the second time, aching and stiff in every muscle, to locate her scattered underwear and sneak out of bed. Shaking, despite her body's overnight return to normal (at least) temperature, her stomach doing flip-flops.

She'd crept into the bathroom and locked the door . . .

If an early-morning pee came upon him, tough luck.

. . . and then stood there in front of the small mirror above the lavatory, watching her faint silhouette take on shape as the light brightened outside the tiny shuttered window.

Rick had always loved mirrors, whereas—except for the one from her father—Nattie could take or leave them. But this was one morning when she was definitely paying attention.

She'd tried for a while with her hair, but it was a lost cause, lying flat against her head . . .

You'd look sharper, Nattie my love, with a shoulder-length cut and a perm.

. . . from the cap and the climbing helmet, and from a day of nonstop wetness. After a while she'd given up, and put it into a single braid.

Then she'd looked in the drawers around the lavatory, because you never know . . .

And found one rusty razor blade, some Chap-Stik, and a dried-up roll-on deodorant bar.

You were expecting maybe skin care products from Oil of Olay?

Hey, screw this, she'd decided at that point. What the hell are you doing, anyway? Within an hour—or considerably less, if you're smart—you're going to be back out in the weather, slogging down the canyon toward the lake. With Cleese and his pals in hot pursuit, more likely than not.

This is not the time to worry about moisturizers.

So she'd climbed into that oversized hunter's garb again, made a rude gesture at herself in the mirror, and quietly unlocked the bathroom door. She then slipped along the hall past the bedroom where Ben McKee lay asleep, and tiptoed down the stairs.

Still quivering, inside and out, which had led to the hatchet job she was currently doing on the can of stew.

If this is what sex does for you, she thought, trying a different angle on the can opener, maybe I was better off living like Harriet the Hermit and studying depth hoar.

Spelled h-o-a-r.

Except that it wasn't the sex. Rick had been very good in bed—Nattie was sure he kept a log of performance ratings somewhere, and graded himself on a scale of probably nine to ten after each putz and George Van Zandt had at least been enthusiastic—for someone looking over his shoulder the whole time—but neither of them had *ever* left her feeling . . . exactly like this.

The last time she'd felt even remotely like this had been the first time. High school, speaking of looking over one's shoulder, and that boy she was going to love forever and have six kids with and write beautiful poetry while he tossed no-hitters for the Cubs.

That was a minor problem. She didn't especially want to move to Chicago.

What was his name? Billy Weatherby, from over in Durango, and her mother didn't like him much, which was probably the main reason—deep down—that Nattie did.

And in those days—the days after Warren Kemper failed to return from that backpacking trip up to Quartz Lake, and the county search-and-rescue team found him slumped over his fly rod at the edge of the water with a sixteen-inch cut-throat trout still on his line—in those days, JoAnne Kemper's word was the law around their house. It was a relationship they'd rehearsed dutifully all Nattie's life, even with the buffer provided by her father. And now, with him gone . . .

There's my way, little girl, and there's the highway.

Which was the end of Billy Weatherby. To the best of Nattie's knowledge, he'd never made it to the Cubs.

Good ol' JoAnne, one grand judge of character. Rick Macon was living proof of that. Even when she saw her daughter in that Denver hospital . . .

Who did this to you? Who really did it to you? It was George Van Zandt, wasn't it? Why are you lying . . . ?

. . . a silent wreck of bandages and bruises and pain, JoAnne had still refused to blame her son-in-law. To look past that handsome face of his.

Rick just wanted to talk to you once more, before those

251

divorce papers were final. That's all. How could you blame something like this on him?

There was nothing more to say after that. The gulf between their separate realities was simply too wide.

Nattie wondered what JoAnne would think of Ben McKee. It might make a useful reverse barometer. If good ol' Joanne hated him, that was a point in his favor.

Two points, after last night . . .

But if it wasn't the sex, what was it? There was no way she really knew this guy. You only knew someone to the extent he wanted you to know him, and in that area Ben McKee was the New World's answer to the Sphinx. That story about the IRS might be true—*might* be—as far as it went, but there was a lot more he wasn't telling.

Like, for instance, who's Shelley?

The best course of action—also the safest—was obvious. Eat some food, a lot of it because this was likely to be a very hard day. Get on every stitch of clothing she could wear and still waddle, because that windchill out there was still well below zero. Pack up those guns, put on the snowshoes, and run like hell for the comm center—Marvin or no Marvin. Get on the radio and call for help, then set up that place like a fort to hold off those bastards until the cavalry arrived.

Then tell Ben McKee . . . *"Adios,* and good luck in New York. Send me some goat-cheese pizza from Elaine's . . ."

And forget about last night. Because God knows I already have.

That was the plan.

And there was no more time to waste hanging around here. This cabin had saved their lives last night, without any question of a doubt, but they couldn't stay much longer. Cleese and his pals were probably early risers.

Nattie finally got a bite with the can opener, though it was rough going on a surface that resembled a war zone . . .

When she heard that noise again.

It wasn't her imagination this time, and it wasn't just

the wind. It was a faint . . . *skittering* kind of sound, coming from over by the pantry.

Nattie put the can of half-opened stew on the cabinet and slowly turned in the direction of the pantry. She was barely aware that she'd picked up the same bread knife she'd used the night before to slice the Spam.

Come on, Nattie. Get real here. Don't go building a simple case of post-coital jitters into something. . . .

She heard it again.

Nattie's first impulse—a very powerful impulse—was to make tracks up the stairs. Wake up Ben McKee . . .

And say what? That she'd heard a noise? Maybe she could bat her eyelashes and swoon at that point while she was at it. Oh, protect me, you big strong man.

Right.

Besides, she wasn't especially eager to see Ben this morning anyway. Nervous as hell about it, in fact. And the last thing she needed, the *very* last thing, was to start it off with a show of weakness. Running up there like some frightened ninny. . . .

Nattie took a firmer grip on the bread knife and walked over to the pantry. She heard the wind, still wailing outside the cabin walls. She heard the creak of floorboards beneath the linoleum floor. She heard—felt?—the sound of her own heartbeat in her ears . . .

And she heard that other noise, too. Clearer now, down low . . .

At her feet. The sound wasn't coming from the pantry at all. It was coming from the trapdoor beneath her feet. It was coming from the crawl space.

Nattie stopped dead still. Her grip on the knife was so tight her fingers were starting to ache.

Nearly all these mountain cabins had crawl spaces beneath them. The climate was much too cold for a concrete slab, so there was an open area under the floorboards of the building. Usually the owner would excavate it out as a buffer against the expansion and contraction of the wooden foundation. Also for a storage space, like a primitive cellar, if it wasn't too wet. And, somewhere inside each cabin, there would be a trapdoor like this one for easier winter access, when the snow was too deep to get in from outside.

But there was something in *this* crawl space. Something moving around.

Reality check, Nattie. She shook her head. There's nothing down there. The snow outside is five feet deep, which means this trapdoor is the only way to get under the cabin . . .

Unless something—or someone—dug their way in.

Where was Cleese about now? And his goons. Maybe they were *very* early risers.

And maybe they'd already visited the wrecked helicopter, and knew about the missing guns. The rifle, and that Ithaca ten-gauge shotgun, which would be devastating in close quarters like this.

A good reason to consider entrance by stealth.

Nattie muttered an exasperated curse under her breath. This entire line of thought was getting ridiculous, taking on a life of its own. But ridiculous or not, she went over to the couch for the shotgun. Slipped the bread knife into her front jacket pocket.

She returned to the pantry, stepping as softly as her heavy Sorels would allow; then she bent down and silently unbolted the trapdoor. Took a deep breath, cradled the Ithaca between her right elbow and rib cage—finger tension on the front trigger—and lifted up the trapdoor.

And stared down into darkness. A square hole leading into blackness that reminded her of the mine. And the musky, nauseating odor of decay.

Decayed flesh. There was something dead in the crawl space.

And that sound again. Skittering, quiet, the *sneaky* sort of sound that someone makes when they're trying to hide.

Hey, drop down on your knees, Nattie my love. Lean way over and stick your head into this hole. Take a look around . . .

Nattie lit one of the candles from the cabinet. When she lowered her arm partially into the opening, she saw a stepladder just below, standing on an uneven surface of half-frozen mud. She leaned forward, watched the cone of light expand.

"Good morning."

"Jesus Christ!" Nattie spun away from the crawl space entrance, dragging the heavy shotgun with her, swinging its barrel around . . .

Toward Ben McKee, who was hobbling down the stairs behind her, dressed in the hunter's garb he'd found the night before. The warmth and color had returned to his bruised face, but he wasn't getting around any better than she was.

He looked at her, and at the gun. He raised his hands over his head.

"I wasn't *that* bad, was I?" he asked.

Nattie lowered the shotgun, a blush burning her face. She stepped sideways out of the pantry and nodded toward the raised trapdoor.

"There's some . . . something in the crawl space," she said. No point in trying to be quiet about it now.

Ben walked over next to her and looked down into the opening for a moment.

"What kind of something?" he asked. "Big? Little? Furry . . . ?"

"How the hell would I know?" Nattie couldn't meet his eyes, which was getting her more angry than embarrassed. "I heard a noise down there; then I smelled . . ."

"Tell me something." Ben took the candle and leaned down, just as Nattie heard that same skittering kind of sound. "What exactly does a porcupine look like?"

"A porc—" Nattie pushed him aside.

"Kind of roly-poly and black? Or maybe gray? Hair sticking up like Don King?"

She leaned down into the hole just in time to see a low, rounded silhouette waddling away from her into the darkness.

"Maybe it wasn't a porcupine," Ben went on. "Maybe

it was a beaver with a bad haircut. One of the things I can't get used to about these damned mountains, you've got all the wrong kinds of livestock running around. Now, cats and dogs are okay. Canaries, even . . ."

"It was a porcupine, all right." Nattie rose to her feet. "Which explains the smell. They're like most other rodents; they find a place to hole-up for the winter, but they don't actually hibernate. One of them died down there, smells like. The Thomas brothers aren't going to be happy about that."

"For a queen of the wilderness, you were pretty jumpy when I came downstairs." Ben knelt to lower the trapdoor. "What'd you think, you had Cleese in the cellar?"

"Funny man." Nattie went back to the battered can of stew on the cabinet.

"Or maybe you were planning all along to light up ol' Porky . . ."

Ben straightened with a groan.

". . . with a load of buckshot. Damn, my legs are sore. In fact, I'm sore all over. How about you?"

"Nah," Nattie lied. "Try a few deep knee bends."

He laughed, a little nervously, she thought, and came over to the cabinet.

"So," he said, standing close behind her. "Once again, good morning."

Get things straight, right from the get-go, Nattie decided. Make him understand that what happened last night was . . . just the circumstances. A mixture of all the fear of that terrible day followed by the relief and euphoria of finding shelter and just plain being alive. Nothing more than that. Nothing that was ever going to happen again.

"Listen, bud." She turned toward him. "We need to . . ."

"Name's not bud," he said, and kissed her. Slid an arm around her waist, pulled her up against him, and kissed her for a long time. Pretty well, too. "Name's Ben."

He let her go, just a little, and glanced at the can of stew she'd dropped on the cabinet.

"Busy?" he asked.

There's no time for this . . .

"Nothing that can't wait," she replied, and began un-buttoning his shirt.

"Remember," said Cleese, "they have those guns. The rifle and the shotgun. Maybe one of the pistols from the plane, too."

"How do you want to play it?" asked Wallace.

Cleese studied the cabin through a ground blizzard whipped up by the wind. The visibility was a bit better than yesterday, when everything was a series of snow-blurred shadows, but it wasn't going to clear completely until the wind died.

"Milt, why don't you get onto the porch," he replied. "Next to the door. Artie, I think you can cover those upper windows from here. I'm going to follow the tracks around back."

Wallace pulled back the sleeve of his snowsuit to check his watch. "Five minutes okay?" he asked.

"Better make it ten," said Cleese. "Just to be certain. Slow and steady's the key. They're not going anywhere."

He moved sideways toward another stand of trees, keeping low, down in the heart of the ground blizzard, watching the shuttered windows of the cabin.

He was feeling much better now, joints warmed up by that long slog down from the mine to the wrecked heli-copter, and then to here, switching out on the two pairs of snowshoes. Any doubts by Wallace and Garza were probably put to rest.

They'd have to do something about that 'copter before they left. It was a major loose end. But that package of C-4 could be used to take care of things. The scattered rubble, gutted by fire just like the Kemper cabin, would get plenty of tongues wagging, but would prove nothing. Especially if there were no bodies . . .

Which was how they'd have to play it, since Natalie Kemper and Ben McKee apparently weren't going to cooperate by lying down somewhere and freezing to death.

Cleese crept in close to the cabin wall, into the wallowed-out tracks already there. He crouched beneath each window as he passed it, shutters or not, and made very certain at each corner. Wallace should be nearly onto the porch by now.

He looked around the corner, at the back of the cabin, where . . .

Where the tracks led away.

Cleese felt his mouth drop open. "Well, well," he whispered.

At the back wall, directly below a downstairs window, the track wallow veered off. Followed a straight line through the snow . . .

Toward a second cabin that was barely visible back in some trees, maybe two hundred feet away.

Two cabins.

Cleese looked at the window, and at the tracks beneath it. He wondered what were the chances those two had spent the night in separate cabins. Jump one of them, you alert the other.

It was an interesting idea, but he doubted it. Who volunteers to be the sacrificial lamb . . .

Or Judas Goat. Tethered as a trap.

. . . in the first cabin? In there alone, isolated, probably with the shotgun. While the other watches through that rifle scope from the second cabin.

Cleese glanced that way. He crouched lower into the windblown snow.

It had possibilities, but he still doubted it. Those two had several chances to split up inside the mine, try something similar to this, but they didn't. They stayed close to each other. It was a pattern.

Another . . . six minutes, and Wallace would be going in the front. If Cleese was right, the big man would find the place empty. But they couldn't take the chance. Better let him go ahead.

Cleese moved into the new set of tracks, still crouched

low. He crossed a small open area, his muscles tensed for an instantaneous dive into the snow; then he entered the trees. When he reached the second cabin, he saw that once again the tracks went around to the back. He followed them to a window . . .

With a broken lock on the outside shutter.

Cleese raised a gloved hand and carefully pulled one side of the shutter toward him. He saw the window had a broken pane, with a red-striped towel stuffed into it. He raised on tiptoe and looked inside.

It was dark in there, the twilight color of a room with no lights on. He could see a kitchen area off to his left, some kind of can lying on its side on a cabinet. A staircase nearby, and then some furniture, farther to the right, grouped around a rock fireplace.

Movement over there, just shadows . . .

Somebody was on the couch.

Cleese smiled, and felt ice crackle in his mustache. Granted he wasn't as young as he once had been, but he still recognized that particular kind of movement.

Which meant that what he was about to do might not qualify as good sportsmanship.

Ah, well . . .

He slowly pulled the towel out of the broken windowpane, then reached up through the hole to turn the latch. He slipped the Glock from his jacket and snapped back the slide to chamber a round before he slid the window open.

This next part was going to require some finesse, but the fact that the back of the couch was between him and those two would help. Also, from what he could see, they weren't likely to be very alert.

Cleese boosted himself up into the windowsill. When he swung one leg through, he felt a sharp stab of pain in his lower back.

It slowed him, just by a fraction.

* * *

Nattie felt a rush of cold air, goose-pimpling the sensitive layer of bare skin where Ben was pushing down her underwear. His hand stopped.

"Ben?" she whispered, just as he moved off her. Her senses, overheated and turned inward by the stimulation of his touch, came back to her in an icy rush.

Jesus. The window . . .

Then Ben was up on one knee, the rifle pointed past the top of the couch.

"Come on in," he said. "And close the window."

Nattie pulled up her underwear in a frenzy of embarrassment—completely out of place, all things considered, but she couldn't help it—and fastened her baggy camouflage pants.

She looked over the back of the couch and saw a man halfway in the window.

"And drop that gun while you're at it," added Ben.

The man bent forward slowly to lay a square-shaped pistol on the floor next to his foot. Then he brought in his other leg and reached for the window.

"The shutter first." Ben kept the rifle pointed, and Nattie could see how steady the barrel was. "Then the window. Just like you found it."

The man followed orders. He even stuffed the towel back into the broken pane.

"You might zip your pants, Ben," he said, and pulled off his ski cap.

It was Cleese. Nattie recognized the voice from outside her cabin the day before. This was her first look at him up close.

He looked like somebody's grandfather, or maybe that western actor—she couldn't recall the name—with a long, lean face and a neatly trimmed gray mustache. His eyes were brown and twinkly, though they appeared a bit tired.

He was about Ben's height, with a powerful frame inside the orange snowsuit, and the kind of square-shouldered military posture Nattie already knew to expect. He looked extremely fit.

He smiled at her. "Ms. Kemper," he said. "We meet at last."

And it was the oddest thing, she wanted to return his smile. Almost did, it was so warm and . . . what? Comforting?

This man who'd spent the last twenty-plus hours trying to kill her. Who'd killed Jack. . . .

"Kick your gun over this way," said Ben. "Very carefully. And sit in that chair."

"Be happy to." Cleese nudged the weapon forward with his foot, then sat on the chair arm. "When you get to be my age, you never pass up an invitation to take a load off."

And he winked at Nattie.

"Where are your pals?" asked Ben.

"I imagine they're around." Cleese was still looking at Nattie. Staring at her, in fact, with an odd, unreadable expression on his face. "Somewhere or other."

Ben leaned down carefully to pick up the pistol near his feet. He shifted it to his right hand, then gave Nattie the rifle.

"Be careful, Ben. That has a round already chambered." Cleese folded his arms across his chest and leaned back slightly. "Notice how light it feels? Most of the parts are made of plastic."

"He's stalling," said Nattie. " 'Til the others get here."

Cleese smiled at her. "I've been wanting to compliment you, Natalie. May I call you Natalie?"

She almost nodded.

"You're very resourceful. Very innovative. The way you got our Ben here down that cliff . . ."

"I asked you a question, Cleese." Ben pointed the pistol at the older man. "Where are the others?"

". . . and then through the mine. Remarkable, really."

Thank you, she nearly said. She realized he was addressing all his comments toward her. Ignoring Ben McKee as though he wasn't even in the room. Smiling at her. . . .

Nattie shook her head to clear it.

"Where are your men?" she asked.

"We split up at the other cabin," he replied promptly. "That wasn't bad, by the way. Your idea?"

"Nattie, take a look . . ."

"I'm curious about something, Natalie." Cleese studied her. "What has Ben told you? About why I'm here?"

"Shut up, Cleese," snapped Ben. "Dammit, Nattie, we don't have time for this."

"Has he told you the truth, Natalie? Frequently he doesn't."

The words stopped Nattie halfway to the window. It's a ploy, she thought. It's like that sweet smile on that Grampaw Walton face, and the flattering way he looks you right in the eye as though your thoughts and opinions are so important . . .

A ploy, stalling until the others arrive.

But what he said. About the truth. . . .

"He told me how you sabotaged that plane," she heard herself saying. "To shut him up before he could tell the IRS about . . . Machtel, or whatever that name was."

"He said that?" Cleese did a mock double-take at Ben. "And how did he know about Machtel?"

"Nattie!"

"Well . . ." She looked over at Ben. Saw his eyes, and felt a sudden surge of doubt. "His job. He accidentally found those computer records . . ."

Her voice faded out, lost in the sound of the wind outside the cabin. Because Cleese was laughing.

"I'm sorry, Natalie." Cleese glanced in Ben's direction and shook his head good-naturedly. "I don't mean to be rude, but . . . he *accidentally* found those records? And you believed that?"

Nattie felt her insides contract, almost painfully, but she snapped back at the older man anyway. "I sure as hell don't believe you. You're the one cut my rope on the cliff."

"I don't blame you." Cleese smiled. "I wouldn't believe me, in your place. But I wouldn't believe him, either. He didn't find those computer records, Natalie. They

262

were *his* records to begin with. Moving that money around, making all those wire transfers to offshore accounts . . . why, that's our Ben's job at Machtel. Or it was, until he ran off with the access codes. And too bad, because he was very good at his work. A real computer whiz."

Cleese looked directly at Ben for the first time.

"The IRS." He shook his head. "Taliferro and Landry? Ben, Ben." He chuckled. "Did you tell Natalie about those access codes? That's *our* money you're trying to steal, Ben. Did you think we'd just let you go? You and Shelley?"

"Goddamn you!" Ben raised the pistol. "You sonofabitch!"

"Ben! Don't . . ."

Cleese just smiled; then he looked at Nattie. "You shouldn't feel too bad, Natalie," he said, and the smile faded. "Our Ben's very skilled at what he does. He uses women, you see. Flashes those blue eyes and that smile, and uses them. Like you, and Shelley. Did he tell you about Shelley?"

"Nattie, listen to me." Ben turned toward her. "Shelley . . ."

And, at that moment, Cleese's arms came unfolded in a blinding orange blur of motion as he leaped sideways from the chair. Nattie saw the flash of reflected silver in the dim room . . .

Knife, she thought.

. . . just as she heard the high-pitched boom of the pistol, deafening her with its sound.

And she saw Cleese—sudden surprise on that grandfather face—slammed backward by the impact of one bullet, and then another. Then another, hit dead-center, smashing into the window.

Glass shattered, exploded outward with the force of Cleese's body. The old man was there—shock on his face—then he was gone in a whirling orange kaleidoscope, prismed by the flying glass and the blowing snow behind him.

Gone, out the window.

"Sonofabitch . . ." whispered Ben, and looked at the knife imbedded in the couch next to him.

"Get down!" Nattie pulled on his arm. "The others, they're out there somewhere."

She grabbed the sawed-off shotgun from a nearby chair and looked around the couch at what remained of the window. A ripped-out hole in the wall, bits of pane and broken glass jiggling in the wind as snow blew into the cabin.

"Nattie . . ."

She pushed his hand away. *Liar.* The word kept echoing inside her head. *Liar, liar, liar . . .*

"We have to get out of here," she said aloud.

"There's no time if Cleese's men are out there. At least we have cover in here . . ."

"For how long? 'Til they torch this place, too?" She shoved the Mauser at him, then turned toward the front door. It was still closed and locked.

For the moment, at least.

Chapter Eighteen

Milton Wallace and Arturo Garza flanked the second cabin, the place where the gunshots came from. They moved in quickly and quietly, keeping the windblown snow behind them. At their backs rather than in their eyes.

Wallace saw the door standing open at the front of the building, and he leaped onto the porch, agile for such a large man. He crouched beside the door, then lunged into the cabin, the HK held low and out in front of him.

The room was empty.

And ice-cold, with a broken window at the back. Even the gusting wind hadn't completely killed the odor of cordite in the air.

Wallace moved sideways, watching the staircase to his right. Over to the window, where he looked out . . .

At the body, lying there in the snow.

There was a blur of movement in the trees to his left, and he swung his machine pistol that way. It was Garza, rounding the corner of the building.

"*Mira,*" murmured Garza, looking down at Cleese. "*La bala ledio en el vientre . . .*"

Then Cleese moved.

"I think it was the chest, Artie," he said.

Cleese's face was as pale as the snow, and he crawled up onto one knee while Garza ran forward to help him. Wallace stood and stared; then a grin crossed his battered face.

"Good ol' Kevlar," he said.

"The miracle fiber." Cleese nodded, then bent forward as a spasm of coughing shook his body. "Remind me—" he cleared his throat and spat into the snow—"to write a nice letter to Du Pont. They advertise this particular model as tactical armor, but I'm still glad it wasn't that rifle."

"You're gonna have some hellacious bruises, *hermano.*" Garza looked at the holes torn through the front of Cleese's snowsuit. "Not to mention a draft. What happened in there?"

"Tell you about it later." Cleese rose to his feet and wiped his mouth. "They're gone, I guess."

Wallace nodded. "Looks like it. The front door was standing wide open . . ."

"It was closed earlier," said Cleese.

". . . but I'll take a quick look-see anyway. Come on in and cover me, Artie."

"Go ahead," agreed Cleese. "I'll check around the outside for tracks. My guess is they're already out of there and running for the lake."

"I'll make it fast," replied Wallace. "Might find you some snowshoes, Gene."

"That'd be nice." Cleese spat into the snow again, then checked to be sure it was clear of blood. "So would a gun. I'm afraid they have mine now."

Garza reached into the pocket of his snowsuit and came out with a black SIG P228 automatic with a rubberized grip.

"Don't never travel with just one pistola, bro." He popped the clip and then passed it over. "I learned that in the barrio. 'Cause you never know, *verdad?*"

Cleese made a complete, careful circuit of the building, but the only new tracks he found were his own, and the wallowed-out, indistinguishable trail Wallace and Garza had made running from the first cabin.

The first cabin . . .

Cleese decided to examine the tracks more closely,

because that wasn't such a bad idea, really. Just the kind of plan Natalie Kemper might come up with.

Expect the unexpected, where she was concerned.

He pictured her again, in that moment when she looked at him over the back of the couch. Green eyes wide. . . .

He glanced up, momentarily disoriented, as Wallace and Garza came out onto the front porch.

"Find anything?" he asked.

Garza shook his head. "Damn place is empty as a redneck's noggin, Gene. We checked all the rooms, looks like our little *periquitos* shared a bed last night . . ."

"Closets, cabinets, the crawl space," continued Wallace. "I even looked up the chim—"

"Crawl space?" said Cleese.

"There's a trapdoor in the kitchen," replied Wallace. "But it's a wash, except for a really ugly porcupine crawling around down there in the mud. Place stinks like three hogs in a closet."

Cleese looked at the wallowed-out trail leading back to the first cabin, and slowly nodded his head.

"Come on, then," he said.

"If they'd bolted this . . ." Ben McKee stood on the stepladder and pushed the trapdoor open. "Do you suppose we'd've developed a taste for porcupine burgers after a few weeks?"

"They were in too much of a hurry." Nattie stood just below him. "Now get going. Sooner or later they'll be back."

She glanced at the rounded silhouette that was barely distinguishable waddling along the far foundation wall. Fortunately for everyone, the sharp-quilled little creature'd had plenty of room in the crawl space for a safe retreat.

Ben climbed out onto the kitchen floor, his clothes covered in the pungent, half-frozen mud he'd burrowed beneath. Also his face and hands.

267

He glanced down at the camouflage gear, now more brown than green. "Guess this stuff really does work," he muttered.

Nattie tossed up the weapons and snowshoes, then crawled out beside him, as mud-caked as he was. She pointedly refused the hand he held forward to help her.

Inside she was like iron. Like the icy wind blowing in that broken window.

"Nattie . . ."

"Get moving," she said, and hefted the shotgun. "I'll cover you out the window."

Because they moved cautiously, it took ten minutes for Cleese and his men to break into the other building, which they found empty. When they finally made their way back to the second cabin, they discovered tracks that hadn't been there before. Fresh snowshoe tracks, leading south from the destroyed back window, the sill of which was now coated with a splattered layer of foul-smelling mud.

"¡Chinga!" raged Garza, staring at the tracks that moved away through the trees. *"¡La cabrona bruja! La puta el diablo, usted se va a morir . . ."*

He spun around to glare at Wallace, and the big man just stared back at him.

"Hey, you looked in that crawl-hole, too, pal," he said. "Climbed halfway down the ladder, in fact. Sometimes you gotta take the shit with the gravy."

Cleese quickly suppressed what wanted to become a grin at the sight of the mud-caked window, and agreed with Garza's angry promise regarding Natalie Kemper. For Genie's sake, it had to be that way, though he found himself growing steadily less fond of the idea.

Especially after seeing her up close.

Within minutes, the three men were moving down the narrow canyon, following the tracks in the snow. As they had done coming from the mine, they made quick stops ever so often to change leads and switch off on the two pairs of snowshoes.

And, since the trail was already broken for them, wallowed wide in the drifts beneath the trees, they made good time.

Out in the open, the wind was like a razor's edge, cutting through even the heavy insulated clothing Nattie and Bon had found in the cabin. The mud stiffened and froze on the cloth, then broke off in clumps as they pushed through the deep snow.

But Nattie wasn't cold. Not like the day before. The continuous shuffle-shuffle movement on snowshoes had warmed up her aching muscles considerably, especially hauling the shotgun, which had no shoulder strap.

And, if that wasn't enough, the steady flame of her anger would have done the job anyway.

Liar. Liar-liar. She matched the rhythm in her head to the steady cadence of her snowshoes, and every breath was smooth hot iron in her throat. *Liar-liar. Liar-liar.*

He'd tried to talk to her a couple of times since they fled the cabin, but she wasn't having any. It would just be more of the same. One certainty she knew from bitter experience was that a liar called out would only continue to lie.

He uses women, you see. Flashes those blue eyes . . .

A falling-out among thieves, that's all it was, this whole sordid mess that had entered her life and so thoroughly trashed it. The little thief—and his girlfriend—steal from the big thieves, so the big thieves send their killer after the little thief.

One no better than the other. No wonder he knew so much about the process of money laundering. Kind of like asking Shakespeare about the mechanics of writing a sonnet.

But he'd saved her life, out there on the cliff . . .

Because he needed her. Just protecting his investment.

And last night, in the cabin? When she freaked out on him, there at first, and he was so . . .

Smart. Leaving the candle lit. And then later. . . .

He played that one just right, didn't he?

Ben's very skilled at what he does . . .

Like lying. And stealing, too. A liar and a thief, headed out of the country, probably, with the key to a sizeable chunk of Machtel's dirty money. Until things went wrong, and he landed in her lap, and she took him in.

Always taking in strays, Nattie my love.

And always getting fooled by the face you think you see. Ben McKee had shown her one face, but not his real one. Not his real face, invisible as the black ice on the walls of Empinado Canyon. Black ice that appeared solid-looking and trustworthy, until you touched it . . .

And revealed the face of a stranger.

The snow had nearly stopped falling now, but the wind was the same. Blowing up ground blizzards that blinded her, swirling snow-devils across the open canyon floor.

Nattie looked nervously from side to side. She knew this section of Empinado Canyon, where it widened some and the cliffs changed over to steep slopes.

She noted the lack of freshly piled snow next to the huge, automobile-sized boulders along Walker Creek to their right. No uprooted bushes or trees, no debris of any sort breaking up the smooth layer of white.

Which was *not* a good sign.

Just keep moving, and keep quiet.

Ben glanced back from where he was breaking trail ahead of her. The mud on his face looked like streaks of manic war paint, and there was brown-stained sweat dripping off the end of his nose.

"Not many trees down here," he said, and shifted the Mauser to his other shoulder. The words came out in a series of grunts as he muscled his way through the heavy snow.

"Nope." Nattie stayed two strides behind.

"Why is that?"

"You don't want to know," she replied. "Believe me."

270

And shut up, she thought.

"Just thinking, is all." He patted the rifle. "If they follow us out into the open . . ."

"Dead-eye Dick. Just think if you had your handy computer. Byte 'em to death, or bankrupt them, at least."

"Nattie . . ."

"Better save your breath, Dick."

He turned, back away from her again, and they settled into the rhythm of the snowshoes. Shuffle-shuffle . . .

Liar-liar.

. . . shuffle-shuffle, moving over closer to the big creek boulders on their right. It was nearly time for them to switch, for Nattie to break trail . . .

When she glanced behind her, and saw the men. Three men, probably no more than a hundred yards back, gradually becoming visible out of the blowing snow. Following in Nattie and Ben's trail, and gaining steadily.

Three men?

No way. It had to be that other guy, the tall one. He didn't die in the mine after all.

Then Nattie saw the dim light reflect off an orange snowsuit.

"Oh, sweet God," she whispered.

"What?" Ben half-turned, and he saw them, too. His eyes widened, oblivious of the stinging pellets of snow.

"Cleese," he said, and that single word was like the sound of an oath. He unslung the rifle, dropped to one knee.

"No!" Nattie grabbed the barrel and pushed it down. "You can't. Not here . . ."

"Why the hell not?" He pulled free, and took aim. "We're out of their range, dammit. I can—"

He never finished the sentence, and Nattie never had the chance to explain. Maybe the pursuing men saw him shoulder the Mauser. Maybe they hoped to panic him into shooting wildly . . .

Whatever, the one in the lead began firing his assault weapon. A high-pitched, chattering sound.

Nattie heard Cleese's voice, carried by the wind. "Artie! Don't . . ."

Then the walls came down.

Rick Macon was out on the comm center's covered front porch, looking across the frozen lake. Visibility had cleared enough to see all the way down to the pump station by the dam.

Macon had slept well, warm and full of food. And now the snow was letting up. This had the makings of an eventful day.

Nattie, he thought.

He'd dreamed of her during the night. And in his dream she was running from him across a white, frozen expanse like an ice skating rink. Gliding, just out of his reach, with her long hair flowing behind her.

And just as he reached out to grab that hair, he awoke. With both his hands squeezed into fists.

Macon looked to his right, up toward where the lake stopped and that canyon began. It was still too cloud-shrouded to see anything that way, just the faint gray outline of the cliffs . . .

Then his eyes blurred suddenly. An instant of double-vision where everything up that way seemed to . . . *shift*.

His eardrums popped, like when the compartment pressurizes in a jet plane. Only harder, much harder. His eardrums popped so hard they sent a jolt of pain through his skull.

And he heard, or thought he heard, a soft, heavy sound, somewhere down at the lower bass end of the auditory range.

WHUMMMP! it said.

Closer—much closer—the sound was a whisper. A long, sibilant *white* whisper as the avalanche came down.

"Run!" screamed Nattie, and pulled Ben McKee toward the creek. "Run, Ben!"

Run for the rocks. Those huge granite boulders left alongside the tree-stripped bank of Walker Creek by other slides like this one.

Nattie floundered toward those submerged, humplike shapes in the snow less than one hundred feet away. She knew she wasn't going to make it.

Trying to get off to one side or the other of the main slide was a second option. She wasn't going to do that, either.

The pressure wave came first, building behind her. In its sudden vacuum of air, she felt her eardrums pop. She ran grimly, as fast as the clumsy snowshoes would carry her, kicking her knees high with each stride. She didn't look back, kept her eyes on the nearest of the boulders.

Almost there . . .

When the slide hit her, a white cloud engulfing all her senses in the same instant, blasting across the canyon floor at over one hundred miles an hour. It slammed her forward and spinning, snow everywhere, filling her mouth and knocking off her helmet.

Nattie felt herself tumbling, head over heels. Try to swim with it, she'd always been told, as if you were on a plummeting wave of water. Try to swim on its surface. She flailed with her arms, kicked with her legs . . .

Then everything was still.

She opened her eyes, expecting only darkness. Instead there was faint light, somewhere ahead of her. And a gray-granite surface of smooth rock.

One of those huge creek boulders she'd nearly reached when the slide hit her. It was only a few yards away, and there was a gap in the snow at its base.

Nattie got her bearings, found she was lying in a more or less horizontal position. She needed to work her way to the rock. One thing she remembered about avalanches was how quickly the snow set up once it stopped. Like cement. Which was the reason most victims died of suffocation.

Or froze to death. Nattie could feel the cold from the

snow all around her, creeping through the insulated layers of her clothing and down inside her.

Get moving, dammit!

She used her hands to gradually widen the pocket of air around her head. Her body, from the waist up, seemed to be loose. It was her legs that were stuck, because of the snowshoes. Jammed in beneath her feet, they weren't going anywhere. And neither was she, unless she got them off.

The air around her head was already beginning to taste stale and hot. Lie still, that was what the safety experts taught. If you have any air, try to conserve it until you're rescued. . . .

Right. Rescued by whom? Cleese and his pals? Chances were, they had troubles of their own right now. Bullets apparently didn't stop him, but she'd bet an avalanche would.

How could they be so stupid? Firing a gun in a steep canyon like this, right after a storm had wind-loaded the slopes above it. . . .

Good ol' depth hoar, she thought, and was surprised when she almost laughed. She wondered if Ben McKee would be interested in another lecture on avalanches.

If he was still alive to hear it.

Nattie shook that thought out of her head. No time for it now. If she got out of this hole, then. . . .

She dug her way down to one of her feet. Unbuckled the snowshoe—its aluminum frame twisted like a pretzel—and slid her foot out. The other one, buried beneath the first, was going to require a little more work.

Take small breaths. Some of the air from over by that boulder was leaching in, or she'd already be unconscious by now. Work slowly and breathe slowly.

Finally she saw the silver-gray frame of the second snowshoe, then its black nylon webbing. The binding had already popped loose, disintegrated under the pressure, so it was only a matter of wiggling her foot free.

Nattie twisted around and began to crawl toward the light. She used her hands, inside those oversized leather gloves of Jeff/Harry's, to widen the hole as she went along.

Don't let it collapse. If the hole collapses . . .

But it didn't, and she began to smell fresher air. She found some smaller rocks and grabbed them to lever herself forward.

To the side of the boulder. It was enormous, about the size of an old tail-finned Cadillac, she decided. One of those vintage Fifties gas-guzzlers they always featured at the antique auto shows her dad had loved so much.

Strange, how the mind behaved under stress. She'd completely forgotten about that.

Nattie finally got her feet beneath her—some pain in her left ankle, the one that had been twisted underneath the other—and stood up. Hard, crusty snow gave way when she pushed on it with her head and shoulders.

Then she emerged into fresh, sweet-smelling air driven by that nonstop wind. This time, she didn't mind.

She looked around her. First at the canyon bottom, filled with layers of ice-edged snow and debris. Chunks larger than the rock that had saved her. The way it *should* have looked earlier if there had been previous smaller slides to relieve the pressure up there on the slope. Now the surface resembled a billowing ocean, suddenly frozen solid, all cracks and crevices.

Then she looked up at the steep slope above her and the gouged-out hollow just below the canyon rim. The spot where this vast slab of cohesive snow had hung, with the weaker layer bonding below it, and ready to fail at the first stimulus. The stomp of a boot, the pressure of a ski . . .

The vibration of a gunshot.

There was nobody moving anywhere.

Maybe I'm the only one left, she thought. A slide the size of this one, it could have taken them all. Cleese and his two men. And Ben McKee.

Just like that. After everything that happened, all the terror and the rage, the . . .

Everything.

After all that, it was over in the blink of an eye.

She suddenly felt like crying, and she didn't try to stop because she didn't want to stop. The tears slid, warm and salty, down onto her mouth. She licked one away, just before it began to freeze on her lower lip.

There's no time for this, dammit. Stop acting like a baby. Two days ago you didn't even know he existed.

And he brought it on himself anyway. On himself, and very nearly on you, too.

But she was remembering the night before. More than that, she was remembering *him*. All they'd shared in so brief a time, and all they hadn't. A man with secrets . . .

A liar and a thief.

Come on, move it. They're dead now . . .

All of them.

. . . and you'll be joining them if you don't get your lame butt into gear, girl. You'll freeze to death out here.

Nattie found some usable handholds in the rock and crawled up on top of it. If she was careful, stayed close beside the buried creek, she could work her way safely out of the slide zone. After that, it was about half a mile down to the lake. Another mile or so to the comm center.

She stood up on the rock, keeping most of her weight on her right leg, and pulled her twisted clothing into place. Brushed snow out of her hair and off her face, and noticed that at least most of the crawl space mud was gone now. She'd lost the shotgun, somewhere under all this frozen expanse. Also her cap . . .

And her old white climbing helmet. Lost along this empty road.

She looked up through the swirling, wind-whipped snow toward the canyon walls and beyond. The high peaks were up there, her refuge for over a year. Hidden from view by the gray clouds, looking down on her, and on all that had happened here.

The mountains don't care. She'd heard that so often it was just another cliché. A logo on a T-shirt hanging in some ski-shop window. But that didn't keep it from being the truth. And it was a bitter truth, never more than now. She and Ben had tried so hard . . .

But the mountains don't care. They're beautiful, breathtaking. They draw the gaze and lift the spirit, and they hide you away from an outside world that's turned all purple in your mind—the color of bruises and of pain.

And so you take them into your heart.

But at times like this, you see their other side, and that side is as cold as their frozen summits. You realize they're looking down on you through the eyes of eternity. And that they don't care if you live or die.

The wind froze the tears on Nattie's face. Tried to blind her. She blinked her eyes . . .

And that was when she saw a flash of color in the distance. Something moving in that jagged, shattered landscape, back up the canyon and away from the creek.

A flash of orange.

"Ogod," whispered Nattie, and ducked down on top of the boulder. "Oh, my God."

Ben McKee had been right about Eugene Cleese. *He won't quit. Not ever.*

Maybe he *can't* die . . .

She slid off the far side of the rock. Kept it between her and that blur of orange a hundred yards away.

Maybe he can't be killed . . .

Stop that! Stop it now. She shook her head angrily.

Two things haven't changed. You still have the lead, and you still have to reach the comm center. Now get a grip, dammit!

She crouched low, and used the boulder for a cover as she picked her way across the crazy-quilt terrain of slab-snow in the direction of Walker Creek. And in the direction of the lake. No snowshoes, no weapons . . . no Ben McKee.

She was aware that she was limping on her twisted ankle, and also that she was still crying. She didn't let either of those things slow her down.

* * *

"No snowflake in an avalanche ever feels responsible," murmured Cleese.

"Say something?" Wallace pulled himself into an upright position and started brushing snow off his clothing.

"Just a quote I read somewhere. An observation on the levels of responsibility, I believe."

Cleese couldn't turn his head to the right. A couple of inches maybe, if he ignored the pain, but no farther than that.

A damaged trapezius on that side, at the very least.

"La cosa no cuajó," he decided. Arturo Garza wasn't there to hear it, but he probably would have agreed. Things definitely were not going well.

Beneath his Kevlar vest, his chest burned with every breath where the bullets had hit him.

"Speak English, dammit." One side of Wallace's face had been scraped raw, cheekbone to chin, by the ice, and he was dabbing at the blood that had frozen there. He was looking more and more like the survivor of a hit-and-run.

"Just thinking out loud," replied Cleese, and stood up very carefully. It wasn't easy, like trying to balance on the ice floes of an arctic sea, but he needed to find out if his legs were injured. Apparently they weren't.

This wasn't Cleese's first avalanche, a fact that had ultimately saved both Wallace and himself. The one before, in the Cascades northeast of Seattle, had been smaller—and Cleese had been wearing an avalanche beacon that day—but it had been an adequate rehearsal.

He realized what was happening as quickly as he heard that first soft sound—like a rock dropped onto a feather pillow—of that massive slab breaking free, followed by the long, hissing noise of sliding snow. He'd yelled at Wallace, who was directly ahead of him, to swim for it. Which made no sense at the time, but the big man had obviously understood. The slide had carried them both, entangled together, tumbling over and over each other. And they'd stopped with Wallace's head upside down, and Cleese directly above him.

It was Wallace's broad back that Cleese had used to push off from, shoving upward as hard and fast as he could before the snow set up. Cascade Concrete, they called it in Seattle.

And he'd popped free, up to his waist. Digging Wallace out before he suffocated had been a bit harder.

Wallace saw Cleese looking around. "He's gone, Gene," said Wallace.

"I know," answered Cleese.

"Why'd he do that anyway? Firing that goddamn gun when they were way out of range? Stupid little shit . . ."

"Artie was always impetuous." Cleese rubbed his neck. A bit more movement now. "Straight ahead and full speed, what the suits like to call a hard charger. It was just his nature."

"Yeah, well, his nature got him eighty-sixed this time. And nearly us along with him."

"I'm afraid you're right." Cleese nodded.

And they'd been so close. The two of them, Natalie Kemper and Ben McKee, no more than a hundred yards ahead. Ten more minutes, fifteen at the most. . . .

Of course, the slide had probably taken them, too. Three bodies under the snow, waiting to emerge with the spring thaw. And another one in the mine, not to mention Marvin Stone. And that helicopter. Very untidy all around.

At least there were no marks on any of the bodies, other than Stone, and he could be transported if it came down to it. A drowning and three suffocations, or possibly broken necks from the force of the avalanche. All were natural occurrences in the high mountains, and though the sheer numbers involved would certainly inspire some headlines, there wouldn't be any kind of proof.

"Gene?" Wallace stood up, swore beneath his breath while one big hand massaged his knee. "Look over there."

"What is it?" At first Cleese saw only the ragged, torn

surface of the canyon floor. Then he followed the pointing line of Wallace's finger . . .

And saw movement. Nearly beyond the range of his vision. A blur in the distance.

"I can't tell which one it is." Wallace stretched to his full height. "But whoever it is, is sure as hell moving along."

Cleese knew which one it was. He didn't have the slightest doubt.

Nine lives, Liam Riley had said.

And it was very odd, but in that moment Cleese wasn't exactly certain how he felt about it. He pictured her green eyes, fierce as a warrior. And that blond hair . . .

Merging images in his mind. A warm, golden beach. . . .

Cleese shook his head to clear it. Saw Milton Wallace watching him expectantly. They still had their guns, the HK and Arturo Garza's borrowed pistol. They still had one usable pair of snowshoes.

And the job wasn't done yet.

Chapter Nineteen

When the snow stopped falling, the coyotes began to howl.

During the blizzard, the pack had gone to ground, into the burrows they dug each summer beneath the boulders and the huge, standing dead evergreens on the west slope above Walker Lake. Curling together, fluffy gray-brown tails across their noses, they rode out the storm. But now, with the snow subsiding to flurries and then finally stopping altogether, the pack pushed its way to the surface. The wind was still blowing hard, with the chill factor well below zero, but the coyotes didn't mind that. They were accustomed to the wind.

They climbed out into a gray-white, cloud-shrouded daylight that was not much brighter than dusk. They slowly descended the deep drifts through the trees toward the frozen lake, the alpha male in the lead, alert for all the sounds and scents around them. And, as they traveled, they called out to each other.

Their sound—their howling—overrode the roar of the wind. Their sound rose into the air to mingle with the last of the dying blizzard; then it echoed across the basin to the trees on the other side and back again. It was a sound indescribable to anyone who'd never heard it—shrill and ululating, and more utterly wild than even the storm itself.

Some have said it's the loneliest sound of all.

From time to time, Nattie looked back over her shoulder at the two men nearly a quarter of a mile behind. She tried not to do it often, just enough to be sure they weren't gaining, but the temptation was always there.

It was strange. She saw them, and they obviously saw her. She was breaking trail for them, in fact, bad ankle and all. But they stayed back there, slogging along, occasionally stopping to bend down for a few moments—sharing one pair of snowshoes?—and then changing leads. Each time that happened, she gained more ground on them, but they never hurried.

It was their patience, that methodical, patient stalking, that came the closest to unnerving her.

She was out in the open basin now, Empinado Canyon behind her, with the frozen surface of Walker Lake on her right, and a steep, tree-covered slope on her left. A pack of coyotes had begun howling, over there somewhere across the lake, and the sound was all around her. Louder than the wind.

A desolate sound.

She was exhausted, moving in a mechanical daze after a mile of wading waist-high snow that clung to her and pulled on her with every step. And her ankle was getting worse. She was beginning to suspect more than just a sprain.

Still, it went on, didn't it? Nobody in a hurry. Three tiny dots—one separated from the other two—moving through this vast open bowl. There was an unexpected downside to that. Too much time to think, about the past and the future. If there was one.

She was thinking at the moment about Ben McKee and, by an odd bit of connection, about her father as well. Nattie had been sixteen years old when Warren Kemper went off on that final fishing trip, and there was something about that day she'd never told anyone.

How they'd fought, she and her father, that morning. Bitter words in raised, angry voices concerning—what else?—her mother. How he could defend JoAnne, time after time, was amazing, especially considering the way she talked about him to anyone who'd listen . . .

But he always defended her. Even though there was mostly silence between them anymore, and, very often, silence in the house. And what they were thinking and what they felt they kept to themselves, at least when Nattie was around.

But he always defended her.

So Nattie and her father parted in anger that morning, a teenaged girl and the man she loved more than anyone or anything. And she never saw him alive again.

Which brought her, by that odd bit of connection, to Ben McKee, buried under the avalanche back in Empinado Canyon. Their last moments together had also been filled with bitterness, with her anger and his lies, and now he was gone. Someone else she'd never see again.

"The most important thing about any lie is its motivation, Nattie." Someone had told her that once, a long time ago . . .

And she was fairly certain that someone was Warren Kemper.

There were things she'd tell her father, right this minute if she could. Things she'd whispered to a still, artificially smiling figure inside a polished casket, but that wasn't really the same. Things she'd say now, if she could, to Warren Kemper. And to Ben McKee, too.

Some of them were the same things.

Ben McKee kept to the protective camouflage of evergreens up on the ridge as he followed the two men ahead. Cleese and the big guy. It appeared they'd had another casualty.

But not Cleese himself, of course. Shoot him, drop an avalanche down on him . . .

No silver bullets, that was obviously the problem. Silver bullets and a stake through the heart, maybe a clove of garlic to go in his mouth.

283

Ben could barely see Nattie in the distance, out in the frozen white vastness of the basin. Cleese and Jumbo weren't gaining on her at all, despite a slight limp she hadn't had earlier. If anything, they were losing ground.

And so was Ben. For one thing, the snow was deeper up here next to the trees. For another, the damaged snowshoe on his right foot kept wobbling with every step, trying to throw him off balance in this treacherous footing along the slope of the ridge.

Everything considered, the fact he was here at all, still in the game so to speak, was mind-boggling. The avalanche had carried him between the boulders and down to the creek, banging him across various rocks in the process. When he'd regained consciousness after a few minutes—or maybe more than a few—he was lying on his back and listening to a faint gurgling noise that he eventually realized was coming from below him. The sound of water moving beneath the stream's iced-over surface.

The slide, partially blunted by the boulders along the bank, had carried him so far he'd outlasted it more than anything else. There was very little of the original snow where he'd wound up, just a loose five- or six-inch cover he was able to dig through for air. Freeing his feet, encased at an awkward angle by the snowshoes, had been more difficult. By the time he'd finally stood up and saw Nattie, she was probably out of earshot in that wind. Since he saw Cleese at the same time, he'd decided to keep quiet.

They'd trudged right past him, those two, on the other side of the boulders at a distance of about fifty yards. The big guy had a machine pistol in a sling at his side, and Cleese . . . you could be sure Cleese had a weapon somewhere.

Like that knife. You take your eyes off him for one second. . . .

Ben had lost the Mauser rifle, somewhere on his tumbling ride to the creek, which was too bad because he could've made really good use of it right at that moment.

What he had left were Cleese's pistol and the snowshoes, one of them with a twisted frame.

He didn't trust the range on the oddly shaped little gun. It was a nine-millimeter automatic of some kind, and was probably useless at any real distance from the two men. Besides, if Cleese was still wearing his bullet-proof vest—that was what it *had* to be, unless he wanted to stick with the silver bullets and garlic theory—then firing at him from that range would have been a waste of time anyway. It would have meant giving away the element of surprise—Ben's only real advantage—for the extremely remote chance of landing a head shot.

So he'd wiggled the damaged snowshoe back into place on his Sorel boot, and got the binding snapped. It flopped around some, but it was better than nothing.

And here he was now, trailing the killers who were trailing Nattie Kemper. Still alive, and still in the game. He remembered the feeling he'd had after the plane crash, when he stood up in the shattered passenger compartment with the blizzard roaring outside and realized it wasn't his time. Not quite yet.

"I'm a survivor," that was what he'd told Shelley the night she'd laid it all out for him. When he'd finally realized there was no rear exit to this one.

She'd flashed that sardonic Shelley-smile at his comment, which wasn't surprising if you knew her.

"That remains to be seen, Benjamin," she'd replied—kind of amusing now in a black sort of way . . .

All things considered.

A wave of shivering hit him as the wind sprayed snow down onto him from the overhanging trees on his left, and he tried to remember how long it was since he'd been truly warm. . . .

Last night, that was how long. With Nattie.

Out here now, with the wind ripping at him, carrying with it those unearthly howling sounds from across the lake, last night seemed a distant memory. Or maybe just a fantasy, a trick of the mind.

But those two, Cleese and the big man with him, they

285

were no fantasy. He'd continue following them, and he'd do what he could when the time arrived. He'd learned a little about that from Nattie. How a person—man or woman—should behave under pressure. Something he wished he'd known earlier in his life, before there was a need for rear exits. But he'd also learned some things about himself in the last day or two. Encouraging things.

It was a remarkable story she'd told him, lying there in his arms last night. A story of terrible fear and pain, and of rare courage. And when—if?—he spoke to her again, he had a story of his own to tell. Less remarkable, certainly, and much less courageous, but at least it would be the truth.

And, in the meanwhile, he'd do what he could.

He stayed near the cover of the trees, and he struggled to keep pace with the figures out in the basin. Moving alongside the frozen lake toward a dark, regular shape there in the distance.

Up ahead, a rectangular outline caught Nattie's attention, pulling it away from the somber thoughts inside and the desolate howling sounds all around her. It was the comm center, no more than a hundred yards in the distance. She felt a surge of adrenaline, one last burst of energy from a nearly empty tank.

She was going to beat them to the comm center by at least ten minutes, maybe more, but what then? If the place was deserted . . .

And it must be. Otherwise, why was Cleese so patient in his pursuit? Because he knew she'd find no help there.

Maybe Marv had a gun somewhere. Maybe back in his private quarters. Nattie had never been a fan of guns, but she'd damn sure use one on Cleese . . .

Why? He just pops back up.

. . . if she could find one. And there was the radio, of course, although by the time anybody could arrive, get in here with a helicopter or snowmobile . . .

Snowmobiles! Nattie floundered to a stop.

Marv had snowmobiles, several of them, and suddenly remembering that was the most encouraging thought she'd had since the avalanche came down. Snowmobiles . . .

For the first time in a while, she began to believe she might make it after all.

The comm center was getting closer every step, enlarging in her view, and Nattie saw something she hadn't noticed before. There was smoke coming from the stovepipe.

Ben McKee had been wrong. Marvin Stone was alive. In fact . . .

She saw him, still a small, heavily bundled figure in the distance—if anything could make Starvin' Marvin into a small figure—coming out onto the porch. She had to warn him. She tried to run, but the heavy, waist-deep snow held her like molasses.

"Marv!" she yelled. He was downwind, so maybe it would carry her voice. "Marv, it's me! It's Nattie!"

Which was when the figure on the porch waved back at her, then turned toward the door.

"Look out, Marv!" Nattie cupped her hands around her mouth. "Look out, they have guns . . ."

But he was already gone. She wasn't sure he'd heard her. She glanced back at the two men far behind.

He must have heard her. That was why he'd gone inside, to radio for help. Nattie drove herself forward with renewed energy. He'll call for help; then we'll jump on a couple of those snowmobiles and leave ol' Bulletproof Cleese behind.

She saw a snowmobile track, where someone had recently circled away from the building and then returned. She struggled over into it, and found herself in ankle-high crust rather than waist-high powder. She began to run, limping some, but it felt like flying after all that time in the deep snow.

Across an open area that was a grassy, flower-filled meadow in the summer. Up onto the covered porch and through the front door . . .

"Nattie my love," said Rick Macon. "I've been looking everywhere for you."

Nattie stopped just inside the door. She heard the wind blow it shut behind her. She knew her mouth had fallen open, but there was nothing she could do about it.

This isn't real. A dream. This is *not* real.

He was standing in the center of the room. He'd removed the heavy coat, and he was standing there in a tight black knit top and black jeans. His legs were spread slightly, and his massive bodybuilder's arms hung loose at his sides.

This is not real.

He smiled, and took a step toward her. "Aren't you glad to see me, Nattie?" he said.

His big hands curled into fists.

And that was when it happened, something so strange that at first Nattie thought it was part of the same dream. Something so completely unexpected, bubbling up from . . . *somewhere* inside her . . .

She laughed.

It stunned her, the unimaginable sound of her laughter, breaking the silence of the room. She nearly put one hand over her mouth, but it was too late.

She did it again.

And saw his smile change over to that dark scowl she remembered so well. The scowl that had always reduced her to helpless terror, because it came just ahead of those harsh, cruel words. Which came just ahead of the fists . . .

But she suddenly couldn't help it. The laughter. Seeing him, standing there like some pumped-up, malevolent Ken doll. The reason he'd run back inside was to lose the coat and brush his hair, for God's sake. So he could be right there in front of the mirror when she came in, posed in the act of trying to appear unposed. Dressed in black, and giving her The Look.

Laughter bubbled up inside her, bursting its way through the unbearable tension of the past two days. Maybe it was as much that as anything.

"Turn a little to your left, Rick." She got it out between gasps for breath. "That's your good side, remember?"

He was staring at her, and his eyes were wide with disbelief. Looking at her like she'd gone crazy. But he was no longer moving toward her.

"What are you doing here, Rick?" She wiped her eyes. "Where's Marv?"

He tried again. "I was looking for you." He let his voice drop to a familiar rumble of low menace, and she realized with a jolt how that was as staged as the rest. "I've been looking for you for a *long* time, Nattie."

And she nearly broke into another fit of giggling. Saw, for the first time she could remember, a trace of uncertainty flit across his handsome features.

And thought . . . Was I actually afraid of this fool?

He was staring at her, clenching and unclenching his fists, a vein pulsing in his thick neck. Common sense, as well as painful memory, told her this was dangerous ground. But after what she'd been through in the past two days. . . .

He doesn't know what to do next, she thought, while they studied each other. He had it all planned out, but now someone's switched scripts on him. I was supposed to cry or beg or run away. Or maybe all three . . .

And then he would have been on me. Just like before.

"You little bitch." Macon murmured it, then spoke louder as he took a step toward her. "I think you need reminding . . ."

"If you touch me, Rick, I'll kill you." She stood her ground and stared into his eyes. "One way or another."

And watched him stop again. This muscle-bound bully who'd beaten her nearly to death . . .

Because she hadn't fought back.

"You haven't changed, have you, Rick?" she said. "Not at all. But I have. I'm not the same. You might want to keep that in mind."

"What's that supposed to be, a threat?" He was still standing there, still unsure. "If I were you, Nattie . . ."

"If you were me, you'd be dead, Rick. Several times over. The reason I'm not is because I'm *not* you. Did you see those two men following me?"

His eyes shifted toward the window.

"Those men are after me, Rick. If they catch me, I *will* be dead, just like you've been dreaming about. But there's a difference. The difference is they'll kill you, too."

"What the hell are you—"

"You think you're a bad guy, Rick? I used to think so. Well, I'm telling you that you don't know what bad really is, but there's an old man headed this way who'll be happy to show you."

"Who . . ." He swallowed convulsively, and she saw some sudden realization pass behind his eyes. "Who are they? What do they want with you?"

"I don't have time to discuss it." Nattie started past him, toward the back room. "I'm leaving here while I still can. You might want to do the same."

His expression changed again. From its original anger to what may have been fear—Nattie couldn't be sure because she'd never seen Rick afraid—and then to something more familiar.

A look of calculation.

"I have a better idea." He stepped sideways to cut her off. "Maybe I should be the one to leave . . ."

"Dammit, Rick, get out of my way."

". . . and you should stay here and wait for your friends," he finished, and lunged for her.

It was pure luck, because Rick Macon was much quicker than Nattie. But this time he missed.

One hand caught for a second in the sleeve of her coat, but she yanked sideways and pulled him off balance. He fell, full force, into the side of the antique piano.

While she ran for the back door.

"What the hell is that?" asked Wallace.

Cleese stopped and listened while the wind blew across

him, carrying with it the sound of the coyotes still howling from the other side of the lake.

"Your ears are probably better than mine, Milt," he finally answered. "But I believe it's 'Camptown Races.' "

"Doo-da," grunted Wallace.

Without discussing it, they fanned out and approached the building from two sides. Cleese took the SIG from his pocket and quickly checked the auto-loader clip, then popped it back into the base of the grip and chambered a round. The P228 wasn't quite the weapon the Glock Seventeen was, but he was comfortable with it. Thirteen shots should be enough for anyone.

He approached the front porch in the snowmobile track that someone had laid down. He was glad to see it, since it represented a way out of here once this business was concluded.

Up on the porch, where the music was louder . . .

Camptown ladies sing this song . . .

. . . and over to the window. Cleese crouched low, his head to one side, and looked in at a section of the room. He saw the file cabinets, with the Mr. Coffee on top, and part of the north wall.

Camptown racetrack five miles long . . .

He ducked beneath the window to its other side. Saw the woodstove and the threadbare recliner, and the south wall where that big topo map had been. The map was gone.

He took a deep, unexpectedly painful breath, let it out slowly, and stepped dead center in front of the window, the pistol pointed into the room.

The radio set was there, its rear cover removed and the circuit boards torn halfway out. At the back of the room, the old player piano sat beneath the mirror, keys blindly following the imprint of the music roll.

G'wine to run all night . . .

Cleese stared at his own reflection in the mirror, his shoulders and head snow-covered, with the storm blowing past behind him, the pistol pointed directly at his mirror image . . .

In an act of reflex, he nearly fired.

There was a man lying on the floor next to the piano. Crawling to his knees, reaching up to grab the bench.

Cleese moved quickly to the front door, pushed on it, then sprang into the room.

Which was empty, except for the man on the floor. Cleese stepped forward, his eyes on the inside door he knew led back to Marvin Stone's living quarters.

The man was sitting on the piano bench now. There was a jagged gash near his hairline, and blood smeared his forehead.

He looked at Cleese and mumbled something, inaudible because of the piano's noise and the howling sounds through the front door just before the wind blew it closed.

Cleese made a shushing motion, gloved hand over his lips, then slid sideways toward the back room. The man tried to struggle to his feet, but Cleese pointed the SIG at him. The man sat back down.

The door to Stone's quarters stood halfway open. If Natalie Kemper was in there, and if she had the Glock. . . .

Cleese looked at the man on the piano bench, sitting there with his eyes dazed and half-shut.

"Could you come with me for a moment, please?" asked Cleese.

The man was about Cleese's height, and very powerfully built. He didn't much want to come along, but he did it anyway. He went through the door first, Cleese directly behind him.

There were no shots. Just the wind, louder again, and the music from the piano.

The back room was dark, the shades pulled down above a rumpled bed. There were several places to hide in there—a closet, a bathroom, another door next to the fridge . . .

A door that was standing open. Windblown snow made a delicate white fan across the worn carpet.

Nattie tried to avoid looking at Marvin Stone. She kept her back to that woodpile as much as possible.

Another life, the life of someone she'd cared for, snuffed out in the unstopping, manic madness of the past . . .

Thirty-six hours. She glanced at her watch, and saw it was almost noon. Over thirty-six hours since the little jet glided down in the darkness above her cabin.

It felt like forever.

There were two snowmobiles in the shed, just as she'd remembered. One was a big Arctic Cat Thundercat, nearly new, sitting near the front door. It had an extended single seat to accommodate Starvin' Marvin's considerable bulk, as well as a huge nine hundred c.c. Suzuki engine and electric starter. All the bells and whistles. The other was smaller and far less grand, a battered Kawasaki that reminded Nattie of her old Polaris.

She didn't have much time. Those two were probably here by now. She wondered if Rick had made it out of the comm center. Compared to Eugene Cleese, Rick was no more than an overgrown child.

No time to worry about that. If something happened to him . . .

She'd feel guilty. Which made no sense, of course, especially considering that final betrayal he'd attempted just now, but there it was. Old habits were hard to break.

But . . . oh, God, what a feeling. Those much-too-brief moments in there. Staring her dark demon of a hundred night's lost sleep right in the eye and knowing she was no longer afraid of him. Cautious, of course—she'd be a complete idiot otherwise—but that old heart-stopping, gut-grinding fear, his voice whispering inside her head, all that was changed now.

Because she'd changed. And she'd seen what *real* demons looked like.

A pivotal moment in her life, though it had wasted precious time that might have had her away from here before Cleese could arrive. There was the chance she'd pay dearly for that moment.

But it was worth it. Whatever happened.

Two snowmobiles. One to leave on. . . .

Nattie had opened her coat, and was ripping a long, thin strip off the tail of her shirt when she heard the shots outside.

Wallace stood at the open door that led into the back of the comm center. Dark in there. The faint sound of that piano music. . . .

He was also looking at a well-worn track, cutting through the deep snow and out toward a large wooden shed about fifty feet behind the main building.

Probably the shed where Cleese and the others had stashed that radio operator while Wallace waited in the helicopter.

Cleese was inside the comm center by now, and there'd been no sounds from in there, other than the music; so Wallace decided to have a look in the shed. He thumbed the selector that converted the HK to full-auto. There was no telling what kind of weapons the woman might have, including Cleese's shotgun.

One faceful of buckshot was more than enough.

Wallace stepped into the tracks for easier going and moved toward the shed. Right behind it was where the tall evergreens up on the ridge grew down closest to the lake. They were whipping back and forth, buffeted by the wind, their movement constantly distracting the edge of his vision . . .

Just in time to see something back there. A quick movement catching his eye, despite those mud-stained camouflage colors blending with the browns and greens. The woman, running for the trees . . .

No. Running his way instead, toward the shed. It was the man. Ben McKee.

Where the hell did he come from . . . ?

Wallace swung the HK up, and fired off a burst. A

294

chattering, high-pitched sound that was mostly muffled by the wind. He saw McKee change direction, clumsy in the snowshoes, as gouts of snow blew out around his feet.

Then McKee raised his arm—something dark, a pistol?—and returned fire. A burst of heat whizzed past Wallace's face, and he ducked sideways.

Then McKee was gone, hidden behind the shed.

And, on the far hillside, the coyotes went silent.

"Milt?" Cleese emerged from that open back door. "Did you get her?"

"Him," corrected Wallace, and retreated a few steps toward the main building. "It was McKee, Gene, and he had a gun. He's behind the shed."

"Maybe that's where she is." Cleese moved up next to Wallace. "In the shed."

"Bonnie and Clyde, together again," grunted Wallace, and they were just starting to fan out when there was movement at the corner of the small building. Ben McKee darted into view for a second, then dove headfirst through a door that someone opened from the inside. Cleese's response was as quick as Wallace's, but from fifty feet away the nine-millimeter slugs only stitched a splintered pattern across the door as it swung shut.

"Well, horse-shit," mumbled Wallace, and dug another banana clip out of his gear. *Cuernos de chiva,* Artie had called the clips. Goat's horns.

"Better pull back." Cleese took hold of his arm. "We know she's in there now, and she may still have that Mauser."

They retreated to the back door of the comm center and studied the shed. It was a rectangular wooden building, about fifteen feet by twenty, with a pitched roof. There was a wide lift-up, garage-type door in the center of the long wall, and the smaller door Ben McKee had used on the shorter wall facing them.

"Those must be the only entrances," said Wallace. "If there was some other way in on that back side, out of the line of fire, he'd've used it."

"Like a window, for instance." Cleese nodded. "That should mean we have them covered from here."

"Y'know, it's mighty cold." Wallace's battered face creased into a grin. "Maybe they'd appreciate some heat out there. A bonfire'd warm us *all* up."

"Not to mention getting rid of those bullet holes," replied Cleese. He glanced back at the comm center. "But there's someone I'd like to have a talk with first. It's what you might call a curious situation, Milt."

Nattie was in Ben McKee's arms. She didn't know how he'd survived the avalanche, or how he'd gotten to the shed, and at the moment she didn't care.

She may have whispered, "You're alive." Remembering her wish from earlier, out there in the basin, she may have said several things a lot more personal and potentially embarrassing than that. She didn't know, or care.

She just held him, and was held by him. And if he *was* a thief and a liar . . .

The most important thing about any lie is its motivation, Nattie.

At that moment she didn't care.

"What's that for?" Ben leaned back slightly, and looked at the strip of cloth in her hand.

"It's a fuse," she answered, and let him go, too. She pointed at the two snowmobiles parked next to the large main door. "I was going to soak it with gas and light it. Use it to blow one of them through the roof while I made a run for it on the other one." She shrugged. "Kind of a diversion, I guess."

"It's a plan." Ben nodded. "You don't think we can hold them off from here? There aren't any windows, just the two doors . . ."

"And it looks like we have one gun between us, 'cause I lost the shotgun in the slide. I think the only thing keeping them back right now is they don't know that."

Ben looked around the inside of the shed. "Is there anything else in here we can use?"

"Couple of axes. Some mechanic's tools. Maybe that old chainsaw over there, if you think they'll hold still long enough."

Ben was studying the two snowmobiles. "So," he said. "How do we do this?"

"We'll have to take the small one." Nattie didn't mention that she'd originally developed her plan as an escape for one person. " 'Cause that Thundercat won't fit through the side door. It's nearly four feet wide . . ."

"Nattie." He took her arm. "I have to tell you something."

She saw the look in his eyes. Realized what was next: "There's no time." She put her hand over his, and gently pulled free. "Tell me later. Tell me while we're sitting in a hot tub in Ouray."

"There may not be a later." He followed her to the Kawasaki. "I made myself a promise, back up there when I was trailing along behind Cleese. That if I found you again, I'd tell you the truth . . . about Machtel."

"I don't care about that," she said, which wasn't the truth at all. "Help me push . . ."

"I lied to you." His voice stopped her. "What I said in the mine was a lie, at least partly."

"I know." There was no time for this. But there'd been no time to face down Rick Macon, either, and she'd done it anyway. "I knew that when you were telling me."

"But only partly." His eyes held her. "And part of what Cleese said was a lie, too, trying to drive a wedge between us, or else distract us so he could reach his knife. The money laundering operation at Machtel, I was part of it. Just like Cleese said. I can't make any excuses for it, except I was young and . . . God, Nattie, it was so much money. And I was needing very badly to get hold of some money right about then . . ."

For a moment he seemed lost in memory.

"I guess you could say they found me in a moment of weakness." He shook his head. "But Cleese was lying when he said I was ripping off Machtel. Jumping the country in that plane with their access codes. Taliferro and Landry *were* IRS, and I was going with them to New York, then on to Washington, just like I told you, to meet with a government unit established to bring down the corporation. I was going to help them."

"Why?" asked Nattie. "If you were a part . . . ?"

"Because they had me, that's why." He smiled ruefully. "I should probably say something noble at this point, right? About realizing the error of my ways, wanting to make amends. And I do, Nattie. I swear to God. But I won't lie to you anymore. The reason was because they had me cold, thanks to an informant of theirs. So, one of their agents turned me. Pure coercion. Get us the hard copy on those offshore accounts. Download it from the Machtel computer to our computer in Washington. Either that, or see how you like the climate around Leavenworth, Kansas. It was a deal for full immunity from prosecution, Nattie, and I took it. But Cleese found out. He always found out. There was another guy, Will Carter. He was the informant who rolled over on me, just before he ended up with a knife through his spine, courtesy of Cleese."

"So . . ." Nattie hesitated. "Who's Shelley?"

"Shelley Gallatin." Ben's face darkened. "Bureau of Internal Revenue. A real hard case. She was the agent who turned me, the one who was running me at Machtel. Ambitious as hell, and screw the consequences for anyone else involved. Will Carter would tell you about that, if he could. She even moved me into the beach house she was renting in Malibu. More convenient for her."

Nattie wasn't sure how to react to that part. "Sounds like a dangerous woman," she said.

"Oh, she is." His voice was bitter. "In Shelley Gallatin's world, the end always justifies the means. *Always.* In that way, she's exactly like Machtel. Or was, might be more accurate. I called her place from the safe house before the plane left. Cleese answered the phone."

"You think he killed her?"

Ben glanced over at Marvin Stone's body, partially hidden behind the woodpile. That was answer enough.

"My God," murmured Nattie. She pictured Cleese, his twinkling grandfatherly eyes, that gentle, unruffled voice . . .

His hands, moving in a blur of motion for his knife.

And he probably had Rick by now. She realized she hadn't even told Ben about Rick being there.

Everything was happening so fast.

"I think I was probably expendable, too," said Ben. "Just like Carter. But I found out about him. What happened to him. So I downloaded the information Shelley wanted onto a single disk instead, and then hid it from her. Which meant she had to protect me, get me on that plane, whether she liked it or not."

"Then, Cleese is after the disk, too."

"He doesn't know about it. If he did, he'd never have sabotaged the plane, and he'd be trying to take me alive right now, which obviously he's not. I told you Shelley was a hard case. Tough as nails. I guess the disk turned out to be her private joke on Cleese, there at the end. I hope she got some satisfaction from it."

"Then, Cleese thinks all he has to do is get you, and it's all over. Ben, you could've made a deal with him . . ."

"I'm through making deals, Nattie. Making deals was what got me into this mess in the first place. Anyway, you can't bargain with Cleese. I told you, I know the man. Bottom line, I'd wind up just like Shelley, and he'd have the disk, too. I like it better this way, which is why I mailed the damn thing to New York. To myself, more or less, care of General Delivery at that big post office in Penn Station. I didn't use my own name, of course . . ."

He smiled faintly. "I mailed it to Eugene Cleese. Shelley probably would've had a laugh out of that."

He looked at her. "So now you know everything," he said. "What fell out of the sky on top of you night before last. I should probably say how sorry I am you got dragged into it. And I am, except . . ."

"Except what?" She looked into his eyes.

"You know what," he answered.

Chapter Twenty

"She went out through the back," the man was saying. "I tried to grab her . . ."

"And she kicked your ass for you." Milton Wallace grinned from where he was standing lookout by the back door. "We know the feeling, pal."

The man clearly didn't like that, but he let it pass. He had one of those Muscle Beach physiques and a darkly handsome face, even crusted by the blood from his forehead. Cleese had never been particularly impressed by these hard-core barbell types. It was his experience that they were rarely as tough as they looked.

"Why were you trying to grab her?" he asked.

The man looked at him. Looked at the SIG. Managed to form a sickly grin.

"She's my wife," he finally answered. "She ran out on me a while back, after . . . after we had a disagreement."

"I don't know Natalie very well," said Cleese. "But so far her judgment has been excellent."

The grin faded some. "Listen." The man held out his big hands, palms up. "I don't know what's going on here, and I don't want to. I have my snowmobile with me, so why don't I just get the hell out of your way . . ."

"You want to leave," said Cleese.

"Hey, this is none of my goddamn business, right? I don't know you, or anything about you. And I don't want to."

"I see." Cleese nodded. "So it's all right with you if we continue to pursue your wife."

"She's my *ex*-wife, okay? That's a part of . . ." The man shifted his eyes back and forth between Wallace and Cleese. "Listen, I'm going to tell you something."

"Please do," replied Cleese.

"Okay. The truth is—" the man grinned again—"I'm after that little bitch, too. Just like you are. She got me into some bad trouble a while back, and I owe her. Big time. I was up here looking for her anyway. So if you guys beat me to her . . ." He shrugged. "No big deal. Just one more reason for me to forget I ever saw either of you."

And he winked.

Cleese smiled. Winked back at him.

"You said you have a snowmobile here?"

The man nodded. "It's parked around the side of the building. Listen, I'll be out of your hair before you know it."

"I believe you," said Cleese.

"They're going to come running." Ben fed the gasoline-soaked strip of cloth into the fuel tank of the larger snowmobile. "When they hear the engines start up."

"That's the idea." For the second or third time, Nattie compared the width of the Kawasaki to the side door. The older snowmobile was nearly a foot narrower than the Thundercat, but it would still be a near thing. "Remember, crank it up first, then give that door chain a pull. *Then* light the cloth."

"One-two-three." He nodded.

She watched him hit the electric starter button on the Arctic Cat's dash panel. The high-pitched clatter of a cold engine drowned the wind noises from outside.

"Doesn't want to start," he said.

"Use the choke."

The engine kicked into life, and the gas-fumes smell of a half-flooded motor mixed with carbon monoxide in the shed. Ben revved the accelerator a couple of times, then went over to the greasy chain used to raise the main door.

Nattie pulled the Kawasaki's old-style cord starter as the door slid up a foot or so from the floor. She could see the snow on the other side.

Ben took one of her waterproof matches and struck it on the edge of the little box. It flared briefly, then went out.

"Shit . . ." His voice was inaudible above the echoing racket in the shed, so she read his lips. "Come on, dammit . . ."

"There are plenty more!" she yelled, but doubted he could hear her either. "Take your time."

Not too much time, though. She revved the Kawasaki, and held the pistol ready in her other hand. Tried to watch both doors.

The second match caught, and Ben cupped a hand around it. Then he touched it to the end of the rag.

It flamed up, just as Nattie saw something . . . a shadow of movement outside, below the main door.

"Come on!" she yelled.

Ben ran toward her. Behind him, the blazing cloth fed into the gas tank. Behind him, the door was rolling up. . . .

Nattie saw a pair of snowbooted feet out there, moving forward. Spreading into a crouch. . . .

Ben was on the back of the Kawasaki. They were accelerating across the dirt floor toward the side entrance, the tread spitting back chunks of frozen mud . . .

Just as the other snowmobile exploded.

It all happened in a blinding flash of motion and sound. The Kawasaki hit the flimsy side door and smashed through it, Nattie ducking low as splintered wood flew all around her. At that same instant, the shed blew outward at the front. Brilliant orange and yellow and red, a deafening boom of sound . . .

And they were outside, grinding slowly . . .

Much too slowly.

. . . through deep snow. Nattie felt Ben's arms around her waist. His body covering her from behind. She had a glimpse of someone—Cleese?—crouched off to one side. Firing at them . . .

The bulk of the comm center loomed straight ahead as the snowmobile gathered momentum. She red-lined it, cut sharply to her left. If they could round that corner. . . .

More shots whizzed past. A thud of impact . . .

Then the corner of the building. They flashed past it, out of the line of fire for a moment . . .

And Nattie saw a dark form sprawled next to another snowmobile. The face . . .

It was Rick.

. . . was turned upward, toward her as they passed. An expression of glazed surprise . . .

Ogod. Rick . . .

. . . then they were past the body. Past the building, and floundering down a long slope toward the lake.

Forget it. The voice was harsh and insistent inside Nattie's head. It's done, so forget it. He did it to himself this time. It wasn't your fault . . .

Get out of here. Keep yourself alive. And Ben.

Nattie drove the small engine to its limit, felt it struggling in the heavy snow. Down toward where a road paralleled the lake in summer. The road out of here.

There were no more shots behind her.

"Are you okay?" she yelled back over her shoulder. Ben's arms tightened on her waist in reply.

They picked up the approximate path of the road, and Nattie found the remains of a snowmobile track. She steered over into it, and their speed increased with the easier going.

Probably Rick's, she thought. From when he came in . . .

Forget it!

The track was straight and steady. Alongside the frozen lake on their right, down toward the dam and beyond.

It was the road out of here, to Ouray eventually, over twenty miles away. Nattie checked the fuel gauge in the center of the console between her knees. Still on full, but she should throttle back some. Save on gas as much as possible, especially carrying two people. Only she couldn't do that, because . . .

Cleese would be coming. She glanced back toward the comm center, and the smoke billowing from behind it. She hadn't figured on Rick's snowmobile. One person, if Cleese left his goon behind, riding a larger, more powerful vehicle than this one.

It wasn't over yet.

They were approaching the old stone and concrete dam now, the spot where the waterflow of Walker Creek had been cut off between two cliffs to form the lake. Nattie steered away from the jagged outcrop on this near side . . .

And felt her vehicle lighten suddenly. It bounced forward in the track.

Ben McKee's arms were gone. No longer around her waist.

She slowed, and looked back. Saw the still figure lying in the track behind her. She made a sharp U-turn, snow flying in a circular wake, and returned.

"Ben . . . ?" she said.

He looked up at her, and tried to smile. The snow around him was darkening with a spreading stain.

Cleese had already decided this was going to be his last job.

He pulled a smoking hunk of the shed door off Milton Wallace, glancing briefly at the man's destroyed face and the oddly flattened shape of his head near one temple. At the wood splinters, some over six inches long, protruding from the bloody spots gouged into the dead man's white snowsuit.

Cleese's own orange snowsuit was singed with tiny

304

burn-holes from flying debris, and the left side of his face felt blistered. Like a bad sunburn.

Definitely his last job. Machtel wasn't big on retirement plans, especially for someone in Cleese's branch of the corporation, but they'd make an exception for him. With the private records he'd kept over the years, he was more dangerous to them than a dozen Ben McKees. But smarter, though. That was the difference. There'd be nobody coming after him.

Cleese looked around for Wallace's HK assault pistol, but it was nowhere in sight. Not surprising, considering the force of that explosion. Where there had once been a wooden shed, now there was nothing except burning rubble scattered up the slope toward the trees. That, and what was left of Marvin Stone's body, over there in an area of smoking ash.

The HK was under the snow somewhere, probably close by, but there was no time to look for it. This may be Cleese's last job before retirement, dealing with this particular enemy who'd betrayed a trust, but it wasn't finished yet. And Machtel no longer had anything to do with it.

They knew who he was. Natalie Kemper and Ben McKee. If they escaped, the walls of the fortress would finally crumble. The world would see inside. Genie would see inside . . .

That dark place where her grandfather lived.

Cleese rose to his feet and ran, his entire body aching with every step, through the heavy snow toward the corner of the comm center. Wallace would have to stay where he was for the time being.

An incredibly sloppy job, this last one. A body in the mine, another up the canyon beneath the avalanche, three more here. Wreckage everywhere.

The message was clear enough. Time to pack it in, Gene. You're getting too old.

He rounded the corner and saw movement in the distance, down toward the lower end of the lake. They had a big lead, but they weren't out of sight yet.

And they might slow down some more. He was fairly sure he'd hit at least one of them.

Cleese popped the SIG's clip. Thirteen shots should be enough for anyone, and he still had seven left. He hurried past the sprawled body in the snow . . .

I'll be out of your hair before you know it.

. . . and climbed onto the seat of the Yamaha.

I have enormous respect for you, Natalie, he thought, but I can't say much for your taste in men.

And then he went roaring out into that gray-white emptiness, the color of a recurring dream of death, one last time.

Nattie couldn't get Ben back onto the snowmobile. He tried to help her, but his strength was gone. The front of his muddy coat was slick with blood. The pants, too.

"Get out of here," he said, and his voice was hoarse. "Dammit, Nattie, he'll be coming. Cleese . . ."

"I'm not leaving you," she snapped. She pulled one of his arms over her shoulders and managed to stand up with him. "Get on the back. Right now."

"Can't hold on." His head lay against her. "Just . . . fall off again."

"Then, I'll tie you." She propped him next to the machine while she searched the storage compartment. "I'll tie you to me. I did it once before, remember?"

He smiled. "How could I forget?"

She saw blood at the edge of that smile. At the corners of his mouth.

Ogod. Oh, please God . . .

She heard a sound in the distance, from the direction of the comm center. A snowmobile.

Ben heard it, too.

"Get out of here," he mumbled. "You still have the gun. You can make it, Nattie."

But there was no time. No time to get him back on. No time to secure him to her. No time to crank the Kawasaki again and get up to speed. No time . . .

For a lot of things.

"Stand up." Nattie got Ben's arm over her shoulder again, and encircled his waist. "Now listen to me. Are you listening to me?"

"Yes, ma'am." A ghost of a smile.

"We're going over to those rocks. Right over there. And you're going to help me, 'cause I don't have time to haul your butt over there by myself. Understand?"

"Gotcha," he said, and a trickle of blood slid from his mouth. Dripped down onto her arm that was around his waist.

The sound in the distance was getting closer.

Nattie started for the edge of the dam, where the beetling brow of rock was the only cover anywhere near. Ben tried to help, but she was dragging him far more than he was walking. Pain knifed through her ankle with every step.

Nattie heard the snowmobile coming. She didn't look around.

They made their way through much shallower snow, less than knee-deep here, up into the rocks. And then over to the far side. Out of the howling wind.

Where the concrete and stone dam marked the end of Walker Lake. There was a sheer dropoff back there, with a jagged cliff overhanging the ravine. A hundred feet below them, the frozen creek—buried beneath lake water for over a mile—reappeared, cutting its way down a narrow canyon.

To Nattie's right, as she moved forward through the notch, the cliff joined the dam itself, a vertical cement wall. Near the bottom were three huge floodgates, frozen open, ready for the torrent that would fill them in the spring. Crossing just below the top of the dam was a metal catwalk. It connected with a locked-up pump station on the far side.

Nattie was pretty sure she remembered a shortwave radio in that building.

"Gotta stop." Ben sagged against her. "Nattie, I can't . . ."

"See the catwalk? Ben, look at it. If we can get across the dam, over to the pump station, there's a radio . . ."

"I can't." He slumped between some rocks.

And she knew he was right. Here, on the edge of this rocky cliff, was not the place to board the catwalk. It was a ten-foot jump, maybe more, from here. He couldn't make it, not in his condition. She wasn't sure she could either.

The snowmobile noise was close. The wind screamed above her head, there in the sheltering rocks, and brought her the sound of an engine idling. Cleese had reached the Kawasaki.

The engine died. Just the wind now.

"Nattie." Ben's hand was on her arm. She crawled in next to him. Took the pistol out of her coat.

"Nattie, you have to go now." His grip was stronger than she expected.

"I already told you . . ."

"Don't be stupid." She looked down, and saw his blue eyes losing their clarity. "You have to go. If you don't . . ."

He coughed deeply, a racking cough that brought more blood to his lips.

"If you don't, all this was for nothing. Nattie?"

"What?" she snapped, but her hands were gentle on his face.

"Remember." His eyes closed. "The post office at Penn Station. A package for . . ."

His voice faded out.

"For Eugene Cleese," she whispered, and bent down to kiss him.

Cleese crawled up through the rocks, with the snow blowing past his head. Icy-cold, gray-white and cold. The tracks were easy to follow, even without all that blood.

At the top of the ridge, he found a cleft to look through. Down the other side . . .

Where a single figure in camouflage gear was climbing

out toward a point on the cliff. Cleese saw the ravine below, and the catwalk that hugged the upper edge of the dam.

"She's going to jump for it," he said, and stood up. He raised the SIG and lined up its front sight along her back. Not an easy shot, with the distance and the wind, but makeable.

Squint one eye, but don't close it. Wait until she stops completely to set up her jump. Okay. Right there . . .

Life and death, they're meaningless, boy.

He felt the trigger beneath his gloved finger. Right there where her shoulders meet that single braid . . .

Of blond hair.

Life and death . . .

Cleese lowered the gun.

"I'm getting too old for this shit," he said.

And climbed through the cleft in the rocks.

Back out in the wind again, Nattie slid one foot over the edge and measured her distance. Maybe not ten feet, maybe eight or nine, and down about three. That would help a little.

But there was no place to get a running start, and the rock was too slick. Icy-slick beneath her feet.

She didn't look down, into the ravine where those floodgates jutted out above the creek. If she missed, she'd probably land on top of that nearest one, a narrow, upraised square of concrete nearly a hundred feet below that would snap her body like a twig. . . .

Just concentrate on the catwalk. Visualize yourself jumping. Landing on it. Remember to grab the railing as soon as you hit, because that metal's as slick as these rocks . . .

. . . coated in black ice she couldn't see. Like the walls of Empinado Canyon. Like the hidden face of a stranger.

Ben McKee. She'd been wrong about him. She'd put a stranger's mask where none existed. Except in her own doubts and fears.

And this . . . this was only ice on some rocks and a metal catwalk. Nothing more.

She wasn't sure why she looked back up the cliff, back to where Ben was. She'd promised herself she wouldn't . . .

But she did, and that was when she saw the man standing there, watching her. The orange snowsuit.

Cleese was up there in the cleft. Next to Ben. Looking down at him.

"Are you satisfied?" she whispered, and felt the wind freeze the tears on her face. "You bloodthirsty sonofabitch. Are you finally happy?"

He was climbing down toward her.

Nattie wiped her eyes, and turned back toward the catwalk. You can do this, Nattie. You can do it. It's a high leap, but it's not that far. Downhill all the way, girl.

What was that she'd yelled up at Ben in the mine? "Trust me," she'd said.

And he had. He'd taken it on faith, and he'd leaped out into the blackness, trusting her that the cables were there.

Compared to that, this was nothing.

Nattie jumped, felt her damaged ankle give way as she pushed off. It spun her sideways, but she had the distance. She hit the catwalk, and sprawled along its frozen length. Scrambled to her feet and grabbed the pistol from her pocket.

Cleese was nearly to the point of rock. She knew he had a gun somewhere, but she didn't see it. She limped backward along the catwalk, her pistol held ready.

He reached the rim, up there a little above her and less than twenty feet away. He stopped, and looked down at her while she stood looking back up at him. She saw the bullet holes in the orange fabric of his snowsuit. Three holes, their edges frayed and ragged, centered over his chest.

Maybe he can't die . . .

From somewhere on the other side of the dam, the coyotes were howling again.

"We need to talk, Natalie," he said.

"You stay right where you are." She pointed the gun at him.

"Natalie, this can be fixed." Cleese's arms were hanging at his sides. "It doesn't have to go this way."

"You liar." She heard her voice trembling, and felt tears burning her eyes. "All you know how to do is lie. That, and kill people. You're very good at lying and killing, aren't you, Mr. Cleese? Is that all you're good for?"

"No." She saw that gentle smile of his. "No, there's a little more than that. You don't know me, Natalie."

"And I don't want to."

"No." He shook his head in agreement. "You don't. But I know you, after what we've been through together . . ."

"Together? Goddamn you, don't even use that word . . ."

"But it's true," he said. "Together is the best way to describe it. And because I know you, much better than you'll ever understand, I have an offer to make."

She remembered his soft voice, grandfather's voice, from that morning. She also remembered the knife.

"I want your word on something, Natalie." He looked down at her from the point of rock. "If you give it, I'll know it's the truth, because I know you."

"What the hell are you talking about?" Nattie saw her hand, the hand holding the pistol, was starting to tremble. She tried to will it steady.

The howling sounds increased, borne on the wind.

"Here's my offer, Natalie." Cleese held both hands, palms open, away from his body. "I'll be going back up the cliff, and out of your life. I'll leave that little snowmobile for you, right where it is. I have a few things to do here, some tidying up, before the weather clears; then I'll be gone."

He smiled at her. "You get on your snowmobile and drive out of here. Out of the basin. You forget all about me, your word on that, and I'll forget all about you. Forever. No return visits, wherever you go. What do you

311

say, Natalie? This is a one-time, take it or leave it offer that I've never made before. To anyone. And that's not a lie. I have my own reasons for making it now, and I'll never make it again. You decide."

Nattie looked up at him, windblown and waiting on that pinnacle of stone and black ice. Standing up there and offering her life to her. He wasn't lying, somehow . . . instinctively, down inside the deepest part of her, she knew that.

"Ben . . ." she said.

"I'm sorry." He shook his head.

Ben. And Marv and Jack. And Rick.

Nattie took a deep breath. Looked up at him, looming over her on the point of rock. This relentless, deadly old man . . .

"Fuck you, Cleese," she said, and saw his smile fade. "And fuck your deal, too. You make another move toward me and, bulletproof or not, I'll shoot you dead."

"I'm sorry to hear that, Natalie," said Cleese.

And jumped for the catwalk.

The pistol bucked in Nattie's hand, recoiled so quickly she wasn't even sure she'd fired. Cleese twisted in midair, missed the catwalk with his body, but grabbed the railing with his hands. The entire structure creaked and pulled itself slightly away from the wall of the dam.

Nattie's feet went out from under her, and she fell onto the icy metal. The gun flew from her hand over the edge as she slid forward, down toward the open end.

She got one arm under her to stop, fingers wedged into a floor seam, and crawled to her knees. Found herself looking into Cleese's eyes, less than ten feet away.

He had one hand hooked over the lower railing. He reached with his other for the top as the catwalk shifted again with a screeching sound. He mumbled something, smiled at her for a moment, and she saw the blood on his face, pouring down out of his gray hair.

Just before he fell.

Nattie didn't watch him fall. She didn't look down at all until she'd crawled up the canted slope of the catwalk to a level spot. She'd have to go all the way to the pump station before she could recross the dam up on the concrete.

It seemed very still to her suddenly. Only the wind now, and that was nothing. Nobody was afraid of the wind.

When she finally looked down the wall, she saw Cleese, his back bent at an impossible angle across one of the floodgates. She thought his mild brown eyes were open, but she couldn't be sure at that distance.

She wondered why he'd called her Genie.

Epilogue

Summer brought the hummingbirds back to the high San Juan. Glittering little buzz-bombs, green and red and blue streaks of hot temper and courage. And the disposition of a wounded badger.

If hummingbirds were the size of eagles, there'd be nothing else left alive in these mountains, or so Starvin' Marvin Stone told Nattie one time. Not even Leo and Laura.

She squatted a little lower, down next to Jack's grave, and surrendered all the air space above the blooming blue-and-white columbines to the tiny tyrant zipping angrily back and forth past her head.

The other flowers she'd planted, scarlet foxfire and purple-shaded western larkspur, were also beginning to bloom there on the grave.

"You must have a green paw, Jackie," she whispered, and held one hand, palm down on the warm ground. "Who'da thunk it?"

After a while she wiped her eyes and rose to her feet, still stiff and painful from the lingering aftereffects of frostbite and a hairline ankle fracture, and walked through the tall, green meadow grass toward the glass-fronted weather array. It needed repainting. Some of its wooden surfaces showed scorch marks even now, five months later.

The cabin-site looked a lot better, at least. With the charred wood and propanel hauled off to one side, it was possible to envision another cabin there, on the same spot.

Or maybe closer to those trees, she decided. A new location, still near enough to the weather array so it could be easily reached during the winter . . .

By whoever would be in the cabin.

"So it's definite." Ben McKee looked up at her when she approached. "You're not staying."

The man assigned to him, Qualls was his name, had wandered off into the flower-filled meadow with Peaches the Wonder Puppy. A tactful man, Qualls.

"Nope." She studied Ben, sitting there with his back against the trunk of an old Douglas fir. He looked different, and not just in the way of someone you haven't seen for months. It was more than that.

He wasn't very vigorous, but that was to be expected. "You think I look like hell now," he's said, right after Qualls helped him down off that very gentle mare, "you should've seen me when I got out of surgery. Hypothermia, frostbite, bullet holes. University's a teaching hospital, you know, and those medical students were all standing around taking dibs on my various parts.

"Even the tiny little ones," he'd added with a grin. And watched her blush.

Ironically, it was the same hypothermia which had almost taken Ben's life originally that ultimately saved him that day, by dropping his body temperature and slowing his loss of blood until the Flight For Life helicopter battled through the waning storm in answer to Nattie's urgent summons on the pump house's shortwave.

"So, if you're not staying, what are you going to do instead?" He shifted slightly to remain in the sun, never too warm, not even in July, at eleven thousand feet.

"I don't know yet," Nattie replied. "I just know I don't . . . *need* to stay here anymore."

She looked up past tall evergreens toward the high peaks, still snowladen against a cobalt blue summer sky.

Remote. Untouched by it all, by life and death, they looked back down on her through the eyes of eternity.

"Look for a teaching job, maybe." She shrugged. "Get some use out of those two degrees in English."

"Seems kind of tame," said Ben. "By comparison."

"You obviously haven't spent much time facing a room full of adolescents on hormonal overload. Anyway, I don't have to decide right now. I want to get the cabin rebuilt first. That'll carry me through August."

She studied him some more. "You made the news, you know. Back in April when they returned all those indictments against Machtel. I take it you got your immunity."

"And a bodyguard." He nodded. "At least for a while. I'm not real popular with *either* side at the moment, thanks to that trick with the computer disk. The advice I got was something like, maybe you should consider another line of work, and another name while you're at it. And another location, somewhere off the beaten path, until cooler heads prevail."

"So here you are."

"Here I are," he agreed, then looked over to where the new lumber was cross-stacked with the precut logs at the edge of the clearing near Nattie's tent. "I've been considering carpentry. Healthy, outdoor exercise to help me get my strength back. What do you think?"

Nattie sat down next to him on the ground. Looked into those familiar blue eyes. "We could discuss it." She smiled, but not *too* big a smile. Make him earn it, that was the plan. "As long as we have a few things clear right up front, bud . . ."

"Name's not bud," he said.